MAGEBREAKER

A SLICE OF LIFE FANTASY

DECLAN COURT

CONTENTS

CHAPTER

ONE

The wind was a spray of jagged ice and a cold so fierce it whipped any heat from my bones. I trudged up the snowy road, struggling to keep the hood over my face, into the mountain town.

No sane man was out in this weather. The broke? The desperate? Here stood I. I gritted my chattering teeth and squinted at the ice covered buildings that still stood.

Erast.

What a famed and wondrous town. When the mountain range here held mines worth working, it had grown from a camp into a shantytown filled with miners, sordid men, wagons of prostitutes and gambling halls. When the mines dried up, Erast had died meekly. The boards and nails of its makeshift structures were broken down into firewood. Now it remained in the snows on the tall mountain peaks, barren and hollow, like a wound nobody had even bothered to stitch shut.

They used to beat you to death in the street here for the steel in your belt. Now, the lazy bastards that remained would probably just knock you in the skull and leave you to freeze. People used to have standards. Bad standards, but standards.

I waded through the snowy street, towards the battering sound of a sign swinging wildly in the blizzard. The wooden post clattered, hung by a single iron ring. Whatever name it once held had been erased by the years of bottles flung at it.

I banged on a wooden door and pulled the frost-caked cloth from my face.

"Let me in!" I yelled over the storm.

"*Whoosit?*" I heard a voice faintly over the howl of the storm.

"Davik! Tell him it's Davik!" I screamed through the wood.

I heard the words through the door. "*Says it's Mavik. Some large fella'.*"

"*Mavik?*" another voice deeper inside answered.

"Davik!" I yelled through the slats in the door. "Hurry up!"

More grumbling inside. I cast a look at the icy street. Erast was so poor, you didn't even see chimneys burning. Impoverished ghosts flitted behind the windows, not waiting for better days, just waiting for less-worse ones.

The door unlatched and swung open with the blowing wind. I stumbled inside, into the arms of a large and muscled creature that stank of shit. Long teeth and surprised eyes gazed down at me before he shook me off.

"He's got a sword!" the bugbear turned to the tables inside.

My contact laughed. "Who doesn't have a sword, Billy? Let him pass."

I stepped aside as the bugbear shut the door, drowning the howling wind to a faint hiss that rattled in all the gaps and holes of this place.

There were ten figures hunched around tables, plus the doorman. The hearth was bare, unlit, with a flue that kept swinging and catching like a drunk blacksmith at an anvil.

Someone had sacrificed the countertop bar for firewood, and it looked like they had already run out. Only two feet of it survived, and they were already taking strips of it for kindling. An ugly, sallow bartender sat behind the lone three bottles sitting atop it. Displeased at my arrival, or his long-term guests, I couldn't tell.

It was spring, if you'd believe it. But the rains had brought a blizzard this high up in Erast. Several candles lit the tables, illuminating men in poor weather gear stooped around them. I knew a ranger once who showed me you could stay alive with a candle in the cold, draping your entire cloak around yourself and letting it warm you.

"Davik, glad you could join us," a voice called from the empty hearth.

I was breathing hard. My trek through the storm had been the lovely ending to a miserable journey.

"You too," I said with numb lips. I shook the snow from my hair, dropping my hood, and stepped further into the fine establishment.

I approached the table where Stroud sat with a half-orc and another bugbear, each of them with playing cards in their hands and a dice cup between them.

"Sorry we missed you, down in Swinford," Stroud said with an impish grin. "Have to say, I'm surprised to see you."

"I figured our lines got crossed." I took my cloak off and slung it over the back of an open chair across from him. The men around the tables were lean, too little food, and I saw the black promise of frostbite beginning. "Didn't want to miss you before your birthday."

"What did you bring me?" Stroud asked. He had dark teeth from a lifetime habit of chewbags, and small eyes a bit too close together that had always reminded me of a rat. His fellow cardplayers looked anything but pleased at my joining them.

I sat down in the chair, frozen leathers creaking, and raised my hands. "Ta-da."

The half-orc to my left sniffed the air, his nostrils flaring and coming in my direction. "Oiled his blade, boss."

Stroud held up a finger. "Well, Davik here and his people are professionals, Lum. I'm sure he oiled it for the cold. Keep that nice metal safe. Bring it here, Billy. Let's see how a professional takes care of his weapons."

Billy the bugbear approached me from behind, reaching down and grabbing my sword. I didn't move, keeping my eyes on Stroud and the soft 'fuck you' smiles we traded across the table.

The bugbear growled and pulled the sword whole. He set it on the table in front of his boss.

"Now would you look at that," Stroud said, eyes alight. He held up the sword for all to see. Even in the dim light of the room, it was like an artifact of the stars come down to visit. "Elven, boys. Belonged to a royal named Venthren, so the story goes."

My sword was blue metal and gold filigree along the scabbard and pommel, slightly curved in the dueling style of some Elven court.

"Tell us, Davik. What grand adventure earned you this little trinket?" Stroud grinned. "Did you rescue a princess? Was it in some dungeon, dark and deep, calling your name?"

I shrugged, grinning. "Took it from a fellow who did me wrong."

Stroud tsked, shaking his head and looking at the scabbard. "Must have been a grievous sin."

My smile slid from my face, and I stared at Stroud. "He didn't pay me."

"Now that's wrong, I tell you boys. Nothing worse than a scoundrel." Stroud pulled the blade out of the scabbard,

4

revealing several inches of its shining blade. He raised an eyebrow. "Freshly oiled. You were right, Lum. You expecting trouble, Davik?"

"You have to take care of your equipment."

"Oh, I'm sure. That's the soldier in you. Always keeping a tight kit."

"I can show you, sometime. If you like." I leaned towards him. "It'd be nice if you used some oil next time before you try to fuck someone on a deal."

Stroud flashed another smile. He was a leader of men, as poor and mangy as they might be, in this shithole winesink. Hiding out in a forgotten town that had been a forgotten camp.

"And here I thought this was my birthday present. Davik, come now. Don't let the cold outside get to your mood. Get Davik a drink, Billy. Darkshire always liked a drink. Isn't that right?"

Chuckles came from around the room. My mind tracked where each sound came from, who had moved from the tables and who hadn't.

I felt the shift of the bodies behind me rising. The value of my sword was more than this crew earned in a year together. It could buy a small town. The bugbear and half-orc at the table stared at me hungrily. I doubted the Erast butcher was open for business. And if I became the next meal it would likely make their human comrades sleep easier. Meat was meat.

The bugbear walked over and sat a cup in front of me that smelled like chemicals in a tannery. I made no move to take it.

"Davik, you hurt my feelings. Whatever is wrong? We've done business before. To think, I wouldn't welch on my debts. You wound me."

Wouldn't welch.

Stroud would draw this out. When you're hiding out, with nothing but a candle to keep you entertained and half a deck of playing cards, amusement is scarce. Any captain lost on his course fears his crew, and a man like Stroud was no different. That sword in his hands would buy him time, buy him confidence. Buy him all the things his little mind was reeling to come up with.

"My mistake," I said, reaching towards the deck of cards. "What are we playing?"

"Pauper Kings," the bugbear sitting to my right sneered a mouthful of fangs at me. He was a big boy, bigger than the half-orc.

I drew several cards. "What are the stakes?"

"What have you got?" Stroud asked with a smile.

Then I heard the entrance latch being tested lightly. To keep me in.

"Just what you owe me," I said, staring at the four cards in my hands.

Stroud placed my sword next to his chair. "I'm not sure how that's supposed to work, Davik. I gave you a job. I was so excited! The illustrious *Darkshire*, doing business with me!" More laughs came from around the room.

I stared at him over my cards. "Don't call me that."

Stroud continued, looking at his men. Eager to get the show going. "But imagine how disappointed I was. Finally, thought I was stepping into a new echelon. Word came down you had quite the mishap, didn't you, Darkshire? Heard you got most of your crew killed. We're real sorry about that. But in what world do I pay you when the job wasn't done?"

Men were standing now. The show was set to begin. The bugbear to my right turned in his seat.

"There was no job, Stroud. Nothing on that ship. Except forty crossbows with men holding them. Seems like someone tipped them off they were going to be robbed."

Stroud sipped his wine or water. "Well Davik, you're a

professional, aren't you? I thought a few surprises would be in your wheelhouse. Did your people forget their armor?"

I thought back to the seven dead traveling companions on that ship. Skewered alive by crossbow fire. The ambush had been surgical and cold. My compatriots had been low to middling in skill and experience. But they hadn't deserved to die like alleyway dogs.

"Want to hear what I think?" I asked.

More footsteps came behind me. The old intimidation tactic, the rustle of a hand on your wallet and the demand to know what you're doing with their money.

I continued, "I think you wanted a move up, sure. But not with me. That ship belonged to the Silver Hands, and I bet you thought they would be in your good graces when you tipped them off I was coming for their cargo."

Stroud grinned. "That's quite the theory."

I looked around the room, marking each man. "Where's Brenner? He didn't make it out of Swinford?"

Stroud's eyes blazed, like I had just outed a secret. "He's coming. Got our payment."

I sat back in my chair, like there wasn't a care in the world. "See, I think you bit off more than you could chew. The Silver Hands don't like rats, Stroud. Even ones that come to them first. Once they fended off the attack, they knew what you were up to. I get cargo out, you win. I die, you win and you're a new favorite for them. But you didn't know they didn't leave loose ends. When they started trimming your little garden here, you tucked tail and ran up here to hide out. From them. From me."

Stroud raised his hand, holding everyone back. The orc to my left turned to me, the steel helmet of a human soldier too tight on his head, the metal bent to make room.

"It's a good story, Davik. It captivates. Look at you. You used to take contracts from princes and walked with the heaviest names in the lands. *Darkshire, Darkshire,* he'll knife you for a loaf of bread! Then I see you, some little ragtag group behind you, I think. How sad that the mighty fall. You were my hero, man. But here you are, telling stories in a little bar like a minstrel on the road. What happened?"

I raised the cup to my lips, sniffed it, and set it back down. "Always time to pick up new hobbies. You know the difference between you and me, Stroud?"

"What's that?"

"I always know who I'm dealing with. And what they're capable of."

Stroud nodded. "I'm a little short on coin, Davik. Why don't you come back next week, once Bremmer arrives?"

"Oh, that's alright," I said. "You can keep the coin. I didn't come here for that."

"Yeah?" Stroud asked.

We stared at one another. The room was a bowstring, ready to snap.

"Yeah," I breathed.

The half-orc rose first. Taller than me, larger. Green skin and a body sheathed in rippling muscle that had never had to do anything but be born to earn it. I shot from my seat, snarling, and drove a fist into his helmed head. The sound of metal, the feel of it crumpling under my fist as it dented up to my wrist into his skull. Blood poured out from the brim of the helm over his face like a sick waterfall.

"Story's over," I snarled at Stroud.

The bugbear produced a knife, flying towards my right ribcage. I spun out of the way, grabbing the cup on the table and planting it into his jaw. The sound and sickening crunch of teeth breaking filled the room like tumbling dice. Louder even than the howling wind outside trying to get in. Men yelled.

The bugbear screamed until I swept his legs out and rammed his face down on the table into a sloppy mess.

Stroud scrambled back to the wall. I spun, a mace flourishing in my right hand like a magic trick. The flanged head swung out to my closest enemy.

It met a man's head and downed him. I roared and surged forward into the mass of bodies trying to rush me.

The winesink turned into a den of frenzied murder. One man shot from a table, trying to tackle me—I flipped him over my shoulder and flung him down into a table, turning it to kindling.

"Get him!" Stroud screamed as I swung out with the mace again, the old army drills coming back to me even after all this time, the soft ditty of a terrible marching song. The only one we had ever had.

War's we wage'em!

A man in sheepskin grabbed my left arm, thrashing at me with a spike of metal. I gripped his wrist, squeezed until I felt his bones pop, and drove his dirk into his stomach and ripped upwards.

"Fucking get him!" Stroud screamed again.

A young man, too young to have known better than to fall in with Stroud, ran at me with a broken billhook.

Brave, braver than his partners. I slipped his stab easily, darting to the left. I brought the morning star up in an uppercut and shattered his jaw, dropping him to the ground.

Mages we break'em!

Two men freed their swords, short blades. Good for indoor work. They spun on either side of a table, flanking me.

"Come here!" I called out, teeth flashing at the one on my right. I feinted towards him with the mace, and spun as his partner drove his blade towards my spine, sliding the sword edge along the leather of my armor until I was face to face with him.

He tried to bring the sword up under my armpit, but my left fist collapsed his orbital socket, crunching the soft jelly of his eye into crimson with a savage blow.

His partner stabbed me in the back. I grunted as the blade bit through the thick leather, pushing towards my kidney inch by inch. I gritted my teeth as Billy the Bugbear roared and charged me.

I grabbed the blade with my left hand, twisting it, wrenching it free and ducking as the bugbear bore down on me. I disarmed the man who had stabbed me and sliced out with a quick backhand, drawing the blade in a steady *chop!* across his throat. His hands dove up to where his skin split, trying to keep his throat together.

The sword clattered out of my hands as Billy tackled me. The bugbear was on me instantly, crashing me into the wooden floor, frozen slats of wood splintering and shattering as he rammed my head into the ground. Fist after fist crashed into my face.

Day's we save'em! Oh!

I reached up, growling into his snarling face and grappled with a heave, rolling on top of him. Someone broke a clay pitcher over my skull, but I was driving fist after fist into the bugbear's face. I grabbed his matted hair and slammed it into the floor in a crumple of frosted timber.

Another blow came for my head and I ducked, grasping out, gripping the sword I had dropped. Billy grabbed the blade, holding it up. A man came from behind me and jumped on my back, pushing me towards the blade.

How foolish, it would go through me and into him...

People can be shortsighted. The bugbear was strong. Freakishly so. But I could see in his eyes the fear, the surprise that I was stronger. I smiled down at him, blood running from my scalp, and smashed the pommel of the sword into his nose, turning it into a river of blood. He let go for just a second as I raised it up in a rebound into the eye of the man on my back, holding him there with one hand as the short sword slid through one side of his face and out the other part of his head.

The bugbear snarled and sank his fangs into my thigh. I screamed, because it **fucking hurt**, and then I smashed the pommel down on the top of his skull, impaling him with it until he yelped and his body twitched.

Huffing, I stood, turning with the short sword in my hands. A single man stood between me and Stroud. He held a short spear up, jabbing at the air while Stroud pushed him towards me.

I lumbered closer. The sword flipped in my hands, and I held it in the *mordhau* grip, turning it into a mace. Against an armored man, I'll take a stone on the end of a stick over a blade. They don't look so valorous when you get their feet out from under them and burst them like a fruit.

"You can go," I growled, mouth full of blood. Must've bit my cheek. "I just need to talk to **him.**" I motioned to Stroud behind him.

The man looked around, then at the door. He gave me a look, and I nodded. As he stepped towards it to leave, he shrieked as Stroud impaled him from behind with my sword.

"Boss!" the man groaned in disbelief. Stroud wrenched my blade back out of his own man.

"You little worm," I spat.

Such a petty act got my blood going. My body was aching, cuts and bruises and bites and a stab wound to be inspected soon. The runes in my bones hummed, searching for any magic to counteract and absorb. Any mage to locate.

But there was none. This was the world of those who dealt in blood and the things that drew it forth.

Stroud laughed, swinging the blade. "Never could find good talent."

The wind whistled through the cracks in the little building, full of dead and dying men. I snapped forward, quick and smooth, gripping his hand over the handle and the other on the blade.

I pushed the sword-edge up to his neck, pressing him against the wall.

Stroud struggled, flailing. He gasped as I brought the blade to his throat, the inevitability of it like a slow-moving guillotine. Then he sneered and spat the words at me.

"There's no gold! You fuckin' fool. Was never... gonna pay you. Darksh—"

I pushed forward, bringing the bite of the blade into his throat. He stared at me as the steel parted his windpipe, turning whatever words he was going to speak next into a gurgled cough.

"I know."

CHAPTER
TWO

W hat had taken me a day and a half of straight marching uphill took me four days downhill. The wind and snow were against me, and the billhook to the back was in a place I could barely reach to stuff clean bandages in. Luckily the armor had chewed most of the barb.

The bugbear bite on my thigh slowed me the most. The punctured muscle was agony. I tried to move quicker, racing against the dirty saliva that promised infection.

I leaned into the wind and snow. The blizzard never stopped. Stroud had been right, there had been no gold. Two silvers, eight coppers between the lot of them. Nothing of value. Nothing worth carrying except my wounds.

The storm caught me the second day hard. Blind and lost, no chance of a cave or shelter. I found the broken hollow of an old tree that would stop the wind on three sides. I lit a candle, drew my cloak around me and huddled over it while my wounded body shook with the cold.

Stroud's word came back to me.

Used to take contracts from princes and walk with the heaviest names in the land...

I shuddered and leaned forward, holding my cloak around me against the howling wind. The candle flickered, then I felt its warmth. A single little flame, heating the canopy I held over it. The air smelled of wax.

Feelings, smells, even sayings remind you of old times. Better times, worse times. Hunger reminded me of the war, and of childhood. Kneeling in a city street, a begging bowl in my hands as life walked by. Growing up and dying at the same time. One force of nature fighting against the other. I remembered humans and elves walking by, laughing at the dirty beggar boy.

I had thought Death itself came for me that day. I knew him, even as a child. He had been red, eyes afire, horned. I had looked up at him with tired eyes, ready.

But it hadn't been death. A demon walking down the street on his way to collect on an infernal bargain had stopped. He stared down at me, mouth agape.

"And these fools call **me** a demon," he had said, the shock at my state plain in his voice. I looked up to what I had thought was my end. His face transfixed in pity. He knelt before me, and I leaned forward, ready to be taken.

A single claw reached out and placed a whole silver ingot in my bowl. His fingers burning etches into the wood as he withdrew his claw. Eyes that promised torture and eternity saddened for me.

"Stay alive, boy." Then he vanished. I had held the silver ingot, hot in my hands, believing it had been a vision. But my begging bowl held the burned mark of his touch.

Beggars retire in the graveyard. Unless they close their open palms into a fist for survival. The beggar starves while the thief eats.

The wind raged against my shelter, and my cloak shook, but I held it closed. Unable to truly rest, to let my guard down.

"Never knew how you could stand this," I breathed the words in chattering teeth.

The cold always reminded me of Trolf. I had been fifteen then, maybe older. Birthdays are for those who have families and people to count them. When my begging bowl had become a club. When my eyes shifted into the hunting look of a petty criminal watching for a soft purse and hard skull to crack. Eventually they turned elsewhere, outside the city, to stories of gold.

The candle between my legs turned into a campfire in my memory.

It had been my first time out of the city. Out in the wilderness. It had been my first crew, and I was a hang-around, agreeing to a third of a share of whatever we pulled. We had been doing small stuff then. Protecting merchants, hunting down the odd artifact. Running with our tails between our legs when someone returned crossbow fire. The bravado I carried as a street brigand had been laughed away by my new partners when I didn't know how to build a fire.

I would have made more with another crew, another outfit. Had a better share. But Mira had caught my eye, and my hormones demanded we stay. She was bratty, nineteen, and I didn't know it then, but she loved the attention I gave her. Nothing else.

An orphan and a beggar are self-conscious at the best of times. When you don't know what you're doing, whether in a group dynamic or with a woman, you second-guess yourself constantly. You pretend.

Trolf had come upon our group. A barbarian from the ice tribes up north. He had been campaigning and questing for ten years. Aside from his ridiculous name, he was everything our group needed. Strong. Intimidating. Sure of himself. He took to us easily, and everyone looked to him to take charge once our leader died of a fever.

Everyone in the group was older than me, and they got off on seeing me chase after Mira like a little puppy. One night while Trolf was oiling a giant greatsword, Mira was tending to his wounds. We were talking about the next job, the next destination. I don't remember.

I was burning with jealousy, of course. Thinking of new ways to grab her attention.

Then Trolf looked at Mira. "Do you wish to share my bedroll tonight?"

This brought a few chortles around the campfire. Sick grins and knowing glances. Mira looked mortified, she tried to laugh it off nervously, the bandages still in her hands.

My face burned with shame. I felt everyone glancing at me, laughing at the street-kid from the city. The burn of indignation was like a knife.

I realized in that moment I was pretending.

Pretending not to care. Pretending it didn't bother me. Feigning against what I was feeling so a group of people I didn't like would appreciate me.

Make no mistake, I was terrified. If I lost, I'd be left behind. Wounded in a wilderness I barely knew how to navigate, much less survive in.

But I couldn't take it.

I threw a knife into the ground, right between his feet. A gesture I had picked up in the minor gang squabbles of the alleyways. My heart had been thundering. My bladder threatening to spill. I was so damned afraid. Afraid of the moment.

But I was more afraid of nothing changing. That I'd settle —grateful for whatever life gave me as long as it wasn't more punishment.

"Challenge," I spat the words out and stared at him.

Trolf measured me for a moment. Mira took the chance to stand and scurry away. My act did not amuse him. Nor was he a fool. You don't live long with a blade as your career taking anyone, even some pissant, lightly.

"Hands," was all he said.

The next morning, I stepped into a clearing while my "friends" gathered around to watch. **Mira** was watching. But it quickly came to me that it wasn't about her. It wasn't about anything but defying what might happen.

We circled up, and I felt the strangest gratitude when Trolf fell into a fighter's stance. He didn't showboat. He didn't gloat. He took me seriously. This type of challenge was common where he was from.

When Trolf hit me, it wasn't a punch, and it wasn't a slap. It was a smack. His gigantic hand rung my bell. I saw the glint of stars in the daytime, my ears ringing. I heard the whistle of something that wasn't there.

My feet flew from under me. When I pushed myself up, one thought had stirred in my wobbling skull.

Not that bad.

I fought him like a wolf trying to bring down a direbear. He beat me until my skin split, blood trickled from five different places. But I kept coming. I littered his body with bruises, his muscle felt like armor. He kept putting me down, trying not to kill me.

Finally, when I staggered towards him again, something dark rose in me. Something that had been there the first time I had robbed a man. The same thing that years later would guide me during conscription, fighting in close quarters.

I landed an uppercut you could've written a song about. It was very poetic, the young hopeful against the barbarian. His chin went skyward. Spittle flew from his mouth. Everyone let out a gasp.

Then his icy eyes settled back on me. Letting me know I had made a mistake. When he hit me, he hit me as an equal.

I remember nothing after that.

I woke up later that night. My compatriots had dragged me back to the fire. We couldn't travel that day, and I learned later there had been a suggestion to leave me. Trolf had broken Jarrod's jaw for that.

Around the campfire, no one spoke. Nobody laughed either. Trolf ate his ration as if nothing had occurred.

When I sat up, I groaned, feeling lightheaded.

"Where do we head to next?" someone had asked Trolf.

The barbarian had shaken his head, then nodded to where I sat.

"Ask him. He's the only one with any balls among you."

Mira had come to me. Checking me, putting salve on my wounds. When I stood up in the late evening, she was there, steadying me.

"Lets get you rinsed off," she had said and took me down to the river. As far as her medicinal skills, she knew little. But she wrapped my ribs by the water, sliding close to me, pulling me tight.

"He almost killed you," she had said. Her face held a strange mixture of gratitude and interest.

I had smirked in the failing light. The soft breath of twilight covered the surrounding woods. I had lost, but I had won. Against myself. Whatever was in me wasn't interested in pretending anymore.

My body was a bruise, but it felt like it was carved out of stone. I had conquered the adrenaline of challenging him, of waiting a sleepless night, of going with everything I had against a stronger opponent. I was alive. The same way I fought off a possible fate in the poverty of my youth, I would do the same thing here. My thoughts were instantaneous. I knew exactly what I needed. What I wanted.

I slid my arms around Mira and pulled her into me.

"What are you doing?" she whispered. But she didn't pull away.

"I want you," I replied, the truth feeling right as I spoke it.

Mira had looked away. Not in shame. She was making sure we were alone. "You're hurt, Davik..." But then she looked at me in a way she never had before that. I no longer was some kid from the city chasing her. She was looking at a man and what he'd become.

Mira kissed me. As she did, I suddenly knew what I had always known—that it was better to be battered and strong than unscathed and weak.

I lifted her dress. I was tired of looking at it, wondering what was underneath. I filled my hands with soft flesh, and she melted into me.

Some men fall to drink, or they spend their coin on clothes or paid company. Others seek power and glory. They want crowns and conquest. They all have their own path.

We fell back into the moss by the river. My ribs screamed with pain, but the rush of recent combat fueled me. The only bedroll she would share would be mine. I strode into her until she moaned my name through the woods.

It was the look in her eyes as we lay there afterwards. She was fixated on me, gazing into my eyes like some treasure she had discovered. I felt I had finally figured out a puzzle. There was no chasing her, she would chase me.

I knew what my path was.

· · ·

WHEN THE STORM BROKE, I rose and made my way down from the mountains. My limbs were sore, my body sluggish from being so long in the cold. I kept moving, flexing my toes and fingers, warding off frostbite.

It took another day, but as I descended from the high altitude, the weather became warmer and warmer. The wounds on my back and leg slowed my travel. On the road among the more civilized areas, I passed small encampments and farms. One morning, a farmer driving his wagon pointedly looked away when I called to him for a ride. Hoping I vanished lest I bring ruin to his house and home.

Couldn't blame him for that.

After another day, I found the last of my crew exactly where I had left them. They were youngsters, too scared and skittish after the ambush to go anywhere. Except in my shadow.

Ciaran spotted me first. A shy kid of nineteen. He was sitting around a dead campfire in the early afternoon.

"Davik! You're back!" He stood with a grin. This had been his first foray into anything dangerous. The son of a fisherman who stared at the sky and had wanted more. His face fell when he saw me limping. "Nellie! Come quick."

Nellie came from behind some trees, straightening her trousers. My greeting from her was a scowl. Her hand was bandaged. A gift from a bolt that had punched through it. I had barely gotten her off the ship alive. She had been on one job prior, which had seen little action. As far as fighters went, she wasn't one. Compared to Ciaran, she was an esteemed veteran.

"Did he pay you?" was the first thing Nellie asked. She stood next to Ciaran, arms crossed.

These two didn't need to hide out. Nobody knew who they were. They could vanish and go off. Back to whatever lives they had had.

"This was all he had," I said, and tossed the coins into the dirt between us. I fell down, sitting heavily next to the camp waterskin, and took long gulps. It was so much warmer here.

Nellie picked up the two silvers and coppers. "That's it? He held out on you?"

"Nellie, stop," Ciaran pleaded. "Can't you see he's wounded? Let's bandage him up."

But Nellie wasn't having it. The brown-haired girl sneered at me, weighing the coins. "Where's the rest of it?"

"That's all they had," I repeated. My feet were pulsing. Too much marching.

"How do you know?" Nellie asked.

"Because I went through his pockets after I killed him. And his people. Believe it or not, they were worse off than we are. Which is what I figured when I went up there."

"Wow," Ciaran said quietly.

My story did not impress Nellie. "What you figured? What you figured! Why would you go up there if you knew he didn't have our money?"

I stared at her. "Not all debts are owed in coin."

"How long do we last? With this **shit!**" she tossed the silver back on the ground.

"Nellie, it's better than nothing." Ciaran turned to me. "Right, boss?"

I groaned, pulling a boot off. "Not really, kid."

"He stole it," Nellie hissed. "Stole the loot and probably buried it. Only came back because he's hurt. We're out here starving, and he buried the payoff."

"He wouldn't do that," Ciaran told her. "Stop it."

"That's Davik of Darkshire, Ciaran! He got everyone killed! Probably on purpose, so he could keep it for himself. He'll kill us too. Unless we..." She shot me a look.

I held my hands up, begging her to continue. "Go on, say it."

Nellie didn't answer.

"Let's just calm down. Figure out what we do from here," Ciaran said, as he looked at both of us. "The silver isn't much, but it's enough. We'll head to town and get some supplies."

I chuckled at that. Few supplies to be had with that amount of coin.

Ciaran had a good heart, which was why I didn't expect him to survive long in this business. If they left, they wouldn't be coming back from getting supplies. And if they did, it would be to kill me in my sleep for my sword.

Nellie kept staring at it. Probably debating if I had some stash of gold hidden somewhere, which would be ludicrous. It's the type of thing an amateur suspects. If I had a big payout, why on earth would I be back here with these two?

I nodded to Ciaran. "Give me a hand with the bandages before you go."

"Of course," Ciaran started towards me.

"I'll do it," Nellie snapped. "Go try to sling another squirrel if you can, Ciaran. We'll leave it for him."

"Right," Ciaran said. "Right."

The young man left and Nellie walked towards me, helping me with my leather armor and bloodstained pants. She tugged them down. The dried blood peeling from the bite made me grit my teeth.

"What did this?" she asked.

"Bugbear," I grunted as she unwound the dressing.

Nellie bit her lip, wincing at the sight of a deep wound. "Can you get around, much?"

"Walked here, didn't I?" I stared at her. She kept her eyes on the punctures made by the fangs and smeared some salve on. The red tinge of infection was flaring around each bite mark. I saw the wheels in her head turning.

"It won't kill me, you know."

Nellie looked up. "What?"

"That infection, you're hoping it'll kill me. Save you the trouble. It won't. Won't take the leg either, now that we've salved it. Looks like you'll need to find your backbone."

Nellie stood up and turned to our camp pack, grabbing another set of bandages. "I don't know what you're talking about."

She wasn't a pretty girl. Most that fall into this line of work at this level aren't. But when you're in the woods for a long time, around the campfire week after week? The odds are good, but the goods are just odd.

"You'll get him killed," I told her.

Nellie turned from where she was bent over, throwing me a look. "Killed getting supplies? Paranoid, much?"

I sat back against the boulders. "Won't take long, convincing him to finish me. Longer than you think, and less than he'll believe. But you'll get it done. Can I give you a word of advice?"

Nellie rolled her eyes as she turned back to me, but her cheeks were burning. "What's that?"

"Go home," I told her. "That sword you keep eying on my hip isn't worth dying over. Go back to where you came from. Or he did. Take him with you. Go work a farm, a mill, something."

The twenty-year-old ignored me, binding my leg with fresh linen. She was a conniver, a schemer, most people were. Was it worth it to kill me? Probably. Would they pull it off? Absolutely not. Ten men in Erast could attest to that. Stopping these two would be like swatting gnats.

Gnats I felt responsible for. I may have saved their lives, but one thing was true, I should've smelled that ambush a far way off.

I looked at her. "It's true, you know."

"What?" Nellie asked. She still wouldn't look at me. She made a show of tying the bandage.

"Got everyone killed," I said. "That's on the leader, whether it's an avalanche or an ambush. Question is, what are you going to do about it?"

Nellie looked at me, kneeling between my bare legs. She glanced down. When she had first joined my outfit, she had given me plenty of glances. Bastard that I was. A big name, a reputation does that.

"What do you want me to do about it?" Nellie asked softly. How funny, sex and murder go hand in hand.

"I want you..." I leaned forward, my face coming close to hers.

Nellie inhaled. I smiled.

"To go home."

Her eyes went into a swift rage. She stalked off.

I reached for the waterskin, wishing it were wine, and stared at the trees. Spring was here, and ending. The heat of the day rose, and it would keep climbing. These two didn't know how to forage, they didn't know how to hunt or trap. They'd make poor road thieves and get themselves strung up.

"C'mon," I heard in the distance. Nellie had found Ciaran.

"What about the squirrels?" He asked.

"We need to make it to town and back. We can hunt on the way."

"Alright, one second."

"Ciaran—"

"Just a second!" He told her. Then he came jogging up out of the trees towards me.

"Need anything else in town, boss?" He asked.

24

"No, kid. I'm set. Go ahead."

"Okay." He turned to jog away.

"Hey Ciaran," I called him back over.

"What is it, boss?"

"Anything happens to me, do me a favor, alright?"

"Sure," Ciaran said. "Anything."

"Don't sell my sword in Swinford. Don't take it to a fence. Alright? Just take it to a jeweler. With a storefront. Get the gold for its inlay and that's it. Don't go further than that."

Ciaran gave me a puzzled look. Then he shook his head. "You're going to be fine, boss. Don't worry. We'll get supplies."

"I'm sure you will," I said as I sat back. I nodded to Nellie, who waited, arms crossed and scowling. "She's waiting for you."

"Right." Ciaran jogged off.

I gave it three out of ten if they came back at all. Taking the measly silver and hitting the road.

I sat there, drinking water and staring at the trees. How many times had I done this? Started over?

Used to take contracts from princes and walked with some of the heaviest names in the land...

Most of my friends were dead. And when I tired of them dying, I stopped making them. The last few years had been a card shuffle of faces around the campfire. Fighters, thieves, burglars. Warlocks with a taste for narcotics and mages I could barely tolerate.

If Nellie and Ciaran came back, I saw what would happen. We would summer here, feeding off the woods and maybe some nearby farms. She'd coax Ciaran along until he made a move on me. But his heart wouldn't be in it, and I'd slay him dead. Ciaran was just a young lad, like I had been before conscription. No thaumaturge had ever carved runes into his bones and under his flesh.

Or it would go the other way. We'd rebuild. Heal up. By the time we hit a new city or town to fill the roster and find some work, I'd have Nellie wrapped around my finger.

It all felt... stale. Something I had tasted too much, and I didn't have the stomach for it.

I looked down at my blade in the scabbard. Plenty of people had wanted it. Stroud had been the last of a long line of names it had scratched out. Scratched in crimson.

I had had enough.

I left them the sword, planted in the dirt. And my ruined leather armor. I scratched a note on the boulder behind it with a rock.

Yours.

We all make symbols, we're all authors of our own little effigies. An unworn engagement ring flung into a river. A father's shield laid to rest on his grave. Four coins from the lands of all your dead friends into the hands of a bartender.

A sword in the ground.

Letting something go. Letting someone go.

Starting something new.

I walked off into the forest.

CHAPTER
THREE

I spent the rest of spring in the woods, making my way slowly to the Midlands. There was no trajectory. No goal. My days became the flurry of traps and hunting small game. Of fishing in rivers with what string I had in my pack. In that solitude I was beholden to nothing and no one. I lost weight. My body grew dark from the sun. I sought to break a cycle.

I held no interest in a life of hermitage. To survive in nature is to engage in the world of competition and brutality. One day, as spring ended, I moved further south to leave the wilderness.

I walked for two days to the edge of the forest. Then I came across a town.

Oakshire. When I walked into its borders, the irony of the name wasn't lost on me. It was a town in a vast valley of farms at the edge of a forest. The snow melts atop the brutal mountains beyond, and it plummets down, but as it reaches the Midlands it slows, widening and warming, until it's gentle enough that the children of Oakshire play in it.

I strode into the town with no obvious goal. There was no one here to meet. No shadowy contact to rub shoulders with,

27

no crew to link up. I viewed it as a traveler does, and the quaintness of the place was no longer something I viewed at in passing, like a portal to another world. I could stay here. As long, or as little, as I wished.

There was no blending in. Even without armor, without a blade on my hip or a mace in my belt, I was a vagabond. The look of a likely escaped prisoner who had ducked from the razor's kiss for too long. At a storefront, I saw a man lighting a pipe with the strike of a flint on some tinder.

Sparks make me nervous. If you fought the Collegiates and the damned blue mages in the Summoner War, you know what I mean. You can spot a veteran of the Summoner War by the way they flinch at the sound of thunder, or dive on the ground when lightning crests the sky. Storms make my fists clench. I paid a fortune for two rune stones that heat tinder enough to catch flame when you face them towards each other.

If you've never seen cavalry and armored men hit with chain lightning from a dozen mages, good. When they come to your village to conscript you to fight them, follow my advice: just run. Run for your life. If they catch you, well, a noose is better than being a charred corpse. A corpse seared so hot it glasses and glitters along the battlefield like a macabre jewel.

War is hell, and wizards are in charge of the weather. I never minded sorcerers. I've known my share. Sorcerers can't help it. Warlocks and clerics have all made their pact. But those dangerous people who read books older than time and spit spells that tear men apart... they deserve little mercy.

Take the short drop.

Stay in your village. Don't go out to make exotic friends. They end up stabbing you in the back.

My life had been one of conflict for hire, of hired conflict.

But I had never built anything. I have never sewn a field or handled a plow. I've never sat down at a dinner table around a family. I ate the meals of my life on march, in trenches, or around campfires with adventurers that are long gone now. Off to a well earned grave, or a new life.

The wind blew, and my cloak that draped out of my bag fluttered behind me, trying to pull me back. Everything in Oakshire had a new-wood look to it. Polished and lacquered timber.

I could be something else here, even just for a while. I went where any great adventurer goes when encountering a new town. I went where the lost, the damned, and the drunks go.

The tavern.

Most towns have inns. It's a place for travelers. You piss in the rushes in the corner of the room, and trip over a dozen other bodies in the darkness. It's a good place to get robbed. Not by dashing thieves, but by other traveling farmers and merchants, especially when you're an outsider.

Fuck inns.

A good tavern has music sometimes. It has pretty girls. Or pretty-enough girls. It has rumors, and jobs, and a myriad of customers in the cities. There's an air of mystery, of a story starting.

A pour-house or a winesink is where you go to drink. You bring yourself and your reasons. I knew a cleric in the war who did more with a surgical saw than he ever did with his prayer book. A battlefield surgeon. He told me what happens to a liver when you drink too much. I didn't believe him. So then he showed me, literally.

See here, kid? That's fat. Man, get's a tolerance, his liver responds. Grows like this.

Please put it away.

I helped him out one month, assigned "light duty" from a wound. After a week, I begged to be sent back to the front. Tending to the dying is not for the faint of heart or the strong of heart. It is for the heartless, and the soon to be heartbroken. It shows you there is nothing glorious about battle or war or fighting. For a month, I watched a man cut others open to save them and he rarely succeeded. I held their hands while surgery was done with little more than a prayer to a god that wasn't listening. They pissed themselves. They wept.

The last thing anyone deserves is me there as the last thing to comfort them.

Summer was here, and I with it. I was a bit off kilter, too much time in the woods. But I felt a strange solace as I walked the streets designed for people. Nature is uneven, there are no flat places, only inclines and declines. To be on solid enough ground was a gift. Maybe the whimsy of the moment took me. Eager to speak to a person again.

I nodded to an elven blacksmith who scowled at me. His forge was cold, his hammer laying on the workbench near him.

"Have you any work, sir?" I bowed a bit when I asked. "I just came from-"

"Fuck off," the elf growled and reached for his hammer.

"Absolutely," I agreed and wandered back into the road.

So much for the call of destiny.

There was a bookstore, where a woman stared at me through the glass with a frown so strong it could have been a shield wall.

"Blessings to you," I said with a nod through the glass. Her scowl continued.

For a few coppers, I'd dust off more than her books if she needed. The woods make for a miserable dating life.

I saw families walking, and young couples. Humans and half-elves, tieflings and firefolk. There were farms and orchards and mills off in the valley's distance. But here in town, there were homes, houses, shops. A place for people to spend money and their lives.

Not a place you needed a swordsman. Which suited me fine.

I saw a bakery ran by a couple of timber dwarves. There was a cafe where a deep gnome smiled and polished cups while talking to her morning customers.

Before going to the tavern, I headed to the temple I saw at the other end of town. In my experience, it's an important first stop. One that can be your life or death. You never know if they worship a god of bountiful harvest. Or perhaps you find a new religion that's taken hold, one ready and needful for sacrifices.

As I approached, I saw a faded symbol of a cut jewel and a key. I hadn't seen it before.

A young man was tending to the weeds in the little lawn out front.

"Is the cleric in?"

He turned and doffed his cap. Good manners, to doff your cap to trash like me.

"No sir, I'm afraid not today. They are in meditation in the wilderness."

"Thanks," I said. "Any work around these parts?"

The young man put his rake down thoughtfully, the type of movement someone does when they actually think about their response.

"Maybe in town, sir, the county harvest festival's coming end of season. Brings lots of travelers."

"Thanks," I said and looked around. "Lots of folks pray here?"

"Some do, sir." He nodded.

"Can I ask you a question?"

"Of course," the young man walked towards me.

"What's this temple for? What deity or demon?"

The young man blushed, whether from my words or the superstition of mentioning the other plane.

"The Mistress, sir."

"Mistress, right. Of course." I nodded. Not knowing what deity that was.

He waited, unsure if we had finished speaking. I eyed him carefully.

You have to be careful when probing about a faith. It takes deftness. You can't tip your hand. There is a delicate balance at work when sourcing information properly. Like springing a lock in the dark of night.

"You eat people?" I asked.

"Sir?"

"People. Do you eat people here? Or sacrifice them?"

"No..." the young man stammered. "That's... no sir. The Mistress faith isn't like that."

"What about sacrifice? Do you cut their hearts out, or anything?"

"No!" The man looked worried. "Do... they do that? In cities?"

"What about strange rituals? Huh? Bloodletting maybe?"

Now the young man was full on blushing. "Not at all. All the Mistress requires is honesty, sir."

"Right," I said. Then I broke into a smile and raised my hands. "Just joking."

The young man stammered a laugh. I laughed.

Then I grew serious.

"You can tell me, you know... if you've eaten people. You think I'll judge?"

"Sir, nobody eats people here."

"Of course," I said with a wink. "Of course." I walked back into town.

Better safe than sorry. My investigation into the subtle dangers of town complete, I went back towards the tavern.

As I did, the smells of the cafe made my mouth water. The

hint of nutmeg and lemon curd wafted from the storefront. I made a note of it on the mental map I was drawing, in case I happened upon some coin, or more likely, rifled through their trash. It had been a long time since I ate something that wasn't trying to run or flop away from me.

The tavern didn't have a name. It was two stories, in a bit of a chaotic, charming style of build. Spiraling roof shingles, the rickety rookeries and off-center angles. The windows were thick and pulsed with a magic that reinforced their strength. I felt the runes in my bones hum a bit as we passed them, pointing them out to me.

I donned my best smile and wandered through the front door. It was early morning, the hour where you get workers who were up all night getting a drink in before hitting the sack.

The tavern was empty of patrons. The stairs to my right led upwards to a hallway of rooms. It opened to look down on the seating area. An enormous fireplace, the kind that costs you too much firewood, sat along the wall in grey rock. At the back, the kitchen clanked with the closing of oven doors. It smelled of wood, of frothy taps and spiced potatoes.

The bar was a fallen tree, lacquered to maintain its flowing effect. The oak countertop was a small city of taps. Behind the bar, bottles glowed in the morning light.

But none glowed as bright as her.

The she-elf was pale skinned and painfully beautiful. Even if I hadn't been in the wilderness for some time, I would have still been mesmerized. There's beauty in the world, but it's fleeting, subject to the denigrations of time and man.

Not her. Her hair was spun gold, like the fields I had seen outside. Two small silver bands kept it neatly away from her temples.

"What can I get you?" she asked, her voice carrying a hint

of feigned disinterest, though her silver eyes betrayed her curiosity. She had been watching me since I walked in.

She was putting inventory away, a marching line of bottles arranged in near-perfect infantry lines on the countertop.

There is no voice like that of an elven woman. It's the kind of voice that pulls you deeper into a dream. She could've been centuries old, or only twenty-five. She wore a simple dress of autumn orange, the kind a farmer's daughter might wear, or a teacher, but with thread and linen so fine a king would don it.

"My name is Davik, ma'am."

The elf stared at me. For a moment something passed her face, not fear, not exactly. Recognition? She moved with the easy confidence of the ageless.

"What'll it be, Davik?" she asked, staring at me with one hand under the bar.

"Are you the owner of this tavern?" I inquired.

She squinted at me for a moment, like an actor whose partner had just forgotten their line. Her hand relaxed and came back to the bar.

"That depends," her voice floated towards me. "Are you a tax collector?"

I shook my head. "Of all the crimes I've ever committed, I never fell so low as to collect taxes."

She stood straighter now, both hands resting on the bar. A mountain of cleavage pursing between her arms, a serious stare in her eyes.

"What are you doing here, in Oakshire, Davik?"

"Looking for work," I replied. If I had felt out of place on the street, standing so close to her was comical. I needed a razor and a series of showers. "And you are?"

"Sariel," she said, waiting as if I was supposed to recognize the name.

"Nice to meet you. I like your tavern."

"How long have you been in the woods?"

"Since spring," I said. "Since most of my traveling companions parted ways."

"Explains some rumblings I've heard." Her silver eyes swept over mine. "Of missing chickens and a man creeping around some farmer's lands. So you're a thief."

I felt the chance of work and maybe a fresh hay bale to sleep in fade away.

"I've been many things. But I won't be blamed for the work of hawks and foxes."

"A veteran," Sariel's eyes flashed. We both glanced at the conscription brand burned into the top of my left hand.

"Aye, even that."

"In the Summoner War," she said. It wasn't a question.

I didn't hide the hate in my voice. "I fought in it, alright. And even more pointless ones. For land and religions and causes... and mages who should've left well enough alone."

Sariel raised an eyebrow. "Were you at Breakspear?"

The name of that place stole the light from the room for me. For a moment, I heard horses screaming. Before the battle, it had been called Kingspear Valley, the last confrontation and rout that ended the Summoner War.

I bit out the words. "That's my business."

"Just trying to figure out if we once crossed paths." The elf woman shrugged. "Lotta men boast about being there."

"I don't." If I never thought of that damned place again, it would be too soon.

"So, you say. Tell me, veteran, what caused the vanguard to break the lines that afternoon? What happened, if you were there?"

I stepped towards the bar, my body locked in anger. She was calling me a liar. Questioning if I had actually seen it.

"It wasn't afternoon," I said. The bar seemed to fade away,

replaced by things I didn't want to see. "It was morning. The Celestial Archon offensive fell, and the Collegiate wizards tore their souls from them."

Davik, they're dying, look at them!

"And what did you do when you heard their cries across the battlefield?"

My face was a mask of fury now. I leaned in close, spitting out the words dripping with venom. "I covered my ears, lady, like every other man. Then we were overrun. By everything. By the Embriel."

Sariel nodded, satisfied. "I know. Sorry. Like I said, lots claim to have been there. Here, have a drink."

"I'm not here for a drink," my voice shook with emotion. I was an open chest she had pried apart, more upset by what I saw inside than her intrusion. "I'm here for work. To trade labor for coin. For food."

A girl came in from the back and swept somewhere to my left. She was in the corner of my eye. Sweeping slowly. Lost in her own world.

Sariel gestured towards the girl. "I have the help I need here."

Perhaps the coldness of her bruised me even more because of her beauty.

"I see that," I said without looking. We were in a duel, neither of us willing to budge.

Slowly, she reached below the counter and set out a glass tumbler and dark bottle.

"Don't have work for you here, veteran. But have a drink. That stamp earned you that. Take the corner, the girl will light the hearth. Just don't pass out in here."

It was tempting. I was angry. Wrathful. And no one needs a better start to a session of burning himself down than the kindling of righteous indignation.

But when I looked at the bottle, I wanted it and I didn't.

"No thanks," I whispered. I turned from the bar, the girl was sweeping behind me. I moved past her.

"Excuse me," I snapped.

When I looked up, I couldn't believe my eyes. I had been so furious with the elf.

The girl was a most-orc. Dark brown hair, skinny for one of her race. Twin tusks jutted from her bottom lips, lips so plump and pink they resembled an orchard yield in the morning. Her dress was a bit ragged, unclasped at the back by a single button. One green shoulder bare where her strap had fallen.

Her eyes were dark and a bit sad. Sad for me, I realized. She wasn't large like many greenskins I had known. She was delicate, a small thing.

"Excuse me," I said again, softer this time. I was taken in by this girl, by her gentleness and slightness. "I'm sorry," I found myself saying.

"Tis' alright, sir," Her voice was shy, and light. Brown eyes blinked and looked at me.

"No," I said, feeling the shitheel I was. The tavern owner had dressed me down and exposed me. Whatever facade I had come in with had been melted away.

I reached into my pocket and pulled out my last iron coin. I handed it to her.

"I'm sorry," I repeated. She took it, confused at my gesture.

I cast one last glance at the owner behind the bar. Then I turned and left.

CHAPTER
FOUR

At midday, I sat by the river, staring at its flow. It wound south toward a valley brimming with farms, likely feeding a dozen fields. It had a purpose. It supplied something. It had value.

I watched it and did what all rotten men do when they don't get what they want—I felt sorry for myself. The biggest joke of all. Behind me lay countless maimed and slaughtered people. They all had deserved it. But maybe I did too.

I heard footsteps approaching, the rustle of brush. I didn't turn. Paid it no mind. I had no blade or armor.

The footsteps grew closer, steady along the same path I had come. Nice to be wanted.

A bundle in a sack landed near my feet. I didn't bother to see who threw it. It didn't look like heads. That's always a plus. It smelled of cheese.

"Sending me on my way?" I asked aloud.

Sariel, the innkeeper, approached and sat near me. Far enough that if one of us swung, we wouldn't reach each other.

"Consider it an apology, though if you're like me, you rarely speak them aloud."

"Don't see it in here," I murmured, pulling a small loaf of bread from the sack.

"See what?" she asked.

"Your apology."

The elf nodded to herself. "Suppose I deserve that. Sorry for pressing you so hard back there."

I pulled out a block of soft yellow cheese. It smelled sharp, nutty, with a bit of hay. I picked a long white hair from it.

"Sheep," Sariel said.

"Thanks." I tore a hunk of bread and offered some to her. She bit off a piece, tearing it away from her face, and stared at the river with me.

I hadn't eaten in a while. Didn't know when or what I'd eat again. We sat like that, ignoring each other. As the food hit my belly, I felt a bit of strength return.

"I rarely keep men around, to be honest."

"Don't blame you. You look like you can handle yourself. And if I had a most-orc working for me, female or not, I'd likely not hire men either."

Sariel smiled, her eyes squinting as the sun broke beyond the clouds, painting us both in light.

"Vorga is a more innocent creature than I ever was. She picks up spiders and carries them outside."

"Sounds like a druid in the making," I said with a full mouth. "What can I do for you?"

Sariel huffed and picked a long blade of grass. She spoke while twirling it in her fingers.

"Before I even think about giving you a spot of work, I need to know. What are you? Wanted? Hiding out?"

"Unwanted, more like." I bit more cheese off and swallowed.

Sariel flicked the blade of grass away and reached for another, slowly, as if plucking the right words to ask me.

"Are you Darkshire?"

I stared at the loaf of bread in my hands.

"Where did you hear that name?"

"Most in town wouldn't know it. But I've only been here a few years. Heard lots of stories. Darkshire, he keeps a sorcerer in a trunk, only lets him out to kill his enemies."

I grinned at that one. Little bastard had deserved it.

Sariel continued, "Darkshire walks the land with a chain behind him, stealing women and girl folk. He murdered a prince once and stole his bride. He was hired to defend the siege at Rochdale, only to open the gates himself and let the enemy in."

"Quite the story," I said.

I'll never forget those gates opening and what poured inside. We would've had a chance. Maybe.

Boss, the Lords are leaving!

"Darkshire will knife you for a piece of bread."

"Lucky you," I said. "Already have your bread."

"Do you steal?" she asked.

"Only if I'm paid to. But not from my employers. Nor my allies. Nor small folk, save the wayward livestock when my people are starving, but only from those that can bear it."

"Do you kill innocent people?"

I snorted. When I had been a boy, I watched my mother get robbed not by brigands or highwaymen, but by our neighbors once my father died. If you put those same people to the sword, they'd call them innocent.

"I never put my skills to work on anyone that wasn't in the trade."

"What trade is that?"

"Killing." I looked at her. "Adventuring. Guild contracts.

Grand quests that shake the pillars of the world. Depends on who sings the story. I served a prince once, hired me to protect his betrothed. When the contract was over, I left him a knife right here." I tapped a finger under my left eye.

"That doesn't speak well to your ethics for gainful employment, does it?"

Maybe it didn't.

He had hired me alright. But the little border prince had always loved to preen. They assigned me the task of guarding his betrothed, a favored daughter of some lord who couldn't pay his rising taxes. For a full year, I scared off any guards with silver tongues, which wasn't really needed. They all feared him. He used to take me to his meetings with the guilds of his realm to intimidate people.

The contract ended the day of their wedding. It had been a bright affair. Yellow flowers everywhere, her favorite. We never spoke much; she was a gentle girl. Nice to me, though. Polite. Her soon-to-be husband just liked having such a heavy name around to show off.

We had been set to renegotiate my contract the day after their wedding. I was hungover, of course. A night of too much wine that ended with one of the newer chambermaids and me in a closet.

I went to her room by pure reflex. It was where I usually started my shift. She was weeping in the closet. I'm no hero. Could never be mistaken for one, either. But some things set you the wrong way. I saw what he did to her, and I saw what her life would be like.

I found him in his study. We negotiated a new contract, right there on his desk. A contract of life and death. His hands frantically clawing at my head as I held him there and slowly slid my knife through his face. He always wanted to see how strong I was, to see if some stories were true. *Be careful what you wish for, prince.* Then I left him there, the blade biting out the back of his skull, nailing him to the desk, right on the parchment he had drawn up.

I slew two gatemen on the way out with her, and the rest let us pass. Took her to her father, told him to hide her. To say I took her. Of all things, the bastard was upset I brought her back, couldn't understand why. Because they were married.

The prince's father hunted me for months after that. Never understood how a man could have a prince for a son and not be a king. Torches riding up and down the roads, among the towns, gripped in the armored fists of knights. The story spread that I stole from her, of course. That I lost it to jealousy and abducted her.

Was the first time I had been proud of myself that entire year. After the fall of Rochdale.

"I suppose it doesn't," I said. "But most people have nothing to fear from me."

Sariel sat on the hill next to me, and I looked at her. I made no effort to hide it. She was beautiful. The most beautiful thing I had seen in a long time, and the way her dress clung to her thick body, the hourglass figure of perfection made my heart beat faster.

"Are women safe around you?"

I chuckled at that. "Oh, definitely not."

She gave me a pointed look.

"I've never harmed any woman that wasn't trying to kill me," I told her.

"You lay any unwanted touch on any of the girls at my tavern, we'll have a problem."

"What if it isn't unwanted?" I asked slowly.

Sariel laughed. "They're big girls. You know what I mean. Or I'll put you down, human."

"Does this rule apply to you?" I asked. She looked at me, weighing my words.

"You're a rogue alright."

"You didn't answer the question."

"Maybe," she said with a shrug. "Maybe not. Guess you'll have to see. I'll pay you. Two silvers a week, twenty after the festival as a bonus."

Used to take contracts from princes and walk with the heaviest names in the land...

Yet here I was, negotiating for a pittance. I could turn tail today, wander into Daggar or Trinth even, and have work by the end of the week that would net me a hundred times that.

But she wouldn't be there.

"Three a week, and forty."

Sariel rolled her eyes. "Three a week, and twenty-five. But if you're going to work at the tavern, there'll be some rules."

"Alright," I said. The wind blew the grasses we sat in; her dress rose from her ankle to her knee, and when I saw her cross her shapely legs, I felt my cock twinge.

"No drinking on the job," she said.

"Bartender who doesn't drink? What is this, a fairy tale?"

Sariel laughed. "Oh, you're no bartender. You ever gone dry? Or needed to?"

"Oh sure," I said. "When I run out."

She glared at me. "Come now. Tell me the truth."

"Never had an issue with the stuff."

"No? Never?"

"What comes out of my mouth always got me more trouble than anything I ever put into it."

That brought her a laugh. "We'll see how long you can keep it up, human. Rule two, no stealing."

"Easy," I said.

"Rule three," she leaned forward, pulling her knees to her

ample chest. I had rarely seen a more buxom woman, and never one in such a shape as her. "No killing."

"Eh," I said.

She turned her head. "I mean it. No blades, no killing. You were a Magebreaker, weren't you? I saw the scars. I didn't think there were many of you left."

"I was" I said. "I still am. It's not something you can turn off."

"Wasn't kind, what they did to you all." Whether she meant my own armies or hers, she was correct. Kind didn't factor into anything for Magebreakers. Not in making them, not in using them, and certainly not for the last of them that were captured.

"That why you're giving me this job?" I asked. "A battle-elf who feels bad?"

Sariel held my gaze. "Embriel is what we preferred to be called."

Of course. I hadn't seen it at first. It was rare to see an Embriel without their armor. Silver and black, like a storm coming towards you. Usually sitting prim on their mounts, never afraid to dismount with those long sweeping swords.

Of the many kingdoms and factions of elvenkind, not all live up to their names. I've known wood elves who couldn't find their way out of a forest, and Feyth'a High Elves who tugged on your shoulder in a tavern, begging for a drink, far exiled from a sparkling city.

But I'd never known an Embriel to be anything but a killer. Their homeland had been destroyed, so the story goes, by some Elven race that they in turn wiped out and no one knew the name of any more. Embriel music was the war drum. Their economy was conflict. Regimented lives, marriages arranged based on the union of companies and legions.

And they had fought with the Mage Collegiates in the

Summoner War. Whether for money or shared ideals, I never knew.

"That a problem, for you?" Sariel asked.

It wasn't, in truth. I knew veterans on my side, bitter at the loss we had suffered. I thought it foolish. Those mincing lords that had conscripted us and put us to field—they made me what I was. They were who I had hated.

"War's over," I said. "For me, at least."

That seemed to suit her. You'd never imagine her leading a battalion of bloodthirsty warriors.

"Three a week, ten to start," I said. "Tax, for an old enemy. And I get my own room."

"Three and four to start. You get a barn."

"With hay."

"With **some** hay."

"Meals?" I asked.

"Crew meals. Lunch and dinner. Breakfast, you're on your own. The girls and I eat together each morning at the house."

"What else?" I asked.

"Go ahead," Sariel smiled.

"Go ahead, what?"

"Ask."

"Do you want to sit on my face?" I asked.

She laughed at that. I liked her immediately. There were all kinds of women in the military. Some tried to be one of the boys. Others floated from lover to lover. The best of them never hid what they were, and knew how to manage men. She was that. She didn't rattle easily. And a bold statement or a bit of forwardness wouldn't coax her forth, either.

"Ask," she repeated.

"Why?"

Sariel leaned back into the grasses. "I was there too. At Breakspear. I saw when the line broke. I'm a veteran. I did...

messed up things during the war. The things you said no to, I wish I could say the same for some of those. What you suffered, like so many others, a lot of that was me. I did some not very nice things. I picked up bad habits, and it took me a long time to rid myself of them."

We sat in silence for a bit. My new employer. This gorgeous woman. There was something she wasn't saying... something hidden.

But we're all entitled to our demons, and the feeding of them. I knew that better than most.

"Your employees know? The townspeople?"

Sariel shook her head, golden hair sliding back and forth over her bare shoulders. "I don't hide it, but they don't know. I don't touch a sword. I don't sleep in armor anymore. I just run a little sinking tavern."

"I see," I said.

I wanted to be close to this woman. In this little town with its shops and slow life. The type of woman who oozed sensuality, like a predator drawing in a wayward prey. Many men want many things from the women in their lives. If I had Sariel, all she'd have to do would be to wake up in the morning.

The moment ended. She stood up and reached down with a hand to shake. "C'mon veteran, I'll show you your barn."

I grabbed the hand that had once waged war against me. A former enemy. She yanked me upwards. Strong, stronger than I had thought.

"With **some** hay."

CHAPTER
FIVE

"So if I'm not pouring drinks, what should I be doing?" I asked as we walked into town. Sariel was almost as tall as I was, which was a change for me. It was hard to tear my eyes away.

I gave myself a week before I was fired.

"To put it in terms you would understand... shit-work."

"Shit-work," I echoed.

"Mmm." Sariel nodded as we walked. "Busboy, dishes, carrying things, including drunk patrons. Changing keg taps. You are a guild initiate of the Busboys and Barbacks Brotherhood. Membership numbers: you."

"I'll pass," I said. "Never was one for paying my guild dues."

"There, we can agree."

We walked back to the tavern. Inside, the orc girl, Vorga, was bringing in bundles of firewood. I watched her dark hair, her lithe frame.

"My office is downstairs, past the bar. The outhouse is outside. Guests want hot water, which we boil in the kitchen and you take up there. Try not to burn yourself. There are eight rooms for let upstairs."

"How many employees?" I asked.

"Vorga and Jessa are waitresses. We call her Jess. She comes in later. She's betrothed and likely to leave us soon to be a young housewife. Tyra runs the kitchen in the back. There's a method to her madness. Her helper, Brim, is here. I'll introduce you. Karley tends the bar. She'll be here soon."

"Come on, you need to know your way around the back-of-house." Sariel waved me to follow her. She slid behind the bar and I followed, passing dozens of bottles of spirits and liquor. One caught my eye. A brandy bottle of clear glass with a swollen pear inside.

"How do you get the pear in there?" I stopped.

Sariel didn't turn back as we continued into the kitchen. "You put it over the stem and it grows inside. Takes patience. A few friends of mine at the orchards in the valley do it for me. We brew here too, now that the old brewer retired."

In the kitchen, a faen-girl was hard at work, staring at a bubbling pot. Her hair was the color of molten rubies in sunlight. Like most races of the Faen, she descended from fairies who had mated with humans. You could spot them if you looked hard enough, the shape of the eyes, the glint to their skin. Most didn't have wings. They were smaller in stature, like a halfling, almost.

"Tyra, this is Davik. You'll be seeing a lot of him. He'll be bussing tables."

"Hey," Tyra smiled and turned to me. Big green eyes on a freckled face beckoned me forth. Her skin had a slight sparkle to it, like most Faen emanate. Her hair had several ringlets of beads and crystals on her coppery flesh.

"Hey," I said. "A pleasure."

"You drop your plates and such over here." Tyra jerked a

thumb in slow motion to the sink behind her. As if there was anywhere else. "Brim will take care of the rest. He comes in later."

"Thanks. Nice to meet you."

"You have kind eyes." Tyra reached out and touched my shoulder. I felt a strange warmth come over me. Like everything was going to be alright.

"Hmm," Tyra's eyes peered at me, confused. "Something in you is... resistant, isn't it?"

She wasn't wrong. My old profession, or designation, limited the use of magic on me in any capacity. That said, it had been a long time since I felt such a feeling. Her magic was non-threatening, natural, not contrived. Maybe that's why I felt more of it. When she touched me, I felt like I was standing in a sunny meadow, and everything was alright.

The feeling didn't disappear when she removed her hand; it faded slowly, like a candle burning out.

"Magic doesn't necessarily work on Davik," Sariel explained. "It's a... holdover from his old job."

"Oh, that's sad," Tyra said and meant it. "Welcome to the team." She turned back to her pots and began stirring randomly, dipping from one to another. Her dress was bound tightly across her heavy chest. It shined with the steam and sweat of the kitchen. The long line of her prominent cleavage jiggled as she stirred, an amber pendant nestled between the crook of her flesh.

"Follow," Sariel commanded and led me out back. I watched her tall form, that motherly sway to her.

"You have quite the staff here." I caught up with her as we exited the rear entrance. I wondered at my luck. When you have a career like mine, there's no shortage of female companionship on the road. But those drawn to a life of adventuring, of hired violence, are not always the most pristine of beauties with a level head. The years take their toll.

"I have a soft spot for hard cases," Sariel said to me. "Those hiding, those running. Those just wanting a slowness."

She toured the back of the property for me. Where the dwindling woodpile was. Where deliveries were to be unloaded.

Surprisingly, there was a bathtub smack dab in the middle of a failed garden, close to a wooden shack.

"Is that going inside?" I asked.

Sariel shook her head. "I had thought about it, maybe as a draw for travelers. We use it sometimes, as do some guests. Takes a bit to fill up and boil."

"I can take it upstairs if you like," I offered. The tub was five feet long, claw-footed. Cast iron wrapped in a ceramic with a patina to it.

Sariel raised her eyebrow. "Let's not throw your back out on the first day."

The tub would be no issue, but I think she knew that. If she was an Embriel, she'd killed many of my kind and knew how many men it took to take one of us down. If you loosed ten enchanted arrows, only one might land true. They had made us stronger, more durable. Soldiers and fighters who could withstand the onslaught of spells and sorcerous assault—that grew stronger the longer they fought, for some reason. It had taken the Collegiate too long to figure out why.

What did our command do to reward us? Fine armor and magical swords? No. Those that had survived the thaumaturgist's engraving procedures pulled the carts they didn't want to tire the horses with. We were animal labor. Spell-fodder.

They did nothing for our flesh, either. A blade split the skin of a Magebreaker same as anyone. The runes were a tuning fork to find and hunt casters in the thick of battle. Arms strong enough to hold shields for hours. The warlock told me any procedure to protect the flesh would've suffocated a humanoid. I doubted he was qualified to work even on farm animals.

Sariel spun and called out to a woman walking on the road. The figure was squinting her eyes and covering her violet skin with a bladed hand.

"Well, nice of you to join us, Karley!" Sariel called out.

I looked up and saw a female Drow who looked like how I felt. Her hair was silver, medium-length, and she walked like a stalking cat. She was sporting a hangover and wobbled like someone trying to keep from falling into the sky.

"Fucking hells," Karley groaned, carrying a bag under one arm. She wore leather pants and a black blouse wrapped close around her small torso. "Keep me away from that goddamn Tiefling next time."

"Did he make you breakfast?" Sariel teased.

Karley snorted and sat on a barrel, holding her head. "I hate summer harvest season."

I was being intentionally ignored. The drow had full lips, a beautiful face with sharp lines and dark eyes outlined by hair as pale as snow. The body of an athlete. If Sariel was an hour-glass, Karley was a fluted champagne stem. Thin, lithe, with a little bubble butt and sauntering hips. She carried herself like the mean brat who ruled the roost in the town school. The kind of girl young men would take too much abuse from because she was sexy.

"I'm going to throw up," Karley groaned.

"Serves you right. You spent half your weekly wages last night betting that Tiefling you could out drink him. They can burn the booze away inside them."

"He played me, alright." Karley looked up from her hands to her boss. Our boss. "I just walked three goddamn miles from his 'Mansion in the Woods.' Some mansion. It was a broken-down wagon."

Sariel smiled. "Tieflings can tell a tale, that's for sure. This is Davik. He's the new guy."

"Mmm." Karley stood and walked toward the door. "I gotta grab a bite before anything."

If she heard Sariel or not, I didn't know. I watched her walk into the doorway. Her tight little ass pressing in that black leather.

I like my coffee like I like my women... ignoring me.

"She puts on a show since you're here," Sariel explained. "But the chatter about spending the night with a Tiefling? All talk. Every night she'll chat up someone at the bar, but when it comes time to take the evening elsewhere, she sneaks off home. Never seen her follow through once."

"How do you know that?" I asked.

"Tyra, Vorga, and Karley live with me at my house. Karley's a tease. You'll help her plenty, but don't let her push you around into doing too much. She can be a brat."

"Strange," I said. "To pretend."

Sariel bent over and grabbed a piece of errant firewood, then tossed it toward the woodpile. "Everybody's something, right? Either what we are, or what we pretend to be. Now, what else should we show you?"

"The shower," I said.

Sariel smiled softly. "I'm glad you said that because you need one bad. Saves me owing you another apology. Water's ice cold, which is always a pain. But people don't want a moderately handsome vagrant bussing their tables."

Moderately. I'd take it.

"Pump it a dozen times." Sariel pointed to a pump jack next to the enclosure. "This valve reroutes water to the shower here.

I keep it for the girls. You can use it, too. If you hit this valve, it comes out of this outpour spigot."

"Does water run to the building?"

Sariel shook her head. "It was an option, but it was too expensive. Contractors wanted a fortune to pipe the place. Besides, I was worried about flooding. Get used to this apparatus, because you're going to be hauling buckets inside when Tyra needs them or there's cleanup."

"I'll leave you to get a rinse off," Sariel said. "Then I'm sending you to the Temple. I want the cleric to take a look at you."

"Magic won't work on me," I said, unbuttoning my filthy shirt.

"Elina finds a way..." Sariel stared at me, as if thinking about asking me something.

"What is it?"

"If you're going to be here, I need to make sure you follow the rules. I'm not everywhere."

"Right, but we already talked about this."

"It's something I do with new hires. Though it's been a while since we had one. Elina will cast a charm on you. It alerts me if any of those rules we discussed get broken."

"Magic won't work on me," I repeated. I was irritated at this blatant lack of trust, despite understanding her need for it.

"Elina can likely can find a way," Sariel said. "Look. I've got a lot of young twenty-plus-year-old girls here. Lot of patrons and customers. You're Davik of Darkshire—"

"Don't call me that." I stared at her. "Please."

"Anyway," she continued. "I trust you enough to hire you. But it's another thing to have you so close. I don't want to regret letting a wolf into the pasture, Davik. Take it or leave it."

"If it doesn't work?" I asked.

Sariel shrugged, beautiful and golden. "Then it doesn't work and I'll have to keep a closer eye on you."

"Fine," I said.

A smirk came over Sariel's lips. "Elina is also a barber of sorts. Tell her you want a shave."

"Okay," I said. In my experience, barbers were surgeons when there was no cleric, simply because they had a sharp set of razors. "Strange that a barber can't cut hair well."

"I said she's *like* a barber. Some sort of training with her religion."

"God of razors?" I asked.

Sariel smiled. "Something like that. I have a feeling she might be able to make the spell work."

"You gonna track my location, too?"

"No, just if you steal or cause the untimely demise of someone. Here, give me that shirt. I'll have Tyra give it a quick scrub." She held a hand out.

I slid my shirt off, and she watched the patchwork of scars along my flesh. The ones taken in battle, in work, and the deeper, straighter lines from the procedure.

Her eyes traveled over me, the mounds of muscle and scar. I was not pretty to look upon. Despite my larger size, after my time in the prisoner of war camps, I never could put on enough weight to be portly. My body held a leanness to it that battled with my muscles, stretching my skin tight.

"Did it hurt when they made you?" Her voice trailed off, her silver eyes sliding up the surgery points.

I wasn't going to answer that. I had already spent my years after the war brooding. It was over.

"I'm going to get undressed now," I said as I reached for my belt.

"Right," she murmured. It wasn't lust in her eyes, not all of it. Something else. Not pity.

Regret?

She snapped back to reality when I unclasped my belt.

"Right," she said. "See you when you're done."

I stripped down and walked behind the shower enclosure. Whoever had built it was about as good of a hand as I would be at carpentry. A shaking pipe ran up the wall that rattled like it was going to attack me. I pulled the chain and the icy water hit my flesh.

Cold, cold like the streams of a mountain. I held the chain-pull down, letting the water spray over me. I was caked in dirt, in sap, in the spring I had finished in the wilderness. My skin was sun-browned.

I used a fresh cube of soap and a rag, lathering myself. Even on the poor stones that made up the drainage, you could see the filth washing off me.

The tap ran dry, and I used a fresh towel hanging on the privacy stall that came up to my waist. Made for shorter folk, I suppose.

The benefits of running water, of soap and a towel were monumental to me after so much time away. I felt more like a person. A person standing in a new world, on uncertain ground, but a person nonetheless.

My pants felt even dirtier after I put them on, but it was an improvement. I walked out barefoot, letting my feet dry. Sariel stood by a series of barrels stacked behind the tavern.

"Look at you," she said when she finally turned towards me. "There's a man under the dirt. Who knew?"

"I think you did." I looked around. "So... where to start?"

She threw my shirt at me. It was still damp, but much cleaner. "Here, we'll get you a new one soon. Off to the cleric with you, brigand." She shooed me away. But that's the last place I wanted to go.

"Listen," I began.

"She'll be coming back now," Sariel said as she turned back to the inventory. "Her shift at the brothel is over."

"The brothel?" I clarified. I had seen no brothel in town. Such places didn't escape me. They are extremely offensive, and I make sure I know where they all are, what times they open and close and their rates, just to make sure I don't accidentally walk into one.

"Yep, she should be back now."

I left Sariel there, a grin on her lips as I walked off to the temple for a proper introduction to religion.

Only halfway there did I realize I had left my boots.

CHAPTER

SIX

I approached the temple as the sun crested into the pinnacle of the day. The shower had transformed me from a vagrant to a haggard barbarian walking barefoot down the road.

"Good afternoon." I nodded to a mother walking with her toddler, the young boy babbling and giggling as he ran down the walkway of Oakshire. She shot me a look of befuddlement and worry.

"Just off to the temple." I pointed in the direction. She grabbed her child and picked them up.

I'm a man of the people. I always have been.

Like a wanderer of old, missing a prized staff, I approached the temple. The young man had called the deity "Mistress" but I wasn't sure if that was a name or a title when addressing this goddess.

I walked in quietly, feet padding on the smooth stone floor. The small temple was empty, save for several wooden pews, a speaking platform, and the symbol of the deity.

"*Did someone steal your shoes?*" A voice echoed.

I spun, wondering where the otherworldly voice came from.

"Hello?" Confidence is key when speaking to gods. Perhaps I had given offense. Maybe they were the god of the shoes. The Archon of the Shod. The Stepping One.

"Out back!" came a mirthful voice. The same one that had spoken to me. I leaned over, staring at the temple altar, and saw an exit to the rear of the building.

I walked past the altar, outside into the bright sunlight. Ducking through, the smell of fresh flowers greeted me and a well-tended garden. Jasmine perfumed the air.

A smiling halfling was sitting on a stone bench. Around the garden were decorative rocks and green shrubbery with bright flowers. The little garden backed up to a high hill. It was quite private and peaceful.

"Are you looking for someone?" a halfling woman asked.

Like any halfling, Elina was the height of an adolescent human. Her skin was a rich, medium brown, and in the garden's light every inch of her looked smoothed and radiant. But in that darker complexion, her eyes were startingly lovely —amber irises, like molten chrysalis. They sparkled with a warmth when they met mine, a silent welcome in their glow.

Her hair was a cascade of tight curls, framing her face and falling past her shoulders. Though her frame was small, she was curvy. Her stature accentuated her build. A pale cleric's dress, sensual and thread-thin, encompassed her from her bust-line down.

I was ready to convert.

Her feet, too short to reach the ground, swung back and forth gently under the bench. The faint incandescence of swirling moon-ink tattooed the right side of her body from ankle to behind her right ear, dull in the daylight of this little garden grotto.

I'm looking for the prostitute-cleric.

"I'm looking for Elina, the cleric."

"Maybe you found her. What's that you have in your hand?" A wry smile fixated on me.

I opened it, handing her the gold ring with the ruby.

"Sariel's ring," Elina whispered, looking at it. Then at me. "Do you work there? New hire?"

"Yes," I said.

If this was a working woman, she was one of the finest I'd seen. The type of body and smile that made you empty your coin purse when your mother had sent you to the market for flour and you return empty-handed with a dumb grin on your face.

A story I knew well.

"What's your name?" She asked. Her voice was bright, patient.

"Davik."

"Come sit next to me, Davik. You don't look well."

I slid in next to her, a bit too close. She smiled and turned, crossing her legs and sliding those dainty little feet across one another. A lone ringlet of hair swung across her face.

Whatever they put in the Oakshire water, I approved.

"You have a sickness in you, Davik."

"I do," I agreed. Whatever she thought I had, I definitely had. I was infected. Sick. Dying.

Elina leaned forward, eyes turning wide. "Did she explain what this charm does?"

"Yes," I said. "Maybe. Why don't you tell me?"

"This is a deal-struck charm. It will alert her via this ring if you break any of the agreed upon rules you made with her. The more serious the violation..."

"Not to be rude," I cut her off. "It won't work. I have... certain attributes that make such enchantments ineffective."

Elina raised an eyebrow. "Do you mind if I try something small?"

Divine magic differs from primal or learned power. Yet, all are lessened against Magebreakers. When I'm near clerics or paladins, I don't feel the same magnetic pull towards their presence, as if I were a hunting dog. Their casting offends me less.

The halfling raised her hands and murmured a spell under her breath. Her palms filled with the spectre of a blessing.

She spread her hands to bless me. I felt my skin prickle in response, the runes within me finding the frequency of the spell, like a safecracker listening to a tumbler...

There.

The surprise in her eyes was clear as her spell dissipated from my body.

"Was that a blessing cantrip?" I asked.

"It was," she said slowly. "How peculiar. I've heard of races that are resistant to magic, but yours is so... reactive."

"Mine is deliberate," I clarified. "Or was, when it was done to me. And others."

"Peculiar," she said again.

"So," I said, making to stand. "Likely a waste. Shall we get to the shave, or do you offer other services?"

Elina peered at me. "Sit with me a bit, Davik. Do you know much about those that follow the Mistress?"

"I don't," I admitted. "But I love learning about new religions."

She smiled softly. "There are fanatic branches, of course. Women who take the scriptures too far, who left the order. They bind men, treating them like cattle, milking them until they wither."

Moo.

I glanced down at her thighs, so thick and supple. That

dark lust came upon me, the one that I had found and never let go. The need to reign. The need to claim. To conquer.

Elina beamed as she saw my hard-on slipping down the left leg of my trouser.

"I help people here in Oakshire, as my first station out of the temple in Trinth. You know the city?"

"Port city," I said, remembering. "Not far from here."

The halfling cleric smiled. "A cleric of the Mistress is an advisor, a teacher. She serves her community in many ways…"

Be smooth. Be deft.

"Sariel told me you worked at a brothel?"

Elina laughed. "I think someone was pulling your leg, Davik. There are no brothels in Oakshire. My facet is single-sided. Do you know what that means?"

Damn. Sariel had me on that one. A full season in the wilderness had left me starved for a woman. Oakshire was a river of them, each as lovely and different as the next.

"I don't," I admitted, turning to face her. "Teach me."

"The Mistress believes in honesty and love. The love of a couple across decades, centuries even. The love of two people for a single evening. The love of one who may never have it returned. We are taught that every soul is a jewel, carved into facets that fit into our lovers. Some fit well, some hurt because they don't fit and we try to make them. Some are temporary. The rarest are multi-faceted. I'm a cleric with a single-facet like most. I can have only one lover to devote myself to. Do you understand?"

I didn't understand.

"I understand. This is fascinating."

Elina touched my shoulder. She smelled of jasmine and soft sweat from a day of strolling.

"Deep things ail you, Davik of Darkshire."

I felt a jolt suddenly. Not from her saying that name. The

surrounding air took on a crackling feel, and my runes were screaming in my flesh and bones. I felt the presence of deep magic. A source. My skin itched with its presence.

"The Mistress whispers to me of your tale. Other men broke lands to wear crowns, but none have been hungrier than you to wear one."

I spoke gently, so as not to give offense. "I have never hungered for any crown."

"You have. One made of will, of desire and subjugation. Kings wear many rings, but the rings you always sought to envelop you were made of flesh. On another plane, you would be a terrible force to be reckoned with."

"And that means?"

The halfling smiled at me. "It means you might be multi-faceted. A river that feeds many. Like the one that feeds this valley. You're a crown that can hold many jewels. More than that, they shine brighter as you encompass them. Reach their potential."

"My powers come from prayer, lent to me by the Mistress. It is a sensual faith. Too much is repressed by the world, shamed, shunned, and forced to grow in darkness and fester. You've been in the woods a long time. What made you come forth?"

"I was looking for a change."

She regarded me. "I like you, Davik. I think you step away from the thing that follows you, your other name. The one you don't like me saying. If you were to come to me for counseling, it would be to help you explore the true capability within you. Not the runes or the power in your body, but in your heart."

"I don't think I need such services," I said. "But I thank you."

Elina put a hand on my leg. "My meditations today told me of your coming, that someone would arrive. When I writhed under my touch, I saw a dark figure stepping into sunlight. I think that's you."

"You pray, by..." I glanced down.

"I do," Elina said. "As do others. I'm a healer to the sick, though my power is fledgling, I'll admit. Not everything needs a spell or a cantrip. Some things that block us simply need to be spoken out loud to someone we trust. Don't you worry about adjusting to a life in a tavern, filling your hand with dirty dishes that once held swords and gold?"

I shrugged. Elina was beautiful, truly. There was a quaint honesty I enjoyed with her, and as one who never trusted the bastions of religion, I found her quite tolerable.

That said, I was not eager to share time speaking what was on my mind. I stood up, preparing my excuse to leave.

"I also believe the deal-struck charm could work with the Mistresses' help... if we were to be bound while performing it." Elina looked at me shyly.

I sat back down. "Bound as in..." I wanted to make sure I heard correctly.

Her foot raised, her shapely leg glowing with the magic ink in her flesh. It slid along my crossed legs, up towards my groin.

"Joined," she purred. "I am in need of a lover, Davik. This valley is filled with older men, or those too young or inexperienced. It's one of the duties of my faith, and as my first station here, for over two years I've been without a candidate. My spells grow weaker."

Despite the lust rising in me, this might be dangerous territory.

"This entails, what, from me?" I asked. "Precisely."

Elina stood, running her hands down her body. "Just being honest with your body and mine. I'd read your facets, Davik. I think by knowing them, the deal-struck charm could work well."

I stared at the beautiful woman, inviting me to share her bed. But you have to be safe. You have to ask the important questions.

"Do you-"

"We don't eat people, Davik." Elina laughed and stood from the bench, raising her arms to feel the pulse in the grotto. She cocked her head, listening to something I couldn't hear. "The Mistress thinks the spell can be completed, if you're comfortable. She's interested in seeing it work."

Had I stopped at this temple before the tavern, I likely would've been an acolyte. But Sariel was still fresh in my mind. If she found out...

"Sariel would not be surprised that you and I enjoyed each other. She likely sent you here not for a shave, Davik. She was probably doing a favor to me, offering you as a candidate."

"You are a strange town," I said.

Elina walked towards me, hips swinging. She spread my legs apart with her thighs and came closer. "You're afraid dining on one dish might mean another is taken away... but you might be surprised to learn that there's more to people than you'd believe. So what do you say, Davik? Shall we give this deal-struck charm a try? See if we can bind the unbound Magebreaker?"

I had been alone for a long time. I knew some men grew tongue tied around women. After I had killed my first man, and I really saw how fast it can all go, I never bit my tongue again. I ran my hands along her hips, the silken cloth rising.

"I have always," I murmured. "Sought to be bound."

"I'm single faceted, Davik. If we are to join, it is with you and none other. But you do have a great malady in you. I want to see you often. Not just for a celebration of the flesh. If you're to change, to grow, you might need someone to talk it through with."

I nodded, sliding my hands up to her ass, as if I had known this to be true my entire life. "I was thinking the same thing. Maybe even daily."

"Maybe," Elina agreed.

I slid my hands under her dress, across her shaved calves and higher.

"I'm very sick."

Elina smiled. "There is a path out of the woods for you."

The halfling pulled Sariel's ring back out and placed it on her own finger where it joined several others on her hand. "You remember the promises you gave Sariel?"

"No stealing."

Elina nodded. "That's a good one."

"No killing, no blades."

Elina's hand traced up to her neckline, where her dress hung from a silvered clasp around her neck. Her round breasts were straining against the fabric. Her body was a canvas of curves.

"When you take me," Elina whispered, sliding closer to me. "Take me as your body tells you. Your instinct. So I might read what's within you."

She touched the clasp at her neckline. The dress fell to the ground in a satin whisper.

Plump, heavy breasts spread across her short frame. Her soft eyes coaxed mine from the heft of her hip. Her quim was shaved bare, her lips inviting.

Elina stepped between my legs on the bench, her belly and breasts nearing my face. She looked down at me.

"Start slow," she whispered, almost trembling. "I haven't had someone..."

Neither had I. Not for a while, since the winter.

I ran my hands down her back

Elina ground against me. Her hands reached down and tugged on my cock through my pants.

"It's been so long since you saw the light, Davik," she murmured.

"Shh," I pulled her down into my lap and kissed her. There was a hunger in her that matched mine. Our lips met, our bodies pressing against one another, trying to become one. Seeking what they needed.

Her hands gripped me now with need. She slid down me, feet reaching the ground, running her bare breasts over my pants until she knelt.

"I've only had tools to practice..." she murmured and smiled. "Do you mind if I taste it? Do you enjoy a woman's mouth on you?"

The thick lust of dominance came over me, and I didn't fight it. If she wanted to know me, then she would. I stood and pulled my cock out of her pants and held it in front of her face. Elina's eyes half-closed in desire, she bent forward, guided by my hand under her chin.

"Ask your beloved Mistress" I huffed the sacrilege words and fed myself to her.

Elina looked up at me, pouting with need, wanting me to watch her wrap her lips around me.

She gripped my cock with one hand, steadying it in front of her. "Sit back, Davik. Let me practice some of my forms."

I did as she asked, though what I really wanted was to fill the garden with the sound of her throat. The cleric tugged my trousers down and placed my clothes under the bench. Then she turned back to me.

"So strong..." She gripped my member and pointed it skyward. A spell escaped her lips to her goddess and the rings on her fingers began to hum and reverberate.

"Oh," I groaned. Vibrating rings.

"I must know you for the binding to occur," Elina murmured. She pressed Sariel's ring into my hardening flesh and slipped her lips around my tip. A long groan escaped her lips. The groan of someone starved for something for so long. I swelled in her worshipful mouth.

The halfling knelt and twirled her tongue. She fed on me in a myriad of exercises.

"It's so good, the real thing..." Elina murmured and then dove down, taking me into her throat. She shook her head rapidly, gurgling and making my body arch.

"I fucking love it." She stroked me, twisting her hand in a spiral, kissing and tasting my shaft with her eyes closed. Her sincerity was intoxicating. "Ughnn," she filled her mouth again, opening her hand over her lips and striding it down to my base. Up and down, twisting, twirling.

"Mmmghhh," she moaned with a full mouth. Then a loud pop as she sucked my tip and pulled it from the saturation of her lips. Amber eyes stared at me. She tapped my cock against her tongue, laughing in joy as she did.

"Davik," she giggled, stroking me, then her smile broke in lust and she fell on me with her mouth bobbing up and down. The rings on her fingers vibrating faster, the ruby one from Sariel increasing in heat.

Her eyes locked with mine. She was teasing me, sucking and slurping and licking, but I needed more. The strange sensation of vibration and heat and... something else. Something almost icy traveling through my body.

I didn't care.

I grabbed a fistful of her hair and guided her down. Not forcefully, but with need. I filled her mouth with cock, then I met her throat and she gurgled praise and grabbed my member with both hands. There was no intimidating her. Her mouth and throat became a slobbering cacophony of gags and she fucked her own face with my length.

The sensation was enticing. She twirled her head and took me down her throat, her nostrils flaring and snorting as she withdrew, then returned, coating my shaft with thick slop and silver saliva.

"Such a sturdy boy," Elina murmured and stroked me rigorously. The ring continued vibrating, as if it was seeking some melody to match with an orchestra.

My eyes were full of wonder. A halfling priestess kneeling and serving me. I bent down and groped her ass, spreading her thick cheeks until I felt the edge of her muscled hole. She moaned on my cock and I teased her while she picked up the pace.

She was sucking my cock as if there was nothing else in this world. Her technique was a cascade of sensation, her hand covering her mouth and spiraling out, down, with that sacred twist some women know how to do.

I felt myself converting.

Yet that lust rose in me again. The need to dominate, to suppress. I would enslave Elina's very goddess and make her nothing but a tight ass for me to split open as I deemed fit.

"Hmmmm," Elina murmured on me, as if seeing what I saw.

The vision fled. I shuddered and stood from the bench.

"I need you," I instructed her.

The cleric's eyes flashed at me with demure understanding. She was meeting the monster within me. Elina withdrew herself and stood, tilting her body from side to side. Her glowing tattoos mesmerized me, racing up her leg and side, cresting under her neck.

I wanted her. I wanted this priestess.

She stepped up onto the bench, each foot straddling either side of my thighs.

I filled my mouth with her sweet cunt immediately. Her body was short, tight. I gripped her hips and swung her towards me. She spread her legs and positioned herself over my mouth.

The last thing I saw before I plunged in was the heft of her tits and little belly, that beautiful smile looking down on me.

Then I was smothered in the darkness of her folds and flesh. She strode against my tongue, gyrating. I reached around eagerly, fishing my finger through her deep buttocks as she slid along my mouth. She tasted of wonder. That sweet musk and tang filled my senses. I spread her labia, seeking, until I found that sweet button that can lead to a woman's ruin.

I locked onto her with suction, and she strode against me in joined friction. The halfling was moaning something to her goddess as she rode my mouth. Her palms slid over her heavy breasts until she reached down and gripped my hair.

The lust grew in me. I wanted to lift her off the ground like a doll in my hands and fuck her until she spurted and groaned and begged.

Despite what she had asked, I held myself at bay.

I broke away from her. "Give it to me,"

"The Mistress provides," Elina murmured. She held my chin momentarily. I remembered someone else doing that, once, long ago. But I couldn't tell you who.

She stared into my eyes as her short body squatted down. Her thick thighs were now rigid with exertion as she lowered herself.

Elina, Cleric of the Mistress, squatted onto the tip of my cock and put her arms around my shoulders. She stared into my eyes, a smile on her face, then a silent groan as she slid over me. Swallowing me with flesh.

I eased up into her, needing her. I filled my hands with her ass again and guided her down. She was so much smaller than me, but I needed her to take it all.

"Davik." She shuddered and sank onto me. "Yes."

It was like sliding into a hot vise. Whether from her stature, her religion, I didn't know. But she was tight. When she rose to impale herself again, I saw the soft flesh of her entrance gripping me.

She took me to the hilt, her cheeks spreading as she squatted down. I buried my face in her plump breasts. She raised one, feeding me like a babe, a beautiful dark nipple rolling in and out of my mouth as she took me. She was milking my essence. She was drawing from me. The spike was only half-sunk. Holding, but denying me.

I stood, taking her in my arms and holding her against my body. I held her up against my chest and fucked her in the air.

"Yes, yes, yes!" she cried out. "Fill me!"

"Take it," I growled.

"I'm going... to..." she stammered. Each syllable was spilling out of her as I took her passionately.

"Yes," I said, the cleric of this temple draped in my arms, impaled on me. I saw in her the moment and the yearning.

My need broke away from me. I would consume her here in this garden. I'd break her with desire until she called out for her goddess and—

The feeling was like a hand rested on my back. Just for a split second.

I slowed down, holding Elina up to look at me.

Her eyes floated, and then finally, focused, staring at me in a strange wonder. We kissed, tongues sliding, before she put a hand on my chest and broke from me.

"Lay down, please," she said, remembering the charm. "We can... finish this."

I did as she asked. Laying there on the stone and moss. The halfling squatted above me, her dark flesh shining with sweat, and she positioned my manhood up, guiding it into her.

She rode me, facing away like that, her ass thudded in thick steady slaps onto my hips. Elina galloped, holding one hand on my knee and the other steadying her swinging breasts. I was in heaven.

I laid back as she increased her pace. Then she laid forward, spreading her legs, her rear still facing me. The hop and gallop turned into a long sliding stride, shifting her body back and forth like an oar in the water. I witnessed her swallowing me again and again. The grip of her so tight, only the slickness of her lust for me allowing it to occur.

"It's so good," she groaned. She slid back again, my cock-head pressing against the angle she wanted, and she trembled, stunned for a moment as and then she shuddered on me.

"Good." I spanked her, my hand sending her cheek jiggling with a swift crack. She groaned in greedy lust, shifting from the glide to the gallop again. Her ass popped and rolled like a dancer twirling fire on stage. Her cheeks clapped as she took me, the sight of her quim straining to take me slipping in and out of view.

I reached up and carefully withdrew. Elina sensed exactly where I wanted her next. She laid back on the moss and stone and smiled at me.

"Come here," she whispered as I settled between her legs. Then she wrapped her arms around me.

The cleric reached down and guided me inside. I put her short legs on my shoulders, pinning her to the earth. A smile spread across my face.

"Take me, Davik," Elina groaned. The ring on her finger was vibrating again on the back of my shoulder.

I slammed into her. She was so slight, so small, but thick

enough to take a proper fucking. My lust boiled over when I looked down. Her body locked in heaving grunts, her pussy at my mercy.

I took her as a beast would. I filled the grotto with the sound of my hips slapping against into hers. I was grunting like an animal finally freed from my cage.

Elina rubbed her clit frantically, then pressed the vibrating ring against herself and I felt her approaching. I picked up the pace, matching her rhythm.

"Come on this cock, priestess," I ordered.

"Dav-Davik... oh Mistre—"

I covered her mouth. She was gripping me so tight, and then I felt her spasm, the small spray of wetness from her release.

"Oh..." Elina cried out. "Dav-Davik."

The feel of her so slight and wet on my base drove me to feral heights.

I was approaching. I felt it far away, like an attack on the flank. My line would break soon.

"I'm going to cover you in my come," I growled.

"Yes, Davik. Cover me. Show the Mistress. Show me what you can do."

I felt the same hand of something otherworldly come over me. My orgasm had been in the distance, but now it was thrust on me. It came on me before I was ready. I grunted and bucked inside her.

Elina pushed back from under me, taking my cock out of her hot pussy, and with that ringed hand, she milked me as I released all over her. That icy feeling that had been traveling through my veins left me, combined with the hot seed and the heat from the ring.

I'm not sure I've ever come so hard in my entire life.

We both moaned. I spurted rope after rope of silken seed across her quim, then her belly and some cresting her chin.

"Elina..." I whispered.

But then her eyes flashed. Her tattoos were glowing.

"*Binding,*" she said. But it was as if there were two voices within her.

"Elina?" I asked again.

"*Be done,*" she finished the spell.

It was an invasion. Slipping past the runes in my body that were carved into my bones and in the flesh itself. Elina kept stroking me, holding my shaft. When I looked down, the ring was glowing, but beyond that the icy sensation returned, making me shudder. It swirled through my body.

Wind blew through the garden. I couldn't look away from her. Divine magic fell down on me like a hammer. My body locked, every muscle. My calves were seizing.

The spell finished, but it felt like two, not one.

The presence finally left the garden, and I felt my heart begin to beat again.

"Such a fire in you," Elina murmured, kissing me. I fell against her, exhausted. Her hands held my back, holding me close. Our bodies were flush, and the only sound was our breathing and the heart I heard beating rapidly in her chest.

"Thank you," Elina whispered. I looked up, kissing her. "I've... been waiting for this."

"It worked?" I asked.

Elina ran a soft hand over my face. "It did. It took a coupling, and the attention of the Mistress herself, to get a simple spell past you. But it worked. And as for us... my facet faces you alone."

Binding... be done.

"Elina," I said, shocked by the severity of the words. We had just met. I had just come here today.

"Shh," Elina smiled. "It's not what you think. Less. But more at the same time. I'll explain later. You're not bound to me. Come see me tomorrow, if you can."

The halfling slid Sariel's ring off and placed it in my hand. Elina reached down to the cooling ropes of seed on her and rubbed it into her flesh, her tattoos pulsing with light as she did. As if her power came from it, or what had brought it forth.

"Come see me tomorrow," she repeated.

CHAPTER
SEVEN

Oakshire had livened up now that it was past midday. Farmers, orchard keepers, and millers all were coming into town to sell some of their harvest or drop off orders at the differing shops. Had I had my silver upfront, I would have stopped and eaten at the cafe.

Coffee had been around since before I was born, but potatoes had come to the continent when I was a boy. I remembered seeing the strange new crop at the market with my father and mother. All of us standing around passing the potato to one another like it was a dragon's egg.

As I walked back to the tavern for my first day of work, there was a jump in my step. I still felt like I was in a dream. I had slept with women soon after meeting them before, but Elina held such a grace to her. It had felt like her body read mine, and as I walked, I couldn't believe the tightness of her embrace. For a cleric of love, she had been so vocal. As if the sensation had been new. It had almost been as if...

No, it couldn't be.

I kept walking.

I've been waiting a long time...

I shook my head. I had misheard her, of course. Elina was in her mid-twenties. A cleric of love. Such a possibility wasn't in the cards.

Entering the tavern, I saw the bustle of patrons coming in at midday for a drink or a spot of lunch. A traveling family of dwarves sat by an opened window, sipping ale and feeding their children. The morsels of misplaced food littering the ground.

Vorga, the orc girl, walked past me, smiling as she did. I was taken by her grace, by the smoothness of her step. She wore a small smile as she worked, talking with the family, bending low and playing with their young children.

I walked towards the bar.

Karley, the drow girl, was preparing bottles for the evening.

"You missed the crew meal," she said.

Nice to meet you too. "Anything left?"

"Nope." She checked the handle on one of the taps, frowning.

"Got any coffee?" I ventured.

"Got any coin?"

"Not a penny."

"Well then." Karley's eyes flashed as she gazed at me, letting me know how unwelcome I was. "You'll have to figure that out. You want coffee, go to the cafe. Maybe wear your shoes next time."

I smiled to myself. The tough girl attitude didn't hold weight with me. An attitude like that serves as armor to protect something underneath.

Before I could bite off a barbed retort, Sariel poked her head out from the kitchen. "Knock it off, Karley. Get a pot on for him. No one drinks the stuff but me."

"Alright." Karley turned from me and bent low to look for

something. I looked down and saw that violet flesh poking from between her black blouse and the crack of her little ass. For such a thin girl, she had a rear on her. The edge of a thong strap poked out as she did.

Karley looked back over her shoulder with a bemused smile. "Gee, having trouble finding it. Might take me a while, guy."

"Name is Davik," I said.

"Mmhmm." Karley turned away, making a show of not looking for any coffee.

"Come back here, busboy!" Sariel called to me.

"Excuse me," I said and stepped behind the bar.

Sariel motioned me into the back of house. "You were gone longer than I thought. You have my ring?" She asked me.

I gave it to her from my pocket.

"She makes all new hires wear it," Tyra sang over her shoulder.

"No shave?" Sariel asked me with a cheeky grin.

"Hilarious. Didn't have time, with the spell and all."

Sariel looked me up and down. "Your boots are back here. Put them on and come meet Brim."

I did as asked, pulling one boot on after another. I'd be due for a new pair soon. They were so raggedy and traveled; the heels were worn into slight bumps of leather. I couldn't remember when or where I'd gotten them.

Tyra was prepping a course of food for the travelers. Her red hair tied up in a bun to keep it from the steam. A sour-looking gnome was standing on a stepstool behind her. His arms were crossed, and he was scowling.

Sariel motioned. "Brim, this is Davik."

The gnome looked over at me slowly, chewed like he was going to spit, then turned back to watch Tyra bustling over the stoves.

"Mmm," Brim said.

I was making friends everywhere.

Tyra was spinning among the stove and oven and chopping ingredients like a leaf in a firestorm.

"Do you have a second?" Sariel asked me.

"Sure," I said and walked with her towards the back of the storage area. Her golden hair swung lightly as it draped over her shoulders, and I found myself just enjoying the closeness of her.

"Here." Sariel palmed the four silver coins into my hand. "As agreed. A deal is always a deal."

"Thanks. So, that ring, the spell and all..."

"Are you wondering how long I'll keep it?" Sariel asked. "Trying to time your grand robbery? Bad news for you, Davik. There's not much to steal here, just debt and a rundown tavern."

"Aside from what we talked about, does this charm do anything else?"

"You have a real distrust of magic."

"In my experience, it's warranted."

Sariel didn't jibe me on that, knowing my background. "No, it doesn't. It's just a precaution. The things I have here, the people, I have to make sure they're safe."

Suddenly, I heard a whisper in my mind.

You'll die here. This place will be your ruin. Run now.

A cold shiver went through me. I looked at the ring.

But Sariel scowled and leaned over, staring at the kitchen. I turned around and saw Brim the dishwasher muttering in the doorway.

"Knock that off, Brim. Don't be an asshole."

You'll die here and nobody will fuck you. You are ugly.

"Brim!" Sariel yelled.

The gnome scowled and went back inside.

Ugly-man.

"Brim's clan are psionics. Telepaths. That's why he doesn't speak much," Sariel explained. "That and he doesn't want to. Don't let him fool you."

"Such a pleasant fellow. I was worried. I thought the ring was speaking to me."

"That would be strange," Sariel said. "Who wants talking jewelry? So, veteran. You ready for your first day? Big new chapter. Quests of dishes and mugs of ale to carry."

"Maidens to charm? And townsfolk to sing my name?"

"Oh yes. Nothing in the realm will be the same. After the battle today, you can rest in the grand keep of your chambers."

I liked being close to her. I liked her sarcasm. When I was near Sariel, it felt like standing next to a sunrise. The perfection of her face, her body, all that golden hair.

"You don't talk like most Embriel."

"That so?" Sariel grinned. "Had many conversations with battle elves?"

"... Yes."

Her face fell for a moment, remembering I had been a prisoner of war under her people.

"Right, of course. Sorry. But you're correct. My first command was half Embriel, half human. It's where I learned your language. Suppose a lot of it stuck with me. Embrien can be so sharp to speak. I don't miss it at all. So, ready to work?"

In truth, I couldn't tell you if I was ready. But I was ready enough to try. It may sound simple and small, but a quiet start in what many would call "honest" labor was refreshing.

Like any other grand quest or mission, mine was simple. Keep it tight, be aware of your surroundings.

And don't get stabbed.

❧

"The little fucker tried to stab me!" I yelled.

"Davik, just back up, calm down!" Sariel shouted.

"Fuck you!" I pointed at the gnome.

"Rahh!" Brim growled. He was standing on a barrel, waving a meat fork back and forth like a rapier.

We were in the middle of what they called the dinner rush. Patrons filled the tavern as drinks flew and food marched in and out of the kitchen. My hands were never empty.

"You little shit!" I walked towards him. "You're going in that fucking oven!"

"No one is going in any ovens!" Sariel replied. She held her hands up between the two of us.

A moment passed where we stared at each other. A duel as old as time.

Gnome vs. Man.

Tall vs. Short.

Busboy vs. Meat Fork.

Our boss held her hand out, and Brim reluctantly handed over the meat fork.

"Davik is the busboy, Brim. He hands you dishes, you clean them."

The gnome peered at me. His words entering my mind.

Ugly-man.

"I can get in your head too," I warned him. "But it'll be metal, not some psychic nonsense."

"Rahh!" Brim growled, holding his hands out like a martial artist.

Sariel took the tub of dishes from me and slammed them in front of Brim. "No more bullshit, Brim. I mean it. Do your job."

Brim grumbled something and turned away, grabbing a dish and sticking it into the sink.

"Yeah, clean those dishes, you little rat!"

"You," Sariel stated. "Out front."

Tyra was standing in front of the stove, completely oblivious to the war going on behind her. She was staring at the series of food orders scribbled down on pieces of paper with charcoal.

I stomped out of the kitchen. My first shift at the inn was going extremely well. I had broken several cups. I cleaned up vomit. A gnome had almost planted a meat fork in me.

Karley was leaning over the bar, chatting with the female bookstore owner I had seen when I first came to town.

"Excuse me," I said as I tried to slide past her.

She kept talking to the bookstore owner.

"Coming through," I said and slid behind her.

As I did, she leaned back, pressing her ass against me. Her pants were thin. Like spidersilk. I could feel the soft curve of her as she ground against me. I looked over to Sariel to help me out, but before she noticed Karley stood back up and kept talking to her friend.

"Night is winding down a bit," Sariel said in my ear as we made it past the bar.

It didn't seem that way to me. The music was getting louder; the drinks were flowing. Jessa and Vorga were flying between tables with platters of food and drink.

"You sure?" I asked.

"Yeah, once this last turn comes, it'll die down."

"Turn," I said with a nod.

"It means the rotation of people at a table. Once they finish and pay, that's a turn."

"Alright," I said. "What should I do now?"

"There's a family just arrived. They have little ones. Take this key, grab their trunks outside the front door and take it up to room four."

"Room four," I repeated. She slid the key in my hand.

"Room four," she slapped me on the back and spun back

into the bar to run food from the kitchen. I watched the battle-elf who once commanded legions go check on a kitchen of potatoes and stews.

Funny how we end up.

Outside, I was glad to be out of the commotion. There was a controlled chaos to the tavern, not unlike a melee. Tackling the tasks at hand wasn't difficult, it was the conflicting directions from all my new coworkers.

"Davik!" Tyra always sighed as I brought a tub of dishes to the back. "Can you run these plates out?"

"Busboy," Karley would say. "Run this bottle over there. Take four tumblers too."

"Which ones are tumblers?" I'd ask, but she would already go to another area of the bar.

"There you are," Sariel would exclaim. "Someone spilled their food by the hearth. Can you grab a mop?"

And on and on it went from all of my new coworkers.

When the turn ended for the night, the patrons emptied and the serious drinkers stayed in the tavern. I had to escort one older man out, and Sariel told me to walk him home.

"Sorry about that," he grumbled as we walked, me half carrying him.

"Don't worry about it. Happens to the best of us." I shifted his gait and we walked the streets of the town. Boots on cobblestones and plankways.

"Think I got a bit on your boots," he huffed as we crossed the promenade.

"Need new boots anyway." That was true enough. And it hadn't been the first time my boots were dusted with the consolation prize of too much drinking.

"Got a pair ye can have, lad. Yer' a good lad."

Good lad. I wasn't so sure about that.

"How long you lived in town, old-timer?"

"Since the wife passed. Couldn't work the farm no more. Kids all grown up... most of em."

I didn't pry. I knew people lost children to poor harvests. To working tenant-farms and having to give all their yield to petty lords. Or plague, or disease.

"Goddamn Summoner War," he huffed. "Useless damn thing."

I couldn't agree more. Whichever side you were on, if you had made it out, you knew.

"What's your name?" I asked.

But he didn't respond. I glanced at his face. Long whiskers, mutton chops like a man I used to know who had taught me how to fish in the village I was born. A kind man. I remember he wore cavalry boots, and I had asked him about them. About being a great warrior and soldier.

Just fish, kid. Only good thing I learned in the cavalry was how to fish.

"Devon," the old man said.

"Nice to meet you, Devon."

"His name..." the old man whispered. I heard the lump in his throat. His eyes were glazed, far away. "My boy's name had been Devon."

I didn't know what to say to that. His body sagged a bit, like the memory and the grief fell on both of us.

"Shouldn't have let him go. Shoulda broke his damn leg to keep him from going."

"Come on, grandad." I hoisted him back up. "This your place?"

He nodded. I looked up to a little house on the end of one of

Oakshire's streets. There was a staircase on the left side leading up to the second story.

"Get a single-level next time, will ya?" I pulled him towards the steps.

It took a bit of maneuvering, but I got him up to the door. I could have taken him in my arms, but no self-respecting man wants to be carried like that. On a battlefield? Maybe. Not from the bar. I had to search through his pockets for the key.

"Nice place." I heaved as I pulled him inside. He could do to lose a few pounds. I looked around at the modest accommodations. The old boy had done well enough for himself. Likely sold the family farm and land, saved up over the years. After his wife passed.

But it lacked that thing we need. I don't know how it's decided, but there are houses and there are homes. This was a house. It was a room with furniture in it. A place for living. For waiting.

I walked the old man to his bed and plopped him down as gently as I could.

"Boots..." he whispered.

"Not taking your boots off, my friend. Some things I draw the line at."

"Take the boots by the door. They were... Devon's..."

He was snoring after a moment. Blissful. There's no slumber like that of the drunk, but there is no worse morning after either.

I shut the door quietly and left him in his room. His son's boots sat near the door, as if the boy would be back any moment to slip into them.

I've taken handouts, and I've taken bribes. I've taken things that didn't belong to me.

But I never took a man's memories. I imagined him waking up from his blackout and seeing that he had given his son's boots away. Boots he would give anything to be filled by the boy he missed so much.

I left them where they belonged.

AT THE TAVERN, I came across Vorga sitting on a bench outside the windows. That beautiful green skin illuminated by the light pouring through the windows inside.

"Mind if I join you?" I asked. I felt somber after taking that old man home. Time around women is time well spent, and I won't listen to anyone who says otherwise.

"Please," Vorga said.

Vorga watched me with dark eyes. She had a single booted leg up on a box of supplies near the bench. Her long skirt lifting slightly, showing the shape of her calf.

I noticed she was holding onto a little novella, reading in the window's light.

"What do you like to read?" I asked.

"Myths," she said and glanced at me. "Stories about creation. Different cultures. This one is about hungry demigods."

I raised an eyebrow. She had been so short spoken before. I expected the chopping cadence of speech from so many orcs I had known who grew up among their clans.

We often mistake someone's second or third language as a sign they aren't sharp, but that's not true. You should hear me try to prattle on in hill-dwarven, all I can really say is *Let's talk about this* and *Just put the crossbow down.* I once met a full-blooded orc who was mayor of a sea-town. He could move an entire crowd with an address. When he spoke, it was like someone wove silk through every listener's ears.

"What do you like to read?" she asked.

I leaned back on the bench, watching the Oakshire street in the warm summer evening. "I'm not sure if I've ever read a book for pleasure. Where I... worked, there weren't many books."

"There's a bookstore that Helena runs. You could go there." She looked away. "If you wanted."

My gods. Had there even been an orc girl so delicate? A bookish girl reading fairy tales.

"I might do that," I said.

"What do you think of the tavern so far?"

"It's nice," I said. "Different. A bit chaotic."

She laughed at that. I enjoyed hearing her laugh.

"You're doing well," she said. "You broke a few things, but it happens."

"Yeah." I rubbed the back of my neck. "I'm sure I'll hear about it."

"Sariel's nice," Vorga said. "She was patient with me when I first came here."

"How long have you worked at the tavern?"

"Three years, almost. Came here when I was seventeen. You should've seen me. Trays weren't safe in my hands. Sariel forbade me to carry more than a plate until I got used to it."

I laughed. "Seems like you're doing great now."

"It's nice here. Sariel's been very good to me. She always tells me I can look at moving out of the house whenever, but I don't know. I like being around people." Vorga looked away, picking her book up but not opening it. She was nervous, which was adorable.

"I should get back to it," I said.

"See you." she looked at the same page that hadn't moved since I strolled up.

I stepped to the bar. Karley leaned on the counter with her elbow, a bored look on her face.

"How's it going?" I asked.

"Hmm," she murmured.

"Excellent," I said.

"Sariel wants to see you. She's in her office."

Karley was the type of girl to look bored constantly. Like nothing amused or excited her.

I had seen her throughout the night working with customers. Underneath this bored demeanor was someone looking for attention. She was aware of everything around her and pretended not to be. I'd bet the hangover this morning when she had walked in had been half an act.

"What?" Karley looked over at me, her chin still resting in her hand.

This type of girl ate town boys alive and hung them high and dry. She wanted to me to say something flippant, or biting, or even complimentary.

I smiled softly, like I knew a secret. Then I turned to head to Sariel's office.

"What?" Karley asked again. She wasn't used to this, someone not playing her game, or playing a better one.

I knocked on Sariel's office.

"*Give me a second,*" she said through the door.

"Alright."

I leaned on the wall in the hallway. My mind drifting to that pleasant and heated time with the halfling. Elina felt like a fever dream that had happened to someone else. My mind was chewing on the moving pieces of today. I kept thinking of Vorga. Of her soft skin in the light of the warm tavern.

Oakshire was such a difference from the world I came from. When I thought of a life constantly on the move, I missed nothing about it. Not the plunder, not the company, not the ships and alleys and dungeons filled with things that try to kill you.

"Come in," Sariel called through the door. I opened the door to her office and stepped inside, shutting it behind me. A force of habit. You never know who is meaning to sneak up behind you.

When I turned around, Sariel was standing on her tiptoes, reaching up to a shelf on her desk, looking for something.

Pale orange cloth, so fine, outlined her broad hips and the enticing heft of her backside. I could see the sweet curve of either cheek under her dress shifting. So large and inviting.

"Need a hand?"

She smiled over her shoulder.

"Can you grab that step stool, hold it steady for me?"

I looked around the office. The stool was a little foot rest with four legs, maybe six inches high. I grabbed it and went to hand it to her, but she leaned forward and raised a single foot.

"Okay," I said and knelt down.

One pale foot stepped onto it. When she lifted the other, she reached back and steadied herself on my shoulder.

"Thanks, just keep her steady." Sariel leaned up, searching on top of the desk. I held the stool as she went on her tiptoes again. Her calves rippled with strain, the muscles sliding like oval gems under her skin.

"It's here somewhere," she whispered as she rummaged. Her other hand held a fistful of the front of her dress.

If the cloth along her back had been form fitting before, it was now a second skin. She raised a single foot while she leaned forward.

It was beyond inviting. It was one of the classier yet more lurid displays anyone had ever done for me. I stared at that shapely elven flesh.

"Got it," she said.

The spell broke, and her foot settled. I stepped back and offered a hand as she climbed down, but she waved me away.

"Thanks,"

"Find what you were looking for?"

"I did." Sariel opened a folded piece of parchment and looked at a tally of deliveries. "Damn. I was right. We need to push more cider in the tavern, its set to turn at the end of the season."

"I'm sure Karley will get it done." I glanced around the office. There was a single chair for her to use, and it didn't look like she had other people in here often. "You wanted to see me?"

"I did. You can take my chair if you want."

"You go ahead."

Sariel sat, her dress coiling around her. The cleavage on display was cruel, and I was straining my eyes not to be distracted. Former enemy or not, she was a formidable beauty. She belonged in a story that Vorga would read. Stepping nude from a lake, delivering a magical artifact to those of better character than I.

"How was your first day?"

"Good," I said. "Not what I'm used to. But well enough."

"You did well. You don't have to skulk so much, by the way. It's okay for patrons to see you."

Had I been skulking? Maybe. Just felt more natural to be out of sight. To bus the tables and move on.

I've held fortunes, letters of marque, and even land that I gambled away. I've had chests of gold and jewels and a sword worth a small town. It never meant much to me. You could only buy so much with those things, and the things that came free when you were flush weren't worth the price of the attention they brought.

It still felt strange not wearing a sword. You'd think I'd be used to it after a season in the wilderness. But now that I was around people again, I reached for steel that wasn't there. I was off balance without it, steadying myself on churning tides.

"Anyway..." Sariel spoke to fill the silence.

"Anyway," I said.

"Crew seems to not mind you. That's good. And it was helpful having you around today. So tomorrow we'll do more of the same. Come back two hours past midday. We don't need extra pairs of hands before that."

"Alright." I slid my hands in my pockets. "Karley seems to just **love** my help around here."

Sariel chuckled and swung back to her desk. "She puts up a good front. It's not my business and I won't share hers, but her background isn't exactly what you might think it is. All I'll say is that she probably leans more into the idea of being a prickly drow than ever being around some."

"The little hangover act today?" I asked.

Sariel's lips pursed. She seemed pleased. "Caught that, did you? Keep an eye on her most nights. She'll drink too much, but she has to force herself. Try to let the patrons down easy when they're waiting for the flirting bartender that never shows up to go home with them."

"Little old to be playing games," I replied.

"She's twenty-one. What do you expect? She hasn't even played the game. Despite what she wants others to think. The fishnet stockings, the skirts, the tight pants... it's all presentation. We had another drow come in here once, and she watched them the entire time, probably taking notes on how to act."

"Not been around her own people much?"

Sariel nodded. "Something like that. Or men."

So I had been close.

"So, what do you think?" Sariel asked.

"About Karley?"

"About the tavern. The job tonight."

"It was good. I broke a few items."

"Oh, we all heard it," Sariel laughed. "I just wanted to check in after your first day. We'll do a shift meal after close, a late dinner if you're hungry."

"Sure," I said. "Was there anything else you wanted to talk about?"

Sariel looked down at the ring that would alert her to the deal-struck charm.

"Everything looked good. That's all."

Like she said, that was all.

CHAPTER

EIGHT

M y first weeks at the tavern were fraught with small mishaps and mistakes. But like any job, they lessened over time. I found my rhythm and footing in the tavern. In a strange way, it felt good to be part of something bigger than myself. I had my own role to play. I could be depended on. Over time, Karley began calling me by my name when I didn't respond to anything else. The war with Brim settled down into a quiet feud, with either side threatening to violate terms of the treaty at any time.

It was the longest I had stayed in a place in a long time. While not glamorous, the barn was comfortable and there were no animals. Sariel told me she had planned for it to be storage, but it never got busy enough to utilize it.

I would work all evening, less of a busboy and more a reactionary force, sent to dispel spills, settle down arguments, run food when needed, heft heavy sacks for Tyra. I moved belongings, luggage, even the errant child that ran too close to the fireplace.

After the bar closed, we would sit down for a shift meal

together, eating close to or past midnight. Jessa, the human girl, usually went home early, and we rarely interacted. She was half-checked out, looking forward to her marriage and life as a stay at home wife.

The work was simple, chaotic, and honest. The money was a pittance, but it was enough. I never felt the need for more. I bought a fresh shirt, new pants and paid the Oakshire cobbler to refit my boot heels.

At night, I would sleep in the barn among the bales of hay. Most rooms were taken up by travelers on their way to somewhere. Every now and then, one of them knocked on my sleeping area asking for something.

One morning, not long after I started, I woke at dawn to the gentle knock of Tyra. Bleary-eyed, I opened the door and she smiled at me as the sun rose behind her mountain of red hair.

"Come on," the faen girl whispered. "I'm taking you to breakfast."

It became a little ritual. Not every day, but most. We would walk to the cafe and bakery together.

"These morning jaunts have caused a bit of uproar at the house," Tyra giggled.

"Why's that?"

"Because Karley is on her own to make her own breakfast."

"I'm surprised, honestly. That you'd buy food for yourself, you're such a splendid cook."

Tyra smiled and drank her coffee. Both hands cupping the big porcelain mug. "Davik, it's so nice to have someone else cook for me. You have no idea. Besides, I don't bake like they do here. Isn't it nice not to bus your own dishes?"

I agreed. And in the mornings of Oakshire I would sit with her, chatting about small things. About the women, the gossip in town. Like me, she was an outsider. Where I was tolerated, she was loved by all.

Later on, I would realize she wasn't just taking me for company, she was doing me a favor. Introducing me to the town, showing I wasn't some frightening stranger.

It was impossible not to like Tyra. There was a softness to her, a genuine enjoyment of life and people, and those mornings with Tyra, sitting and eating pastries and drinking coffee together while the world woke up, were the first true stitches that wove me into Oakshire.

After breakfast, Tyra would walk back home and not return until the late afternoon to begin her cooking shift. Sariel came early in the mornings. Brim slept in the back of the kitchen, squirreling away somewhere.

In the mid mornings I would visit Elina. She would tell me about her time here, about the visits she would make to people in town. Ailing husbands, sick babes. But much of what she visited people about was to discuss issues in relationships, to navigate messy breakups, and more than that, to address issues of the heart and bed.

When the halfling and I walked, either on the trails outside of town or among the streets of Oakshire, she would tell me more about her religion. About the Mistress. When the mood took us, and it often did, we would fuck. She was always eager.

"Only you," she moaned one morning near a stream we had walked near. "Only you, Davik."

I liked Elina a lot. But when we weren't wrapped around one another, she sometimes spoke to me like a physician, trying to understand me, trying to see if she could help. Maybe it was her nature.

Eventually, she admitted something.

"It's not just that I enjoy my time with you," she said as we walked one morning. "When we join... my power grows. The

Mistress bestows more upon me, from the essence of our union."

"So I'm a mana pool for you?"

She shook her head. "You're a person, Davik. You're my lover. You aren't a commodity. But when we join... it's a prayer to my goddess and deity. It's stronger than when I meditate."

Meditation, I learned, was something that involved her hand between her thighs, and one in her mouth as she pleasured herself. There was never any move to convert me. I respected that. She just wanted me to know who she was. Our dalliance was friendly, but I worried, because sometimes she would look at me as if I was the only man on earth. I didn't want to lie to her.

"You don't understand," she would say when I broached the subject. A soft smile on her lips. "I'm yours to take. You just haven't taken me yet."

She was right.

In those weeks, Sariel and I passed each other, seemingly too aware of one another. She was polite, but distant. Hiding behind a facade of helpfulness, or making sure I was settling in. Something was on her mind, though. I caught her looking at me often. Her face would be tragic, as if some terrible sin had been committed.

It worried me.

"What do you think it is?" Elina asked when I brought it up to her one morning.

"Maybe I did something," I said. "Something in the war. To someone she knew? I don't know."

"You can just ask her, you know. The Mistress loves honesty. You've become a more honest lover since we met. At least with me."

I rolled my eyes at that. I wasn't sure what passed for honesty when speaking with your body. She placed her hand on me. "I mean it, Davik. You're multi-faceted. You're not meant for one pairing, but many. I feel you and I, but this thing can't grow until you do. The Mistress brought you to Oakshire, I'm sure of it."

I was more sure being sick of a life of adventuring brought me, but I said nothing.

"It's her business," I told the halfling cleric. "I won't pry. We all get our secrets."

"They all have them at the tavern," Elina mused. "I do hate to see Sariel alone. She fills the house with the other young women, but nothing to warm her bed as the years pass."

"She's not had a man?"

Elina shook her head. "Not in her time here. She doesn't talk about her past."

My relationship with Elina was one of the body and tongue. She wanted to speak and discuss as much as she wanted to practice her ministrations with me. Beyond that, I didn't know where our path led us. There weren't expectations she laid out. She seemed to simply enjoy our time together.

When I wasn't working, or with Elina, I enjoyed the quieter moments of Oakshire. The cafe, the little market. Sometimes I'd wander down the road to the valley and the farms below, meeting other citizens of Oakshire.

A free pair of hands was a welcome sight to any farmer. I was offered plenty of side work I had never intended to take on. An old widow in a cottage on unworked fields waved me down one morning as I walked. I thought something was the matter.

"The mill! Come quick!"

I jogged over to her cottage, and she beckoned me towards the rear. Then the ambush occurred.

"What is it?" I asked.

The old woman grinned and nodded to a pile of black soil,

freshly delivered.

"Don't suppose you could give us a hand moving that to the garden beds, do ye?"

I laughed at that. She had me. So my morning burned away under the rolling of a wheelbarrow and laying a half ton of soil in the vegetable gardens of Mabel Prise, con-woman extraordinaire.

As I finished, she waved me over to her cottage and served me chilled tea on the front porch.

"Go no coin for ye', young man."

"Don't worry about it."

The old woman gave me a scoffing look. "Do I look worried? The hells I'd be worried for? Not my fault you got whistled out of a morning."

I liked Mabel. She was a conniving, foul-mouthed old crone. Quick to take advantage of any well meaning passerby. She was my hero.

"Where do ye work?" She sat and kicked back in her rocking chair. In a moment, a pipe was between her teeth and she was lighting it with a candle.

"The tavern."

"For that buxom she-elf that runs it?"

"Sariel," I said, sipping the tea and watching the valley. She had quite the view from her property.

"No wonder you work there. Those tits could bring the calves wandering into town."

I laughed at that.

"Big lad like you, wasted in a tavern. Look around," she said and pointed a crooked finger at a series of farms and houses. "Harvest has been good this year. So good the damn farmers thought only about money and not about winter. They're shorthanded. Their lazy sons ran off to cities to make soft money. Air-headed daughters everywhere."

"Is that so?" I mused.

But Mabel wouldn't be humored. She cast a furious eye at me. "Listen, boy, to what I'm telling you. Mabel isn't some dusty ole gam-gam. I'm not giving you coin, I'm giving you a goldmine. Every plow-pushing softhead is scything his fields, hoping to get it all done in time to sell. But this summer will end quick, mark my words. So busy they're buying firewood from two outfits. Leasing their own lands to them. But you know what?"

"What's that?" I asked.

Her eye twinkled. "The kindling vendors don't do squat. They never come fell any of it, not often. Drives up the price. They're waiting on this valley. Once the snows come, woods are too cold to chop. Wood's unseasoned. They'll jack up the price and eat into all the profit these boys are racing for. They think they're harvesting their fields for themselves, but the food and firewood outfits are who they'll be paying."

"That so?" I looked around. Every field was full of farmers yielding their crops, or shepherds moving flocks around.

"Underhanded, most of em."

"Why would anyone buy firewood? They have trees in their plots."

"You damn young people, you don't know nothin' about land. Firewood outfits have bought rights to most of the valley. They come and these fools sell the rights to it, thinking they'll get their free timber that's processed from their lands. But they never process it."

"So?" I asked. "Why are they afraid to go pull their own timber?"

Mabel tapped her temple. "The kindling outfits send them letters, telling them when winter comes, they'll deliver a few cords. But then they don't, so they send their other outfit to offer services. Right hand vanishes, the left hand appears. The bastards put a lien on their land, saying if they touch any of the timber, they owe them for the entire plot. Scares em, so the other outfit picks their pockets."

"Why doesn't the constable do anything?"

"Do what?" Mabel laughed. "It's all legal. It isn't a crime to separate a fool from their money when they sign it away. It's just evil. Thieves used to pick your pockets. Now they take homes with a quill. Even the constable is subject to imposing the lien. Farmer can't pay, so he gives up land, or risks losing his farm."

"Come on." I put the glass down. "How would anyone know if they pull a few trees down?"

"They mark it with a spell of some kind. So I'm told. Could be horseshit. But all the farmers believe it. The closest patch of free forest is few and far in between."

I stood up and walked to the edge of the porch. Then I turned and saw the back of her house, leading to a large swathe of the forest.

I raised an eyebrow at her. She cackled.

"Now you're thinking like a businessman. Come, take a seat, let's talk a divvy?"

I MET MANY OTHER FARMERS, their wives, their children, their families. The same faces I'd see in the tavern. There were tieflings and humans and half-orcs, and every denomination in between. All were obsessed with reaping a grand harvest. With the full family working, they'd often head to the tavern for Tyra's cooking.

I met widows and widowers. I met children forced to grow up too soon and take over family estates they were overwhelmed by.

It was true what Mabel had said. Most landowners had agreed to lease their timber on their land and hadn't understood the fine print of the agreement. Half were signed onto Crescent Timber, the other half to Hearthwood Holdings. If Mabel was right, the squeeze would come in winter.

Nothing had been agreed upon with Mabel, but I was considering spending my time away from the tavern on her land. It was one of the largest holds in the valley. Many had tried to offer her pennies for the right to lease it, which had pissed her off so much that she refused everyone after that.

One evening after the dinner rush, I knocked on Sariel's office.

"What is it?" she asked.

"Where do you get your firewood?"

She looked up at me, puzzled. "I buy cords from Crescent. They're pretty awful, too. Always late. I've got the invoice right here."

"Nevermind." I waved her hand away from having to search through the invoices.

"What are you up to?" Sariel asked. I shrugged.

"Nothing that violates your rules. Don't worry."

"Mmhmm," she said, the suspicion plain in her tone. "Sure."

That night, the tavern musicians didn't show up. The crowd was yelling for music, trying to get Jessa to sing in front of the hearth. She ran away to the kitchen.

"Again?" Sariel asked as she came out of her office. "They didn't show up again?"

"Did you pay them?" I asked her.

"Damn right I paid them," Sariel growled, her silver eyes growing furious. "Fucking bards!"

Karley looked away, eyes wide. Sariel was staring at the empty spot in front of the fireplace. It wasn't just the minstrels not showing up. Each day I found her at her desk, diving deep into the papers and the invoices. Meat deliveries. Ingredients for brewing. Liquor. Vegetables. One vendor would be late, so she'd have to buy from another and pay a rush fee.

Sariel glanced at me. I shook my head. "Not a chance," I said. "My voice would empty the tavern."

Then it happened. The night would have been fine. The musicians kept a crowd going, but we already were almost full.

Vorga's voice broke across the distracted crowd. Hands clasped shyly around her stomach. Her face was a mixture of anxiety and being so unsure. Vorga cleared her throat, holding her eyes shut for a moment.

When her song came, it was one of those moments. One you always remembered. It was soft, sad, and with a nervous tremble that painted the room in the sweetness of her bravery.

> *Raise your glass, my friends, to the brew of our land,*
> *From the soil, from the oats, where our proud labor*
>   *stands.*
> *It's not the finest, nor richest, yet it's our to claim*
> *Made in Oakshire, I am, where summer reigns*
>
> *Here in Oakshire, the days may grow cold,*
> *But in a warm tavern, stories are told*
> *We laugh, and we sing, as our spirits delight,*
> *In the glow of a hearth, staving off the night*
>
> *Raise your glass, my friends, to the brew of our land,*
> *From the soil, from the oats, where our proud labor*
>   *stands.*
> *It's not the finest, nor richest, yet it's our to claim*
> *Made in Oakshire, I am, where summer reigns*

So here's to the ale, and here's to the rye.
To Oakshire's spirit, under the frosty sky
We stand together, when the cold winds blow,
In the heart of the valley, where the brave hearts
    glow.

She walked around the room now, smiling, nervous as all hell, but everyone was captivated. Vorga moved her hands to have people join in the chorus. The entire tavern began nodding, as if this were some old song they knew from back in days of old. The patchwork of voices joined.

Raise your glass, my friends, to the brew of our land,
From the soil, from the oats, where our proud labor stands.
It's not the finest, nor richest, yet it's our to claim
Made in Oakshire, I am, where summer reigns!

Applause broke out, several people stood. Was it the finest song ever penned? No. But Vorga had been brave, and what she sang was a song any town could get behind. For her, an outsider who lived here, it was a testament to her love of this place.

"Holy hells," I murmured to Sariel as we both clapped.

Her eyes were wide in wonder. The elf shook her head. "I never knew."

Vorga blushed deeply and several people passed coins to her, which she refused. The calls came for an encore. But she giggled, following Jessa's route, and ran to the back of house. When she got there, Tyra wrapped her arms around and her and spoke to her. Even Karley was clapping, smug behind the bar.

"Looks like you got everything you need, right here," I said to Sariel.

CHAPTER
NINE

Summer ended too quickly for Oakshire. Autumn approached like a coming storm, the treelines shifting from green to the flurry of gold, red and yellow. Farmers of the valley hurried to finish their fields.

The anxious feeling grew even more when travelers stopped in Oakshire, bearing heavy carts from their own harvests. Despite the low prices, Sariel bought nothing from the out of towners, preferring to do business with Oakshire locals.

Though the harvest festival wasn't until mid-autumn, I learned it was common to store yields in the mills and granaries near the Tawney fairgrounds where the festival was held.

Ugly-man, worst busboy. Brim's voice sang in my mind.

"I heard that," I said to Brim as I set another tub of dishes down next to his growing pile. "And I see that meat fork down your back, Brim."

The gnome scowled at me

Tyra set her head on my shoulder when I came next to her

at the stove. "Davik, wanna trade? I'll clean up out there, you cook. I'm having dreams about cooking and it's not even busy season."

"You're doing great." I put my arm around her shoulder. The faen girl sighed and went back to her pots. "Cafe tomorrow?" She asked.

"You know where to find me," I said, winking at her.

Out on the tavern floor, the turn was in full swing. Traveling farmers had copper to spend and Karley was a blur behind the bar, her violet skin coated in sweat from the mass of bodies inside. Bratty as she could be, she knew how to work a bar.

"Keg!" she called to me.

"Which?" I said, sliding behind her.

"Dowager Brew."

"That bitter stuff? I don't get it."

"Thank you, Davik. Brewmaster. Tastemaster. I wonder, if it meets with your approval, could you just change the damn keg!" she shouted.

I leaned close so she could hear me over the clamor of the tavern. "You're cute when you're angry."

I ducked a swat at my head and went down into the cellar via the ladder and changed the keg in the dark. When I came back, I didn't have to ask if it was working since Karley was already filling mug after mug of the stuff.

"Davik!" Sariel called me over towards the front door. "Can you get this luggage upstairs?"

I threw a bar towel over my shoulder. Now I felt out of place without it. When I'd picked up the habit, I didn't know, but it was like a part of me.

Used to take contracts from princes and walk with the...

"Right this way," I said to the family with two tired children at the base of the stairs. I lifted two sets of trunks and showed them to their room with two small beds. "Water's here. Ring this bell if you need it refilled or any extra linen."

"Thank you," the half-elf mother said with tired eyes as she walked into the room. It looked like they had had a long day. Her husband followed, two sleeping children hanging onto him.

The man set his children down on the bed gently, both of them rolling over despite the noise down below.

"My appreciation," he said, reaching into his pocket. I held my hand up. "Keep it. Better spent at the bar down below. Can I have the girls bring some drinks up? Plates of food?"

"Please," the half-elf woman smiled and held her children on the bed. "That would be lovely."

"Welcome to the... tavern," I said and bowed.

So maybe I was enjoying my time in the world of hospitality. There was a real selfless pleasure in seeing things taken care of, in seeing weary travelers having a bit of an easier day.

Sariel came from another room in the hallway. Our dealings had been businesslike, and I noticed that she always had another task to accomplish when we were alone. Sometimes she would call me into her office, something on her mind, and then cut our talk short. As if she changed her mind about something.

"Great job," she whispered as I passed her in the hallway. Her beautiful face was hidden in the dim light upstairs. As I walked by her, she stopped me, reaching out and touching my long hair.

"Everything okay?" I asked.

Downstairs, the music was in full swing, the instrument players picking up the pace. I heard the march of boots from Vorga and Jessa, flying food out to the travelers.

There were a million things to do. To clean, to carry, to help with. But for this brief moment, her wrist on my right shoulder, her fingers holding my hair, I stopped and breathed her in.

"You need a haircut," she murmured. Her silver irises stared into mine.

"Yeah," I said slowly. She stepped a little closer. I felt a roaring need to take her in my arms.

The door to the room we had just shut opened, and we stepped away from each other. The half-elf mother came out.

"*Nela sira, linwe me? I hini...*" the woman said when she saw Sariel. I know a little elvish. She was asking for linen.

"*Tancave',*" Sariel replied, smiling.

The half-elf nodded to me. "*Ma sina tye herven?*"

Husband.

Sariel bit her lip for a moment, then shook her head.

The half-elf woman smiled. "*Lo na vanima, gerthad edain, u-erui, u-ura.*" Then she shut the door.

"What did she say?" I asked, hoping to rekindle the moment.

"Just for linen," Sariel said. She made to go downstairs and then stopped. "She said... humans aren't so bad."

"What do you say?"

The Elven beauty stared at me. "Stick around after we close. I'll cut your hair."

"I'm really good at getting my hair cut," I said. "Some say the best."

Sariel laughed and walked down the stairs. I went to follow, but the door opened behind me again. The half-elf woman looked around and called to me.

"Could you help my husband move the bed towards the wall?"

"Sure," I said and walked back into the room as quiet as I could. The human male nodded to me in appreciation and we lifted the bed off the floor, the children asleep in their pajamas, one girl and one boy, until we set it against the wall.

"I'll get that pillow," I whispered to the mother, and she smiled at me. I shut the door gently behind me to drown out the noise of the band downstairs.

A haircut sounded mighty fine. I felt a warm glow inside me in anticipation of being alone with her.

I had been so lost in my daydream that as I went downstairs, I hadn't heard it. The pinpoint shift of the room. The feeling of merriment was replaced by tension. The murmur of jokes and chatter had come to a halt.

The mood had changed, and I saw why from my vantage of the stairs.

Two of the four players were still playing, too drunk to see what had caught everyone's attention.

Four armed men, in leather and some scale, were standing and grinning on the tavern floor, just past the staircase I stood on. They were to my right, and I watched them as they stared at the room.

The man in front seemed familiar. Really familiar. Had we worked together once? Or against each other?

He was shorter. Human. Stocky. A thick neck with a shaved head and the bright pink scarring of blades littered his skull. The man to his left looked like he had taken a mace to the face once upon a time, and his jaw never sat right again.

Everyone was staring at them. I heard rumbles from the tables. Two families picked up their children and headed to the door, pausing when they realized the men blocked the only exit.

I peeked through the railing at the bar. Karley looked scared. Sariel came out from the kitchen, Vorga fetching her, and her face set in anger when she saw the men.

There was the battle-elf who broke the lines at Breakspear.

"We're full up for the night," Sariel stated.

Forty sets of heads and eyes went from Sariel to the bald man at the door.

"Just looking for a bit of beer. Little wine. Maybe a place to sleep." The leader smiled.

I knew that smile. I had seen it many times and worn it even more. The smile when you have the upper hand, when you're among prey.

Mercenary is a nice term for a shitty profession that attracts an even shittier person. Cutthroat. Vagabond. Highwayman. They're all interchangeable. Mercenary's can guard princesses, or gold. They can also raze villages and enslave.

Sometimes they even call themselves adventurers.

"Sorry," Sariel said. "As I mentioned, we're full up. Can't help you."

"Can't or won't?" Mace-face said by his boss's side.

Sariel scowled. "Won't."

The leader raised his hands. "My apologies, madame. We look meaner than we are. Not all of us are born beautiful, like yourself. We don't want any trouble. We're protectors, see. And there's been lots of banditry on the road to the mills and granaries. We provide security for travelers."

"The constables of three jurisdictions handle that," Karley said from the bar. She looked like she regretted it the moment she spoke.

"Did they, though?" The leader looked around the room. "My name is Gulrith, I protect wagoners and vendors on the road from falling to harm. We're just looking for a bit to drink, then we'll be on our way. If anyone requires our services, well, I'm sure you won't get in the way of folks seeking security, would you?"

I knew this grift. Never used it myself. I was an honest killer, at the least. They swagger into a tavern. They extort travelers to keep them safe on the road. Even if you pay them, they may rob you if they see something they want. Or someone. They're serpents, feigning the need for one coin so they can see how many more await when they pluck them from your corpse.

I peered over at Sariel, catching her eye. They hadn't seen me on the stairs. They were too focused on the tavern floor. Focused on taking control. She shook her head very slightly, her finger tapping on the ruby ring by her side.

I guess I was to play by her rules.

"No soliciting," Sariel said. "Sorry, we are full up tonight. But take a few bottles for the road. My thanks for keeping those roads safe."

Sariel nodded to Vorga, who grabbed several bottles of wine Karley was setting on the bar.

Vorga walked forward, unaffected and unafraid of all of this. Maybe she didn't understand, maybe she didn't care, but she was grace incarnate as she crossed the tavern floor and held out the bottles to the mercenaries.

"You think it's green inside, too?" one man in the rear joked with his friend.

My hands tightened on the rail, begging me to turn the tavern into a warzone.

"Well, aren't you sweet," Gulrith said to Vorga as he took the bottles. "And a pretty one, to boot. Are you wed, girl?"

Vorga shook her head. "No."

"A pity." Gulrith raised the bottles in his hand at Sariel. "Another time, innkeeper."

"We shall see." Sariel's eyes were two silver gravestones.

They sauntered out the doors and into the streets of Oakshire. Likely to cause a bit more harm. Rustle a few feathers.

The music picked back up but, but the mood was lost. I

kept waiting for Sariel to make a move. To gather me and some others, to go sort this out.

She moved among the tables, trying to lighten the atmosphere. Even with her grace, her never-aged beauty, it was a lost cause. These were civilized folk. Here for trips to granaries. Bandits were some of the worst of their fears, and they had just walked out of their dining area.

When I caught up with Sariel, she was nonchalant.

"You get the towels?" She asked.

I nodded. I had to speak up a bit since we were near the musicians. "What do you wanna do?"

"Bit early to close up. Just stay close by, keep bussing tables. And I may have you run some food from the kitchen when the orders are ready." Sariel leaned against the hearth. I saw the sweat on her neckline, her chest heaving.

"I meant." I leaned forward to speak the words in her ear. "What do you want to do about what just happened?"

She didn't look at me. Rather, she stared at the tavern, as if holding onto a dream that threatened to vanish upon waking. "Nothing, Davik. They're just looking to scare a little coin. You've been out there too long. Not everything is a storybook."

I disagreed. "They'll come back."

"Maybe, maybe not. If it happens, it happens, we'll deal with it."

"You got any steel? Anything tucked away in a trunk somewhere?"

A strange look crossed her face. Shame. "I don't... I don't use that anymore. Those things."

I didn't want to deal with these men with a kitchen knife and a rolling pin.

"Is there a constable in town?"

"Not anymore." Sariel shook her head. "Never stays close. The shopkeepers keep an eye out sometimes."

"Let me watch the door—give me a knife or something."

Sariel shook her head. I couldn't believe what I was witnessing. Was this denial? Was I being too paranoid?

"We had a deal, Davik. Remember? Is today the day?"

Irritation filled me. It was one thing to be wishful, but this was reality. "Today the day for what?"

She looked at me. "When a deal isn't a deal."

I felt a stillness in that moment. The music, the room, the patrons, it all faded away a bit. I saw in that moment a woman who had taken a chance on a man like me. She was trying to help me. Maybe she was trying to make up for what she did in the war. Make amends. I saw a person whose soul had been maimed. Maimed so badly that it only healed if I did.

"No," I said. "A deal is a deal."

"Good," Sariel said. I could see this was a relief to her. A great relief. Something that had threatened to disappoint her was staved off.

For now.

"Busy night," I said to Vorga as I walked out to the front of the tavern.

"Pretty exciting," Vorga said, and patted the seat next to her.

"Let me sweep first." I motioned with the broom and began the slow battle of bristles and dust on the wood deck.

Vorga was reading her same book.

"So," I said. "How many times have you read that?"

The girl laughed. "Too many." She flipped it over, looking at the back of it. "My... stepmom got it for me. She was a teacher. Right before she passed. I was seventeen then... so, I've been reading it for three years."

"Sorry to hear that."

Vorga smiled. "It's okay. She was a bit older."

"Doesn't it ever get boring?" I swept closer. "Reading the same thing over and over?"

"To be honest, I like it. I love books, but they're so expensive, you know? My mother used to buy so many books. She called herself a promiscuous reader." The glow of the tavern lit her face, her eye and tusk catching the light.

"How did she—" I began.

The sound of glass smashing cut me off.

Vorga jumped up. But it wasn't that close. Just across the street in the darkness. Someone standing and throwing a bottle down on the cobblestones.

A bottle flung at the ground.

I knew the song well; I had performed my own rendition many times over the years. It wasn't the sound of a drunk wandering home and dropping his liquor. It was someone who had been watching us. Watching the tavern. Someone who wanted us to hear.

Vorga peered at the dark. "Was that—"

"Shh," I said. "Get inside."

I heard the whinny of a horse, climbed too roughly, and the clop of a shod hoof on the street as they rode off.

North. In the hills.

Vorga put a hand on my arm. I was gripping the broom; the wood creaking in my hand and threatening to splinter. Her soft touch made my muscles go slack, and I forced a smile on my face.

"Many people drink too much," Vorga whispered. I watched her face.

"You're right," I said. But my ear was fixated on the sound of the hooves. Distant now. But the bright tin of metal striking the stone, then muffling as they exited town.

North, then northwest. Towards the hills.

"I'm glad you're here," I said to Vorga, who still held onto my right arm.

"Yeah?" she asked, brown eyes looking into mine.

"Need you to protect me." I grinned.

She shoved me—her face breaking into the glee of the surprised. "You better be careful, Davik. Otherwise, nobody protects you from **me.**"

But her hand lingered on my chest, and I didn't move it. I slid mine over hers. "Brave of you, tonight. What you did."

"Just dropping drinks off," Vorga said. Inside the scuff of chairs being put up was the signal the night was over.

Her hand slipped out of mine and I let it go.

"I should go check inside," I said.

"Okay," the most-orc said. "I should too. Tyra may need a hand."

We left the moment there, punctuated by a broken bottle and a silent threat.

I walked to the bar where Karley was leaning on the counter with her elbow, a bored look on her face.

"How's it going?"

"Mmm," she murmured.

"Excellent."

"Sariel wants you to close up tonight." Karley slid the keys to the tavern across the bar.

I took them. "You okay?"

She gave me a puzzled look.

"Looked a little rattled earlier, when those men came in."

"Oh fuck off," Karley stalked away.

"G'nite Davik!" Tyra called from the kitchen.

You die tonight, in your barn, ugly-man. Brim's psychic message echoed in my head.

"Goodnight, Brim!" I called to the back of house.

I'll burn your barn. With fire.

"Goodnight," Vorga said to me, smiling as she walked towards the kitchen with her roommates.

"Goodnight, Vorga."

Sariel poked her head out of her office. "Davik, grab a white tablecloth when you get a chance?"

"Sure," I said. "You got it."

Vorga left. I watched her go for a moment.

I went to the storage area after the girls had left and fished out one of the few white linen cloths. When I came back to the tavern floor, Sariel was waiting for me, the front door barred.

Silver blades in her hands.

"I thought you said no blades?" I said.

She was deadly serious. "Sit down, Davik."

"You know what? Let's not do this," I said.

"Sorry." Sariel shook her head. "This has to happen."

"I won't let you win," I warned her.

Sariel spun the scissors in her hand and pointed them at me. "Give us your pretty scalp, human."

I sighed and walked forward, handing her the sheet. Then I surrendered to the chair.

"I've got you now," Sariel cackled.

"Just get it over with."

"Foolish boy," Sariel purred and held the steel in front of my eyes. "You thought you could get away."

I rolled my eyes. Sariel chuckled and ran a comb through my hair and began the haircut.

"You look like a barbarian. You're scaring the customers."

"I knew a barbarian," I said as she snipped my long locks. "Trolf."

"You lie. That's a made-up name. Sounds like a kid's story."

"Swear to the heavens," I said solemnly. "Trolf was a good guy. An ice tribesman. We eventually parted ways."

"You steal his woman?" she asked in a murmur as she snipped another lock of my hair.

"That's not why. He just couldn't take the heat. Said it was too hot for him. He barely wore anything. It would be autumn and he would be sweating."

"Well, I'm sure he's happier up north with his people."

There's an intimacy to someone cutting your hair, I learned. Most of the time, I cut it with a knife once a year. I would throw water in it for meetings, tie it in a long ponytail or wrap, or just let it hang around my shoulders.

"I hope you know what you're doing," I said. I really did. I'm not a vain man. I've been called rugged. Which sounds like the ugly house next to handsome. After a few bottles of port, a woman once told me I was beautiful. Right before she threw up in my lap.

I have that effect on the ladies.

It was like a tickle, but deeper. Feeling her run her fingers through my hair. Sariel moved all around me.

I shut my eyes, enjoying the tingle of her.

Sariel stepped forward and straddled my legs. Her dress parted where it was split, revealing all that flesh.

"Stay still. This is the hard part." Sariel leaned forward, trimming the hair in the front of my scalp. My hair was hanging in front of my face, and she cut it just in the middle of my nose.

She slid forward, thighs wrapping around mine.

I didn't dare move. I didn't want this moment to end, for the perfection of it to shatter. She smelled like soft things, of cities made of stone that were older than my species. Of oils and a perfume that was like a poem about flowers. The never-aged, in all their wonder. We humans are so different, so fleeting compared to that near-immortal flesh.

"How do you like it here?" She whispered, sliding closer.

I opened my eyes.

She leaned forward, pulling my hair between her fingers.

Snip, snip, snip.

"I like it," I said. "Town is alright. The tavern could use some upgrades."

"High praise," she chuckled. Her chest swung in front of my face as she cut.

"The contents within are... to my liking."

"I'm glad to hear it." She slid closer. A single breast, carried only by the stitching of the maker, and a single string over her pale shoulders pressed against my chest.

Sariel combed my hair. "You know, I was proud of you tonight."

"Proud?" I asked. "It's just luggage."

"On the stairs. Keeping the peace. I was proud of that. For a second I thought you would... that we would see Darkshire."

"Ah," I said. They almost had. I had considered it greatly. At the moment, the most beautiful woman I'd ever seen was straddling me. That was enough for me.

"Did they ever call you anything?" I asked.

The scissors stopped. She held my hair taut, where she had been about to trim.

"Once, back then. I haven't heard it aloud since the war."

"Where did you go after?" I asked. "If you've only been here a few years."

She pressed her finger to my lips. Looking down at me, a face framed in golden hair. Pointed ears, slender and perfect. She stared at me.

"Almost done," she whispered. She came even more forward, her thigh against my groin.

The flesh of her leg, her hip, it was right there. It needed to be touched. Something that beautiful just can't be looked at.

Sariel raised her leg from off of me. "Just hold still..." she whispered. This wasn't sex, and it wasn't just a haircut. It was something inbetween, something restrained. Something we both felt and could taste but didn't dare name, because if we did, we would know it. Break it.

Sariel's chest was rose and fell. The silk of her blouse rose slightly as her nipples hardened. The already straining fabric drawing just a bit tighter.

"I have to get this part... here," she said.

My fist tightened around the left arm of the chair as she slid over it. Her dress parted, and she shifted around my forearm and up to my elbow to continue cutting my hair. I could feel the heat between her legs, just inches above my arm.

Sariel knelt on her left leg between my legs

I did not move. I was gripping the chair so fiercely I felt the wood crack under my fist.

I had to. I just had to.

I reached over with my right hand towards her left hip.

"Don't want you to fall," I whispered.

Sariel didn't say anything. She was staring at my hair, cutting it.

I guided her hip lower, so slowly, that slowness when you're with a girl for the first time that you're not even sure you're moving or not. The silent advance of the unacknowledged need, before the dam breaks.

She followed me, lowering herself, until I felt the velvet cloth over her quim press against my forearm. That sweet heat, that lust in her that she had been hiding was mine to feel now.

Sariel stopped cutting for a second. I wondered if I had moved our dance too quickly, too soon.

Then she ground against me. The cloth of her silken panties sliding along the muscles of my arm, all the way to my elbow. I guided her with my right hand on her hip like a slow dance.

Sariel ground against my arm. I was wrapped in silk and thighs and the heat of her elven flesh. She rode faster. I gripped the arm of the chair harder, my muscles straining to press against her.

"Yes," she whispered.

The words were thick in my throat. "Take your time..."

Sariel sat down harder on my arm, grinding with more pressure. Barely any chance of hiding what she was doing now if anyone walked in. Her fingers laced through my hair, pulling it tight.

I turned into her, and she pressed her breast into my face and I was covered in satiny darkness. My lips were open, and she rode my arm, wetting it, clenching her thighs around it and rocking hard enough that the chair began to squeak.

We were silent for the travelers upstairs. Silent for this tavern, and all those nights working near each other.

I opened my lips and the top of her breast was mine to taste. I didn't want to break this for her, to grip her arms and pull her into my lap. Not yet. This dance was too wondrous to disturb. My cock was straining in my pants and she pressed her thigh against it and I gripped her hip and tasted the flesh of her chest as she rose up... slowly.

I felt her legs trembling. She ground harder, rising up.

"Almost... done," she moaned. Another piece of my hair was cut.

Her eyes shut and she lifted up, bringing her breast to my face. My chin would slide the edge of her blouse down, and I knew what she wanted. I knew it more certainly than any other lover I had ever had.

This was a small step for her. Forbidden, to whatever rule she placed in herself. Right when she arrived, her dress would be pushed down and her nipple would be in my mouth. I'd pull her into me then. Taking her. In the chair, on the floor, it didn't matter. I wanted her.

I gripped her hip as she ground slow and hard, coaxing herself there.

A long strand of my hair was her rein now, the scissors forgotten in her hand, each blade on either side. My scalp stung as she pulled it harder. I extended my tongue against her sliding breast, so large and plump and she began to shake as she was nearly...

Bang! Bang! Bang!

Someone pounded on the door.

Sariel yelped, and when she did, she cut my hair so deep I felt the cold steel on my scalp. The fresh cut of skin. I was so dazed, so lost in the moment,

"Shit!" she said, as if her parents had arrived. Silver eyes looked down at me.

"We're closed!" I yelled. I grabbed her hip, stopping her from leaving.

The banging continued.

"*Please help, elf maiden.*" The voice of a girl came through the door.

"Gods dammit." Sariel stepped off of me, but I grabbed her again. The moment was gone, right at its pinnacle, and I knew there wasn't any rescuing it. Not yet.

"Wait," I said.

"Davik, they need..." Sariel was straightening her dress.

"It's a trap. Do you recognize that girl?"

Sariel bit her lip, staring at the door.

"*Please! My father is hurt!*" the girl said with another bang.

"I'll check," I whispered and rose from my chair. "Just wait."

I ripped the linen from around me. I felt dizzy. The heat of the moment had taken me somewhere else. I stalked into the kitchen, my cock half-hard and very much still in my pants.

It was my dire hope it was a trap. Because someone was going to die for interrupting my haircut.

Near the barn out back I grabbed wooden shovel I had seen earlier. It would have to do.

I crept around the front of the building, passing the bathtub in the little garden and the shower and storage area. On the gate at the side, I climbed quietly over and peered into the street in front of the tavern.

There was a young girl banging on the door, looking around wildly. The street was dark, the moon behind cloud cover. A wagon was parked across the street.

I crept behind a wagon. I heard a pair of people struggling.

"Knock again!" a voice hissed urgently. I imagined a man holding a knife to someone's neck.

I emerged from the side of the wagon behind them. The shovel raised to stave in someone's head.

An older man was sitting on the hitch of his wagon, head down. His two horses shifted at my approach. I could see the bruises around his neck and bald head even in the dark street. His wife had a hand on his shoulder and motioned to the girl again.

"Please help us!" the girl cried out.

The wife turned and saw me just as I dropped the shovel down to street level and yelped.

"Get away!" she cried.

"Whoa, whoa!" I held my hands up.

"Get back, Ella!" the father spun around, and I saw his face had been beaten to a pulp. One defiant eye still shone through, his big broken hands up, ready to defend his family.

"Easy now," I said. "I work at the tavern. What happened?"

They told me. It was no wild tale. And one you can probably guess. Once Sariel heard me speaking to them, she opened the door. I nodded to her to bring them inside.

"Go head in, I'll help your husband, ma'am."

The older woman watched me for a second, figuring on whether or not to trust me. The way I had crept up on them had spooked her. But she went inside, and I stood in front of the father.

"Let me give you a hand, lean on me."

"I'll get blood on yer shirt, young man," he grumbled but gave me his arm.

"Wouldn't be the first time. Don't worry." I made to let him lean on me, as I did often with drunks, but he collapsed quickly.

"Here we go," I hefted him into my arms and carried him towards the tavern.

"Yer shirt," the man repeated. Then he looked around, confused. "You carryin' me?"

It might sound silly to some, but these were hard-working folk. They likely had a shirt to last them years, so I understood his fixation on dirtying mine.

"I won't tell if you don't," I said and walked forward to the tavern.

I should buy a cart, start charging to take men from place to place.

"Looks like you gave them a piece," I grunted as I carried him towards the tavern. In truth, he wasn't that heavy for me, but I wanted to save him a bit of pride.

Carrying unsteady men was becoming my new job. Maybe it was payback for all the times the situation had been reversed.

"Gave em' what they asked, the coin," the father groaned. "Didn't want any trouble. Then the bastards tried to take Ella to the woods. I wasn't having it. Got her out of their arms and she ran with. The men looted the wagon and threatened to burn it, but gave me a dance party instead."

He winced when we hit the steps. Ribs were cracked, most likely. Probably the bones in his face, too.

"These men," I asked quietly. "Four of them? Leather and scale?"

"Aye," the father grunted as we took another step.

"You do any damage?"

"Couldn't reach my cudgel in the wagon. Dotted an eye, maybe."

"You did good, old fella."

"Lost the purse," he wheezed. "A full year for nothing."

"Got your family, kept them safe. That's all that matters."

"Aye." he looked up as we walked through the doors to the tavern. "All that matters."

"Is he okay?" Sariel said as we walked into the tavern. The large man like a baby in my arms.

"We need Elina," I said under my breath.

Sariel sent the wife to fetch her.

Within an hour, the tavern was a makeshift little hospital. Three families came from their rooms and looked down from the balcony.

"What happened?"

"Was it bandits?"

"Everything is alright," Sariel said to the people on the walkway. "Just an accident. Let's give them some privacy, please."

But gossip and prying eyes aren't so easily shaken off. Not among farmers, shepherds and millers. In the end, many stood to watch from the walkway above the tavern floor.

Elina came, dressed in her silver robes bound against her body. She spoke softly to the family and tended to the older father.

"His ankle is broken," Elina confirmed after I had helped him onto a table for her to inspect. "Ribs too. The bruises on his face are so swollen, its keeping his skull fracture from spreading. He'll need the Mistress."

"Can you heal him, Elina?" Sariel asked. "Do you have... powers?"

Elina glanced at me, and Sariel noticed. "I've done my prayers today to the Mistress. She can ease his suffering."

We watched as she laid hands on him and I saw the swelling in his face go down. The air buzzed with divine magic, Elina's tattoos glowed brightly in silver up her body.

After a moment, it was over. Elina nodded, and the father was fast asleep. I saw the swelling on his face recede.

"You can stay here till he's rested." Sariel held the mother by the shoulders.

"They took our coin. They took all of it!" the mother broke into tears.

"It's no matter. Don't worry about that." Sariel shut her eyes as she hugged the crying woman. The daughter was sitting quietly, a faraway look in her eyes.

"What are we going to do, mama?"

Sariel came to me as the mother went to comfort her daughter.

"Help them upstairs, take them to room three." She pressed the key in my hand.

"Can he wake?" I asked Elina.

The halfling nodded. "He can. Get him up there, and then I'll bring the girls. Put pillows under his foot. It'll help with the swelling."

I woke the father and made him sit up.

"We're going upstairs, my friend."

The older man eyed the rickety stairs with a proper amount of distrust.

"I got it, I'll carry you." I waved him to give me his hand.

"Nice of you lad, but I don't think you're—whoa!"

I took his left hand over my shoulder and my right one through his legs and rolled him on top of me on the side of his good ribs. He was twenty stone easy.

I carried him like a speared boar over my shoulders. I felt that old strength in me singing out. My back straightened, my jaw set, and I climbed up the stairs with him bouncing on my shoulder.

A few exclamations went up from the guests of the tavern.

"Yer half a horse, lad," the father said from my shoulders. Putting on a good humor for the onlookers and to save his embarrassment. "We slip some bridle on you and tack. You can come plow my fields for spring seeding."

"Try not to talk," I said and took the steps. "Give your ribs a rest."

Each step produced another groan. Once I got him to the room, I nodded to the father of the two children I had met earlier.

"You mind?" I jingled the keys in my hand at him.

"Sure!" he jumped forward, eager to be part of the tale they would all be telling in the morning. He unlocked room three and followed us in.

"Grab some of those pillows off the other bed," I told him.

I settled the father down and propped his foot up.

"Thanks," I told the visitor, nodding to the door.

"Holler, if you need anything. Anything at all." He fumbled for the doorknob.

Once he left, I turned to the father in bed. He looked much better, but he would be in pain for a few days at the least. He was lucky Elina had been here. Ribs heal. A cracked ankle could end a farm and the family with it.

"Hope you're ready to repeat that tale. I suspect they'll start knocking tomorrow."

The father groaned as he rubbed his side.

"You need anything?" I asked.

The man shook his head, his whisker furrowing as he chewed his lip. I could see his mind racing. His eyes fell on mine in defeat.

"Lost the whole take. Two harvests turned into a sack of coin. All gone."

"You're alive. Your daughter and wife are safe. You saved them."

"I killed them," he huffed. His eyes glassy and I looked away to save him the shame. "Too cheap to spend the coppers on a room for the night. Tried to save pennies, and I lost it all."

I didn't say anything. There wasn't anything to say.

He looked at me. "What are we going to do?"

You'll heal, then you'll struggle. You'll lose your home. Or you won't. Maybe your lives.

I patted him on his good leg. "Rest up. Nice elf lady downstairs is going to take good care of you and the family. Just rest."

I left him there and went downstairs.

What are we going to do?

By now, the watchers from the balcony had come downstairs. They should have been putting their arms around the mother and daughter. Instead, they were clamoring to Sariel and Elina as if they were the town elders.

"The roads aren't safe!"

"How are we to travel now?"

"What if they come back?"

Sariel and Elina were trying to calm the small crowd. I nodded to them and raised my hands.

"They won't be back," I told the crowd. "The bandits

headed off, somewhere south away from the constables. Some transport town. I forgot the name..."

"Tilbrook?" a man asked.

"No, that wasn't it. Some place with ships."

"Eatherton Bay, in Trinth!" A man ventured.

"That's it," I said.

"How do you know this?" the wife of the man I had just carried asked.

"Your husband heard them shouting about it as they rode away. It's probably why they didn't take the wagon. Likely didn't want to pay to load it on a ship, and wanted to make time to the town."

"He didn't say anything like that to me." The wife looked down. Then up at the crowd. "But... I did hear them shouting something as they rode off."

"These types are like that. They don't stay long. They know the constables will come for them," I said.

"Is this true?" Sariel's soft voice cut through the crowd.

Whatever she had locked away inside herself, she had stipulations for me. Elina watched me, too. I knew that the ring she held would tell Sariel the moment I killed anyone or stole anything.

"We won't see them again," I assured her.

"Why's your hair like that? Looks like a bird took a bite out of you?" the daughter asked.

Everyone looked, and I reached up to where Sariel's scissors had dipped too low. I felt stubble there.

"Was it bandits?" A man asked.

"Worse," I said. "Drunk barber." Sariel looked away, deciding to re-stack the chairs at that moment.

The crowd groaned after Sariel refused to open the bar back up.

"They'll gossip all night," she whispered to me.

Elina helped the mother and daughter upstairs.

"All done here, folks. Please head back to your rooms. I'm going to lock up." I waved the crowd back to their rooms upstairs. Couples and families shifted, finally making their way back to their beds.

After a while, Sariel came to me. "I'm going to head back to the house with the girls. Make sure they're safe. Brim will keep an eye on the place."

"Sounds good," I said. "Walk you home?" I was miffed the haircut had ended before we could continue. And I saw her drawing inside herself again.

"Halfway," Sariel said with a soft smile.

We made our way on a route from behind the building, out near the woods. The pathway curved around a few ponds, and on the south side of the river I saw the dim glow of her house where the girls were sleeping.

"Davik..." Sariel broke our silence.

In the moonlight, she was like a figure from the stars. Her pointed ears, the soft wisp of her blonde hair. It was cold and her immaculate flesh was covered in a cloak of emerald green. She kept it open, and I saw the sliding fullness of her bosom. I regretted that our moment had ended.

"If you're looking for a tip for the haircut, you're sorely mistaken," I said.

Her eyes turned serious. Worried.

"Those men weren't heading to Trinth, were they? I know you wanted to calm everyone. But you promised. No blades, no killing."

"I intend to keep it," I said. And I did.

She smiled. In that moment, there under the half-moon-light, she wasn't an elven commander or an innkeeper. For that moment, she was a beautiful woman asking me to keep a promise.

"No killing," I said again. "And they won't be back."

Sariel nodded. She reached out and touched my arm. Disappointment filled me, like the lungs of a drowning man. The touch was just acknowledgement, not a promise of anything. She would steal away, hiding from me again.

I watched her walk all the way to the house. In a town where people were just trying to make a living. She was avoiding what we could be. What she had been. But I didn't fault her for it. And I wasn't going anywhere. Oakshire was worth more than anything I had ever owned. Or wanted to. So was she. So were all of them. Worth so much more.

Worth protecting.

CHAPTER
TEN

I walked quietly in the forest. It was the deep night. I had been following the scent of a campfire for almost a mile in the dark.

North, then northwest.

I clutched the farmer's cudgel in my hand. It felt right. It annoyed me how right it felt. Like it was taunting me.

Knew you'd be back.

With the deep treeline on the hills, there was almost no light. Almost. My eyes were wide open in the dark. The closer I got to my quarry, the more the old marching song rattled around my head.

Wars we wage'em!

Mage's we break'em!

Days we save'em! Oh!

I shook my head, trying to keep that old infantry song out of my mind.

I had jumped off the road almost two hours ago and was making slow, steady time. For half an hour I had gotten turned around, the wind throwing the scent off for me. Once I caught the smell of smoke again, I knew I had them.

It was autumn, and even with bare feet, it was hard to keep completely quiet on the forest floor.

I saw the soft glow of a dying fire. Right on the edge of a little flat ground. As far as hiding places went, this was a prime one. But a smart crew would have forsaken the fire. An even smarter one would have been long gone by now. But the drunk are sloppy and lazy. Only somebody looking for you who wanted to find you could get here.

Which explained why I was here.

I would have rather had a sword. Or even better, a short mace and a shield. Those were my preferred. Maybe two or three backups with spears to skewer the little rats in their bedrolls.

I've known and worked with some of the heaviest names in the lands. I've seen a paladin that could level a temple with his power laid low by a knife in a tavern doorway from behind. There are swordsmen out there who fight like a poem, like a dance. They fight like they are making love. It's art.

People asked me after he died. How did it happen? The man had slain champions of the underdark. He'd banished demons under the banner of his deity.

He hadn't been looking.

The best fights are the ones you win. And the ones you win are the ones that are in your advantage. You can prattle on about fair contest, but for those who are in the trade, we take every edge we can get.

What's fair about fighting someone better than you? What's fair about fighting some elven lord who has practiced for centuries?

Not a damn thing.

Winning is what counts.

Four drunks can swarm a schooled fighter in an alley.

Four men can tackle a mage before he mutters his second spell.

Fighting four men, and leaving them alive and you unscathed? Damn difficult.

But promises are promises. And today, at least, a deal was still a deal.

I gripped the cudgel in my hand. It was a foot and a half long, dark rowan wood, with a single iron band around the head. Good for dispatching the odd farm animal, or breaking an arm maybe to quell a bar riot.

It also was not a blade. I hoped very much the deal-struck charm on me recognized that.

I crept up to the edge of the camp light. Three of the mercenaries were sleeping. A fourth was failing on watch, and I saw the hunched figure of him, drunk and asleep against a tree.

Looked fair to me.

I had bound my face in dark cloth. I kept to the outside, circling the campfire. My eyes were set on the guard on watch. The fire flickered.

I crept closer.

My eyes set with grim resolve. I felt the need for the slow work to begin. It was foolish to do this without killing anyone. But there was an old part of me that wanted to see if I still had it.

Wars we wage'em!

I was within arm's reach. His helmet was against the tree. In the dim light, I saw he was young.

I lashed out and swung the cudgel into his jaw. Holding back, so as not to kill him. There was the crunch of battered bone and he slumped down. I kept my eyes on the campfire. No one moved.

Waiting. I felt nothing. No flicker of the deal-struck charm in me.

I moved his body and positioned his leg on the stump he had been sitting on. With a sick heave, I broke his femur while he was unconscious.

Hard to be a bandit and rob the small people of the land with a broken leg. If you got to a cleric or healer in time, you could walk normally again. If not, well... that there's the price of being an asshole.

I crept towards the campfire. I could get one more before the alarm rang. I crawled over to the sleeping figure closest to me. His eyes opened when I covered his mouth with my hand. He started hollering and struggling, but I was much, much stronger. His two hands couldn't even move the one I had over his mouth.

His eyes went wide when I raised the cudgel in my hand.

"Shh," I hissed. "Or I'll do em' both, get me?"

If he agreed to this whispered parlay, all he gave me was a jabbering plead. But I could hear the thunder of my own heartbeat in my ears.

Mages we break'em!

I brought the cudgel-head down like a whip across his kneecap. The crack sounded like a nut being split. He howled in my hands and struggled so hard he squirmed away from me.

"Gulrith!" he screamed.

A sleeping figure rose in the middle. It was the one with the mace scar on his jaw. I leapt away from the screaming mercenary and pounced on him. I landed on his chest and sat on him, trapping his arms as I pounded the cudgel into his right leg over and over and over. Bones cracked, then fractured, and then shattered as I maimed him.

"Sorry bout' this," I grunted and whipped the short cudgel

from left to right, knocking his off-set jaw to the other side in a thick crunch.

Gulrith was up. Halfway out of his bedroll. He was good. Not good enough to set a proper watch. But out of sleep and on the attack instantly. He snaked out with a blade without missing a beat. No exclamation, no wondering why.

He shot his fist forward. The punch-dagger slid an inch into my side.

My left hand gripped his forearm, keeping him from going deeper. Behind us, his men were yowling.

Our eyes stared at each other. He was straining, trying to summon everything he had to get past my grip. He had his other hand around my shirt, trying to pull me over onto the blade.

He peered at me.

I gritted my teeth and squeezed his forearm. I felt both bones in his arm flex as I brought them together. The soft click of them meeting before they broke under my grip.

He stared into my eyes. Realization came across his face.

"Darkshi-"

Snap!

I slapped the punch-dagger away from him and crawled on top of him, pinning his broken forearm to his chest and staring down at him.

To his credit, he raised his other hand in subjugation. A good mercenary knows when he's beat. He knows he'd rather live to fight for more coin another day.

"Alright, alright!" he hissed.

"This valley is off-limits..." I whispered.

"Of course," Gulrith nodded. His broken arm didn't set him howling like the other men yammering near us. One clutching his face, the other his leg.

"Don't come back," I said.

He nodded. "I swear..."

I squeezed his arm, and he clenched his teeth in pain. Then he nodded to drive his plea forth.

"Look at me! Won't ever come back. I swear it. You'll never see us again."

I nodded. Satisfied. He breathed easier when I let go of his arm.

Then I broke his leg.

CHAPTER
ELEVEN

"How did you get this again?"

Elina peered at the wound in my side. A thread of catgut slid through my skin and I felt the tug of the last portion of the injury closing. My skin was red from the boiled wine she had poured into the wound to clean it.

She moved one of several candelabra closer to inspect the stitching she had done. The air smelled of drying blood, cooling wine, and the paraffin of candles.

"I fell," I said.

"Onto?"

"A... nail. In the hay. In my barn."

I had woken her before dawn, my side killing me when I made my way to the temple.

My lover didn't look too happy with that response. She peered at the wound, frustrated that she couldn't use her healing powers on me. Even after warning her not to waste her reserves, she had tried, and the look on her face when the spell shimmered and dissipated as it hit my skin was disheartening for her.

"You know, Davik, when you speak to a priestess on private matters, she can't disclose anything."

"Is that true?"

"It is. Following the Mistress is a delicate thing. She was an outlawed deity in so many cities and towns. Much of our duty is in private tutoring, in matters of reproductive health, in the affairs of the bedsheets."

"I know," I said. She looked up at me from the altar I was supine on. I knew her spell failing had bothered her greatly, and despite everything inside me, I would give her the truth.

"I might have... bent the rules Sariel set out for me a little."

Elina sat back, putting her tools away. "Did you kill those men?"

"No. But... there were some broken bones involved."

Elina shook her head. "Davik, Sariel sees something in you. I think, and I can say this because it's just what I think, not what she's told me—I think she's trying to make up for what she did during the war. So many people couldn't look at themselves again. She considered following the Mistress, but I think deep down she wants to punish herself."

I rolled up, my side screaming. "What are you saying?"

"I think that it's important to her you... turn a page. Because maybe she can do the same."

"I get it, Elina."

"I don't think you do," Elina said, and a dark curl fell across her face. "You're conflicted. The facets inside you are spinning, never sitting still. We haven't joined lately... and even the last time we did, my powers were waning."

"It's the runes," I explained for the dozenth time. "When they made me-"

"Davik," Elina whispered, eyes pleading. "It's not just the runes. You're pulled in different directions. I am not one to preach monogamy, I'm one to preach about truth. Your soul can supply so many. You think you have only a small capacity. If you would just let yourself feel it, then you'd see. People that join and bind with you will circle your star."

I pulled my only clean shirt over my head. What she spoke of wasn't unknown to me. I had been hiding our union from Sariel. My mind filled with the scent of her from the night before. Now, when I tried to reach for it, it was tainted in bloodshed. Tainted by the lie of staying true to what she asked of me.

There had been no blades, except the ones that entered me. No killing. But I was still lying to her.

"I won't apologize for protecting her." I pushed myself off the altar and stretched a bit. "Nor you, nor this place."

"I'm not asking you to." Elina grasped my hands. "Honesty, truth, Davik. It's the path out of the woods. Your lust and hunger were shaped by a lifetime of hardship, and you mistake it for sickness. Just be truthful with her."

I wasn't sure about that.

"It's... not that simple, Elina. This isn't a song or tale. My time at the tavern, I can't destroy it. I won't go back to what I am."

"You can't live a life cloaked and pretending. Look what it's done to others."

"If you want, I can help you with your powers, Elina... you just have to be careful."

The halfling cleric lingered on her tools, considering it. "It won't work, Davik. I'm... guilty too. I should've told you."

"Told me what?" I asked. The sun rose outside the stained glass of the small temple.

"Acolytes wait until they're stationed, and they weave themselves into communities. We are a very liberal, free faith. The single-faceted like me? We choose our partners carefully."

"Okay..." I said. This wasn't making any sense to me.

"This was my first posting."

"Yeah, you had mentioned that." I shrugged.

She kept staring at me.

I stood up. "Wait... but you've been here for years."

"It's a small town, Davik! Everyone is married. Or old."

"I saw plenty of young guys walking around,"

"The jewel of my soul didn't move in the slightest for any that made advances. It's just, you were so forward, and dominant when you came here. I could see the dark hunger inside of you. The string of lovers, of conquests. I thought... why not one more?"

"What are you saying?" I asked.

"You were," she whispered. "My first."

"Oh hells Elina," I choked. "You're... I didn't feel exactly. I mean it was..." I trailed off, trying to find words that wouldn't reduce what I had felt our first time into the tavern chat of men.

"Implements of meditation, Davik. Like those I teach or give to of age women here. You broke what remained of my crest physically, but in my soul... you claimed it. My power grew. I can't be a priestess of devotion and love without... loving and devoting. I'm sorry, I should have told you. The more you're conflicted about Sariel, the less I gain from you. You're withdrawing."

"It doesn't make sense," I said. "The things you were doing. The... the technique. I didn't feel you break-"

"We practice! And... the body has its needs. We're taught to see to them, with tools... with items of the Mistress. It's part of our training. Part of our counseling. So many women of age come and have never explored themselves. We don't show them, exactly, but it's the job of a priestess to teach. I don't just peddle birth control. The women at the tavern even-"

"Enough" I threw my hands up. I was pacing now. "What does this mean, you and me?"

"I'm devoted to you. I chose you."

"Forever? Are we..."

Elina laughed. "Davik, I'm just bound to you. Until you leave here. Until you don't... want me anymore."

At that moment, she was tragic. I wanted to take her in my arms and tell her such a thing wasn't possible.

So I did.

"I don't see that happening," I whispered and held her close. A moment ago, she had been tending to my wounds, but now she melted into my arms. Despite priesthood, despite deities and spells and goddesses, she was a woman unsure of where she stood with her lover.

"You don't have to tell me what I want to hear," she said in my arms.

I drew her closer to me and kissed her. The world stopped for a moment, as it does when a beautiful woman is in your arms. Elina and I were more than friends. She spoke about things I knew existed, but had never believed truly. Love for a partner. Devotion of clutched sheets and soft communion.

As we broke, standing in a strange lilting dance in each other's arms, she looked up at me with tears in her eyes.

"The Mistress isn't the wife, Davik. She lives in every wife. In every moment you walk closer to a woman you desire. Me, Sariel, any others. You don't leave one to have the other, you bring them all to you. It's the path. You're a good man."

"A few men in the woods might disagree with you."

Elina squeezed my arms. "But the people you helped and protected wouldn't. The Mistress isn't jealous, and neither am I. If you join with Sariel, or any others, or even all the others... that might just be what you need. Enough to sate you. And instead of a string of conquered and subjugated bodies and souls... you might know love."

Love.

She broke from me, standing back. "Davik, just go with what feels right, not what feels compulsive. See where it leads you. Be honest, be open. You're a dominant yet sensual spirit, one of the strongest I've ever heard of. But you've denied yourself the peace of comfort and love for so long. You seek the void in your vanquished foe, whether you're taking steel or flesh to them."

I raised an eyebrow.

"What does this mean for you and I?" I asked.

She shrugged. "It means whatever you decide it does. I'm bound to you. But you have to decide what your life looks like. What your soul looks like here in this place. Just do what feels *right*. I'll be here to talk it through, to serve you if you wish."

I watched her in the dawn light of the temple.

"Or not," she said.

I was in no rush to head to the tavern before we opened. I walked with the secret of what I had done. Wounds weren't the only thing I had taken from the woods.

The large sack of coin sat comically in my pocket. The farmer's lost purse. While the mercenaries had howled in pain, I had taken their arms and armor. Four short swords, two spears, three knives and three breastplates. I hid them in a dried ravine in the woods.

In days of old, I would have left no one alive that might come looking for me. Yet I had. They were maimed, yes. Severely damaged. But they had their horses and the coin in their own pockets. Whether ill-gotten or not, I had left it for some reason.

No stealing.

It was doubtful the deal-struck charm would have alerted Sariel to anything outside her ownership or the tavern. Yet it had felt wrong to me, so I left the bandits their own coin. Their arms and armor were mine by codes more ancient than man. The rite of conquest.

I took breakfast at the cafe. The girl behind the counter gave me the eye, despite how haggard I looked and felt.

"Threw this in for you." She raised a large almond pastry for my plate with my coffee.

"Thanks," I said, taking it. Maybe marriage options were more limited in town than I thought.

"Heard that father you carried was a right ogre," she said with a soft smile. "Glad you helped him."

"Much obliged."

She leaned towards me, smiling wider. "I think it's handsome."

"What is?" I asked, looking down.

"Your hair. The bald spot in the back. Is it from a scar?"

I reached up, feeling where Sariel and I had been interrupted. It was a hefty chunk of missing hair. My scalp was almost bare from the closeness of the scissors.

"Yeah, something like that." I raised the pastry to her. "Thanks."

Even in my time here, I had forgotten that a town ran on gossip where little happened. I said nothing, taking my food and coffee outside while she watched me.

Other denizens of the town were there too, and I heard their murmurs as I ate.

"Heard the young man found them ravaged and dead on the road."

"Chased the bandits off too, killed one and pulled the wagon himself into town."

"I heard that too."

I finished my breakfast quickly and left. As I walked to the tavern, Elina's conversation circled in my mind.

The more you're conflicted about Sariel...

I saw the bookstore opening.

The shopkeeper Helena didn't look too pleased as I entered as her first customer of the day. I wouldn't take any of the farmer's purse, but I did have my own silver from my weeks here at the tavern.

"We sell books here," she said the moment I entered the store.

"I figured," I said. "From the sign and all. You're Helena, yes?"

She crossed her arms and looked around, as if scanning to see what things of value she should position herself near.

"Do you have any books on... myths? Or legends, maybe?" I asked.

This question seemed to catch her off guard.

"Well, yes. Are there types of myths you're looking for?"

She had me there. I must have shown my frustration, but she helped me out.

"If this is for a friend?"

"It is." I nodded.

She smiled. "I'd suggest a small tome on elementals and their own myths. They're stories of great deities clashing among the stars. It has to do with astrology. Lovers, betrayals, wars among the celestial bodies. There's a pretty girl in town who has been eying it for a long time."

"That sounds like just the thing."

She smiled and fetched the small book.

"How much is it?" I asked.

The woman looked at the tag. The leather was hand woven. The pages had a red sheen to them when pressed together. I knew little about books, but this looked to be a good one.

"Eight silvers." She spoke the hard price, her face softening in understanding if I couldn't afford it. That was more than what I made in two weeks at the tavern. "We can also put it on layaway."

"Eight it is," I said and reached into my pocket.

THE TAVERN OPENED early that day. When I came in through the back, Tyra was standing next to the kitchen window, her fiery hair done up in a bun. The sunlight made her skin sparkle. The busty girl smiled at me, the shape and lilt of her faen features encased in skin pale as cream.

"Hey hero, you missed breakfast."

"I cheated on you. I went to the cafe early. Couldn't sleep."

"That's okay," she said with a wink. Then fluttered her eyes. *"Davik's such a strong boy, carrying that man. Do you know if he's wed?"*

"Very funny," I stepped forward.

Honesty. Elina's words came back to me.

I kissed Tyra on the cheek from behind. "Appreciate you."

The faen girl smiled and looked over her shoulder at me. She reached back, grasping my wrist.

Her magic flowed into me. I felt a pulse of gratitude. And gladness. Like a blanket thrown around a cold child. It was her way of telling me how glad she was I was here. Our friendship was one of comrades, but as I felt her, I knew there could be more there if I wished.

The thought rose in my mind of what it would feel like to

be inside her. To feel that faen magic cascading in emotion as she bit her lip. Despite the wound, I never felt clearer and more lustful than after winning a fight.

"You're... full of vitality today." Tyra giggled and let go of my wrist. "Hotter than my stove."

"Sorry," I said, realizing she probably felt what I had for a second. "Can't help it, dashing fellow that I am."

Tyra slid two plates of food into my hand. "Try not to get anyone pregnant on the way upstairs. This is for that poor wounded man."

Perfect. I took the plates and walked past Karley at the bar.

Brim growled at me as he walked by. He was carrying a set of clean rags from the laundry to the bar. I saw the meat fork in the back of his belt and we traded barbed looks.

"Morning," I said to him.

Ugly-man.

Karley was out on the tavern floor, taking an order from a family staying at the tavern. She glanced at me as I walked past, seeing if I was looking at her. I marched upstairs.

I knocked on the man's door with a tap of my boot.

"*Who's there?*" he asked.

"Got food for you," I said into the door. "I'm coming in."

"Alright," the man said.

I leaned down and unlatched the door handle with my elbow. When I saw him, he looked better than he had last night. Yet the look of defeat and the sense of ruin permeated the room.

"How are you feeling?" I asked as I sat the food down on the bed next to him.

"Better, aye. Not sure how long I should stay here..." he looked away. Likely hadn't slept much the night before.

"I went back to the road where those men robbed you, looking to see if they left anything."

"Did you?" He perked up.

"Mmm." I pulled the heavy sack of coin out of my pocket. "This belong to you?"

His face lit up. "Yer pulling my leg! Is that it? How did you get this?"

I tossed the heavy purse to him and he caught it, inspecting it, opening it to feel around for coins.

"They must've dropped it on their getaway. It was about fifty yards up the road, just sitting there. Lucky I spotted it, before some traveler."

"Oh lad." the man moved to get up to shake my hand, but I pushed him back to the covers. He gripped my hand fiercely. "Thank you. Thank you, lad. I can't tell you-"

Then his eyes peered at me. He looked down at my bruised hands.

"Banged it up, moving your wagon out back."

The older fellow nodded, leaning back into the pillows, holding the satchel of coin to his chest. "You seen my cudgel around? When you moved it, I mean?"

I shook my head. "That, I didn't see. Wouldn't know what it's for anyway, right?"

"Right." The man chewed his whiskers. Then nodded. "Thing always has a way of walking off."

"Didn't want to tell your wife about the coin," I said. "Never good to worry the women folk, you know? Just leave a man's business to himself."

He looked down in gratitude. "Keen eyes, you have. Spotting this." He jingled the pouch. "Lucky, you did. Let me give you a spot of coin. Please."

"Against tavern policy, I'm afraid. Wouldn't want my boss to know I violated that. Tip your bartender and waitress."

"Thanks lad." The man smiled at me. "We'll make it. Thanks to you."

"Just a busboy, bringing things back to where they belong. Girls will be up soon to check on you. And that lady cleric."

I left him there, shutting the door behind me. As I walked onto the stairway, Karley poked her head out as if she had been waiting for me. Today she was wearing a black blouse, smudged shadowy lipstick, and a short tight skirt in fishnet leggings.

"Boss is asking for you," she called up.

I walked down, sharing a look with her. Tyra had been right. I was feeling lustful after last night. It felt good to come out on top of four men, and better that they deserved it. Women can always tell when you're feeling it. It shows in your walk, in your swagger.

"Thanks," I said. Keeping my eyes on hers. The drow girl had such a thin frame on top, but with a shapely rear and amazing legs in her stockings.

"Do you need anything?" I asked.

"Keg four is acting up, if you want to take a look." Karley was glancing at my chest.

"Didn't ask about the bar," I said and walked past her.

She chewed her lip for a moment, selecting which spiteful retort to spit out. But I left her where she stood and went to Sariel.

"Morning," I said in her office.

"Morning," she looked up in her chair. Today's dress was pure white, almost silver, like her eyes. If yesterday had been clingy, today she had squeezed into this thing. I shut my eyes for a second and wanted to shake my head.

Go with what feels right, not what feels compulsive.

"You look beautiful today." I folded my hands behind my back, like I was standing in parade rest.

The compliment seemed to take her aback. I saw her eyes searching me, prying.

"The wounded gentleman in room three is going to stay awhile. Vorga will bring the meals, but he may need a hand getting up and down the stairs."

"No problem," I said. "Anything you want me to do in particular today?"

"Just keep an eye out. It's going to be busy as hell today."

"More travelers?"

"There's a story, and a wounded man to tell it. Just you wait and see."

I waited for more, but she looked at me as if everything was business.

"Do you need something, Davik?"

I walked towards her. "Sorry we were interrupted last night."

Sariel shrugged. "I owe you an apology for that bald spot in the back. The knock startled me."

If she wanted to pretend nothing had happened, that was her business. But I was not going to have any of it.

"I feel like something went unfinished last night," I said. She stared at me with unblinking eyes. "And I don't think that's right. So tonight, why don't you stay after closing? It's my turn to treat you to something."

"Tonight..." Sariel said, looking away now. She began to push some invoices around. I leaned forward on the desk, placing my hand over hers.

"Yes, tonight. You and me."

She looked at my forearm, the same one she had been grinding against the night before.

"I don't think that's such a good idea."

The possibility swung in the balance. The smart move, the polite move, was to give her space. Sit around. Maybe things would align once again.

If you want things to change, then you have to change them.

"Meet me after closing. Once the girls leave."

"And if I don't?" She whispered.

"Then you might be condemned to a lifetime of good ideas."

SARIEL WAS RIGHT. The tavern bustled that evening, and for the first time we had a line of people waiting for seats at tables, glaring at customers eating Tyra's fare, wishing them to hurry. Finally, things settled down, and the turn ended, with the night sliding into people nursing their drinks and listening to the musicians Sariel hired.

During a break, I found Vorga out front. As always, she read her little book.

"Vorga," I said. "I got you something."

The orc girl looked up, taking a moment to come back to the present. I heard someone once say that readers live hundreds of lives. I thought in that moment, seeing her, that if you were truly to understand someone, you would have to read everything they ever had, in the same order, at the same pace.

She was beautiful enough for me to give it a go.

"I got you this. I saw it in the store and thought you would like it." I pulled the thick little tome out of my belt and held it out to her. Glad to be rid of it in my waistline.

Vorga stared at it, then at me. As if there was some punchline. Her lips were so full and pink. Freckles on her pale green skin and the darkness of her eyes and lashes made me want to see this moment forever.

"Really?" Her voice was disbelief. "You got this for me? I can borrow it?"

"It's yours. I thought you might like something new to read."

She reached out and took the tome.

"It's about the mythology of elementals, of what they believe. If you don't like it-"

"Yes." She looked up when she cut me off. "I like it. Very much. But this is too much. Books are so expensive."

"I think they're worth much more in your hands."

The gratitude in her eyes had me planning a heist of the world's libraries. I'd haul books back on wagon carts and hand them to her one by one to see that delighted look again.

"Do you want to take this one? To borrow, even?" She held out her own little novella.

"That's yours. I'm not much of a reader. I suppose I prefer to hear words instead of reading them. A bard, a good story-teller, that's more my style."

She looked down at both books in either hand. Like a beggar staring at two coins that slid into their bowl, amazed. A smile broke across her face, and the light in her eyes was something I'll never forget.

"I have a library now," she whispered.

"You do. Do you have a shelf to put them on?"

"Oh yes, I know just the place." She stood up and put both books on the bench. "Thank you Davik."

She threw her arms around me. It was an eager embrace. Her cool arms wrapped around my neck and she buried her head over my shoulder. It took me by surprise. I leaned back, sort of lifting her, and hugged her back.

"I'm glad you like it," I whispered.

She slid away from my neck, the touch of tears in her eyes. Her soft voice was tinged with the heaviness of emotion. "I love it. I'll get you something one day too. I'll get you a storyteller."

I chuckled, not used to this type of attention. I've marched and stood in infantry lines, and I've stalked the deepest dungeons with torches and steel in my hand. But the pure joy of this girl, the gratitude of her, I found myself glancing away.

"Don't worry about that. Maybe you can tell me what the book says. Read to me sometime."

Her eyes lit up. "Yes! I'll read it to you."

"Hey, you don't have to-"

"Shh!" she grinned and pushed me. Maybe a bit too hard, not knowing her own strength. "I'll read you all the stories."

"Yes, you do that," I said.

"I should get back inside. I have to put these away in my bag. We can't let them get stained."

"Okay, see you."

She walked back inside and turned again to look at me. The shy orc waitress, the bookish girl was gone for a moment. Something else burned in her eyes. And it burned for me.

"Thank you," she said again.

Do what feels right, not what feels compulsive.

Maybe Elina was right. Maybe the pursuit of one woman didn't mean leaving the other. Or perhaps it was just time to stake my life here, in this tavern, in this town.

The thoughts melted from my mind as the night picked up again. More travelers came. People checked out of rooms, they checked in. I pumped more and more water outside to carry in.

"Tyra, another batch, please." I nodded to the giant pot we heated water in.

"Davik! I need my stove!" she said. The orders were piling in. Piling in so much, we had both servers now writing orders instead of yelling them to her.

"Sorry!"

"Ugh!" Tyra threw her hands in her hair.

Karley walked back from the bar. "Hey Tyra, can you put up

six more potato friers on in a basket on the fly-"

Tyra turned, face red and eyes bulging. "Write it down! Write it down Karley!"

"Whoa! It's just some-"

"Do you see this!" Tyra held up all the slips of paper that were sitting in a pile on the cabinet next to her stove and oven. "Put them on the bottom. They'll come out in a while."

"Alright!" Karley huffed and stalked off. I saw her take charcoal and scribble quickly. She stalked back in and shoved it under the papers. "There!"

"Fine!" Tyra shouted.

"Fine!" Karley shouted.

"Rahh!" Brim growled from his sink of dishes. He had his own battle to fight. The dishes around the sink were a siege upon his domain, and as fast as he scrubbed I kept burying him in more.

I enjoyed it immensely.

Tyra spun back to her stove as the music picked up outside. She looked completely flustered.

"I'm sorry Davik, just put the water in the pot here. I'll try to make room." Tyra's eyes slid over to the stacks of paper. Then her voice choked up when she opened the stove door. "I need more firewood."

"Hey, don't worry about it. I'll bring you firewood first. Then I'll heat some water outside."

"Thank you," Tyra said and shut her eyes. She looked like she was about to cry. The feeling of frustration and being overwhelmed was shared with me, in her tingling magic.

I put my arm around her, and she sighed and leaned her head against me.

"We'll get through this," I promised her. I grabbed the giant pot of water, freeing up her stove and carried it outside.

The woodpile was running low. Very low. I needed to go

take that old woman Mabel up on her offer. We were running through more cords per week than ever before. The amount of fuel we needed to run this place was mind-boggling. Sometimes it was a quarter cord a night. Between water and cooking and the fireplace, we were burning money.

I split two logs and set a bundle down for the stove inside. As I was cutting the last of the batch to make a fire to boil water, Jessa, the human waitress, poked her head outside.

"Hey Davik, we need some help bussing inside."

I left the axe buried in the stump and grabbed an armful of wood.

"Be right there."

I filled the wood for Tyra, and then the rest for the fireplace on the tavern floor. Before I could get it roaring again, Vorga called out to me.

"Davik, can you bus those two tables over there?"

"Yep!" I turned and went and started grabbing dishes. I didn't even have my tub to carry them, I just kept stacking them on my hands and arms. I squeezed past Karley, tending a full bar.

"Hey, we need two beer kegs changed. The red ale and the spiced brown."

"I'll get right on it," I grunted and rushed past her.

In the kitchen, I buried Brim in more dishes. Instead of a growl, he looked up at me in amazement. I had seen that face before on men who saw the enemy host arriving, with their size stretching to the horizon.

"Sorry, guy," I said and left him.

Damn you, Ugly-man.

"Davik! Can you bring the food to the bar?" Tyra pleaded with me.

"Yes." I reached out and grabbed several plates of steaming food.

"Order up!" I shouted to the tavern floor so Vorga and Jessa could come fetch whichever order this was.

Karley was a blur behind the bar, bending down, grabbing bottles, pouring glasses.

"Need those kegs changed!" She yelled behind her.

"Coming right up," I said and slid past her. Before I went down into the cellar, I knocked on Sariel's door and opened it.

"What is it?" Sariel was staring at several letters in her hand, a look of morbidity in her eyes.

"Getting crazy out here, Sariel. We might need a hand."

"Alright," she nodded, not looking away from the paper. "I'll be right there."

"Meat is running low, too." I informed her.

Sariel shook her head and cursed. She set the papers down like they were death omens and shut her eyes. "Alright, Davik. I'll be right there."

I trudged down to the cellar. The chaos of the night was getting to everyone. But the busier it got, the more centered I felt. That quiet feeling came down on me, the ability to track multiple targets at once. I had always been good at protecting my blind spot. Once I had spoken to a duellist about it and he had told me he felt the same.

'You have to look everywhere and nowhere. Look where you can't see.'

It had saved me many times. Swiping a spear or sword blow away from where I had felt it coming. Keeping track of multiple enemies in the treeline, in the dungeon. I could always feel where they were.

Now instead of enemies, I had tables and kegs and plates of food.

'The real trick to mastery,' he had said, oiling a one-sided sword. *'Is to make the entire battlefield your blind spot.'*

I smiled in the cellar's darkness. It was cold and damp, a

pleasant relief from the heat of the tavern from so many bodies.

I changed the two kegs and left the empties. I would drag them up later and pile them for our brewers to refill.

Sariel was at the top of the stairs when I came out, walking past with two armfuls of food.

"Gonna need more specialty kegs from the brewers, boss." I smiled, and I reached out to give her a hand.

"Of course," Sariel huffed, biting her lip in frustration. "Why not?"

"Everything alright?" I asked.

She didn't answer. She was like that all night. It wasn't like her to be so distracted.

The tavern became so crowded and bursting that I had to start turning people away from the door. The musicians were lively, and people started dancing, spinning about, knocking tables and food aside. A fresh order clattered to the ground and Sariel had enough.

"Davik! Sort that out!" she snapped.

At first I thought she meant the mess, so I grabbed my broom.

"No!" she took it out of my hand. "That!" She pointed to three men who were way over-served and being rowdier than the rest.

I walked over. One man was dancing on a table, drunk, laughing with his friends.

"Fellas, we're gonna ask you to keep it down in here. It's too crowded for all that."

The two men in the seats waved me off and kept clapping for their friend on the table.

"Alright, let's get down." I reached up to give him a hand.

"Piss off!" he cackled and kicked my hand away.

Do the right thing. Not the compulsion. Do the right thing.

"Hey!" I shouted over the noise. "Please, get down."

The man kept dancing, living it up.

I reached out and grabbed his wrist and yanked him down. He was a big man. I snarled in his ear.

"Get off the fucking table!"

He tried to pull away, but he couldn't. I tightened my grip around his arm. Then I hoisted him over my head like a barrel, he flailed in my arms.

"Hey, let go!"

Several more people turned to see me holding him over my head. They cheered. Calling for me to spin him.

"You gonna calm down?" I called up to him.

He kicked and flailed in my hands. But he wasn't going anywhere. His friends came forward to grab my arms, but I warded them off with a glare. "Don't."

"Alright!" he conceded. I set him down.

"Just," I breathed. "Stay off the tables."

One of the man's friends nodded.

I walked off to the hearth, grabbing another set of dishes to take back. Vorga glided by me, stopping.

"You okay, Davik?"

"Yes," I said. Before I could continue Sariel waved to me from the bar.

"Room two and four need to check out. Can you get payment from them?"

"Sure," I said and spun instantly around. Not a problem.

LATER THAT NIGHT, things finally calmed down a bit. Tyra got the kitchen under control.

I went to Sariel's office.

"Come in," she said.

I shut the door behind me. She stared down at her desk, head on her hand, peering at a set of ledgers. Her chest was resting on the edge of the table, threatening to spill out of her blouse.

"How bad is it?" I asked.

"Hmm?" Sariel blinked and looked up.

I nodded to the papers she was staring at. "How bad?"

She sighed and pushed the papers away.

"Pretty bad."

"Tavern's doing well," I said. "Busier than ever."

"Prices have gone up." She held up a paper. "Distillers. Food. Firewood. Transport for all. There's been weak grain harvests outside of the Midlands. Farmers here can sell at a high profit. Grain feeds the horses that pull the carts. So on and so forth."

"You've got to be making a fortune here."

Sariel laughed. "You don't know much about running a bar and restaurant. This place is a money pit. Every year I say I'm going to get it in shape. Every year something changes. The roof leaks. A beam splinters. I feel like I'm on a ship patching holes instead of sailing, just staying afloat. If I stock up too much, it's a low crowd. If I don't, big crowds come."

I watched her search the mess of letters on her desk as if there was an answer to the puzzle.

"Worse than that, they're talking about moving the Tawney harvest festival next year. We won't even be on the main road there. I think they're pressing for advanced deposits, but if it happened..."

"Hey," I said. "It's going to be alright."

"I'm tired, Davik," Sariel leaned back, pressing her fingers against the tops of her eyes. "Can we rendezvous another night?"

"No chance," I said with a grin. "I've got just the thing."

CHAPTER
TWELVE

It would have been easier to do what I was planning at the back of the tavern. Much easier. But with such a full set of guests, I didn't want to risk being interrupted again.

A night of bussing tables hadn't done the wound on my side any favors. But I felt the reassuring tug of the stitching there and knew it would be mostly healed in a week.

After being released from the Summoner prison camp at the end of the war, I had vowed to never be captured again. My young adventuring career had been cut short by conscription before it could truly start. After, I fell in with a strong party. Whatever they had done to make us Magebreakers, I would take advantage. If I could pull a cart, why not a wagon? Why not ten? I had trained religiously. Pushing my body. Run faster. Climb. Lift, drag, fight. As much as I had a distaste for magic, it was in me. They wanted magically resistant spell fodder who were strong enough to break enemy lines and get to the sorcerers they guarded. I would use it. Embrace it.

Now, I carried a bathtub, cast-iron wrapped in ceramic, a half mile from the tavern to the southern path that led to

Sariel's home with the girls. I had filled it with firewood and a pot and chain. Lanterns on strings swung on my arms. I had told Sariel where to meet me.

There along the lake and among the reeds, I set it down and started the fire. Taking water from the lake and boiling it over and over, until Sariel appeared, her house out of sight.

"Wow," she said.

Despite the growing chill, sweat covered my body. The tub was steaming as she approached, a wooden cover over it to keep the heat within.

"This looks like a waste of firewood," Sariel laughed. I looked up from the enormous pot of boiling water and smiled. Glad she had come.

"I figured you gave me a haircut with a disastrous result. Least I could do would be to give you a bath with some semblance of privacy."

"Privacy, huh?" Sariel looked around. "I feel like there's at least one peeping tom here. Can't seem to locate him, though."

I winked at her. "He's close, I assure you."

The steam rose from the tub. The moon reflected on the soft water of the pond. The reeds shuddered under the touch of the breeze, setting the mood for reprieve. More than anything, I wanted her to enjoy herself.

"You promise not to look?" Sariel smiled and tested the heat coming from the tub.

"No," I said and stood. I reached over to the supplies I had carried on my third trip, practically sprinting from the tavern to here. I pulled a bottle of wine and glass from the pack, holding it up to her. "But I promise to pretend not to."

I opened the bottle and poured her a glass. The small pair of lanterns in the trees gave a romantic glint to everything.

"Not bad, busboy." Sariel walked around, her face lit by the crackling fire. She turned to me, a lantern over either shoulder, and smiled. "Sorry again about your hair."

"Me too," I said.

"Looks good on you, though. A bit more controlled."

"So..." I said and stepped towards her. I took the cup from her hands and took a long sip of her wine. "Are you getting in?"

Sariel glanced at the bathtub. Then at me.

"Turn around," she whispered with a smile.

"Do you want me to?" I asked. She reached out and took the cup from my hand, hers lingering on mine.

We were finally alone. Away from a tavern full of prying eyes, of noise and ways to ignore and stare at one another. It was just us, here among the reeds and the crickets. Summer was withering to the crisp touch of autumn.

Sariel looked at me, eyes full of moonlight. Then she took her hand from the cup and raised her hair, turning around.

"Undo my strap for me, would you?"

I pulled the knot behind her neck, soft velvet whispered in the night air. When it fell from her neck, she held her dress to her chest, covering herself.

The elf looked over her shoulder at me demurely. "Remove the cover for me?"

I turned around and did so, pulling the steam soaked wood from the top of the bath. Sariel reached over to one of the several towels I had brought and traded it with her dress.

I watched her in the light of the moon, wishing it were as bright as a burning sun. She covered her body with a small towel clutched close to her chest. Her heavy breasts poured from behind her forearm. I drank in the sight of her wide hips, her hairless body and perfect skin. She was even more desirable, half-covered like this. The length of her pointed ears jutted from forests of golden hair and she bit her lip.

"Turn around," she whispered with a smile. I did so this

time. And I heard her step into the water, one foot after another, until she slid inside with a groan.

"Oh gods," she murmured.

I handed her the wine. She held a washcloth over her chest and let her hair spill back over the back of the tub. Her splendid silver eyes softened as the heat seeped into her body.

"Put this behind your neck," I whispered, holding up a rolled towel. She leaned forward before settling back into the makeshift pillow.

"It's been so long," she murmured. "Since a proper bath. Every time I try, something comes up. This is wondrous."

I had set a little block of soap on the small stand next to the bath with other washcloths.

"Sorry, didn't have a vast selection of towels."

"You're forgiven," Sariel said and slid lower into the bath. Her feet emerged on the other end of the tub, propping one on top of the other. Toenails pedicured and painted the same silver as her eyes.

The bubbles in the water from the slice of soap I had thrown in churned in their froth. She reached forward, sliding them towards her chest.

"How's the temperature?" I asked.

"It's wonderful," she sighed and leaned back. "But might need a refresh soon. Can you put half the cover on?"

"Sure." I turned and grabbed the tub cover. two wooden pieces in half ovals. I walked forward, angling it above her. She slid her feet down as I placed it, covering half the tub.

Sariel looked at me, chest covered. I knelt next to the tub and touched the water where the wood ended.

I walked over and grabbed the oven mitts I left next to the fire. The water in the pot was simmering. I kicked more kindling into the little fire and picked it up.

"Watch out, this is hot," I warned. Sariel sat up, drawing her long legs to her chest.

I poured the pot into the bath.

"Ohhh," Sariel said as the hot water swirled in. "That's nice."

She sank back into the tub, melting. I followed the figure of her body in the water lit by the lantern light.

Sariel opened her eyes as I set the pot down. Her knees were sticking out of the water. She had the same look on her face as when she had given me a haircut. "Will you get my back?"

"Sure," I said. I walked behind her and knelt in the wet grass.

Sariel leaned forward. She glanced over her shoulder at me as she moved her hair.

Women are, in my opinion, another species. If you've ever walked through a room when they're getting ready, and caught sight of one, you likely know what I mean. The way they sit in front of a mirror or a polished piece of metal, doing their hair. Applying their creams. Their perfumes. The softness of them is otherworldly.

I reached forward and took the rag she held up from her chest.

"Hold on," she said and turned suddenly, reaching for the soap. As she did, I saw the profile of her chest from the side. Her breast seemed almost too heavy for her frame, slumping against her body as she rose and turned under its vast weight. The barest edge of her areola slid from the water, pink like a brightberry.

Sariel scrubbed the soap block on the washcloth and handed it to me.

I knelt and slid the rag over the top of her shoulders.

"Mmm," she murmured. "You went to some extreme

lengths to get me naked."

I soaped her and scrubbed down her back. She leaned forward, bringing her knees to her chest again. The outline of her breasts under her cradled arms making my cock hard as I washed her.

"That feels good," Sariel whispered.

I kept scrubbing her, lost in the moment.

"Lean back a bit," I told her.

She turned and raised an eyebrow, but did as I told her. She sunk back into the tub a bit, and I dropped the washcloth over her chest.

"What are you—oh..."

"Just relax," I said, as I massaged the back of her neck. The steam rose from the bath and I pressed my thumbs up and down her neck, then down into her shoulders and went deeper, spreading, kneading the tissues.

"Forget the tavern. We may need to open a bathhouse," she groaned. "It'll outsell the bar."

"Shh," I whispered. I found the strain in her and I eased it forth. When I was halfway down her back, I grabbed her shoulders and gently eased her to lie back.

Sariel's eyes closed as I massaged deeper into her shoulders. Her left arm held the washcloth across the base of her cleavage. A wondrous mountain of elf-flesh flowing over her left arm.

"Might as well enjoy the last of the firewood," she murmured.

"I'll handle it," I promised her. Her body entranced me. It was like touching a deity, a goddess of beauty.

"Mmm," Sariel murmured, letting the moment take over. "What are you doing here? Davik? You should have wandered into town earlier. Are you going to come save me and this tavern?"

"Everything will work out," I replied.

A smile broke across her face. "Tell me more sweet lies."

"Don't worry so much," I said. "Life is good here."

She shuddered in pleasure as I kneaded deeper and deeper, my hands sliding over the front of her. Massaging the top of her chest.

We both knew where this would lead.

Sariel moaned and shifted her legs. In two minutes, I planned on slipping into this tub and finishing what she and I always started.

Then I saw her right hand and arm were in the water, between her legs. Elina's words came to me as I knelt.

I've never known her to keep a man. She denies herself as punishment.

"You deserve to relax," I whispered in her ear. I had never kissed her. Never grazed her cheek. Now my hands were full of the top of her chest and sliding lower and lower.

It turned me on to see her playing with herself in the milky water. I wanted to wrap my hand around her throat and kiss her, replace that hand with mine, but I wanted to extend this moment. This moonlit bath, the sound of crickets and the way the lanterns swung on their branches. She deserved this magic. We both did, before I took her and we fell into one another.

This was a beautiful moment, and life had a short enough supply of those already.

"You deserve to feel good," I murmured into her ear. I kept rubbing her shoulders, and she shifted her legs in the water.

"Dav-"

"Shh..."

Sariel writhed, rolling her hips on her hand under the cloudy water. She sighed, and I slid my left hand along her neck to cup the cheek of her face.

She opened her eyes and looked at me, upside down. I held her face, inches away from kissing her.

Bright eyes stared at me, her perfect full lips pressed into a soft "o".

"Yes," I told her. I moved my right hand down her breast, teasing her with my fingers.

She bit her lip. I held her chin there, making her look at me while she pleasured herself.

"Davik," she breathed my name like a spell.

Her hips rose and rose again. I saw the end of her hand moving furiously. I nodded slowly, giving her my permission, and her face set into the pursuit of what she needed.

I held her mouth, pressing her lips together, and she groaned, her hips rising out of the water, and I held her.

"Ugh, Davik," she moaned my name under the lanterns.

"Shh," I whispered. I slid my other hand into the water, past her flat stomach and down to her smooth arm. My hand found hers, churning the water like a slow oar.

"I'm going to..." Sariel moaned. I slid my hand along her moving fingers, touching her. The lanterns flickered around us. The pond shuddered in a soft breeze, rippling.

"Yes," I told her. "Look at me."

Sariel's eyes opened, her face contorted in pleasure. I slid my hand lower onto hers, to join her between her legs. I wanted nothing more in the world than for her to feel good, to feel safe. From the tavern, the bills, and the denial she heaped on herself.

She stared at me, and when I lowered my head to kiss her, she responded quickly. Kissing me back. She tasted of fruits, and I sank into her, my hand overtaking hers, and I felt her velvet folds. My touch replaced her own, and she responded, grinding against me. I rubbed her, driving her to press against the back of the tub, eyes half-rolling as she kissed and kissed me, tongue on mine.

When she came, she clenched her thighs around my hand, trapping me there.

Our kissing ceased. She was warmth and wetness. And I wanted to envelop myself in her.

When I opened my eyes, she did the same. Then she broke from me, the moment falling like a gift handed to someone that they dropped. She dropped her head, looking away.

"What's wrong?" I asked, seeing the look on her face. Nothing had been overstepped. But the look on her face was of such heavy shame, she was holding back from crying.

"I can't," Sariel said. She stood from the bath.

"Wait," I said.

She ignored me, shaking her head. Not at me, at herself. She wrapped a towel around her. "I'm sorry. I'm sorry," she kept saying. The water shifted as she stood, covering herself and stepping out.

"Sariel, just hold a second."

"I can't do this," Sariel said, a sob in her throat. She reached for her dress. "I'm sorry, I thought I could... but I can't."

I stood up, reaching for her, but she walked away from the tub. Towel firmly around her.

"Will you just talk to me?"

I couldn't believe it. I truly couldn't believe how quickly she had broken away.

"I can't," was all she said as she picked up her shoes and walked off towards her house.

I stood there, calling to her again. Confused. Surprised. And above anything else, disappointed. The golden hair slapped on her back wetly as she jogged away, shaking her head.

So much for what felt right.

CHAPTER
THIRTEEN

I hadn't slept that night, after Sariel and the bathtub. Too much ventured, and too little accepted. When I took everything back to the tavern, I felt like I was rebuilding what she had wanted. Everything was where it needed to be. Not allowed to change. To stray.

The old me would have been banging on Elina's door twenty minutes after that, already half a bottle deep.

Instead, I went into the valley.

I took the broken down cart from the tavern, throwing the double-bladed axe inside. Then I marched down the road, pulling it behind me.

The old woman, Mabel, was likely asleep, and I was in no mood to talk. I pulled the cart past her house and followed the path on her property to the forest.

If you asked some neighbors near those woods, they would tell you some monster was attacking trees before dawn.

I had entered the world of good normal people and maybe I didn't belong. Sariel's avoidance had little to do with me, and everything to do with herself. But I had wanted to be the exception. The key that unlocked whatever was hidden away. I think we all want to be the outlier, the thing that brings them forth. I had no thoughts of leaving. Oakshire was a place I enjoyed. The only place I had probably enjoyed.

My mind went to a place I spent most of my time ignoring. My days in the Summoner War. It's a tragedy that the hardest years of your life weigh so heavily compared to the rest. Wars end. Their memory never does.

I took the axe to the trees. When I shut my eyes, I didn't just hear the voices of a company of men that were all gone. I heard the clink of chain mail, the trudging of boots in mud. A cart creaking on the march.

Wars we wage'em!

Thwack!

Mage's we break'em!

Thwack!

Day's we save'em! Oh!

Thwack!

We had been fools. Those that survived the engraving. We thought it had made us special. Nothing could hurt us. We were strong. We were hearty. Nobody sings that marching song anymore, because nobody is likely alive that knew it.

I swung and swung. I had never been a lumberjack. Never worked timber. Only flesh. But every man knows deep down how to swing an axe into a tree.

Every time I swung, I saw a different man I had killed in the war. A tree turned into a screaming mage, his hands up, face panicking as I bore down on him.

Thwack!

Hold still, this may hurt a bit. And then the falling surgeon's knife on my flesh. I screamed when they pried me open. I felt the dull scrape as they inscribed the runes on the inside of my flesh, pointed outwards. Old outlawed magic. Ancient runes.

Then they sewed me up again, casting the last spell that would, or could, ever heal me again.

Thwack!

There had been a hundred of us. Gathered around a camp posting for the legion. Pissing rain. We had been on march to Kingspear to finish the campaign. We had had the Summoner forces on the run. It would all be over soon.

Thwack!

'*What's it say, Davik?*' Lonny had asked. We had been shield-mates. In the trenches together. You had to dig deep to keep away from the arrows and the damn spells flying everywhere.

'Says Magebreakers - 1st Vanguard,' I had said.

I still remember the words on the marching orders, how the ink had gone all blotchy in the rain.

Thwack!

The Embriel took thousands of prisoners. But they moved us and several companies even further out. We watched the sun disappear as we entered the deep woods. They had knights; they had clerics; they had infantry. But they kept us separate. In the first month, ten men of our thirty starved to death. I held Lonny in a cage of mud. That's all there was. Wire and mud and guards that watched men beg and plead and starve to death. Battle Elves and sorcerers and collegiate soldiers betting on who died next.

Thwack!

Other prisoners got some rations. But many died. They hated us so much. We stopped wondering what the lords who had conscripted so many of us were negotiating.

Thwack!

It had been four months. We pulled the gold teeth from everyone. One man wept when his slid out so easily. A handful of gold teeth traded for a single contraband potato.

Why? It wouldn't stop anything. There had been thousands of other prisoners of war. Many traded back. Most. But the last of us were still here. Even those the Collegiate and the Battle Elves had fed originally, they stopped. In a cage next to ours, we saw a pikeman close to being released, nearly dead.

In one singular act of selflessness, we palmed him the potato through the wire. Twelve skeletons handing the morsel of food they had bought with their teeth. He cried as he ate it. Couldn't look at us for the shame of taking it.

Thwack!

In a wire cage across from us, they pile our dead on the freezing winter ground. Taking their time. Making sure the faces stare at us. A small sign clatters in the winter wind against the posts. A single word, a mockery. The name of that place.

If you want to eat, they tell us. *You can.*

Thwack!

A guard walks by. The season has changed. It's the start of spring. I'm thinner than I've ever been in my life. Than I knew anyone could be. I am alone. The last prisoner. Everything feels slow. I'm fed once a week, maybe. Just to keep me alive. Just so they can watch. A guard taps on my cage. I've tried to escape before, when my body was whole. But one man can't outfight a hundred.

Do you want to go see your friends? A guard sneers.

We both look over to the cage across from mine. The frozen bodies softening now in the rising temperature. Eyes that had stared at me all winter, weeping now as the frost thaws.

Thwack!

I stopped. My body was on fire. The dawn had broken, and I looked up from the battlefield of splintered wood. It was a massacre of tree stumps and branches. Nearly two dozen trees lay fallen. Branches sticking up like rigor mortis in the rising sun.

Sariel's words floated in my mind.

I can't do this...

It was the only thing that chased that damned marching song away. I thought of her in the heat of that tub. The smell of the cheap soap when her body deserved so much more.

Sometimes when your mind is loud, only the exertion of the body can grant you silence.

Men are cheaper than horses. That's what a lord with a bought commission had said once when myself and other Magebreakers were pulling carts on the march.

We engrave them with runes of strength and to withstand. Why not get our money's worth?

Oh, aye. Get your money's worth.

But he was right about one thing: that strength amplified what you had. After the war, I promised myself that I would never be captured again. Not by anything.

If you want to eat... you can.

My runes grew after the war because I fed them. I knew little of what they did to me. I lifted logs, and then stones. I swung axes, then maces. Hammers with heads so heavy blacksmiths moved them on wheeled dollies. I killed men for money. Then groups of them. Any mission or quest, you asked Darkshire. Especially if you wanted a caster gone. Over and over, until I was strong enough to wrap my arms around a shrieking demon lord and break its spine.

I pulled my shirt from my head and tossed it on the cart handle. I trimmed the branches from the fallen trees. Then the bark. The axe dulled, but I continued. Then I split the trunks into sections of three and hurled them on the cart until it was comically overloaded.

A single horse couldn't pull this cart. You would need a team, or oxen. A full bridle and brace.

Or a Magebreaker.

I gripped the handles. The weight was so immense my body wouldn't even tip it down. I exhaled and felt the power in me, built fiber by fiber from every single thing I had ever fought or killed, and pushed down with the inertia of my body. My muscles swelled, rippled, and then locked.

With grim eyes set on the road beyond, I set to it. Creaking the rundown cart, pulling it while it squealed in protest.

When I passed Mabel's house, the old woman was out on the porch, watching me with amazement.

"Guess we didn't need a horse after all," she called out.

"Guess not," I huffed, pulling the cart behind me.

"We'll settle up later," she said, turning back inside to start her day. "Looks like we're in business."

At the main road, I turned the cart around and let it fall again. Two wheels groaning against the weight. I reversed, readying to push it up the long road back to the tavern.

I can't do this...

I heaved against the massive weight and pushed.

THE BACK of the tavern was now half a timber mill. A dozen trees, in varying states, were scattered around the back.

I had no pull-saw, no proper tools, so I set to work with my axe.

Unseasoned wood is wet. It needs two or three seasons outside to dry. But it'll still burn. It'll season faster if you split it down.

Several hours later, the girls came from the house to the tavern. Brim would be inside, holding things down for any guests until the morning shift started.

"Davik killed a forest," Karley shouted behind her.

I looked up. Karley was watching me with a soft smile on her lips, one hand on her hip. Then when she saw me notice her, the smile disappeared, and the bored-girl act started up.

"Oh, wow!" Tyra laughed as she walked up.

"What have you been feeding him, Tyra?" I heard Karley murmur.

I was covered in sweat and sap. My shirt was drying on the cart handles behind me.

"Maybe he's a barbarian," Tyra giggled. "We'll need double the meat order now."

"Probably why the tavern's losing money. Look at him. Looks like he's been eating all the grain out back." Karley's voice held a tint of a dreamlike daze.

I wiped my brow, ignoring them, and split another log. It had taken me an hour to bring the lumber in one cart the miles from Mabel's place.

I threw the split wood into a wheelbarrow and pushed it alongside the tavern wall to replenish our woodpile.

"Hey," Karley said behind me.

I turned around. She held a goblet out to me. I took it and drained the cold water down in three gulps.

"Thanks," I exhaled the words and handed her the cup.

"That's a lot of wood," Karley said. Today she had lipstick that was like crushed violets and swoops of dark eyeliner. Her skirt was tight and long leggings of black and yellow went from her thigh to her ankle.

"I needed to replenish the stocks," I said and walked away from her back to my task. She had been looking for the chance to chat, to say something with her little bored smirk. I left her standing there, holding the empty goblet and watching me.

When I got back to my stump, I looked up at her. "Come here."

Usually, she was the one shouting orders. She fancied herself the captain of the tavern during rush hour. But she came over.

"Grab that next section. Put it on the stump when I split this one."

A drow in the autumn morning light is a lovely sight. I felt full of vigor, of strength. Despite the day's labors, I was brimming with vitality from a disappointing evening. I felt like fighting ten men and plundering a dozen skirts after.

"You've got a lot of scars," Karley said and grabbed the next log to set it down. "You must have been a terrible lumberjack."

I nodded to the stump and had her reposition it. Karley did a little shimmy and bent a too low, trying to tease me with her rising skirt. I rolled my eyes and walked around, then handed her the axe.

"Uhh, no thanks. I'm not in the timber business."

"Go ahead, you can do it."

Karley laughed. It was probably the first time I had heard it in earnest. The lightness of it surprised me.

"Here," I said and stood behind her. "Take it in both hands, one here, one high up. Throw it up high, and at the pinnacle, bring it down. You're guiding it into the fall, get it?"

"I think so," she murmured, tongue in her teeth as she concentrated. I wrapped my arms around her and guided her hands up. She pressed her body into mine like she did whenever I passed her in the bar.

I think she got off on the attention, on the chase. Maybe she got off on teasing all those traveling customers who waited around for her while she escaped home. I had seen many of their faces in the dimming light of the tavern, that slow realization they had been played.

"Now," I told her.

Karley did a little hop and brought the axe low. She was off target. Maybe I had made her nervous. It sank into the log and split it a third of the way.

"Damn," she grunted.

"Not bad," I said.

"Woo! Karley!" Tyra clapped from the shade of the back awning.

"Here, don't take it out, we'll split it by slamming it again. Watch me." I scooted her out of the way and split the log by raising it with the axe head still in it and slamming it home. Then I split the rest four more times.

"Here." I stacked firewood into Karley's arms up to her chin. She buckled a bit.

She looked around. "Woodpile is full. Where should we put this?"

"Follow me." I filled my own armful of firewood and nodded back behind the storage shed. We walked around to the rear and I tossed my bundle down, stacking it along the wall.

"Right there." I pointed.

Karley waddled over and dropped the pile on the ground, where it scattered everywhere.

"Stack it," I said.

She dusted her hands off, the bratty grin on her face. "Nah, we're good right there."

We stared at each other. Then she bent down and hiked her skirt up, the edge of her little bubble butt poking out from the bottom. She waved her hips back and forth, and then she shoved the top of the woodpile down on the ground, scattering it.

"There we go," she smirked and turned around. The surprise was plain on her face when I stared her down.

"Stack it right," I ordered.

A defiant eye regarded me. "Make me."

I spun her in my arms and sat down on the woodpile. As she landed in my lap, she let out a surprised gasp. Then, in a heartbeat, I grabbed her ponytail and bent her over my lap, bringing her ass up high.

"You keep pressing against me in the bar," I growled at her. "I'll drag you down in the cellar and give you exactly what you want."

"I don't know what you're-"

I spanked her over her skirt quickly. Instead of a yelp, she let out a soft groan.

"Yeah." I gripped her pony tail. "You do know."

Karley looked over her shoulder at me with eyes as soft as honey. She bit her lip. "Maybe you should... punish me."

"Yeah?" I asked.

Dark eyes full of need begged me.

I slid her skirt up; her plump little cheeks smooth in my hands, the soft tight cloth of her panties nestled between them. I stared at the soft mounds of flesh. Mine to claim. If I wished. She arched her back, wanting more.

I swatted her once and pushed her up. "Clean this up."

When I stood and she looked at me, aghast that I hadn't pushed her further. But even this little fake tantrum was her trying to control things. Karley blushed as I walked off, leaving her there.

Around the side of the storage shed, I saw Sariel and Vorga standing there, gazing at the pile of wood. My heart hammered for a moment upon seeing the elf again.

"You can cancel the firewood order," I said to her.

"Davik, this is..." The elf looked around at the logs every-where. "What did this cost you?"

"A morning," I said. I wasn't trying to be cold. But between the two of us, it would take a bit of time before things settled back to normal. "The old widow Mabel gave me a timber lease."

"It's too much, Davik. I can pay you when—"

"This is my tavern too," I told her. "I won't see it go cold."

$$\sim$$

VORGA ACCOMPANIED me that afternoon to go see the widow Mabel. We traveled down the road in silence, my mood creating a vacuum as we walked.

"Is something bothering you?" she asked me after a while.

"Not at all," I lied. Then I gave her a fake smile. "Just been a busy morning."

Vorga didn't believe me. But that was fine. Between Sariel in the bathtub and spanking Karley behind the shed, I was glad to get away from the tavern. Karley made a show of ignoring me afterwards, but lingering around wherever I was, trying to get more attention.

"I've never met the widow Mabel," Vorga mused as we walked. I had left the cart at the tavern. There was still more timber to process, but I didn't see more happening today. I couldn't work at night since that would bother the patrons.

"She's a character, that's for sure."

We came to her cottage on the road from town. To our right, the mountains bore the signs of a brief summer and were white-capped in the frost of autumn. It seemed unbelievable to me that somewhere in those lofty peaks was the town of Erast.

And a tavern full of dead men.

"Are you going to visit anyone this summer?" Vorga asked.

"No plans. What about you? Do you have family nearby?"

"Not anymore," Vorga said softly as we walked. Her step-mother, of course. I had forgotten. I left it at that, hearing the hurt in her voice.

We knocked on the cottage door. A curse came from inside as Mabel meandered to open it.

"Back again?" She opened the door, peering at me. "Who's that? Come closer, girl."

Vorga smiled and walked up the steps. She shyly said hello.

"My word girl," Mabel began. I braced for something foolish or grating, but was surprised. "Aren't you a pretty thing? What are you doing with this beast here?"

Vorga giggled. "He's alright."

"Careful," she said and pointed a finger at me. "They lure women by lifting heavy things around them. Next thing you know, you have to piss every ten minutes and your feet are swollen from a babe growing inside you."

I rolled my eyes while Vorga laughed. Mabel scooted to join us on the deck. "Where's the cart? You going to make this girl carry the timber?"

"Just came to pay you," I said, reaching into my pocket. "Would a silver be amenable?"

Mabel waved me off and sat on her rocking chair, motioning for Vorga to take the other one on her porch. "Ten would do it, but not for purchase. I was hoping to see my share of the proceeds. A third is a bit of a rake, but I'm an old woman." She leaned towards Vorga. "And we get to be greedy."

"Just wanted to pay you, Lady Mabel. I don't think I'll have time to do as we discussed that day."

Mabel ignored me, speaking to Vorga. "He felled almost two dozen trees. Frantic out there. I woke and thought there was a thunderstorm. But it was just a sweaty man grunting and muttering to himself."

Vorga looked at me, eyes warm with delight as Mabel continued.

"They get like that, you'll learn. When they come hoping

for a plate and get nothing from you. Are you married, girl? Are there more orcs in Oakshire? I haven't seen any."

"I'm not," Vorga said. "I work at the tavern with Davik."

"Well, good for you. You'll learn. My husband used to get like this one here. Every time the woodpile grew too lean I'd close my legs, and they'd only part when James filled it back up." The old woman cackled, leaning back in her chair. Vorga's sweet laughter joined hers. "I used to get excited, hearing him outside, swinging that axe. I knew it was me he was thinking of splitting like a log. It's good for them, setting them to task."

The two broke into mischievous giggles.

"You're bad, Mabel." Vorga shook her head.

"What's your name?" She asked her.

I walked over and leaned on the porch as they chatted, completely ignored.

"Vorga."

"I heard all sorts of talk about you when you came to Oakshire. These little hayheads will jabber about any such nonsense. Anything out of the norm. I thought they would all have heart attacks when the temple of the Mistress opened. Now look at them. The wives head up there to buy their concoctions to make their husbands little pricks work again."

Vorga laughed. "Do you know the priestess, Elina?"

Mabel waved the notion away. "Of course I do. I showed her how to make some of those herb concoctions. It keeps me in some coppers." The old woman now looked at me pointedly. "But silver is better."

"Were you an herbswoman?" Vorga asked her.

"Of a sort. A long time ago. I was a pretty young thing, like you. I snagged a handsome man. Women used to know all the herbs of the valley. Now they just bat their eyelashes and buy mixtures. I remember that redheaded woman down the road wouldn't listen to me about her headaches. She bought some

Southroot extract from a traveling herbalist. Do you know what that is?"

Both Vorga and I shook our heads.

Mabel leaned forward conspiratorially. "It's a laxative. For livestock. The foolish woman. She drank half the draught! I saw her sprinting down the road to her house."

The air broke into cackles from the two of them. Even I was chuckling. It surprised me to see Mabel's mirth.

"Did they give you a hard time when you came here? Because of your race?"

"Not so much," Vorga said with a shrug. "Sariel sorted a lot of them out. A few farmers tried to stand in my way on the way to work."

"What happened?" Mabel took the words out of my mouth. I was interested too.

"Sariel came bounding out of the house, screaming at them. She took a gardening spade to one of their brows and threatened to bleed him. Then told the others if they bothered me again she'd tell their wives of the propositions they proposed when they visited the taverns."

Mabel laughed. "Oh, I like her. I've never met the elf woman."

"She's wonderful," Vorga agreed. "I had never seen her so angry. She made them apologize to me, and now they tip me whenever I serve them in the tavern. I think they thought she had magical powers, too."

"Leave it to fools to fill a shadow with monsters. That's good. And now? You like it here?"

They talked for a while, and I was glad to listen. About what Oakshire and the valley used to look like. Mabel knew the story of every farm, every family, new and old. She knew about affairs and children who were born out of wedlock. There were tales of poor harvests, of disease, of thieves and crooks. It was like any other town, and Mabel had seen it all.

After an hour and a half, I came back from relieving myself in the woods while Mabel and Vorga shared tea. I cleared my throat.

"Shh," Mabel said to Vorga. "Now a fellow has a declaration."

"As I said," I told Mabel. "I'll pay you for the lumber. But I don't think a firewood business is in the works right now."

Mabel nodded solemnly.

"So if it's alright with you, I'll pay you whatever you ask."

Then the old woman started laughing. I stood there, looking at Vorga as if I was missing something. The most-orc looked lovely sitting on the porch in her dress, a soft glad smile on her face.

"You don't know much about small towns, do you, boy?"

"What do you mean?" I asked.

Mabel shook her head, her gray braid swinging behind her as she leaned forward. "These people talk about everything. They talk about you lifting a wounded man up some tavern stairs like a grand bard's tale. You think they didn't hear the swing of the axe? See a man carrying lumber from my lands? They all came asking."

I stared at her. "And you told them..."

She laughed under her breath. "Well, I told them the truth. I said, if you want cheap firewood, go see the busboy at the tavern. He's got a lease on my timber."

My first customer came the following day. I was outside on my day off, splitting and trimming wood.

I'm not sure if I had an end-goal in mind. I just knew I

needed to keep moving. Sariel and I largely kept our distance from each other the day before. I wasn't the spurned would-be lover, pining after the beautiful girl. She hadn't rejected me; she had denied herself. Some rule, some punishment she doled out for herself, had blocked the link between us. I could understand that.

But I didn't have to like it.

When I wasn't working in the tavern, I was splitting wood. The piles had grown to where I would need to get Aron the blacksmith to hammer together some new cord holders.

But while I was out there between shifts or on my day off, Vorga sat on the stump, the wind blowing through her hair, and she would read the book I bought from her to me.

"Then El'ra, known as Ingeth to her lover, fell from the tower, so rapt was her outrage at her lovers death." Vorga's words were hypnotic while I worked. I sometimes didn't even see the stump or feel the axe in my hands.

"Poor El'ra." I buried the axe into the stump. "Is that the end?"

"It is." Vorga shut the book. "Should I start at the beginning again?"

I looked over at her. I loved her being near. I liked her sitting there, reading, just being Vorga.

"You know what I think?" I said.

"What's that?"

"I think we need a new book."

Vorga laughed. "You're greedy, Davik. Books are lovers, to be explored over and over. If we go your way, we'd have a library instead of a tavern."

"What's wrong with that? Maybe I want a library."

"It's too expensive," Vorga protested. "Don't be so impatient."

She wasn't wrong. Books for pleasure were a luxury item. I

had heard tales of some contraptions certain cities had, where a machine would stamp the words on the page over and over, making dozens, maybe hundreds of books. I told her so.

"A machine-book? Now you've truly gone mad." Vorga leaned back on the stump, arched her back, feeling the feel of the morning sun.

"It's true! Have you ever been to a library?"

Vorga's grew a little embarrassed. "No, I haven't. I don't think that they would—"

"You know," I continued. Later on, I really wished I would have listened to what she meant to say. "Trinth is said to have a library. You can even take the books home with you. Not sure if that applies to visitors. You don't have to be a mage or a wizard. I've been meaning to go there soon for supplies for a new project. Why don't you come with me? We'll take Elina. She studied there."

Vorga looked over at me, weighing if it was a good idea or not.

"What do you say?" I asked.

"When would we go?"

"In a few days?"

"Why are you heading there?" she asked.

I grinned. "I've got an idea for a new project."

Vorga shook her head and laughed, getting up to go inside. "You're trying to stay so busy lately, Davik. You need to relax!"

It was true. Now that the wood was taken care of, my mind had been putting together a hot water project that would dispel needing to boil it. Mabel's words came back to me, about her husband setting to task when he was frustrated.

Maybe we all are the same.

"Davik!" a voice shouted to me from the gate. I looked over at Elina, standing there with the blacksmith Aron. He was a surly elf, and a downright miserable spirit.

I started to jog over to the gate.

"Wait!" I stopped and turned to Vorga who was heading inside. "So you'll come?"

Vorga turned around, holding the book to her chest, her little gown spinning as she did.

"I'll come!" she shouted.

I grinned, then ran to the Elina. "What can I do for you?"

The halfling smiled and cocked her head to the side. "Aron here wants to buy some of your wood."

I raised an eyebrow. "I don't really have much to spare as he might need."

"Davik," Elina laughed. "Look around."

I turned. It was one of those times where you're too close to something, you finally take a step back. The entire back area was littered in woodpiles. Split wood cord by cord, and then smaller piles when there were no storage buildings or walls to stack them near.

"I guess I have some to spare." I looked at Aron, the scowling blacksmith. "What are you offering for a cord?"

"Three silvers," he said.

I laughed. "Crescent and Hearthwood are charging sixteen for a cord. And they have a waiting list. Nobody is cutting wood because they don't have time for harvest. I'm not asking for sixteen, but I'm not taking three, Aron. What did it cost you two years back?"

The elf glowered at me, but he nodded. "Six and two."

Six silver and two coppers sounded right. It took most men a day to break a half cord. I did two and a half a day. Ten coppers to a silver, twenty silver to a gold...

I was calculating how much the heating system was going to cost in Trinth. My plan was to buy several parts separately instead of the entire thing. My estimates were always coming to over twenty gold pieces. I had much less than that.

But you have a little red treasure up in those hills don't you?

The arms and armor from the bandits. I could sell those in Trinth too...

"How many cords? These aren't seasoned, you know." I asked.

Aron held up four fingers.

"I'll do five silvers a cord if you take four."

"Deal." He nodded.

"Alright, pull your wagon up and load it." I gestured to the piles. "The ones in the rear are the most seasoned, but not by much. You'll need to watch out for buildup. It won't be clean burning, but none of that stuff anyone is delivering is seasoned, anyway."

Aron looked taken aback. "The *human* will deliver."

I leaned forward. "The *elf* will load it himself. If he wants my help, it's another silver."

The blacksmith glanced at Elina. It wasn't easy for him to negotiate with a woman here. He was likely trying to save face.

"One silver, delivery."

"One silver, to load and deliver. You unload. Deal?"

Aron stared for a moment, then he nodded. I put my hand out, and he took it.

It took another three and a half hours, but I walked from the blacksmith with one full gold coin and a single silver richer. Aron would likely be the largest buyer of firewood for his forges. I pulled my cart down the main street and by the time I got there, Elina was standing with a bashful-looking farmer a bit on the heavy side.

"Another?" I asked her. She nodded with a grin.

"Sir." he rubbed his hands together. "I came to town for a new axe head. But I saw your woodpiles... what are your prices?"

I laughed when Elina gave me a knowing smile. "You

working on commission now?"

"Just helping out, Davik. We can't let such resources be cooped up, lest they rot, don't they? They have to flow."

"Mmmhmm," I murmured, knowing her meaning.

"This is Rober. He owns a farm on the south side of the valley."

"You got a cart?" I asked the farmer. "I can't spare half a day dragging this load to your farm."

"I do! I do, sir. But first... how much is it? For a half cord?"

I took a gander at Rober's boots, threadbare, and the belt that hung too long around his belly, a new hole being punched in. A man who had been skipping meals for his own family.

"How's your harvest?" I asked him.

"It's been, better. But if we make a good sale at the festival..." the man shook his head. I knew that look. When your luck was running out and choices were getting slimmer and slimmer.

Two stout carthorses were attached to a long wagon behind him. A good wagon for transporting... even traveling.

Two more Oakshire residents were walking up, looking around the back of the tavern at all the firewood.

"Is it for sale, sir?" One asked.

"How much is he charging?" The other inquired.

"Give him a moment." Elina smiled and turned to the two men. "This man was here first."

"So... how much?" Rober leaned in.

"The blacksmith just gave me fiver silvers for a cord. I'll do the same bulk pricing for you, even if you take half a cord. Two and a half silvers."

A look of disappointment crossed his face. "It's a mighty fair price. But I..."

"How about a barter?" I asked.

Rober's eyes lit up. "Sure, sure! I have barley. It's not

processed yet but—"

I shook my head. "I don't need barley, unfortunately. Sariel has plenty. I tell you what, Rober. I'm foreseeing more inquiries. I charge folks a silver to deliver. How about you stick around today, and you do the delivering with that wagon of yours?"

"For a half-cord?" He asked slowly.

I patted him on the shoulder. "For a full-cord. And you keep the delivery silver. Just make sure it all gets done proper."

"That's a deal! That's a deal, young man!" Rober shook my hand furiously. "I can spare the harvest for that sum. I tell you what! I'll have the wife make you pies for you and the girls here. Several pies!"

I chuckled and shook my head. Elina was glowing, as if I had just converted from the most heinous religion to one of peace and prosperity.

"One catch, Rober."

"What's that lad?"

"I'll need to borrow the wagon next week. The cleric here is coming with me to Trinth."

"I am?" Elina gasped.

Rober grinned. His eyes slid over the cords and mountains of wood in the back gate. He looked to make a hefty sum on this. Enough to come out of the year ahead.

"Lad, you chop more wood. I'll chase the carrot myself."

"Where's the boss?" I asked Karley inside the tavern. It was nearly time for the shifts to start.

The drow ignored me, moving bottles for imaginary customers.

I walked towards the office. I didn't knock, I just walked in where Sariel sat at her desk penning a request for a vendor.

"The meat delivery is going to be an issue," she said without looking up. Then she looked up. "Oh, sorry. Davik, what can I do for you?"

We need to talk. Why did you run away the other night?

The weak babble swirled in my head. If I ever felt like hanging up my balls, I'd speak the spell to words like that and watch them vanish.

"I've got a project I'd like to work on. For the tavern. I won't be here Monday or Tuesday after the weekend."

Before, I likely would have asked her if this was alright. I didn't resent her. I felt a bit sad for her. Sariel was a grown woman, she made her own decisions. If nothing would come between us, that was fine. We wouldn't be enemies, but I knew the value I had brought with refilling the firewood that would get us not just through autumn, but all the way to spring.

"Okay, that won't be a problem. Thanks for telling me."

"Vorga wants to come too, to Trinth."

"To the city? Just the two of you..."

"Elina as well, since she studied there. I figured she could show us around. Visit her temple."

"It's going to be hard without Vorga. The evenings are getting busy..." Sariel stared at me. The slight flush of jealousy on her face. Or worry. Or maybe something else... something I was wrong about. She was plainly stopping herself from being too emotional, making a decision just to mess with me. "She deserves some time away. Go ahead. I hope she has a great time."

I took a step towards her at the desk. Whatever sensual tension between us was stifled. She had smothered it, not wanting to let it be lit again.

"There's room on the wagon for more," I told her.

She considered it. "It would be nice, but I don't think so.

What's this project you're working on?"

"It's going to help out here quite a bit. I think you'll like it."

"Well, let me know what it costs. I've been keeping track of how much of your firewood were using to pay you back."

That caught me off guard. I felt a bit of wind vanish from what remained in my sails.

"You, what?"

"It's only fair," she said with a shrug. "I won't have you working for free. If we keep being smart, coming up with some new ideas until festival, we should have enough to fully reimburse you."

"Keep your coin," I bit the words off at her. "I didn't do it for money."

"Why did you, then?"

We stared at each other for a moment. Two people bent on proving something. I thought of all the things I could say. Endearing words. Spiteful words.

What feels right.

"To help you."

Sariel wore a bemused look at that. "You already help me, Davik. That's why I pay you. Why would this be any different?"

And with that, she trampled over the unspoken thing between us.

"I suppose it wouldn't."

"Elina helps you, doesn't she?" Sariel said suddenly.

I raised an eyebrow at that. "Does that bother you? Me and her?"

"Why would it?" Sariel asked, but I saw her holding herself back. "You can fuck whomever you wish."

"Hmm," I said. "Glad, I have your permission."

"She's a beautiful woman. I was hoping you two would link up. That's why I introduced you. Just when you're on the road, be careful around Vorga. She's not as experienced."

Jealousy? From Sariel? I didn't believe it. I hadn't been with Elina in weeks, due to Sariel. My feelings for her. If I wanted, I could use that as a little barb against her.

"She says the same of you," I spoke the truth. "That you're beautiful. And that she hoped you and I would link up."

Sariel looked away, reaching for her quill again. "Followers of the Mistress have an interesting view of the world. Monday and Tuesday, is there anything else?"

I ignored her question. "Things don't need to be awkward between you and me. I don't resent you, Sariel."

"That's nice to hear." She made a show of waiting to place her quill against some parchment. Then she nodded. "Sorry."

"It's alright." I was glad a bit of the heat left our words. "And... for what it's worth with Elina..."

Sariel raised her hand to stop me. Her face wasn't jealous. For a second, I saw the urge of... temptation? No, I decided I was mistaken. "I meant it, Davik. That I sent you there, hoping you'd join with her. She's been unlucky in finding someone to bind to. I'm happy for you. Really."

"Did she say what kind of facet your jewel was?" I asked, trying to further lighten the mood.

Sariel blushed, actually blushed and looked away.

"Oh, really?" I ventured.

She laughed. "You'd need a keg of honeyed mead to get that information out of me. Just get back to work, okay? Enjoy your time away."

As I reached for the door handle, a grin broke across my face.

"There is one other person who may need the days off..."

"ALL I'M SAYING IS that we don't have to destroy each other."

189

My words landed on deaf ears. My strongest enemy, the one who hated me more than anything, gripped the steel in his hand.

"Listen." I sat on a box of vegetables next to the sink. Brim was standing on his stool, glaring at me. "You like it here, yeah? I do too. There's room enough for both of us."

"Mmm," Brim intoned his disagreement.

"I need your help. We have to save this place. You have to come with me to Trinth. I need you to negotiate with some vendors of your kind. "

Brim blinked.

"Okay, imagine this," I said. "You hate Davik, the ugly-man yes?"

"Ugly-man," Brim echoed, eyes flaring.

"Yes. He comes in to the kitchen all the time. He disturbs you. Tyra talks to him. Imagine, you need water, you turn a spout and it comes out. Now imagine, its **hot** water. No more 'Tyra, can I boil water for the guests'. Less ugly-man."

Brim nodded. This was making sense to him. "Ugly-man leave kitchen."

"That's what I'm saying!" I clapped my hands. "But I don't speak your language. You barely speak mine. You come with me. We grab the new system. No more ugly-man in the kitchen all the time."

The little gnome stared at me, then he stroked his chin. "Monday?"

"Yeah."

"Ugly-man leave forever. On Monday."

"No," I shook my head. "Ugly-man in kitchen less. Less ugly-man. It's good, right?"

He pushed his hat up, his white beard furrowed while he chewed on it.

"It's good."

CHAPTER
FOURTEEN

That Friday, I visited Elina at the temple. I waited while she finished speaking with a middle-aged woman, a face I'd seen in the valley and never met.

Elina motioned to me from the far side of the temple. "Just a second, Davik."

I waited, and once they finished, the woman walked out without meeting my eyes.

"What can I do for you?" She asked, smiling.

"I was wondering." I took her in my arms. "Could you use any extra power this weekend before your house calls?"

Elina kissed me deeply. Her hands around my neck as if we were slow dancing. It had been a while between us. She ground against me. Then she looked into my eyes.

"What's the matter?" she asked.

"Nothing." I leaned forward to kiss her again. "Just missed you."

"I've missed you too, but... now isn't the right time for me. My monthly is in full swing. There's a ritual I perform. It's a whole thing."

"I don't mind," I said and pulled her closer.

The beautiful halfling laughed. "But I do!" Then she peered at me again. "Davik, what ails you? I can feel it coming from you. Is it... Sariel?"

"I don't think she's ready," I said. "Maybe she never will be. That's her bag to carry."

Elina nodded, then she gestured to the bench. "Do you want to sit? To talk?"

"Tavern is picking up," I told her. "Just wanted to see you. Why don't you come for a drink? I'll walk you."

"Let me lock up around here, then I'll meet you there. You sure there's nothing you want to talk about?"

"Just make sure your bags are packed for Monday. We're leaving bright and early."

Elina smiled. There was something she wanted to say, but left it alone.

"I heard you spanked someone."

I grinned at that. "Guilty. But it was consensual. And long overdue."

"I heard that too..." Elina laughed. "Biggest complaint was that it was short-lived."

"Careful," I warned her. "You break confidentiality, I'll have to spank you too."

"See you, Davik." Elina watched me go, more worried than she needed to be.

I walked back through Oakshire to the tavern. The days were getting shorter, the nights longer. You had to take advantage of a good morning.

Rober was standing near the back gate of the tavern. He had transformed from the forlorn farmer wringing his hands for a discount to a hustling businessman as sharp as any would find in a city.

Already, a third of the firewood had been sold. I had

brought four more hauls from Mabel's plot, and left her share of the profits on her deck early in the morning before the sun came up. If you walked the streets of Oakshire, you could hear Rober's voice from his twin team of horses, declaring the best deals in Oakshire on firewood.

I went out back and saw his two children running around, making a game of filling the wheelbarrow while the day's customers were already piling up. The air was getting colder; the wind was getting sharper, and people weren't heating their homes as much because of the rising cost of firewood.

That was the yeoman's way. Time was his currency, and the stretch and sweat of his back. I had no children, no wife. I had no home to keep. Just a barn to sleep in and a job around pretty women.

"Good morning, Davik!" Rober shouted from the gate. The yard was already looking cleaner, the woodpiles shrinking as more customers lined up with their own wheelbarrows. "A moment folks! A moment. I must speak with the master lumberman."

Rober swaggered up, a face full of grins. "Quite the haul, yesterday. And more to boast today, Davik. I brought the family to help out. I hope you don't mind."

"No, it's..." I jumped as his son ran across my foot and ran away squealing. "You have a fine family."

"That, I do." He smiled with genuine warmth, watching his herd run around. "Glad I put the hammer to the anvil when I did. You get older, my boy. The hammer doesn't raise the same anymore. Or at all."

"They've got herbs for that," I offered.

Rober chuckled. "Some things are as they should be. In some ways, it's a blessing."

I couldn't imagine it being anything close to a blessing.

"Here's the take." He pulled out a small pouch of rabbit fur and emptied it into my hands.

Six gold coins fell into my grasp. To say I was surprised would not be doing it justice.

"How much did you sell?"

"Twenty cords, in all. Made eight silvers myself, just so you know. You're doing a good thing here."

Six gold would go a long way. A very long way to what I wanted to do at the tavern. I put them in my pocket.

"What are we charging for a wheelbarrow?"

"Eight coppers," he said.

I walked toward the growing line of customers and peeked my head around the corner. It was lining up.

"Make it four coppers for any denizens of Oakshire. One per day, per customer."

Rober laughed now. "Lad, don't throw money away. These are more than fair prices. These folks are glad to pay."

As I thought about it, we charged four coppers for a mug of ale. Six for beer. Sariel wouldn't take my money, even if I gave it to her and demanded she did. But paying customers...

"On second thought, half-off a wheelbarrow when you buy a drink inside."

A few customers in line exclaimed at the idea. It seemed popular.

"How will we, uh.." Rober pulled his collar and looked around. "Track such transactions?"

I thought of a certain little gnome who could do with some more washing deliveries.

"I'll leave a tub. Have customers bring their mug outside when they're done. Just let me know when it fills. Or have one of the kids bring it to Brim inside."

"The little fellow?"

"Yeah." I smiled. "That's him."

Later, inside the tavern, I saw Sariel speaking to Rober's wife. She was a middle-aged woman, with hard years on her face. She held a bundle of pies in a linen cloth.

"Are you Davik?" she asked over Sariel's shoulder.

"I am."

"We made these for you. We can't thank you enough for giving Rober this job."

"Well, it's not exactly a job..." I started to say.

"Pies!" Tyra exclaimed from the kitchen. The faen girl was on us instantly, taking them out of the wife's hands.

"Oh, these smell lovely, so lovely. Is this boysenberry?"

"It is." Rober's wife nodded and looked around the tavern uncertainly.

"Wonderful!" Tyra threw her arms around her. The woman looked taken aback and glanced at me with a smile as the warmth of the faen girl enveloped her.

"This is our cook, Tyra. She's faen, in case you didn't notice."

"I figured. I felt it when you hugged me. I'm Linna. Pleased to meet you." The wife patted her on the back. "I've never been here before."

"Are those pies?" Karley called from the counter.

"Yes!" Tyra did a little dance and took them. "Please, come in. Do you like wine?"

"Ale, is fine..." Lia looked around the room as Tyra dragged her within. "Don't put yourself out."

"Nonsense!" Tyra giggled and pulled her to the bar. "Have you ever been to a place where they waited on you before?"

"I haven't," she said.

Tyra dragged her away, leaving Sariel and I standing there.

She glanced at me. "You should invite Rober in as well. I'm sure he'd like a drink."

"Hard to separate that man from the coin he could make."

Sariel nodded. We both looked around the tavern.

"Tell him he should stick around. Have dinner here with his family tonight. On the house."

"I'll do that. Get ready. I'm offering half off a wheelbarrow of firewood for anyone who buys a drink here."

"That's... generous of you." Sariel seemed to be reaching for words. Instead of filling the quiet between us, she made her way to her office.

Then she turned back to me. "I'm glad you're here, Davik."

I smiled at her. "Me too."

JUST ONE.

It's a fable as old as time. Men letting their wives know they are stopping for a single drink. The magic number that coworkers convince you to share after a hard shift. Just one.

One tankard turns into two easily. It wets the whistle; it gets the foot tapping after a long day, after a good outing of getting firewood on the cheap.

The new offering spread fast in town. Faster than I'd thought it would. It filled the tavern to the brim. It was the best way to put money in the girl's pockets without giving it to them directly. At the end of the day, Rober pulled me to the side while I worked inside the tavern.

"There's the take, my boy."

Eight gold and fifteen coppers were in my hand. I raised an eyebrow. "You been overcharging?"

"The opposite, my friend. Your drink-barrow deal is netting us only sixteen and a half silvers a cord when we used to make twice that. But we've got a ton of business. They're buying halves and fulls. I've got orders for cords to come. You have a waiting list, so I suggest you get a new axe and some help. We'll take my wagon down to replenish."

"You can't be serious," I said.

Rober laughed. "Come with me."

He pulled me outside and showed me the yard. Almost all the firewood was gone.

"Saved those dozen cords you asked for, lad. Had my kids cover them up."

"How did you do?" I asked.

Rober grinned and pulled out his own gold piece.

I clapped him on the shoulder. After a moment, Sariel came out back to where we were standing. Her eyes opened wide. "Oh my, look at that! All your wood is gone!"

"Oh, I wouldn't say gone." Rober laughed. "Come, both of you. Something you should see."

He walked us around the side of the tavern, out near where the bathtub was and near the open gate. There were almost two dozen patrons outside, drinking from tankards and laughing. As the sun went down, several had pulled logs from their wheelbarrow and started a fire in the foot brazier.

"Hope you don't mind. I told them they could start one." Rober motioned to the brazier.

"Aren't they cold out here?" Sariel asked.

"For a tavern owner, my lady, you should drink more. Nothing warms like a good bottle." Rober laughed again.

It seemed almost like a ritual. Wheelbarrows were parked around the sitting men and women. Each would reach for their own supply and throw a piece of kindling into the fire, which brought the clanking of mugs. The call for refills.

People were sitting on barrels and makeshift benches and downed logs. Two women were singing while a man beat an empty cask as a drum.

In between all of them was Vorga, carrying a tray of drinks and handing them out.

"I'm not a tavern man, I'm a farmer," Robert said. "But if I owned this place, I'd think about expanding the outside. A nice outdoor seating area."

"Expansion?" Sariel asked.

"Exactly," Rober said. "You couldn't use that unseasoned wood Davik has been hauling in. But you're making enough money right now, why not? The tavern is set to grow. Folk like to sit under the sky and stars."

"What would it cost?" I asked.

Rober shook his head. "I don't rightly know. I'm no carpenter, Davik. Not a craftsman. But imagine. An outdoor area, a few firepits. People would walk up off the streets. You'd make back whatever you spent in a single summer."

"An outdoor seating area?" Sariel asked, her voice faraway.

"How far does your lot go?" Rober turned and asked.

I didn't know the answer to that myself. We both looked at Sariel. The beautiful Embriel elf blushed like a sheepish girl.

"To the oak over there..." she pointed.

We both turned. The oak she was pointing at was almost two hundred feet away.

"That oak? *That* oak? Oh, mistress Sariel, you've got a bit of land here. Why not expand?"

"Business hasn't been that good," I said, hoping to help her save a bit of face.

"Looks pretty good to me." Rober nodded to Vorga, collecting payment and taking empty tankards inside. "You do it right. You'd have a girl out here all the time serving. Grabbing orders through the window. Expand the bar as a pass-through."

"Could you do it?" I asked him.

Rober chuckled. "I wouldn't curse anyone with me as a woodworker."

"But you'd know a good one from a bad one, right? If I made you a general overseer, reporting to me?"

Rober considered it for a moment. "Aye, that might work. But you wouldn't be getting your copper's worth, Davik, like I said."

"I won't have time," I said. "I've got work to do here."

"Alright, maybe." Rober nodded. He took on the same excitement as when I first gave him the delivery job. "Let's talk about it when you get back from Trinth with my wagon. In one piece."

Sariel smiled softly, but she seemed sad.

"Head inside, Rober. Go have dinner with your family." I clapped him on the shoulder.

"What's that? Oh, aye. Absolutely." The older man walked off.

I turned to Sariel. "What do you think?"

"It's a nice thought. But I can't afford to put the coin to it, Davik. Even after the festival. Bills and all..."

"What would you say to a partnership?" I asked.

Sariel raised her eyebrow. In the falling light of the day, I felt more attracted to her than I had ever been. Maybe the cold war between us had settled into a pact of non-aggression. A breakup of not what had been, but never was. That strange dance of hope and the future and building something, turning to something else.

"I'm not sure," she whispered.

I took a step forward. "Or an investor. You let me operate the timber out here for no cost already. Let me help out."

"You might need a new shirt before you begin this new enterprise." Sariel laughed.

She reached out, touching my shoulder and the solid

muscle underneath. I stared into her eyes and all that lust I had been ignoring came boiling off of me. I wanted her.

"Why are you afraid of me?" I asked her.

She took her hand back, surprised by the question.

"I'm not, Davik. It's just... when the..."

I knew the look on her face. I had worn it myself.

"The war's over, Sariel. Maybe what you did in it can be over too. Just let it go."

Her face softened, and I could see she was still holding on.

"You don't understand," Sariel said.

"I forgive you," I blurted out.

She looked shocked. "What?"

"I forgive you. Whatever it was, whatever things that happened. I was your enemy, once. Maybe we didn't know each other. But I took plenty of bad from you and yours, and I forgive you."

Sariel didn't respond. It was up to her to hear me or not. To believe it.

I left her there, watching the people drinking where we could build something. Expand. Lay new ground. Maybe we could never change the bones of the tavern, but we could add something beautiful onto it. It was up to her, whether it was the start or the end.

THAT NIGHT, the tavern was a merry place. The crowd grew outside. The drinks for the buyers of firewood flowed and gave birth to two more, three more.

The people of Oakshire got good and proper drunk. It was a warmer autumn evening, and we all knew it would be one of the last. Even Karley was in fine spirits, speaking to me again, batting her lashes.

Linna and Rober and their family had a grand time sitting

at a table, being waited on. He made a big show of ordering a bottle of brandy for his wife, who blushed as she was served.

Sariel was softening, enjoying the mirth of the day. Coins were floating in, and Tyra and Brim were working hard in the back. Halfway through the night, we had sold out every room, and the band played louder.

It was a night for locals and travelers together to swap stories, to trade, to argue, and to become best friends.

Vorga and Jessa were outside, taking orders for people out in the makeshift seating area. I was changing kegs quicker than I ever had to before. The beer was flowing.

I'm told it was a traveling band of entertainers. Not minstrels exactly, but carnival-folk. Coin-pluckers, my father would have called them. The kind that drew a large crowd and then set the pickpockets on them while their backs were turned.

I was downstairs in the cellar, changing the last of our kegs, when Karley came trampling down.

"Davik!" Karley yelled.

"Hold your horses," I yelled out to her from where I was hunched over.

"Davik! Come quick! Outside!" Her voice was full of fear. Raw fear. This wasn't the pouty brat that usually tended bar. I spun around and sprinted up the stairs after her.

"What is it?" I demanded.

"Out back, Vorga! Sariel went to help."

I left her standing at the bar and went to the front door. I pushed my way out of the onlooking patrons. The other half inside were too drunk to know something was going on.

"Out of the way!" I grunted and pushed past.

I spilled into the street and saw more Oakshire residents outside. Everyone was looking, leaning over. The telltale posture of a crowd watching something bad about to happen.

I heard Sariel yelling. I ran towards the back.

Rober was on the ground, sitting with a face full of blood from a busted lip and a knock on the side of his head. His wife tended to him, and she looked up at me with wide eyes when I rushed past.

"Tried to stop them, lad. They took my coin..." he groaned.

I ran past him, moving people out of the way. In the street was a procession of three traveling wagons. Bright colors to catch the eye.

When I rounded the corner, my heart skipped a beat.

Sariel was shouting and three men I didn't recognize were holding her back. Several outsiders were carrying armfuls of firewood to the wagons.

"Leave her be!" Sariel screamed. Her voice was frantic and shook me to my core.

I looked up.

Jessa was cowering in a corner with the other people who had been drinking out back. A preening man in leathers sneered at them, drinking someone else's ale.

Vorga was standing in front of the gate, swinging a piece of firewood wildly at the troupers laughing and dodging her, running past with bundles of kindling.

A minotaur pulled a cart of wood beyond her. My cart. He had a large nose ring and a nasty grin. His only clothing was a set of trousers stretched tight under his thick legs. Dark brown fur covered a wall of muscle.

"Vorga, no!" Sariel shrieked.

I knew instantly what had happened. Rober had tried to stop them, and they beat him and took his money. Then Vorga stepped in before Sariel came.

"Hurry up, Bull!" A man with his back to me, in a wildly colorful getup, laughed. "I promised these folks we wouldn't be long!"

The minotaur set the cart down and stepped towards Vorga. He was chuckling. The sound like a deep drum in his chest. He licked his lips and cracked his knuckles, eyes fixed on the most-orc girl.

The world is full of awfulness. I know this for certain, because I was some of it. Maybe I still am. But at that time, I was living in a wonderful dream. A tavern of soft things, of kind folks and pretty girls with their smiles.

This was ugliness coming to visit. This was wrongness and it was too much of it.

I knew a pirate once who told me the greatest feeling in the world was going towards where you needed to go. Whether that was coin falling into your hand, or your ship taking you closer. And no worse feeling than finding what you wanted in pieces when you arrived.

The world is ruled by power. The power to maim, the power to take. The power to stop. The miserable reason behind what people inflict upon each other is that they simply can, so they do. They burn farms. They ruin families.

They steal my fucking firewood and manhandle my friends.

"Davik, no!" Sariel pleaded when she saw me.

I wasn't listening to her. If she had hung her sword up long ago to be a better person, good for her. I grabbed a piece of firewood off the ground and when she said my name, the man in the multi-colors turned.

The timber in my hand came crashing down. His scalp split under the blow, the wood splintering on his face. He crumpled to the ground. He'd live.

I stalked forwards.

"Hey!" one of the troupers walking past with a bundle of firewood yelled. I yanked another piece out of his hands and bent low, cracking his kneecap into kindling. The bundle fell on top of him as he shrieked.

I tossed it away. I reached out and grabbed one of the men holding Sariel back and gripped his throat. I lifted him in the air in one hand, that old power and strength roaring to life inside me.

Here I am again.

I threw him so hard against the gate he bounced off of it, splitting a board before falling to the earth in a limp heap.

"Asshole," I grunted and walked forward, eyes locked on the minotaur in front of Vorga.

The other troupers, and there were several I didn't touch, stood perfectly still, arms full of firewood. Like I was some creature that hunted by movement.

"Don't move," I said slowly as I walked past them.

They nodded. Fear flooded their eyes.

"Hmm," the minotaur's voice was so deep you could feel it vibrate your chest. His eyes floated over Vorga to me. "One with a spine."

"Move, Vorga," I said softly, coming up behind her.

She turned, about to argue that she should stay to help. But when she saw the look on my face, she backed off.

"Put that back," I demanded.

The minotaur straightened up, curling his fists. I felt my vision tunneling, focusing on his snout. His face was as large as my torso. His hands could have wielded a small tree instead of a sword.

A wicked grin spread across my face.

The crowd melted to the sides.

"Make me," he rumbled in a voice of gravel. The horned beast snorted, shuddering, his bloodlust boiling.

Someone was yelling my name. For me to leave, to run

away. But all I saw was the creature in front of me. The way he had walked towards Vorga had purchased his doom.

His feet were cloven, his body was muscle and shag fur. Twin horns on either side of his skull jetted out in sharp spikes nearly a foot long. The beast they called Bull looked down on me, a full two feet taller.

He pounced.

The crowd gasped, expecting my demise.

We locked together.

His claws had shot forward to grab my shoulders, he had fistfuls of my shirt, but I had locked around his arms and held them there.

We were growling, every muscle in my body was locking up, seizing. I felt the rage and hate come boiling through. He roared and pushed forward, but I didn't budge. My entire back was straining with the force of holding him up. He wanted to crush me into the ground.

"Die human," he grunted. His eyes were flaring, bloodshot, staring into mine.

I grinned through my gritted teeth.

Then I hit him.

His snout went skyward, both from the force and the surprise. I had shifted weight, pulling him down as I drove my fist up in an uppercut. I remembered Trolf so long ago. Had I been as strong as I am now, I would've taken his head clean off his shoulders.

Yells of disbelief came from around the crowd. He roared and swiped at me, one long claw going for my chest.

I leapt back, then forward, and hurled my right fist into his belly with a strong pivot as hard as I could. I delivered three more strikes to his stomach before ducking and rotating out of his reach. He was trying to grab me in a bear hug.

I sank backwards on my heels, fists up, motioning to him. It felt marvelous to hit something as hard as I wanted.

He roared and charged me. He tried to grab me again, and I stuck him with a leaping jab right in the snout, driving that stupid nose-ring where it belonged.

He didn't like that. I was soaring through the air in a heartbeat, shove-tossed towards the storage shed. I ducked and landed, rolling on the ground and back into a fighting position as skin slid off my knees onto the ground.

"Come here," I sneered. He roared at me, but I was already charging him.

I tackled him. That brought shouts of disbelief. We rolled on the ground. Each of was snarling and cursing as we were grappling, rolling, squeezing, and pulling. I slid out from under him and got his back, wrapping my arm around his neck to steady myself while I punched the side of his skull and over and over. I was going to drill a hole straight through to his brain.

Huge claws reached up and grabbed me, tearing my shirt away and then gripping me, cutting into me with his claws. I grunted and snarled, holding tight. He rose.

Now I was strangling him. His neck was so large, it took my entire arm to encircle it, but I had him. He gasped for air, claws raking my arms. I heaved back, my fortitude overpowering his.

He screamed as I dug in. The minotaur thrashed. I was digging my boots into his back, trying to pull his fucking head off.

The beast jumped up in the air and brought himself back on top of me. I felt an explosion as we hit the dirt. A thousand pounds of fur and muscle battering into me. The wind left my lungs. I had him, I was going to strangle him to death right here—

A blow came to my back shoulder. I was so surprised, so

locked in, I nearly broke my grip as the firewood in his hand sunk into my back. One of the troupers was screaming in pain.

He had missed my skull, and I turned to see why.

"Get it off me! Get it off me!" The trouper was screaming.

"Rahh!" Brim growled. His feet were in the air, swinging around as he hung onto the meat fork in his enemy's ass.

The trouper stumbled towards me in a blind panic, and I was so wrathful he had came between me and my prey I let go of my grip and backhanded him. One powerful hand snapping his head to the side and he spun to the ground.

Brim growled, pulling his meat fork out of the unconscious man. Before I could say anything the beast broke out of my grip and twisted while I was still on the ground.

He head-butted me. It reminded me of the battering ram at Rochdale, before the same lords who had hired me had betrayed their own city. My skull was the doors of the gate. I saw the blink of stars.

The beast roared again, arching up, driving his horned head towards mine, trying to break my brain and skull in one movement. The crowd shrieked in terror. A murder imminent.

"Oh gods," someone said. It might have been Sariel. I never did find out.

I grasped his horns as he came down. Gripping with everything I could. I was flat on my back, and groaned as I pressed him up. He took a swing at me, but I protected myself by tilting his head to the side and throwing it off course.

I got to my feet, pushing him back. Standing with one foot, then the other. He couldn't believe it. No normal man could have withstood this and lived.

Once I broke contact we traded blows. It had all the technique of two bears on their hind legs mauling each other. I cracked him across the jaw. Then the snout. I dented his skull and brought him to his knees like a rancher with a maul putting down an old bull. He hit me so hard, but I was built to withstand damage. My skin split, I was clawed. But my bones didn't break. Nor did my power. I was formed to weather forward, no matter what.

He fell to his knees, and I gripped his horns again, bringing him close. I kneed him in the jaw, once, twice. The sound of it was dense, like punching a sack of grain.

I twisted, gripping the horns tightly. Every muscle in my body tensing. I felt the runes under my scarred flesh giving me what I needed, what I had earned so long ago. They promised strength, the strength we had cultivated for years. They promised to deliver if I did my part.

"Fucking..." I grunted as I twisted. The minotaur reached up, grasping at my hands, trying to stop me.

"Cunt!" I screamed and snapped both horns off his head.

When I was a boy, my father and I helped a neighbor track down a bull that had broken out of pasture. He hadn't been hard to find. The bull had fallen into a ravine crevice and broken both legs. I'll never forget the terror of that animal, trapped and broken. I remember my old man and the farmers lowering me down with a rope, swinging there, a child on a swing, with a spear in my hands.

Right in the neck, Davik. Ease his passing.

The minotaur sounded like that bull had. He was snorting, screaming, grunting, crying, and shaking his head all at once, feeling up for the horns that were no longer there.

"You're lucky the elf lady doesn't like bloodshed," I snarled and bashed him with his own horn, swinging it down like a club two-handed. The force of it made my ears ring as it struck, and he sprawled into the dirt.

I stood over my conquered enemy. My body was fire and blood. The back of the tavern wasn't a storage area, it was a battlefield. I turned around, ready for more. Eyes mad with challenge.

"Davik..." someone was saying. I blinked. Vorga was looking at me, right in front of me.

I looked over at the troupers still standing there, holding my firewood. Their faces were in shock. I marched up to the oldest looking one, my face furious.

"Alright, alright!" He screamed and dropped the firewood.

"Put it all back." I prodded his belly with the sharp end of the horn. "And give me the farmer's coin. Now."

"Here," he fished into his pockets. "Here, sir."

Everyone remembers their manners when a beating is on the line.

I took the gold piece, and I leaned forward. "Who paid you?"

"No one, we just saw the wood—"

"Troupers don't need firewood. Don't lie to me."

The man decided then that I was a bigger threat than whomever had paid for this idiotic stunt.

"Hearthwood Holdings."

"You sure about that?" I asked.

He nodded. "Just a quick job, sir. They sent the Bull with us for muscle. He works for Crescent Timber."

Both companies, same thing.

"There's no harvest festival for any of you, you understand? No Oakshire. Don't ever come back here. Or next time, it'll be a sword in my hands. And you'll die last. Get me?"

"No harvest festival," the man said with an eager nod. "Absolutely!"

I spat blood on the ground and turned around. The crowd erupted into drunken cheers. Elation. A champion of the town.

But in their eyes, I saw fear. Fear of what they had witnessed. Fear of me.

Wherever I go, there I am...

"Lad..." Rober shook his head in wonder. I looked over his shoulder at Sariel, who was staring at me with a strange look on her face. Vorga and Tyra came up to me, asking if I was alright.

"Davik, I've never seen... are you okay?" Tyra asked.

Vorga put a hand on my shoulder. "He ruined your shirt, Davik."

I suddenly didn't want to be around them. Any of them. I didn't want to be around the merriment and the stories and the retelling of what had just happened. It had taken so much of me not to kill the beast snoring on the ground.

There are times to be around soft things, and this was not one of them. I dropped the horns and locked eyes with Sariel. Maybe the war wasn't over for some of us. I was kidding myself. Maybe you couldn't build something beautiful onto something ugly, and sharp, and wicked.

I walked past the clamoring crowd and took my cart, emptied it, and dragged it off to the valley. I only stopped to grab my axe, buried in a stump. As if it could hide from what it was built to do.

CHAPTER
FIFTEEN

I took the axe to the treelines all night until the world smelled of split wood, of bleeding sap and sawdust. It was easy to throw myself into work. I worked with a butcher's focus, moving from kill to kill. From carcass to carcass.

But what I loved out there among the falling trees only came when I was finished. When I was done swinging and burned through whatever was on my mind, until sweat poured off of me and I would stop. Stop and look up and then I would see it.

A peaceful valley.

Oakshire.

Mountains in the distance. Farms up on the roads. Vast fields, all leading to Oakshire. So far away and clear in those autumn mornings that it felt like I was standing in front of a painting.

And just a tiny bit of that peace would seep into me. I'd sit and stare at it all. A valley of people just living their lives, of girls working in a tavern, with their little stories and their warm smiles.

For those moments, I felt stillness. And I loved this place. I loved it because it just was what it was. Maybe some weary fighter like me had seen it long ago and traded a sword for a shovel. A mace for a hammer. Maybe he had built something.

It's nice to pretend.

In the dawn light, Sariel came to me. The rattle of the borrowed horse's bridle made me turn.

It felt inevitable; her coming here. Like we were each arrows with our names etched upon one another.

"Are you hurt?" Sariel called to me as she climbed down.

I was cleaning my axe head, and it was due for another session at Aron's grindstone, that much was for certain. My shirt was ruined, and I had discarded it long ago. My body was crested with light bruises where other men's bones would have been turned to a pulp.

"They take that cow away?" I asked.

"It took the troupers and the tavern goers to get him on the wagon. You almost killed their leader, too. He was mumbling, and Elina did what she could, but she said it was a serious wound."

"Good," I spat and turned around to sink the axe into another tree. "Fuck him,"

"Davik, you don't have to do this."

I stopped chopping. "Do what?"

"Run away."

I snorted. I kept swinging.

"Talk to me," she pleaded.

"I'm not the one running away." I sank another bite.

"What's that supposed to mean?"

I left the axe buried half into a trunk. "Why didn't you stop anyone yesterday, Sariel? What would you have done if I hadn't been there?"

"They were just stealing firewood," the elf said to me. "Just firewood, just thieves."

I walked towards her. "They look like that to Vorga? You weren't able to stop her. They could have killed her. They could have attacked her, taken her. What then? What if Davik hadn't come running out of the cellar?"

Sariel stared at me, a flash of hate in her eyes. I didn't care. "That's not what would have happened."

"Would. I deal with could. I've always dealt with could."

"Maybe that's why you're so messed up, Davik."

"It's why I'm alive!" I shouted. "I see a man on the road with two partners following me? I wait, then I kill them. You know what firewood is? It's you not losing your tavern. It's people keeping their homes warm enough so their children don't freeze. This isn't an elven city, Sariel. It's full of normal people. Common people. We die to famine, to plagues, we die when it gets too cold and the children get too hungry and you have to pick which one eats and which one doesn't."

"Davik-"

"What happened, Sariel? You were a commander. You could have handled that business, at least tried to stop it. To slow it down. Why don't you just bury or sell that sword on top of your desk—"

Her face contorted, some monstrous sin urging its way out of her. Finally she screamed the words at me, "I crushed the lines at Breakspear!"

I stopped. "What?"

"It was me," Sariel's voice grew grave and I could hear the threat of her weeping. "It was me, Davik. They didn't know what to do. The Collegiate. The Embriel. I said 'send it all'. 'Send the vanguard. Send the mages. Send the heavy infantry first and trample the rest in cavalry.' I rode down my own men. I had to win."

It was her.

"I saved a farm once, when we were on march. Early in the war. I was going to be good. I was going to be *different*. The men were hungry. Even elves get hungry, Davik, despite what *you* may think. They bleed and they die and they turn into animals."

I held up my hands to stop her. "Sariel."

Her face grew red, angry. She pointed at me. "I saved them. I stopped anyone from stealing their livestock. And another. And weeks later, one other. But then the supplies grew thin. *Magebreakers* were attacking us. Slaughtering caravans. Hit and run tactics. So we stole one cow. Then a pair. My men lived."

She walked forward and grabbed my shirt. Her eyes were mad, far away.

"By the end of the war Davik, I saw my men butchered, left as effigies blazing in the woods. I razed villages that hid weapons for your army, for your lords. They were innocent people, just doing as commanded. Common folk. I burned their homes and left them to the wilderness. I hung farmers who were paid to poison our supplies."

She let go. "I was like you, coming out of the woods. I was too ashamed to ever go home. I was too effective. The commander who broke Breakspear, scared of a damn mirror!"

Sariel screamed the last words. Her face was gaunt, horrified. The face of someone on a battlefield. When the lines broke and there's so much mud, you're not sure if you're killing your comrades or your enemies, and both are just as dangerous because they're just as confused.

"I had to become a new person, Davik. I couldn't, I can't... I can't kill anymore. I can't kill another person as long as I live. Haven't you ever wanted to be someone else so badly that it murders you inside?"

I had. And I think she knew I had.

"But then I saw you, Davik. I remembered you. When you came into the tavern, I swore you had come to kill me. And all I could think was, **finally.** Finally, someone knows who I really am. I was so ashamed to see how broken you were."

"Remembered me?" I asked.

Sariel nodded. Tears were in her eyes. "I rode by the camps, towards the end of the peace treaties. For the prisoner exchanges. I knew the treatment for Magebreakers would be tough. Terrible, maybe. But I didn't know... until I saw you. Sitting in that cage. You were so alone."

"Stop," I said.

"It had been five months since Breakspear. The last of the prisoner batches were to include any Magebreakers. Along with spearmen. Lowest of the low. We traded horses and armor before the likes of you."

"Stop," I warned her. I felt the forest disappearing around me. I felt mud under my feet. Terrible, cold mud.

Sariel's face was a mask of shame and grief. "Then I saw you. You were so thin. So frail. I thought, **'This is what I'm afraid of?'** You could see where they cut you. And all that hate left me. I saw that we were just fighting because other lords sought us to. You were the last one alive. And they put that little sign up on the cage where your comrades had been, right across from you. And it said..."

"*Darkshire,*" I mumbled the syllables.

My comrades had starved. One by one. Some had fought for food. Some had turned to darker hungers, and I didn't blame them. There is a hunger so deep and terrible and gnawing that it makes you insane. You'll kill for meat. For crickets. For bugs.

One by one, they died. A starving man dies hard. He wheezes. His body has consumed itself, but he's still so hungry.

The guards had put a small sign, carved with an elven flair, in the cage across from me.

They told me I could eat whenever I wanted. All I had to do was ask.

Darkshire. It read.

Bodies of my comrades, left in the elements to freeze and stiffen. I spent the winter staring at the eyes that used to wink and laugh with me around a campfire.

When the Summoner commandant saw the last of the prisoners off, he said he wanted to meet the last Magebreaker.

"I have your first name here. What's your surname?" He had prodded his pad with a quill made of crystal.

I had stared at the page. The words seemed so fresh, so lively. I wanted to eat them.

"Your surname, Magebreaker?"

"Don't have one..." I said. I didn't want to speak. Speaking was energy. I was a skeleton with skin back then. A swollen belly.

"Where do you hail from?"

I stared at the words. I couldn't remember the name of my father's village. I couldn't remember what he looked like. Or my mother. Or if I ever had parents. My body was eating itself. So starved it had eaten my memories. My childhood.

"Darksh—"

"What's that?" He leaned in.

"Darkshire."

"Very well," he said and jotted it down. Then he looked up at me and shook my hand. It hurt when he squeezed it. I was nothing. There was barely anything left.

"I'm glad we are no longer enemies, Davik of Darkshire."

Darkshire.

That name had followed me ever since. The commandants threw a little celebration for the last returning prisoners of war. The spearmen. Those too poor to warrant their own ransoms. Some lower knights and cavalrymen. Two paladins of a god nobody liked, too. They had walked into a group of cheers, the oaths on their flesh burned away by the enemy. They would never pray properly again.

Then I came. They had had to bring me on a cart. I was wrapped in blankets, I couldn't stop shivering. The idiots hadn't thought to bring any food, so I was chewing oats that the cart horses were supposed to have been eating.

Rumors spin quick in barracks, quicker even than a small town. Stories people wanted to hear. They had been told that I had fought to the last man. That my valor was respected by the enemy. They had kept me locked away, and I was the final bargaining chip in the grand negotiations.

It seemed even in my absence; I had been of service.

They rolled me into the keep. Soldiers, comrades, they all lined the walls. The casks had been opened that night.

"Darkshire!" the keep commander had yelled and gestured as I came rolling in. Like some hero.

The applause was deafening. I looked around, seeing fit men. Men who hadn't had to miss more than three meals since the end of the war. All those lords, the blessed human gentry who had treated and negotiated and stalled for time while men starved to death in camps to save face, to gain land or grain or gold.

I stood on the wagon, steadying myself as we rode in slowly. Then I threw off my blankets and tore my shirt away.

When they saw my body, they stopped cheering. It was like death slew any good humor as it flew around the battalion.

I stared, mad with hunger and captivity, eyes wide and completely insane around the camp of a thousand men. I raised my arms, not in glory, but to show them the lies. What had happened. How many had died with me...

They cheered again. It grew and grew. Until it was all there was. I became the story they wanted. Whatever it was, it stuck.

I had collapsed on the wagons. The clerics took me. They fed me broth for a week, and tied me to the bed because I kept trying to grab their scalpels and fighting them. I didn't want more runes. I didn't want more service.

Eventually, I could walk. I was quiet. Any good soldier knows how to step quietly, how to creep for an ambush.

I became the wraith of the keep. Flitting around. They would see my bed empty and know exactly where to find me.

I was always in the pantries. Among the foodstuffs, the camp supplies. I wasn't even eating. I had to go there. I had to make sure there was food. To count it. To make sure none was missing. To touch it all. To be absolutely certain that the behind that very door, there would be food.

The legend spread of Darkshire, the last Magebreaker. It's a nice title. It was a reputation I rode for a long time, when I became a proper adventurer. It got me out of fights, into jobs. It opened doors for me and blouses too. They would look in my eyes when their spells failed on me and know the story of Darkshire.

It was silly, of course. There were other Magebreakers. There had been a small squad that had been delayed, but when the battle was lost, they were smart and ran.

I spent a season there, getting my weight back. I never spoke a word about what happened. Not until years later, when I met a man who had been in the same camp. When he recognized me, he hugged me tightly in some seedy tavern and wept into my shoulder.

They don't know. They just don't know.

My compatriots at the time had been a fearsome group. A group of real renown. They had thought him a madman. Nothing surprised them more than when the black-hearted

Darkshire held the man and whispered something back to him.

No, they don't. But we do, brother. We do. And those we left.

They were flabbergasted when I gave him my entire take from a recent job. Enough gold to buy a castle and lands if he wanted. But he had taken it and promised me to make a place for men like us, for veterans that only war remembered and the world forgot. Whether that gold went to a series of pour-houses and a bloated liver, or that nice dream of his, I never knew.

I kept bread in my pockets for three years after I left. I wouldn't go anywhere without it. I never ate it. I changed it for fresh bread regularly. Once, in a sea-port town, a pickpocket grabbed a handful of it and before I knew it, my dirk was through his hand.

"Phieran's wrists, Darkshire! He's just a kid!" my partner had said.

He had just been a kid, maybe fifteen. I hadn't even thought about it. Because I hadn't been there. On that dock. I had been in the camps again, back in my cage, staring at Darkshire. The eyes of my dead friends staring back at me. Begging me to cross over and eat that mountain of frozen flesh. The restraint of it had driven me mad.

Sometimes, towards the end, a new face would appear on the pile. It always smiled at me. It knew my secrets. My hunger. My dark wishes. It was Lonnie, my friend.

Even when the Embriel and the Collegiate Mages cleaned out all the bodies before the commandant came to cover their crimes, Lonnie was there. Smiling, always fucking smiling. And he would sing to me.

War's we wage'em... Mages we break'em... Day's we save'em...

But there was a new terrible verse.

Friends we ate'em...

I walked towards Sariel. The axe in my hand.

"I saw you there," she whispered. "And I could have moved you, or saved you. But I didn't. I hated what you did. I hated you..."

"I know," I said.

And I did know. I had seen her, clear as day. I had denied it until now. Memory is a fickle thing, and for many, it is best ignored. But she had been there. A beautiful battle elf on a horse, clad in plate that was a thousand years old. I had thought she was a spirit from the afterworld finally come to take me, to free me.

"I was so ashamed," she whispered. Her beautiful face was a mask of grief now.

"Of what?" I asked.

"Of how little I cared. Of how I knew I should. You were just a conscript, a soldier. And I passed you by, leaving you to die."

I grabbed her dress now. She didn't resist me, and I pulled her close. In training long ago, they had taught us this, to pull a man onto your knife in a trench. The coldest embrace.

"I've had enough of ugly things. War and cages and plunder and sad stories," I told her. I wiped her tears away with my thumb and made her look at me. Almost shaking her. "It's over, Sariel. I didn't survive to think of grimness for the rest of my life. I never tasted anything so good as damned horse oats when I left there. I'm tired of it. That's why I came to Oakshire. It's why I stay."

Sariel shut her eyes, blinking away more tears. I let her go.

I shook my head at her. "If you want to run, keep running. But you're the one in the cage now, and the door is wide open. Aren't you tired of punishing yourself? We only get this one life. Just one."

"Davik, you don't understand. The war—"

I grabbed her now and pulled her to me. My lips met hers, and I held her neck as I kissed her deeply. I kissed her how I had wanted to kiss her so many times.

"Fuck the war," I whispered. "That's over. There's no good or bad, Sariel. There's alive and dead for people like us. And I'm tired of watching you pretend to be dead."

Sariel kissed me. Her body pressed against me. She smelled of the valley, of the oak, of a bright tavern and the soft scents she donned. I slid around her, feeling her at last. My hands ran down her back.

"Davik..." she murmured. I walked into her, guiding her back to the cart. My tongue slid along hers, and her plump lips met mine.

"Say it," I whispered. "Stop hiding and say it."

Silver irises. Eyes of my enemy, so the world had said once. They stared at me in revelation. A secret brought forth because it was too heavy. And once it had moved, a more powerful one spilled from her tongue.

"I love you," she whispered.

Eyes that loved me. They shut as I kissed her, responding in touch. Denied for so long.

Until now.

All those days, those weeks, those looks... they all lead to here. To this soft, warm place I had heard of but never seen. A heaven of comfort and guidance and acceptance that felt so good it hurt. All those glances, those words between us... they had built something. Something you couldn't touch or hold, but you could feel.

A beautiful elven woman wrapped her legs around a shirtless human, and we fell into the back of the cart. Such a simple story. One I thought I'd never know.

Every time she looked at me, I had wanted her. And I knew, somehow, that Elina had been right. That it was different now.

When I reached for the thing I thought I wanted, it was something else.

Something so much better.

Sariel enclosed around me and held me close, our bodies pressing and sliding and grinding against each other. A duel, a dance, our flesh trying to reach out between us, to cast off the clothes that hindered them.

There was no need to rush here. I knew suddenly that I had had so many lovers, but had never loved. I had fucked, and dominated, and drawn out the fixation and the hungry need in so many. But I had never loved. I saw that now, as she pulled me down and I tasted the nape of her neck. The world had told us we were enemies once. What greater defiance was there than this?

We were both scarred from a war we didn't want. From the things we did and did not do. This was not a ravagement of flesh. There was no cruelty or malice here.

It was slow and wondrous. It was the opposite of war. Of hate. Of being alone. It felt like walking out of a prison camp cage into a feast. I wasn't running from anything. I was sprinting towards something.

Our bodies read one another, and they attuned. The pitches matching, the melodies seeking each other until... there...

"Taste me," she pleaded in the back of the cart.

I felt her, with my hand, the ripe flesh of her hip. Then she spread her legs, and I drew her silken dress higher. I slid her tight panties, somehow softer, somehow finer than her gown, from her sweet southron lips. She was bare of hair, prepared for me. A table of flesh and the pouting lips of her sweet quim waiting only for mine.

I tasted her like a dying man finding a spring. Her hands

gripped the cart. She breathed faster and faster as my tongue traced her folds. I loved her with my mouth, my tongue, with suction and friction and her hands left the cart and found the back of my hair and held me there as she arched her hips into me. I tasted the sultry essence of her and could never have had enough.

"Davik," she whispered my name in a valley older than both of us.

I slid my hands upwards, across supple smooth thighs and pushed her legs back, giving me the gift of her. When I looked up, tongue dancing across her beautiful clit, her lips were pursed as if she were frozen. Every lick, every rub, it produced a jolt in her body, and the cart rocked slightly.

I tasted her, filling my mouth with her sweet flesh, and there had never been anything better. She pulled at me eagerly, and I broke from her and kissed her mouth fiercely. Her cunt ground against my bare abs. Rays of sunlight slid over both of us.

"I never... I starved myself of..." she whispered.

"Shh," I told her. It didn't matter. Nothing mattered except her and I. I had never known it was real. Love. Not for me. It was something that existed in songs and at the end of a poet's quill, and to find it was immaculate.

To feel it was like coming home.

Sariel reached down. She flung open my belt line with such raw need. Had anyone ever wanted me so truly? Never.

Not until now.

Her bare feet reached up and slid my pants down. I kicked off my boots, stepping out of my trousers until I was finally unclothed. The second my cock was free, she ground against me, and I slid my length along her, the heat coming from her boiled for me alone.

"Make love to me," she pleaded. Her hand reached down,

guiding me. She spread herself, rubbing me on her, and then I teased myself against her entrance.

Our eyes met. There was something there she was giving me. Trust. Real trust. I was being invited somewhere no one else had been, a place she had starved herself in punishment.

When I entered her, it was slow. The tightness of her, her body responding, readying for me. I slid inside and she braced against the cart. Exhaling.

"Davik," she groaned. Her hand found my back, pulling me in. I didn't want to hurt her. I didn't want anything bad to ever happen to her again.

My girth strained inside her stretching flesh, into silken pink folds until finally I took her to the brink and she cried out in pleasure as her crest broke.

"Yes," she said. And she said it again and again as I strove into her. It was slow. The sky above us, the landscape like a painting and the sun shone on the autumn day as two people made love for the first time.

I sank into her, not just where we joined, but her body. I sucked and groaned with her nipple in my mouth, her breasts rolling with every growing thrust. The heft of them was a gift I pooled in my hand. The heat coming from her loins, gripping me, milking me, made me mutter her name like a prayer.

I was bruised. Battered. Covered in sweat. Something rough inside of something beautiful, and that beauty was her. Welcoming me, bidding me to stay.

She was the loveliest thing I had ever seen, touched, or felt. Now she was mine. Her hands locked around my back, then her calves slid across my plunging waist and she moaned into my ear.

"Come inside me, please. Please, Davik. Come inside me. I'm so close I wa—"

I heaved into her, stretching and taking her. The cart

rocked, the rhythm of it creaking on old wooden axles, and she quivered around my cock. My pinnacle danced on the edge of my senses, but when she moaned those words, it came plunging down like a hunting bird on high.

"Yes," she groaned.

I gripped her hands in mine, fingers interlocking.

"Davik, fill me..."

What I had been holding back, those long weeks, came forth. I spilled into her, filling her sweet core with spasm after shuddering spasm. We both groaned, our muscles straining as I filled her, and I felt her come, swelling around me, easing me forth. Her body drank me in. I had never felt such release met with such welcome, and she squeezed her arms tighter around me as I fell into her, kissing her.

"I love you, Davik," Sariel whispered my name. All I heard were her and my racing breaths, and the birds in the trees so vast behind us, they could never be counted.

CHAPTER
SIXTEEN

That morning, we lay in the cart, our bodies bare and spoke of gentle things.

"Why a tavern?" I asked.

Sariel stroked my arm. "I wanted to be around people. Just normal people. The girls came these past few years. It's a money pit. Don't have to tell you that. But it felt... honest."

I watched the sun rise over her bare shoulder. Her dress spilled across her hips and into the cart. Her heavy breasts fell into the crook of her arm and she looked at me with soft eyes.

"What is it?" I asked.

"I knew the first time you slept with Elina. When word came across the valley about her powers improving, I had a feeling she bound herself to you."

"Ah," I prepared to explain. "It was before you and I..."

"It's good," Sariel said and nuzzled closer.

I looked down at her in my chest. "Good as in, it's okay it happened or that it's..."

Sariel's eyes opened, and she sat back up. "It's good it

happened, Davik. I'm not blind. And I've been around for a long time. But, you're my first."

I knew that, but it struck me how alone she had been all these years when she said it aloud.

She looked away. "I was betrothed to another Embrien commander, another battalion family. Arranged by our families. We were set to be wed before the war contract was signed to support the Mage Collegiates in the Summoner War. I... never came home for the ceremony."

"That was over ten years ago," I said.

Her eyes softened in memory. "I never came close. Not that there weren't suitors. Letters from my family. I kept delaying our wedding. Finally, I just said I wasn't coming home. I starved myself of any touch, any at all. I felt so guilty. How could I allow myself to feel good? Elina tried to help, but I wouldn't hear of it."

"I love you," I said. The words were new, and they felt powerful.

"I love you," Sariel said and touched my chin. "I spent the years after the war watching other women be happy. I developed a bit of a... fascination. Elina was the only person who understood it when I told her. Maybe because I denied myself, I enjoyed watching other women doing the opposite. I've seen you talking to Vorga. I've seen the way Karley looks at you. I... imagine it sometimes."

"You do?" I asked, "Imagine me with others?"

Her eyes flashed at me. "Yes. I'm not ashamed of it. I'm not like those strange men who degrade themselves by loaning out their wives. I want a true love. One so bright and strong, a champion. Where, no matter what, his heart belongs to me. "

"That won't be an issue," I promised and kissed her hand.

"Elina told me about different facets, different souls. She

says most of us can only match to one person. But some men are so encompassing, they fill many. They're a river."

I didn't say anything to that.

She continued, "I don't want to start a war. Not with the girls at the tavern. But you have to be careful with the others. Elina won't mind. She's bound and devoted to you."

"I suppose she is, but I didn't know what that meant."

"I like it," Sariel said matter-of-factly. "I like other women wanting you. Needing you. It's like I have the grandest prize of all. I was never like this, or maybe I didn't realize it. Maybe the war, or the years of watching other people enjoying themselves changed me. But it's what I am."

"You're an interesting woman."

Sariel rolled her eyes. "You've cleaned up nicely since you came here." She reached out and traced a finger on my chest, over scars that crested mounds of muscle. "Just... I can't stand to lose the girls, Davik. I see the capacity in you. It's boundless. My gods, I feel it when you're inside me. Just don't do anything that would send anyone away."

I raised an eyebrow.

Sariel playfully smacked my chest. "Don't be coy with me. I may not be... experienced as others. But I've been alive for a long time. I just don't want anyone spurned. Or denied on my account. I don't want anyone leaving the tavern because their heart broke."

This was new territory for me. Not multiple lovers, but the idea of multiple relationships? Women that knew about each other. The old me would have slept around the tavern, and then walked away as jealousy rose. But what Sariel spoke of was different. She wanted it kept together. Bound tightly.

"Promise me," Sariel said.

"Promise you, what?"

"Nobody leaves."

"I'll do what I can," I said. I slid closer to her and began kissing her neck.

"I wanted you so badly," Sariel moaned as I bit into her neck, drawing her close to me. "That night in the bathtub. I wanted you to crawl in, no warning. I knew you were about to. But I was ashamed. I ran away."

"Tell you what," I murmured between kisses. "We'll have a reenactment."

She stopped me, staring into my eyes. "I'm no one but yours, Davik. Not now or ever. I want the only touch to have been you. I want to belong to you. Just always come back to me wherever you go."

"Always," I swore.

Sariel reached down and pulled me towards her. "It was what I always wanted it to be," she whispered.

"What?"

She smiled. "You."

I took her again, there in the cart. We made love slowly until she clenched around me and huffed my name.

"Fill me again, please."

"Sariel," I groaned. I pumped into her, raising her leg high. I wanted to be closer to her. Deeper. I had never had anyone like this before. It's like we became one thing when we were together.

"You can do whatever you want to me," Sariel moaned in a girlish voice. "Ugh, whenever... you want. I'm always ready. When you're near me. I feel... ready..."

I filled her again, and she clasped around me, holding me close, not letting me leave.

"Mmm," she murmured, eyes shut in bliss. Sariel rested her head on my bicep. "Stay like this, can you?"

"Nowhere else I'd rather be." I kissed the top of her hair.

"THE BOSS HAS a new jump in her step," Karley said.

I didn't look up from my place at the kitchen table. When Sariel had said we should go get breakfast together, I had figured she meant the cafe. Now I was sitting at the table inside her house.

With everyone who lived there.

"How are you feeling?" Vorga asked softly next to me. She placed her hand on my back, somewhere between the bruises.

"Little rough," I said. "Is Rober okay?"

"The cleric saw to him," Vorga reassured me.

"That's good," I said. I still had his gold coin. I needed to get with him today to return it.

"That was... something Davik." Karley stirred a spoon in her coffee, eyes darting at me. For someone who hadn't bothered to dress for breakfast, she seemed to have had time to throw on a little dark eyeliner.

"Pancakes for the conquering hero!" Tyra shouted as she danced up with the platters of food.

Where Vorga had been quiet and inquisitive and Karley wandered around the events of the night before, you could expect nothing else from Tyra but a trumpet blasting.

"Let me give you a hand," I said and pushed myself up.

"Sit." Vorga grabbed my shoulder and pushed me back down. She rose to help Tyra.

"Thanks Vorga, the rest is on the stove," Tyra said with a smile. She grinned at me and put a stack of pecan pumpkin pancakes down in front of me. The sweet mixture of nutmeg, cinnamon and pumpkin dusted with powdered sugar was tantalizing.

"Wow, this looks amazing."

Tyra bent low, her chest giving me a full eye of sparkling

faen cleavage. She made a show of setting the bacon to the side of me. "I think I speak for the entire town when I say thank you, Davik. I'm not sure what we would have done had you not been there last night."

Vorga rubbed my back again as she sat down. I glanced over at Sariel.

She was beaming. The elf bit her bottom lip slowly, enjoying the attention I was receiving.

"I mean technically," Karley pointed out. "There wouldn't be firewood if he hadn't been here."

"There might not be a tavern if there weren't the firewood and the business it brought," Sariel responded. "Or your tips, Karley."

The table was set with servings of pancakes, bacon, cream so thick and whipped it was like a frosting and a glass pitcher of bright orange syrup. All of it was imbued with Tyra, the faen-girl's mood and gladness seeping into every morsel she prepared.

"Thank you, Tyra. I'm absolutely famished." Sariel passed a plate of pancakes to Karley.

Tyra smiled and sat on my left, reaching for the coffee. She kept looking up at Sariel, as if noticing something. Then she slowly looked at me, an impish smile spreading across her lips.

"What?" I asked.

Tyra winked and giggled. "You were up early, Sariel."

"Oh, bills," Sariel said and reached for a helping of bacon. "Vendors. Plus cleanup. I daresay we might not have the sizeable crowd today we had yesterday. It's understandable."

"You think they'll come back?" Karley asked. A flicker of fear danced across her face.

"The thieves? Oh, heavens no. Elina was tending to one of them all night. The rest of the procession sped out of town. But their leader will live. Thankfully," Sariel said and smirked at me. I saw her rub her thumb over the red signet ring.

We ate in small chatter. I felt wonderful. Sariel was mine. I wanted to pinch myself to make sure I wasn't dreaming. But every time I looked up, Sariel was across from me.

Breakfast was delicious. I said as much to Tyra.

"Oh, it's good. But not as good as **some** things." She grinned at me again.

"Don't know why we all had to be here," Karley grumbled at her plate. "We were cleaning up forever last night."

"Sariel came back from her walk. I figured a family breakfast was in order." Tyra reached out and stole the bacon from between Karley's fingers.

"Some of us get up early," Vorga said from my right.

"Oh, she's up early," Tyra said. "Karley just keeps her door closed. I hear such strange things sometimes... maybe prayers Elina taught you?"

Karley's eyes flashed up at Tyra in outrage, her cheeks darkening from violet to deep purple. She did not meet my eye.

"Karley's just upset," Vorga said. "Now you'll know how lazy she is."

The drow bartender rolled her eyes and stood up, taking her plate and coffee to the kitchen. She was wearing a thin tank top across her tight chest, abs flexing as she stood, and the nipples on her small breasts poked through the cloth. When she turned, the dark thong between her juicy little ass caught my eye.

"You're so right, Vorga." Tyra nodded. "Maybe Karley should cook us something some morning."

Sariel sipped her coffee. "I think that's a splendid idea."

"That's a cold chance in hell," Karley said over her shoulder as she walked to the kitchen.

"Put that cake away!" Vorga laughed at the drow.

Karley looked over, confused, then gave her ass a shake. "Came with me, sorry."

I broke my glance, snapping out of my long gaze, and Sariel was smiling discreetly to me. She liked me looking.

"It's not fair, really," Tyra murmured, staring at her pancakes. "Davik misses out on most breakfasts."

"Well, he doesn't live there, does he?" Karley asked from the kitchen, grabbing more coffee.

"Bring that, would you, Karley?" Sariel called to her.

"Maybe he should stop by some more mornings?" Vorga asked, looking around.

"Nah." Karley sat down and handed the pitcher of coffee to Sariel. "Stinks of timber and hay."

"Well, you'll just have to give him a bath then," Tyra teased.

"Can't do it," Karley said with a mouthful of bacon. She made a show of wiping her lips with the back of her wrist. "I'm allergic. Besides, someone has to be here to cover while others go on vacation to Trinth."

"Poor Brim," Tyra said.

Brim. I hadn't even thought of him. "Is he okay?"

"He's a bit banged up. But Elina said he'd be alright. Sariel told him to take it easy today. He's at the temple."

"Probably leering at Elina," Karley said.

Tyra shook her head. "You don't know anything, do you, Karley? For a drow you can't see much that's placed in shadow."

"Fairy words." Karley shrugged. Then she raised an eyebrow as all the women around the table gave her a look. "What?"

"Brim likes **boys.**" Vorga laughed.

"What?" Karley asked. "He's always hanging around, sneering. I'm careful with my skirt because he's so short."

Sariel chuckled. "Brim is an odd little fellow, Karley. But I don't think anything under your skirt would be enticing to him. Brim was married. He had a husband. Poor man is a widower."

"I miss him dearly already," Tyra intoned.

"When's he back?" Vorga asked.

"Today, but still. I'll miss him." Tyra sipped her coffee.

"I'll miss him for sure," Karley said. "Since **some** of us are taking Monday off."

"Oh, you're just jealous." Tyra threw a bun at her, which she caught. "That you don't have anywhere to go on holiday."

Vorga blushed and focused on her food. I turned, and she glanced up at me.

"I think maybe we should postpone... the library. You're injured, Davik."

"No chance," I said and shot Karley a glare. "I'm fine."

"That minotaur isn't fine..." Tyra murmured in a sing-song tone.

"You know," Sariel said, "With how busy it's been, and the firewood business Davik is running, I thought more money in your pockets would cheer you up."

"I'm cheerful!" Tyra protested.

"Eh." Karley slurped her coffee. Then she looked up at me, playing the disinterested tough girl. "What are you getting in Trinth, anyway?"

"Something to upgrade the tavern." I didn't want to give too much away.

Karley stood up again, taking the time to stretch and yawn loudly, her ass facing me.

"Quit showing off," Tyra said to her, and threw a dish-towel. "Cheeks should remain under the table!"

"I'm not dressing up because the human stops by."

"Pants is not dressing up," Tyra said. She turned to me. "She's such a slob, you'll have to excuse her."

I shrugged, and I saw Karley waiting to see if I gave any reception. Her flat stomach, lined with abs, poked out from under her tight tank top.

"I best be going," I said. "I want to see Rober, and check on Brim, too."

"I'll head in as well," Sariel said, standing up. "See how things are. We didn't do a proper cleanup last night."

"Yeah, some of us ran off, that's why." Karley left the kitchen and marched upstairs. Each asscheek jiggling between the dark purple lining of her thong.

Vorga's hand rested on my thigh. "You're sure about Trinth? We can go another time..."

"We're going," I said. "Besides, even you have to be getting bored with that book."

On the way to the tavern, Sariel and I walked slowly, enjoying the warmth of the day. But before we made it far, the rest of the girls came piling out of the house and raced up to join us.

"Boss! Did you decide about the festival?" Karley asked.

"Are we going or not?" Tyra squealed.

Vorga walked behind them, shy. In a stable of beauties and big personalities, it was easy for her to fall to silence. But it was not easy to forget her. I was really looking forward to seeing her face light up when she saw a proper library.

"Well," Sariel said as we walked. It was like towing a bunch of ducks behind me. "Yes, I think so. The extra business we'll get makes sense."

"Yes!" Tyra jumped in the air and squealed again. "Brim is going to be so excited."

Brim excited? I wasn't so sure about that.

"You'll come," Sariel whispered as she leaned into me. "Right?"

"Of course," I said. I hadn't really thought about it. But now, it made sense. A lot of sense. I didn't want to leave the girls of the tavern alone at a harvest festival, not with everything that had been happening.

"I'm still thinking about this morning," Sariel murmured as we walked.

I nodded, not wanting to give anything away.

"I wanted to suck your cock on this walk, but it looks like that'll have to wait." She smiled.

I looked around at the bouncing and scowling girls behind us. "They might hear," I warned.

"I've always wanted to try it," she continued, not seeming to care if they heard or not. "Elina gave me some techniques to practice. But I always thought about you... sometimes I thought about you and me when I did."

"Is that so?"

"Mmhmm," Sariel purred. "Sometimes I thought about you and Elina while I touched myself in that bed, all alone up there. I think you've opened something in me, Davik."

"Sariel, can we talk about-"

"Oh shit," Karley said behind us.

I was so focused on keeping a low profile; I didn't look at the tavern until now. A line of people was forming.

"They're already lining up!" Tyra said. "Sariel, we'll have to get that meat order in soon!"

Sariel's face fell at the sight of customers, instead of it being one of gladness.

"Everyone probably wants to see the hero!" Tyra laughed.

"It's gonna be a long day," Karley groaned.

"Davik." Sariel turned to me. "You head to the temple, go

see Rober and Brim. It might be good for things to cool off a bit before you make an entrance."

"Right," I said.

Right.

"How are you feeling?" I asked Rober as I sat down next to him in the temple of the Mistress. Elina had pulled out a cot for him to lie in.

"Bastards knocked me a good one. For a little guy, he hit like a mule," Rober groaned. "You just missed the family. I sent them off to the tavern for breakfast. Had to get the Linnie away. I love her dearly, but the woman can dote a bit too much."

I tried to stop him, but Rober sat up and placed his feet on the ground. He rubbed his head. He was battered good, but a wink and a smile broke across his face. "Hell of a show we put on, eh? I don't think anyone's seen anything like that before. Hearthwood Holdings will think twice on their bullshit."

"Sure, Rober." I wasn't sure. Groups of organized crime don't just get scared off when one of their hired beasts gets bested. "By the way, this is yours." I handed him his missing gold piece.

"Thanks, my boy. It really is something, having what you worked, taken away from you. But this means a lot."

"Luckily, they didn't get away with anything." I put a hand on the older man's shoulder. "But you didn't need to step in like that."

"Ah hells," Rober groaned. "Wasn't trying to be a hero, Davik. Coin keeps the family alive. You chase wolves from the herd, not because you want the applause of lambs, it's so your family is fed. Do you understand?"

I did. I had seen many men in my lifetime put themselves between their families and danger. Men you would think were meek. But men who rose daily and tilled fields or went to the woods to work and provide? That was a different march than a soldier knew. A march without end.

I remembered stopping once with a group on our way out of a city. We watched a fruit vendor split the head of a thief. It ended like most fights do, in a flurry of blows and peacocking.

"Probably the biggest fight he'll have," my travel companion had said. He was a cleric of immense power. His goddess had bestowed blessing upon blessing on him. I had seen hordes of the most vile creatures shield their eyes from the dedications on his armor.

But he was a pompous ass.

"No magic armor protecting him, or goddess," I had said as we watched. "Just death hanging around every day. Trying to get into his home. Take his children. Steal his coin."

"Is that your new name, Darkshire? Are you Death?"

"I don't steal from farmers," I had spat, and we rode on. I thought of that man sometimes, fighting off a little mob. That was a hero. There was no brave companion to come save him. No powerful spell. Just will. The old animal drive to protect and survive. I made more in a week back then than he would in five years, but who worked harder? Who was braver?

Even I had known the answer to that.

I thought of that morning with Sariel. Of the house, surrounded by the girls. The warmth of that place, the smell of breakfast cooked and everyone just sitting around, eating, teasing.

"Yeah," I said to Rober. "I get it."

"I appreciate you coming by, lad. But I'm going to be alright. The cleric helped me when she could push Linnie out of the way."

"That's too bad you're laid up..." I said.

"Aye, gonna have to rest awhile. Wife is bringing me something from the inn."

"There's such a line outside, and I'll be leaving soon to Trinth. Won't be around to sell much."

"A line huh?" Rober said, rubbing his chin thoughtfully. "Makes sense, it getting cold and all. Everyone wants to see the man who broke a minotaur's horns off his damned head."

"But I understand, I'll find someone else—" I said.

"Hold a moment." Rober pushed himself up. The portly older man straightened his shirt. "Can't have any fool off running the timber business, you see? Damn idiots will give the lot away. It's complicated, tracking the mugs and the discounts."

"Is it? Seems simple enough. Maybe I'll get Brim to do it."

Rober's eyes went wide at that. "Don't be daft! He's a brave little fellow. Crafty with that meat fork. But no sense of people. No sense of *showmanship*, Davik. It'll set me back on my recovery, but because you asked so seriously, I'll see to it."

I chuckled as Rober walked off, stopping to smooth his hair and mustaches in a polished mirror. Whether it was the prospect of more coin, or the chance to be the center of attention in Oakshire that moved him, who knew?

I walked over to Elina's other patient. The halfling straightened up when she saw me, smiling. "He'll be fine."

Brim's eyes were glaring at me as I walked up.

"How are you Brim?" I asked.

"Ugly-man..." The gnome sneered.

"Yep, that's me."

"Fool..."

"Thanks for saving me yesterday. If it weren't for you, that lad would've split my scalp." That wasn't the exact truth. My skull would've taken it, but Brim didn't know that when he had acted.

Brim bared his teeth at me.

"Figured this was in order," I said and withdrew a gold piece from my pocket. "For your help, and when we go to Trinth."

The gnome's eyes practically twinkled when I gave him the coin. He held it in both hands, then bit it to test its grade.

"Trinth?" he asked.

"Yeah, Trinth. We go the day after tomorrow, if you can."

"Can." Brim nodded and turned over in his cot, staring at the gold coin.

Elina motioned with her head to speak with me, and I followed her outside.

"How are you? Can I do anything to help you?" she asked.

I stared down at the halfling. Her mirth, her ability to care for people, just seemed part of her. "I'm alright. I'm... better than alright. Sariel came and saw me this morning."

"Did she?" Elina smirked.

"You knew," I said.

"I saw her riding out. The look on her face. She never left the tavern, you know. I think she expected you to return, and when you didn't, I heard her asking where the timber came from. Which farm."

I took her hand and held it in both of mine. "You're still coming to Trinth?"

Elina looked up at me, like a kid hiding a secret. "I have a patient that may need tending to..."

"Who? The bandit with the rainbow clothing? I don't see him here."

"It's... the minotaur, Davik."

I stared down at her. "Are you crazy?"

"Brim actually found him. They dumped him off the wagon

when they left because he slowed them down. Broke his leg. He can't move. The gnome told me he was just hired muscle. But... he wants his horns back."

"You're joking."

Elina shook her head. "Brim has taken a real... interest in him."

The words of this morning came back to me. *Brim likes boys.*

"I can't." I shook my head and raised my hands. "I can't think about that image."

"He won't do any harm, Davik. But would you give the horns back to him? I might be able to heal them. He's beyond depressed. Too ashamed to come back to town."

This was unbelievable. "No way. That's out of the question."

Elina begged me with her eyes.

"Absolutely not. He's too dangerous, Elina."

"You know..." Elina looked up at me. She could always turn it on when she wanted. "Some people have to have a bit of help, to find their way out of the woods."

"No," I said.

Elina batted her eyes, looking up at me with orbs of amber.

"Not happening."

"It's not a big deal," Elina said as we walked through the woods north of town. "If there's someone else you'd rather take to Trinth—it won't hurt my feelings."

"Oh be quiet, you're coming." I shook my head, the two broken horns in either hand. I was hefting a pack of food and waterskins as well. "How much further?"

"He's just up in this glade," Elina promised. She pointed through the trees up the hill. "Not far."

Elina marched ahead of me, using her staff as a walking stick to help her up the slick moss. I reached forward, pushing against her supple rear so she could climb up.

"Thanks," Elina said and looked back over her shoulder as I climbed after her. "So... did you get any rest?"

"Ask your Mistress," I grunted and pulled myself up.

"I don't have to." Elina grinned. "I can feel your facets shining Davik, you're full of vitality. The more you flow, the stronger the current."

"Yes, yes, jewels and souls and rivers. Let's focus on the murdering horned beast first, okay?"

Elina nodded. A dark spiral of curls shaking as she did. "This way."

We found him splayed out. Those bastards really had left him for dead. Aside from his broken horns, he was clutching his side where I had mangled my ribs. A makeshift splint and bandage was around his leg. My guess was that injury had come when they threw him from the wagon. His chest rose and fell rapidly in a fitful sleep.

"Brim's new boyfriend is a heavy sleeper," I said.

"The poor thing is wounded." Elina walked forward to help. I shook my head again. The 'poor thing' had tried to kill me last night.

"Wake up," I said down to him.

Bloodshot eyes opened and locked onto me. They went wide with alarm.

I held my hands up, horn in either one. "Easy, big fella. Came to give these back to you."

The minotaur looked defeated, broken. I supposed I hadn't ever really stuck around to see what hard defeat did to someone. Most of the time they were just dead, or on their way there.

I bent low and handed them to him. His massive hands

reached out and grasped them, a single claw-like nail protruding from each finger.

"Victory," he huffed. "Is yours."

"No shit," I answered.

"Davik!" Elina turned around.

"What? He tried to kill me."

"The man is... right." The minotaur looked at his horns in his hands. "He bested me. In my herds, to break one's horn is a great boon. To break both means banishment."

"Well, lucky for you, this lady is going to set your horns straight." I nodded to Elina.

"No." The minotaur shook his massive head. "I will have them bound in metal. You must not hide defeat." He cast his bloodshot eyes over to me. "What are you? A champion of some human god?"

"I'm a Magebreaker," I answered.

"This, I do not know." He made to push himself up, and I readied for more combat. Elina begged me with her eyes to stop.

He growled in pain, but he bowed before me on his knees. "You are the breaker. I am indebted to you."

This had all the feeling of some grand ceremony among his people.

"I clear your debt."

The minotaur raised his head. "I was paid to support the weak men who came for you."

"Let me guess, Hearthfire Holdings?"

"Crescent Timber... Limited."

"Why is it limited?" Elina asked.

"I do not know." The minotaur looked back at me. "I cannot work unhorned. I cannot bind what is broken without metal, and a blacksmith, and that calls for coin."

"If you're looking for a donation." I stared down at him. "You can keep looking."

"Davik!" But I shut Elina down with a look.

"I will aid you," the minotaur explained. "You are the breaker. Set the task, it will be completed."

I crouched down, going face to face with him. "I'm not interested. Pack it up, move along."

"You are the breaker," he explained again. "You must let me repay you."

"I'm not much for hired help."

He searched among the ground with his eyes. Elina looked at me again, pleading.

"Fine," I said. "Rest, listen to the cleric. We'll speak again before you go on your way. Do not step into town, or I'll bury you there. Do you understand?"

"I understand, breaker."

It was difficult not to roll my eyes.

"What were you before you left your herd?"

"A guard." He bowed his head. The piety was rich for me, considering his conduct the day before.

"You weren't so somber charging down an orc girl, were you?"

He bowed his head again in shame. "I strayed long ago into the wants and needs of men and their coin. You reminded me of otherwise."

"Let's go, he'll be fine." I motioned to Elina.

As we walked away, he called to the halfling.

"Did the gnome ask of me?"

"Let's go," I repeated, pulling her into the woods.

As we walked back the way we came, hiking through thicker brush and jagged rocks, Elina kept smiling at me.

"Stop that," I said.

"Just nice to see a change in you," she said.

Surely. This deal with Sariel was leaving a lifetime of shoulders to look over. But as we walked, I watched Elina. There was a goodness in her that was so genuine. A piety based in a faith that I knew little enough of, but seemed to want nothing but honesty.

I helped her down from a bank of logs, fallen decades ago. I caught her as she hopped into my arms, bringing her slowly down.

"Thanks," she said. But I didn't let her go.

A river that flows and feeds many...

I brought her into my arms where she belonged. Oakshire was a field filled with ripe fruits, and the woman who loved me told me to take my fill. To not pass up any good things. And so I would listen.

The cleric regarded me, welcoming and inviting as I pressed her against a fallen log, sitting her there. Eyes that were bright with kindness glazed over in lust.

I ran my hands up her shapely short legs, lifting her dress higher. I knelt.

"What are you doing?" she whispered, shuddering.

I spread her legs and looked up at her.

"Praying."

CHAPTER
SEVENTEEN

The road rolled underneath the wagon, Rober's twin horses pulling us towards the road to Trinth. I was driving, and it had taken me the best part of an hour to remember the cadence and timing of driving a team. I was used to riding on horseback or walking. At first I thought there was something wrong with the cart, that maybe we had broken it during all the deliveries. For an hour, my hand gripped the brake, my eyes scanned the calm road for signs of any pebble.

"Davik, you're so tense." Elina turned from the cargo area. Vorga was sitting up front with me, taking in the sights. "It's just a wagon."

"It's a damned devil contraption, you ask me." I gritted my teeth and steered the reins.

Vorga chuckled next to me. "It's funny to see you like this."

I raised a dramatic eyebrow at her, doing my best grand villain look.

"Why is that?"

Vorga shook her head and patted my leg. "Big bad man, breaking minotaurs. Afraid of two little ponies."

"I'm not afraid of ponies."

"Right now, you're afraid of the ponies," Vorga said with a grin. When she smiled like that, her two short little tusks jutted out. It was adorable.

She saw me looking and covered her mouth, apologizing.

"What are you apologizing for?" I asked.

"I just..." she kept her hand to her mouth. "Better to hide them."

I reached up and pulled her hand away. "There, that's better."

Vorga smiled at the road, something suddenly interesting her to her right.

It was a blessing I hadn't had to chase anyone down for us to leave Oakshire on time. In fact, I was the late one. I had woken to Sariel creeping into the barn quietly before dawn. She hadn't said anything, just smiled in the predawn light as she straddled me, reaching back to guide me up her dress.

"I needed you before you left," she whispered as she sat back onto me. The barn was silent save for our quick breaths and the shift of hay.

We rode for a while. I kept a lookout for a bridge we needed to cross before making our way south to the city of Trinth, which sat on Eatherton Bay.

Vorga turned to me. "When I was a girl, my mother, my adoptive mother... she taught me to hide parts of me. To keep me safe. We lived in an area that wasn't as, welcoming, as Sariel is."

"Do the people of Oakshire give you any trouble?" I knew we were in the Midlands, where there were larger human populations. I suppose a life of people moving out of my way made me forget about these things.

I've traveled with orcs, with kobolds, with many number of species. Make no mistake, I'm not perfect. I have my own hangups. Blue mages are among them. Though I've known plenty of fine casters. There were times where Vorga lived in my mind as nothing more than a shy, bookish girl with green skin. Not a *greenskin*. It was ignorant of me to think every other person saw things that way. I had known a half-elf exiled from his people, and I saw how he struggled among either race. Too much of one, never enough of the other.

"You didn't grow up among the tribes?" I asked. We had never spoken about her upbringing before. Not everybody has a happy childhood. Sometimes people moved to become new people, start somewhere fresh.

"I was adopted. By a teacher in a town not very far from Oakshire. She was a single woman. My mother was a half-orc who mated with an orc. She lived among the realm, but told me my father had been of the Storm Brawler clan. They met for a single night... and she fell ill after I was two."

"I'm sorry," I said. It made me reel inside, thinking of her as a small child, wondering where her mother had gone to.

"It's okay. My mom, the woman who adopted me, was a wonderful person. She taught the entire town. I was small enough to pass for a half-orc, but eventually I left after she died. I just couldn't really stand being around that empty house. She had another son, grown, who came and told me I needed to leave while he sold everything."

I kept driving the wagon, not wanting to disrupt her. To prod her forward for more information or to hold her back if she wanted to share more.

Vorga's voice took a faraway sound, "He wouldn't even let me keep any of her books... he sold them for pennies. Last I heard, he was flat broke."

"Good," I said and turned the cart around a giant rock in the road. "Hope he suffers, the little weasel."

"I don't," Vorga murmured, watching the road and hills beyond.

Maybe that's why I was so drawn to her. My answer to such a sad story involved salving the wounds of her soul with a little breaking and entering and some bodily harm.

Yet here she was, not wishing harm on anyone. I had seen how strongly she had stood against that minotaur. The fire in her eyes. Not because she was brave, or had a chip on her shoulder, or had runes put inside her bones long ago by outlawed warlock surgeons. Because taking the firewood had been wrong, and she wouldn't stand for it.

"Here we go," I yelled to my traveling crew. Brim and Elina perked up from the back. I had my gold hidden in several places on my body and within the wagon panels from prying fingers and eyes. What I expected to buy would be expensive.

As far as cities went, Trinth was small. Without the port, it would be little bigger than Oakshire. I knew these small hamlets, these rolling hills. Some people were indentured, working as villein's their entire lives. Asking permission to marry, to bury their dead.

Here in the Midlands, it was a dying practice, but not dead. In some parts of the realms, you called them serfs or indentured servants. What's a man who isn't free to do as he wishes? A convict, a conscript, or a slave. The words mean the same thing, the job duties differ is all.

"Davik, have you thought of what we talked about?" Elina called from the back.

"Eh," I said, taking a page from Karley.

Vorga turned to look, not understanding.

"The minotaur asked for his horns. He was very upset," Elina explained.

I noticed Brim was exceptionally quiet when the subject of the horned beast came up.

"What happens without them?" Vorga asked.

"He'll be an outcast among his people. Likely even as a laborer or a hand for hire, he'll walk in shame. Destitute. It is not far from an orc losing their tusks, Vorga."

Vorga was staring at me, eyes pleading. I glanced over.

"I already gave them back!"

"Did he?" Vorga turned around.

"He did," Elina confirmed.

"What, I need a witness now?" I asked.

"So, what is the issue?" Vorga asked.

"Tell her, Davik."

"You tell her," I said, eyes on the road.

Silence and the sound of a wagon on a bad road was all we heard until I finally broke.

"He wants to work off a debt to me."

"The minotaur?" Vorga asked.

"The minotaur," I said.

"Are you going to let him?" Vorga asked.

"No," I said. "He tried to kill me. He was going to hurt you."

"Davik," her voice slid into my ear again. Beautiful, innocent Vorga. Who never wished a bad thing upon anyone.

I glanced over. "Maybe I'll help him find something. Something **outside** of town."

She sat back, smiling to herself. A wisp of black hair trailing down her face before the breeze moved it away. Brown freckles on green skin.

"Maybe," I repeated.

I was surrounded by too many good people. They always wanted to do the right thing, the kind thing. The soft thing.

"What's that racket?" Elina asked as we hit another bump. The swords and breastplates I had tied under the wagon, above the axles, were rattling from the cart. Brim had crawled under the wagon to help me hide them.

"Probably the axles."

"Axles," Brim echoed.

"Exactly."

We made good time. Or we were until Elina and Vorga declared we were stopping for lunch.

"Why do we have to stop?" I asked. "Can't you eat while we move?"

"Davik, this is a vacation." Elina shook her head.

"This is a trip to the hardware store," I corrected her.

"And the library." Vorga grinned.

I parked and took the chance to check Rober's horses. I inspected their hooves, searching for fractures or any sign the distance was getting to them.

We sat and ate bread and cheese sandwiches that Tyra had made for us.

"The girl can cook, that's for sure," I said.

Vorga laughed. "Sandwiches aren't cooking."

"You know what I mean."

Elina stretched out in her cleric robes, her plump thighs peeking out as she drew her dress back and felt the breeze on her skin.

"So Davik, aside from the hardware store for your secret project, and the library, for our little reader here, where do you want to go in Trinth?"

"Home," I said after swallowing my food. "Less time in a city, the better. Cutpurses, drunks, thieves."

"Well Davik, maybe for some people, that's what a city is. But you know, when things **change**, there are new exciting things. Some people go to a city for pleasure. To learn. To explore and grow." The halfling winked at me.

Sure they did. I had seen those who came to a city for pleasure, pumping away at back-alley doxies between the wine tents. But as I glanced around, I realized I was in stranger company than I had probably ever been. I've eaten as the guest of lords as well as captors, but those were the days of being a hired knife.

We were four people on a wagon, on our way to buy something to improve the tavern. Just common folk. No Darkshire here. No names and processions of reputations. We were travelers.

Still, it didn't sit right with me. In and out, a quick trip to the library. That was the plan. I'd have a hard enough time unloading the steel under the wagon. That would be after lengthy negotiations with Brim as translator.

"If we could stop at the Temple of the Mistress, I'd love to show you all around. The Baths of Flavor would be free for us, and we could enjoy ourselves." Elina munched on her sandwich.

"I don't think so, Elina. If you want to go check in with high command or whatever, please do. But this wagon leaves before sundown. If we have to make camp, we do it off the road, far from prying eyes."

Vorga rubbed the back of her slender neck. "A proper bath would be fabulous."

"I'm telling you, Davik, the bathhouses are unlike any you've ever seen," Elina said.

In my experience, bathhouses were just another name for brothels. I was already on edge bringing Vorga to the city. It was doubtful she had ever seen deep poverty or the sordidness a visit to a port provided.

"I'm not sure," I said.

"It's completely safe, Davik. And more than that, it would be a treat for all."

"No bath," Brim grumbled. "Friends to visit."

"Of course," Elina patted his leg, which Brim looked like he'd rather have lit on fire. "We'll make sure you get time to visit your friends."

"What do you think, Davik?" Vorga asked.

"I don't think it's a good idea. If something happens and I'm on the opposite side..." I began.

Elina laughed. "Davik, you misunderstand. These are private baths. The Temple of the Mistress is a business as well as a faith. It provides environments for travelers and lovers to relax in private."

"Maybe," I said. I still wasn't sure. It might sound like an enticing idea, getting these ladies into a hot bath. But if you let your guard down a little, it's enough for regret to slip in.

"What's your secret project?" Vorga asked.

Even Brim looked interested beyond what I had told him. I sighed and sat back, pulling on the jug of water, enjoying the chance to keep them in suspense.

"Okay, fine." I leaned forward again. "It came to me while I was carrying water to Tyra's kitchen."

Brim made a rude noise.

"Sorry, *the* kitchen. On my first day when I saw the water pump to that little shower outside, Sariel told me how expensive it had been. But it's pretty simple. I've seen boilers that run on firewood before, but that would just mean we're constantly splitting wood."

"I don't think I get it," Vorga said.

"Well, hold on," I continued. "I've seen gnomish glow-stones before. I knew a mercenary once who did a lot of work up north in the cold. He used to break them apart into small pieces and keep them in his pockets. I came with him one time to help him out. One of our party had fallen into the river, under the ice. We got him out, but he was going to die. But this swordsman cracked open one cask of freshwater we had and told us to put him in it. We thought he was crazy."

"What happened?" Elina asked. She crawled forward, cleavage drooping below her. Even Vorga watched her.

"We put him in. Then he took a hammer and broke these big glowstones apart and put them inside. Within minutes, the water heated, it heated so much steam was pouring off of it. It saved him."

"So you're going to build a hot water bath?" Vorga asked.

I smiled. "I'm going to build a hot water heater and pipe it into the tavern. Imagine hot water running parallel to cold anytime you need it. How many travelers would come just for the marvel of it? Hot water in their room, in their basins."

"Wow," Vorga said. "That would be amazing. There's not even water upstairs. Could you put it in at our house?"

"It would be a separate system, but in time, maybe." I grinned.

"Well then, it's settled," Elina said. "You have to see the baths at the temple. It's your duty as a fledgling engineer."

"It'll be research," Vorga agreed.

Even Brim nodded.

"What's your cargo?" the guard asked.

We were moving through the line on the bridge to Trinth. The city was a slow-moving organism, with several spires reaching up to the sky. On the east bank, the port processed a succession of ships and cargo, with tax inspectors and long-shoremen moving steadily. Cargo swung on ropes like dead men, waiting for someone to claim them.

"No cargo, here to buy supplies," I said as he patted me down. Our wagon had been stopped like all the others.

"Supplies for what?"

"A tavern. Brews, metal, piping." I cast a glance back at the wagon. The search was much more thorough than I had expected. On the side of the entrance to the city walls were large ordnances. Apparently, someone had appointed a new sheriff for the city.

BY ORDER OF SHERIFF RODOLF SEARLUS THERE ARE NO WEAPONS ALLOWED IN TRINTH. ALL MUST BE SURRENDERED TO THE CITY GUARD.

RANSOMS AND BAIL CAN BE PAID TO JAILOR BELLICK IN THE CITY CENTER

CREDIT AND TRADE NOT ACCEPTED

That sign gave me genuine worry. If I had seen it earlier, I would have made everyone stay outside the city and I would have headed in alone.

Sheriffs are little more than brigands, high rising men who isolate and attack their political enemies. If you're a farmer, or a villein who has something they want, they will declare charges against you.

Jailors are worse. Most towns and counties don't have constables, let alone sheriffs. The jailor is the real law, and that law is the power to hurt you. They'll grab anyone and ransom their bail. They torture false confessions on behalf of anyone to get a servant or a common man to speak false words against their target. By the time an actual constable or lord comes to examine what happened, you're already hanging from a gibbet.

You'd think jails are full of thieves and the poor. They're full of thieves alright, but they just happen to work there. I've seen jailors turn away hardened criminals with literal blood on their hands because they didn't have enough money for them to extort. They like pretty girls, they like soft lords with too many fingernails.

I knew. I knew all too well. And if the sign posting was showcasing a new sheriff and his jailor so prominently, giving directions in town of where to pay bribes and fines, it was a full-time business. This cargo search was a way to mark you so you could be arrested inside the city. There wasn't enough to warrant eyes on me, but if those weapons were confiscated, then I wouldn't have enough gold to buy what I needed.

But I also knew one thing for certain.

The weapons would be worth a fortune inside.

I could surrender them now, or I could try to get them within the walls.

"Just supplies huh? What's the name of the tavern?"

"It doesn't have a name yet," I answered him. I smiled at the girls and Brim behind me, waiting to be searched. "Do you know who I pay this to?"

"Huh?" the gruff guard looked up at me. I had palmed several silver coins from my stash. I had been tempted to show some gold, but gold often fuels greed and sometimes silver sates it.

I showed him four coins between my fingers. "I was here last time, before this new sheriff. But my wagon had been too heavy. They let me go, telling me to pay a fine next time I came. I think I give this to you?"

There's a proper approach when it comes to producing a bribe. It's a balancing act. A knowing demeanor with a feigned innocence. For a split second, you and the person you're trying to payoff have to become part of a story that exists just for that moment. That it's the most natural thing in the world for them to take the money.

But the most important part is that it's not your money, it's **their** money and you're just helping them find it.

"Too heavy..." The guard glanced around.

The moment hung in the air, and then that beautiful sight of his hand swinging low where no one could see it.

"Yeah, I remember you. Was wondering when you'd come back."

I slid the coins into his hand. Quantity of coin has as much impact as the quality. Let someone feel the weight of currency, count the coins with their fingers. Four silvers were likely a month's wage.

Had I known before coming this needed to happen, I would have found out where the guards drank and began a loud lamentation about trying to get medicine into the city. Medicine is a pleasant lie. When you're asking someone to do something nefarious, it's best to let them believe they're a hero.

"Would love to get in quickly. I have an appointment to keep. Wagon needs to be loaded," I explained.

"Mmm," the guard slid the coins into his belt pouch and eyed me for a moment. Then he glanced over at the empty cart. Whatever I was bringing in, and it was definitely something, it wasn't a large amount.

"Rask, get down and take a look at that damn wagon behind you. Bastard's been here too many times this season."

"Aye boss." the younger guard climbed down from our cart.

"In you go," he said. As I passed him, he grabbed my forearm. "No trouble, you hear?" He held out a small scrap of paper stamped with the Trinth coat of arms.

"Never," I said. I cocked my head and motioned to the group. "Back on everyone."

We passed through the gate. The city of Trinth was cobblestoned streets and businesses and shops. In the distance, you could hear hammers and the bickering of vendors. The horns of ships blowing, urging the harbormaster to let them unload.

"Did we have to pay to get inside?" Vorga asked.

"Kind of," I said, steering the wagon.

"Here," Vorga reached into the pocket of her dress and drew out a little pouch on a string. "Let me."

I laughed. "Save your money. It's fine."

~

"WHAT'S THE PROBLEM?" I asked Brim. I kept turning around, monitoring Vorga and Elina, who were browsing the stalls nearby.

Brim ignored me. Three other gnomish engineers surrounded him and spoke rapidly. The conversation rolled back and forth, morphing from calm discussion to an all-out shouting contest.

"These look nice," Vorga said from behind me. I spun again, watching her inspect a collection of shawls.

Finally, my so-called negotiator and interpreter waved me into the huddle.

"Well?"

Brim explained, "They can do. But they say, tank is too big to heat water, move water, refill. They want to propose something else."

I was stunned. I had never heard Brim speak this much.

One of the gnomish engineers nodded and motioned to a table in his tent. I peered over, seeing schematics that I had crudely drawn up, quickly crossed out and drawn over expertly.

"Tank too big," the engineer explained. "Water heat, leave, water reheat, leave. Too much energy."

I nodded, understanding.

"Glowstone, slow. Slow, understand, yes?" The engineer pointed to the drawing and shook his head. "Nice to warm. Not good for hot."

I frowned. "So what, then?"

The engineer drew a smaller tank, more like a backpack than the large boiler I had envisioned. "Not heat water, then leave. Water leave, heated as leave. Hotter, faster." He drew a long pipe running from the area in the back to the tavern.

"With what?" I asked.

"Pyrocrystals." Thick eyebrows raised, hoping I understood.

"Pyrocrystals?" I asked. "Explosives?"

The engineer nodded. Then scratched a thick hunk of gold that served as his earring. "No bang. Not powder, full crystals." He switched to gnomish and drew quickly all over the map and tavern. In moments, there were detailed schematics and drawings showing how it would work.

"Heat, heat, yes?" The engineer pointed to the small box.

"Heat," I repeated.

"Water still." he closed his fist. "Water on, crystal on. Crystal on..." he searched for the word and jabbered to Brim.

"Crystal on, push," Brim said.

"Push?" I asked.

Four heads nodded. The engineer tapped the small backpack and drew a tank next to it, but elevated off the ground.

"Fall, water fall."

"Hand pump?" I asked and tapped on one faucet in the schematic. I had envisioned a hot water reservoir that sat there, and a pipe from the tavern would use a pump-handle to bring it forth into a bucket.

"**No**," four voices said in unison.

"Pressure," Brim repeated.

The engineer told his friend to grab something, and they brought a faucet out to me.

"Yes, I know. You pump, it goes to the pipe, you turn, it comes out."

"No pump," Brim barked.

They all nodded.

I picked up the faucet, examining. "Magic?"

There's very little more demeaning than four gnomes laughing at you as if you just asked why the sky is blue.

In the end, they sketched out the new system and seemed more excited by the prospect than I did. I had a feeling this was a new type of project they would sell repeatedly.

"Forty," Brim told me finally.

"Forty gold pieces?" I asked.

He nodded, gravely.

"Brim, it's too much. I don't need it installed. Just get the stones from them or the crystals or whatever. We'll do it ourselves."

He shook his head. *Too complex. You cannot build, ugly-man.*

"You know, I'm not sure why I brought you here. They speak better Common than you do. You're supposed to negotiate, Brim. Not rob me."

Brim chewed his beard. He seemed different around his own people. He had a new energy.

How much do you have, ugly-man?

"I have twenty-one," I said. I had figured it would be close enough.

Brim turned back to the waiting gnomes, who were more interested in the schematics than anything. They chattered back and forth.

"Is everything okay?"

"What?" I turned. Vorga had come up right behind me. "Oh yes, absolutely."

Brim waved to me. He made a slight stabbing motion and beckoned me to bring the weapons and armor inside the bundle at my feet. Something I didn't want Vorga or Elina to see the contents of.

"Hey listen, why don't you two head down to the vendor

down there? With the pecan clusters." I fished five coppers out of my pocket and handed them to her. "Grab us some, and then we'll make our way to the temple, alright?"

Vorga's eyes drifted to the sack. But she didn't press.

"Alright, just, don't be long?"

"We'll be right there," I promised.

Once she walked off, I brought the steel into the tent and the gnomes shut the flap behind us. The air took on that quiet hush of illicit transactions.

I pulled out the armor and weaponry. The spears had been too long to bring. The gnomes inspected it all, murmuring to themselves. I saw their eyes light up at the sight of the steel breastplate. This was no common iron trinket.

"Twenty gold," the lead engineer said.

The price of weapons was high, but the steel alone in the breastplate made it worth more than the entire lot.

"Forty."

Brim nodded at my number. He knew a low-ball offer.

"Twenty-five."

Press him.

"Thirty-five, including delivery and installation."

The engineer shook his head. The motion was native to every pawnshop and hawker who just couldn't cut you a deal, no matter how much they liked you.

"Twenty-five," he repeated.

That would leave me with plenty of gold, but I was already thinking about the tavern, the upgrades we could give it.

"Thirty, installation and delivery."

Brim looked over at them and crossed his arms.

They'll bite, ugly-man. They want the breastplate.

The engineer considered it. Then he asked Brim something in Gnomish. They bickered for a moment. Then the deal was struck.

"Thirty gold," the engineer motioned to the steel.

"Deal," I said.

"One week," the engineer held out his hand, and I gave him ten of my twenty-one gold pieces. That made the system forty, and I had eleven gold left over. A hefty sum for a common man. An amount I used to not even get out of bed for when my skills were for hire.

As we walked off, my purse lighter, I asked Brim, "Is this going to work? Or did I just piss all that money away?"

"Will work," Brim nodded. He kept peering around the streets as we went. Seeking something.

Ahead of us, Vorga and Elina waved and called us over. They were watching a juggling musician and eating pecan clusters.

I saw a very slim half-elf male walk by. He exchanged glances with Brim over thin glasses. Then he kept walking, but slower.

"You want to go visit your friends now?" I asked him.

Brim glanced up at me, as if gauging if I was going to give him hell or think any different of him for going to indulge himself. But I had no such reservations. Maybe if the little bastard visited friends more often, he wouldn't be such a pain in my ass.

"Library," Brim said.

"Yeah, this afternoon. See you there. Or just meet us at the stables."

Brim walked off to whatever part of town he needed to go. To be honest, I felt sorry for him.

"You guys ready?" I asked, putting my hands over both the girls.

"Mmm, you have to try one of these." Vorga raised a pecan cluster to me in a little wax paper. I leaned down and bit.

As I did, I saw an old face I used to travel with. He was half-drunk. Wearing a cowl and hood.

Hello Rushe.

I ignored him, silently letting him know not to approach me. Rushe was a strong burglar, good with locks and traps and he had a penchant for fine clothing that always attracted attention. From the sight of him, it looked like that vice had fallen by the wayside. He also had an eye for noblemen's wives, spurring us to leave certain towns and cities years ago under cover of darkness.

Once, before we parted ways, he had been cornered by the guards of a lord as he attempted to leave the bedchambers of the man's wife once too often. When he hadn't shown up at camp that night, the argument among the crew had been to leave. He had gotten drunk, they said, or taken off. But I had a feeling something was truly wrong, and could only convince one person to come with me.

We got there in time. Rushe had been hanging by his wrists, and they were boiling several pots in the courtyard for an agonizing end. He was a selfish bastard. We had no great love for one another then or later. But I still remembered the look on his face as Rayleth and I had walked into the courtyard, hands on our weapons.

Surprise. Surprise that anyone had bothered to come for him.

We covered that courtyard with blood and we couldn't do business in those lands ever again. They had broken one of his hands with a mallet, and it took our cleric weeks to set it right. The group at the time had been upset at this, and no one more than Rushe had agreed that it hadn't been worth it to save his hide.

But Rayleth, that brooding elf-in-exile, his right ear a chewed and scarred massacre, had been the one to quiet them.

Darkshire went back for him. The villain you all scoff at but have no issue when his name opens doors normally closed to us. I'll remember your complaints the next time one of you is captured.

Rushe glanced up at me, a standard scan, likely looking for someone to pickpocket. I turned away, leaning close to Elina. I felt him stutter his walk for a moment, like he was seeing a ghost. I saw him mouth the words *Darkshire?*

Hiding was just my natural instinct for some reason. I had traveled with Rushe for a good amount of time. There was no bad blood. Maybe I didn't want his business to mingle with mine. Or maybe I didn't want any part of my past to touch what I held in my arms at the present.

I didn't look back.

CHAPTER
EIGHTEEN

The Temple of the Mistress proved to be a very welcoming place. When we walked in I saw multiple smiling couples walking out. The beauty of the acolytes and the priestesses would make any man reconsider his faith of choice.

"Welcome, Cleric of Oakshire." A red-haired woman came from behind the counter and embraced Elina. When they broke their embrace, she looked at a bracelet on Elina's wrist and her eyes went wide. "You bound? You told me there was so much trouble in the town finding—"

Elina whispered something I didn't catch. Then the woman looked at me. "Ah, I see now."

Elina smiled. The human woman was a foot and a half taller than her. "Davik, Vorga, this is Kindra. We were acolytes together."

"Nice to meet you," I said.

Vorga smiled shyly.

"Do you want to speak with her?" Kindra asked Elina.

"Is she in?"

"She is. She'd be delighted to see you. And hear of this... new development."

Elina turned to us. "Vorga, why don't you come with me? I'd love to introduce you to the High Cleric of the Mistress. Davik, it's ladies only in the schola areas. Why don't you start at the baths and we'll join you shortly?"

I went closer to Elina. The entire building was clean, an aesthetic of water pouring on stone, mimicked and mirrored by dozens of fountains.

"Vorga will be safe," Elina told me before I even asked. "They may not look it, but monks and acolytes of the Mistress are no pushovers. We'll be fine. Just go, enjoy yourself. They don't eat people."

"Alright," I said.

"I'll guide you," Kindra said in a low, sultry voice. She nodded to another acolyte who took her place at the welcoming area of the temple.

Her dress was one layer, and soft like Elina's. Whatever fabric it was, it was the mark of their order. I saw her wrists were bare. Elina wore bracelets. Her hips shifted, the silk of the cloth rolling over her cheeks as she led me.

We went down a long walkway. To the right and left were differing pools of water. Some were different colors. Some had different scents. I saw two naked older women shriek as they plunged into a pool of water so cold there were bits of ice floating on top.

A cleric walked by. The entire place vibrated with magic.

"Many come from all over, to pay for an afternoon in the baths. Young brides before their weddings. Grooms as well. Travelers, lovers, lords with little to do."

"Seems nice," I said.

It was more than nice. It was somewhere between luxury and prayer. There were areas where people were in meditation or praying before small altars of the Mistress. Right next to nude individuals in the pools.

"The men's baths are upstairs. But up ahead is a private bath for travelers and... friends to enjoy."

Kindra bowed slightly, pulling a key from a necklace that hung between her cleavage. She unlocked a tall door in a perpendicular hallway of six more.

"Please, enter."

I walked past her. The walls were an amber-pink stone. In the little alcove, the passageway beyond led to a wider room, with lounging seats and a love sofa with a violet canopy all situated around a wide bathing pool, with steam pouring off of it as it swirled.

"The privacy salts are there," Kindra pointed to a small stand of clean white towels. There were several containers to add to the pool. "Do you wish me to add them?"

"Sure," I said. Kindra bent and poured the salts into the water.

"How is it heated?" I asked. Now a novice in fluid dynamics and plumbing.

"By spell, of course. There are no hot springs nearby. Please, your clothes." Kindra motioned to a stand for me to put them on. "You must wash before bathing."

She made no motion to leave, so I began undressing.

As I put my boots and shirt and socks under the clothing rack, I undid my belt and looked at her.

"Do you need something?"

"Elina informed me you might like me to shave you."

"Shave me?" I asked.

Kindra glanced down at my groin. "We offer a variety of treatments here. You have never felt the razor or the waxing strip?"

"I'm alright," I said. "I... just shaved recently."

Kindra bit her lip, her eyes sliding over my chest. "I'd offer more... but I am unbound. And I don't seek to be an acolyte forever."

"Makes absolute sense," I said, wondering what she was talking about. "Thanks."

"Let me assist you." She walked forward, eyes glued to my belt.

"I have it, thank—" before I could finish, her hands unbuttoned my pants. Red lacquered nails dug over my hips while she knelt in front of me.

"Oh hells," I sighed.

Kindra stared as my pants drew down, my cock finally freed and flopping in front of her face. Her reaction was surprise, and then she bit her lip again, transfixed, tugging me out of my pants.

"How blessed. The Mistress smiles upon Elina for such a first-time binding."

"Thank you for the help." I stepped out of my pants. "And the Mistress."

At any other point in my life, I would've had this acolyte wrapped around me and pressed against the wall. But the last thing I wanted at that moment was for Vorga to come in and see such a thing. If Vorga hadn't been with us... maybe.

"Is there anything else?" Kindra looked up at me.

They might be a while...

"Nothing else, thank you," I replied.

Kindra stood and made a slight bow. Glancing pointedly at my rising cock again, then she turned and left me to shower.

As I did, taking advantage of the benefits of cold water and hurrying before the girls returned, I realized I may have just avoided an enormous mistake. Elina was friendly to Kinda, but that didn't mean they were friends. She was bound to me, devoted. You never know someone's history.

The "bath" or pool of water was steaming hot. Almost fifteen feet in diameter. I walked into it, naked, treading down the little stone steps. The privacy salts that Kindra had thrown in turned it milky white, like enchanted waters from a fairy tale.

"That's it," I groaned to myself and submerged in the water. They had crafted steps to sit on and I leaned back in the swirling waters, the heat soaking into my bones, warming the knots in my muscles.

My mind drifted. To Sariel this morning in the barn. To Elina the other day in the woods. I had the strange sense that things were good. The heating system would be delivered in a week, which had been better than I hoped. Nobody but Brim saw the arms and armor I bartered. I still had eleven gold pieces.

"Thanks, Sheriff Searlus," I said aloud. Every smuggler loves laws, because they drive up the price of his illicit cargo.

I kicked my legs out and sank deeper, letting the water come to my mouth line. Heat billowed all around me, slowing my thoughts. In my mind's eye I saw Sariel, her beautiful face and smile, how she had shuddered while I took her there in the cart that loving morning.

The feelings I had for her differed from anything I had ever felt. Maybe that's what life should feel like. Like slow mornings and warm afternoons, like pancakes around a table where people smiled at one another. Like her blonde gold hair, spilling like a river in my arms. Any woman I had been with before this had been a relationship of the finest toxicity. It wasn't what we did together, but what we did to each other that had defined it.

Somewhere along the way, I had diverted from the path. Become a creature, a tyrant of lust instead of a simple follower of love. Through Elina, through Sariel, it was like I was picking up where I left off so many years ago. When I was near Sariel, or Vorga, I felt like the scars in my body weren't there. Sometimes I looked at all the girls in the tavern and regretted so many years lost to a life of violence.

I think about you with her. Sariel's words came back to me. *I shouldn't, but it makes a fire in me.*

She had told me that after I returned from visiting the minotaur with Elina. That night in her office when we fucked on her desk. Sariel whispered she loved me and asked me to tell her about being with Elina.

The door creaked. I opened my eyes as Elina and Vorga walked in. My breath caught in my chest at the sight of them. Vorga wore a bathing shift, tight grey silk that ended at her upper thighs. Elina was wearing only a towel.

"How's the water?" Elina called out.

"Wonderful," I murmured. "Come on in, I'll shut my eyes."

Elina laughed. "No need." She walked forward and dropped her towel.

Blessed indeed.

Elina's short stature emphasized everything womanly about her. Her heel to her calf, to her wide hips like rolling hills. Amber eyes, dark skin, her heavy breasts spread as her towel came away.

She watched me watching her and walked slowly. In the corner of the room, rocks sat in a heating contraption and she poured a ladle of water on them.

Steam billowed off the stones, filling the air with haze.

Elina turned and walked over to the pool entrance. Her quim was bare now. She stepped into the waters slowly.

"Oh, that's nice. Vorga, you have to come feel this." Elina's nude form disappeared as she stepped into the bottom of the pool. She laughed and kicked up and swam over to me. "Definitely not halfling sized."

Vorga turned in her bathing shift. She put her long, dark hair up in a bun and smiled at me shyly.

"She's beautiful, isn't she?" Elina murmured, sitting cross-legged on the step close to me.

I didn't respond.

Vorga walked forward, her skin wet from the steam. The bathing shift billowed as she walked, showing her figure. Her high perky breasts, the length of her legs and slow straddle of her hips. My cock stiffened under the water, and I was glad for the privacy salts.

"It's so hot," her little voice seemed to mix with the haze as she slid a single bare foot in. I shut my eyes as she entered the water.

"Too hot for me already," Elina groaned and stood on the bathing step. She drew herself halfway out of the water to sit on the edge. Water dripped from her breasts to her thick thighs.

Maybe the baths had been a grand idea.

"Where's the step?" Vorga whispered, feeling her way around.

"Here," I said and took her hand. She gripped mine, and I pulled her, floating in the water towards me. For a moment, I cradled her in my arms, carrying her. Her bathing shift gripped her flesh when I raised her, giving me a tantalizing view of her body. I sat her down near me.

"Thank you," Vorga grinned. She looked over at Elina, seemingly unbothered by her nudity. "It feels... funny, Elina."

"The water?" I asked.

Vorga blushed and grinned even wider.

"We met with my High Cleric. In the salon... we were shaved and waxed while we waited."

Shaved...

"Did you get shaved too, Davik?" Vorga asked.

"I, uh, no. No I did not."

"It feels good!" Elina said. "You'll see."

"The High Cleric was a very... interesting woman." Vorga leaned back as the waters lapped at her chest. Had there ever been such a beautiful orc? At that moment, I wanted to fill her room with books, where she could sit and read and just lose herself.

"She's very perceptive," Elina agreed. "She gave Vorga some good advice."

Vorga chuckled, a hint of her orcish bloodline adding depth to the rumble in her chest. "A bit strange. She said women need to touch themselves more. Not hide so much."

"Right," I said.

Elina stood and turned to us, waving her hips back and forth. "See, it looks nice."

Vorga laughed. "It feels strange, Elina. To be so bare. I feel... sensitive."

Elina slid back into the water and swam over, sitting next to Vorga. "Don't be so coy. I know there's all those nasty tales you read about in your legends. You play the prude, but do you ever hear what she reads, Davik? Mythology is just smut! All the High Cleric said was Vorga needed to embrace who she was."

Vorga shook her head, shutting her eyes and relaxing. "You human-kind. All you see is sex. I'm a simple girl. A most-orc."

"Davik, would you put more steam on? It's already starting to thin." Elina grinned wickedly.

This was the spiritual advisor of Oakshire.

"I think we have enough."

Vorga didn't open her eyes. "More *would* be nice."

I shook my head and stood, the water still covering me. Stepping carefully by them, Vorga was seated by the steps with her eyes closed, and I tried not to budge her so she wouldn't look.

Of course, as soon as I rose out of the water right next to and above her, she had the perfect view of my half-engorged cock. Her eyes opened, and she blinked, staring right at it, mouth opening in surprise.

Onwards.

I exited the pool and walked over to the rocks. In situations like this, just push through. That's what I told myself. After another ladle, I waited until I calmed down a bit, and the steam billowed off the hissing stones until I turned back around.

Vorga was giggling with Elina, and I rolled my eyes. I didn't hear anything other than "Minotaur" and I stepped down into the pool opposite their side.

"Ah, that's wonderful. Steam helps loosen so much." Elina leaned back against the stone next to Vorga.

Vorga giggled, and her eyes shot over to me. "It does seem to help things grow."

Elina turned to her. "Do you think we need more?"

"You're out of luck," I said. "Show's over."

"I should've brought my purse," Vorga said. "I think you're supposed to tip performers."

"Very funny," I said and shut my eyes, sinking into the heat and water.

CHAPTER
NINETEEN

Whatever happened in the remainder of my life, Vorga's face upon entering the library of Trinth would be enough for me.

We walked into the building as several people were coming down the steps. They kept glancing at Vorga, which didn't bother me as much as it should have. This city wasn't the most multi-cultural. You had gnome areas, goblin areas, you had factions all tolerating one another. I chalked it up to standard tribalism in a city. If you dove deeply into the land owners of land plots in Trinth, you'd see humans ruled here and sought to contain new leaseholders to specific areas.

I suppose I never thought of an area as safe or not for depending on what species you were. When I traveled with people, it was almost never solely humans. But maybe one of the better benefits of the shadier side of life and adventuring was the only substances that mattered was gold and steel. The origins of anything else did not interest thieves.

"Look how big it is!" Vorga exclaimed as we entered the

building. Tall stone archways with oval wooden doors opened and spilled in the day's light.

Her noise brought a stern look from the human clerk as soon as we entered. Vorga smiled and covered her mouth. I was reminded of her on the wagon, covering her tusks, and it bothered me.

The three of us walked up to the counter.

"Hello," Vorga said.

"Shh," the man hissed.

"Sorry!" Vorga whispered, leaning close. "We're visitors from Oakshire. We'd love to look at the library."

"Book borrowing is for city citizens only," the clerk said. "Not outsiders."

Vorga's face fell, but Elina stepped forward. "That may be so, sir, but we're allowed to wander and read while here, correct? I lived in Trinth for a time during some training and used to visit here."

The man kept putting tomes away behind him.

There are people in this world, it may surprise you, who have never tasted a fine beating. They've missed out on the character building it brings. You find it in places of inherited power, in lords and their demonic offspring. In administrative pillars of bureaucracy. Existing to adhere to process and create more of the same.

The clerk turned and grabbed another tome. I felt the urge to reach out and lift him over the counter, but I let it go. I reminded myself that in this city, I was Davik, here to buy pipes and tour the sights. Just another traveler.

But seeing Vorga's face go from happy to disappointed, and now growing sadder and sadder with every moment, made me start running down the list of rational reasons to strike someone.

"Excuse me," Elina said politely again.

Now he stopped, making a show of turning and raising his eyebrow. He still didn't respond.

"We'd like to go inside and see the tomes and stacks."

He gave Elina one of those looks that wondered what this question had to do with him.

"Preferably the novels," Vorga chimed in, trying to lighten the mood of the man.

He exaggeratedly scanned the surroundings, as if putting on a pantomime.

"Do I look like a library guard? Go in, if that's your wish."

I rubbed the pressure growing between my eyes. It's too easy to lash out, it's too easy to break things and intimidate. To play the big hero, keeping Vorga's feeling safe.

Elina looked at me, pleading with me to bite my tongue.

"We'll go in then," Vorga said.

We turned and walked through the open passageway to the vast library beyond.

"Please, remember, no borrowing. There aren't any *greenspeak* books here... since none have yet to be written."

I stopped walking for a moment, balling my fists.

"Davik," Elina whispered.

I walked forward and put my arm around Vorga. "Let's go. These novels have to be somewhere, huh?"

The library wasn't a vast ocean of books. It was a small lake of them. I'll be the first to admit my experience in libraries is limited to little, especially their intended usage. Even I was impressed. Not with the size, but with the function. The citizens of Trinth were sitting at tables, studying, reading for pleasure. The windows were tall on the walls, letting in the light. Glowstones lit the hanging chandeliers and modified candelabras.

More than a few people looked up at Vorga, plainly shocked to see a most-orc in their midst.

I needed to buy her a new dress; I reminded myself for the thousandth time. Something that really fit her well and expanded her selection. Only now did I notice how self-conscious she seemed. Glancing down at her gown. Likely comparing herself to the humans and elves and other species here. One man made a point to keep looking up from his book, clearing his throat, and sighing.

"Did you need something?"

He jerked around, surprised I had snuck up right behind him. I was leaning over the study table, one hand on his chair.

"Sorry, what?" he asked.

I kept my voice low. We were in a library, after all. "You keep looking at my friend. Did you need something?"

His mouth went tight, disgust plain on his face, and made a show of leering at my common clothing. That only made me grin over him. Far as I'm concerned, if there's no blood, it's clean laundry.

Then he saw the keloid scar, that circular brand on my hand of my conscription, and thought better of his witty retort.

"I'm trying to *read*."

"Shh." I leaned forward. "This is a library."

"Davik!" Elina whispered and grabbed my arm. "Over here, come look."

"Be right there," I said, still staring at the man.

He glowered at me, then turned back to his tomb.

Elina's hand slid around my arm and pulled me away. "Come now, Davik. You're doing well. We're all doing well. Let's not ruin it."

"Miserable little rat," I growled and looked back at him. "What's his problem?"

"Come on." Elina pulled me to the rear of the library. "Take a look, leave him."

"What?" I shook her hand off me.

"Look." She smiled and gestured with her head over to the rear of the library.

It was a sight I'd likely never forget. Vorga was smiling to herself, floating between the shelves. Pulling tomes, putting them back. Grabbing little novels and flipping through them.

"Look how happy she is," Elina said.

I did. She was blissful to watch. Just purely happy to be here, to be among all these books. She ran her fingers across the spines of every volume she passed.

"That's what the path out of the woods has, Davik. Moments like these. Simple, pure. Honest." Elina put her hand on the small of my back.

We stood there, watching her for some time. Like a fawn in the glade, not daring to move, not wanting to disturb her. Watching from afar. For a moment, it felt like a family outing.

We spent several hours in the library. Vorga sat and read an entire little novel, and Elina did as well.

"I wish we could borrow some of these! They let you take them home?" Vorga asked Elina after shutting the book.

"They do, but for city citizens. It's unfortunate, but they have to keep track of some of these and they are quite valuable. When I lived here, some of the higher clerics would borrow books from here." Elina laughed. "One of them once spilled something on a rare tome and it was quite the clamor. The library was threatening to ban all students and staff of the Temple."

"What ended up happening?" Vorga asked.

Elina smiled. "The High Cleric invited them for an afternoon to discuss. She said once they saw the beauty of the temple, they agreed coin to repair and copy the book again would suffice."

"Ladies," I said, eying the window and the falling light. "It's about time we head out."

"Oh, I wish we could stay longer." Vorga stood and closed her book.

"Maybe next time," I said.

"You know, Vorga, if you have some titles in mind, I could ask my friends who live here in the city to borrow them for us. Next time we're here. Then we'll just come back and give them the book when it's due. They'll *smuggle* them for us." Elina gave a mischievous wink.

Vorga's beautiful brown eyes lit up. "Really? That would be wonderful. Davik, do you think we could come back?"

"Absolutely," I answered. Though, I didn't relish the idea. The postings about the jailor and the new sheriff worried me. The looks that Vorga kept getting in this city also made me anxious. Nothing had happened, but people were fickle, petty, and prone to snap judgments.

Vorga put her book back, and we headed out the front.

"Thank you," Vorga said politely to the clerk at the front. He peered at her, watching her like a thief leaving his shop, and didn't say a thing.

I bit my tongue and followed the girls out front.

"Brim!" Vorga said when she saw our other quiet traveling companion. The psionic gnome sat on the steps of the library, a long pipe clenched between his teeth. He looked rather relaxed. I looked in the street and saw that same half-elf man we had seen earlier walking off, pretending very hard that he had some place to be.

"Did you visit your friends?" Elina asked, a twinkle in her eye. Elina was a beautiful soul. The more I got to know her, the more her outlook on the world shaped by her deity explained so much. I think deep down, Brim's secrecy made her sad. She likely tried to get him to embrace it, to be proud of it.

I knew little about gnome clans and houses and guilds of the world, other than that of a customer. I had only been adventuring with one, and she died so quickly we never got to know her much. Others were short-term professionals we had hired. Picked for a particular role. They always came as a specialist. Explosives, contraptions, information gathering.

But I knew they were a clannish lot. They had their own communities. It was hard to find one alone in the Midlands, as they were always among their journeymen or brothers or families.

I realized then, there on those steps, that Brim was someone I had viewed as a force of irritation, an anomaly, and not a person. He spoke Common, but answered in simple small words with a heavy accent. A psionic gnome was something I hadn't heard anything of, and he definitely was one. Maybe what drove him from his home, wherever that had been, had something to do with his gentleman caller walking off now.

But we're each entitled to our secrets, whether or not they're good for us. Not all of them come to light. Nor are they meant to.

Brim gave me a brief nod, the nod of two people who respected each other's mysteries.

As we made our way back to the stable to fetch the cart and horses, I realized he might have been the only person to pick up steel in my defense, where we didn't have a common goal or job at the end of it. There had been no chest of gold, no contract payment. No military banner we shared. He planted a meat fork in that trouper in an effort to save me.

If there wasn't too much cloud cover, we'd make it to Oakshire an hour after sundown. Maybe longer. I had promised Sariel that we'd be back in time to take the evening rush.

And I was eager to return to her arms. To shut those silver eyes with a kiss and feel her in my hands, like a dream I kept demanding it proved itself real.

The stableman tried to cheat me as I expected he would.

"One silver and six," he said with his hand out.

The girls were already climbing on the wagon. His stableboy held the horse's reins. The boy's face was so thin, the rags of an urchin wrapped around him.

"It was eight coppers for the afternoon." I stared at him.

The man shook his head. Some infection long ago had left his face pockmarked. "That's for one berth. Your wagon was so large, it took up two berths."

"No, it didn't," I said and reached into my pocket. "You know, if I was ugly, I'd endeavor not to match my behavior with my looks."

"Everything okay, Davik?" Elina called from the wagon, sensing something was wrong.

"Eight," I said again, staring the man down. This was his stable, his stall. But he was in here with me, and I wouldn't be fleeced like some bumpkin in the city for the first time. "Eight is what you said. Is a deal not a deal today?"

The man eyed me, then the girls, then me again.

"Eight coppers."

I handed it to him, in my other hand I held a silver coin. He eyed it greedily as I paid him. Then he took his frustration out on the boy holding the reins.

"Idiot! They're leaving! They'll need the reins, don't you think? How much do you fuck up on a first day?"

I walked near the young boy. He had all the signs of a street beggar. Thin, frail arms. Quick eyes, dark circles from staying up all night looking out for predators.

"How much he pay you for a day's work?"

"Half copper sir." The boy answered. Likely more than that. I respected anyone who could play for some gratuity.

"Find a new job," I told him and handed him a full silver coin. "Make sure he sees you run off."

The beggar boy's eyes opened in wonder, then he deftly pocketed the coin. He gave me a quick tip of an imaginary hat and rushed off.

"Fuck you, Hallasker!" he cried out as he jogged down the street.

"Damn urchin!" the stableman growled. Then he jumped to the side as I drove Rober's two carthorses out past him.

"You're bad, Davik." Vorga giggled behind me.

"Don't know what you mean." I snapped the reins.

As we rode out of the city, Brim in the front seat with me, the girls in the rear, I thought about Sariel and what she had said. That nobody leaves.

Elina was gorgeous, but Vorga was beautiful. Beautiful in a delicate way that you almost don't want to touch because you might leave your imprint. She was a woman grown, and I wanted her. I wanted her innocence and love and to taste that wondrous outlook in life. But more than that, I felt the duty to protect her. You can't protect someone from all the sharp edges of the world, but some, you can and you do.

No lovely most-orc girl deserved me as her first. Or her last. I've been called a myriad of things in my life. If you wrote them down on a list from most meaningful to least, the term *busboy* would be at the top. I enjoyed being part of something larger than myself, even if it was as simple as a little tavern in a road-stop town.

The guards waved us through the gates and I pushed the team forward, keen to make good time back to Oakshire. Maybe stop for a late lunch again while the girls gushed about Trinth.

I smiled as we rolled over the bridge.

"That's her!" A voice shouted behind us. I heard the clatter of boots and spun in my seat, yanking back on the horses absentmindedly.

282

I should've snapped the reins and raced off. Maybe we would've made it. Doubtful, with the crossbows on the parapet. I was too blind, too busy being the new man that went to cities for libraries and supplies instead of contracts of gold traded for blood.

A guard jumped up on the wagon. I raised my foot to boot him off over the side of the bridge into the waters far below, but Elina grabbed me.

"Davik, don't!"

The guard didn't notice. He pulled on the brake lever and the wagon lurched to a halt. The horses cried out as they skittered on the bridge.

That dreadful sound of banded mail and leather reverberated in the air, like a storm approaching. I turned and saw four crossbows pointed at us as the city guards fanned out. On the parapets above, several more trained their weapons on our party.

"What's the meaning of this?" I stood.

A portly man with the mass of someone who breaks faces in a tavern for sport strode towards us. His shirt was filthy, his smile gap-toothed and cruel.

"This her?" He growled behind him. Eyes falling on the back of our wagon.

I stood further, seeing who he was speaking to.

The clerk from the library walked up and nodded. Behind him, a tall middle-aged man with a long mustache and bored eyes watched. His rich tunic was held by a belt of gold banding at the waist.

"Is that her, Arvie?" The man in the fine apparel asked.

"That's her! The greenskin. She stole a book from the library. I saw it."

"She did no such thing!" Elina shouted. "We were permitted to enter!"

"You were not permitted to steal!" the clerk shouted back.

"Calm now." The man of authority walked forward on the heavy step of good shoes. A blazoned star sat on his chest. Sheriff Searlus raised his hands to calm the situation. I stared at the man who ran Trinth.

I hoped this was a common scam they ran. Accuse you of stealing the book. Something they do when you're on the way out of town. I had enough gold to solve this... if gold was what they were after.

I glanced around at the crossbows. The guards looked too skittish for my liking. I could've made noise on this bridge. Littered it with a few corpses, but my party was unarmored. And so was I. The only thing my enchanted bones would do is hold me up as bolts punched into my flesh.

I looked at Brim, and then at the brake lever, and he nodded knowingly.

I won't leave without them.

"She stole nothing," I said. "I was there. You can search the wagon. We have nothing but what we brought with us."

The sheriff sauntered over, propriety and superiority radiating from his demeanor. His nose was hooked like a hawk. "Let's see if that is the case," he said.

Two guards lowered their crossbows and climbed onto the wagon. A third motioned to Elina and Vorga. "Step down!"

Elina cast a glance back at me, begging me to keep this civil. Sariel, Elina, all that path of following what was right didn't seem to be working at this moment.

Brim slid closer to me. Readying to take the reins when needed.

"The cleric has nothing," the guard called out after inspecting Elina and her bag.

"Search the other one," the clerk barked. "She's the one who stole."

"I didn't!" Vorga cried out. The fear in her voice set every hair on my neck upright. I gripped the wagon and climbed down slowly, approaching Sheriff Searlus with my hands up.

"Sir, it's a mistake. The girl stole nothing."

He held a gloved hand up to silence me. Everyone watched as the Vorga emptied her pockets. The jailor walked up, fat and jiggling, a cruel smile on his face.

"Where's your bag?"

"There," Vorga muttered, pointing to her satchel.

"Hey!" Elina shouted, but the jailor emptied her belongings onto the bridge. Her smallclothes tumbled out, and a hairbrush, a small coinpurse, which he bent low to snatch up.

Then the book I had bought her in Oakshire.

"That's it!" the clerk cried out.

"Seize her," the sheriff ordered in a bored tone.

"Wait!" I shouted.

Everyone was moving. The guards moved in on Vorga and she backed up against the bridge. I was afraid she was going to resist and their clubs would come out.

"It's her book! She brought it!" I shouted.

"Orcs don't read!" the clerk spat.

"Even you can't be as foolish to believe such a thing!" Elina snapped, fire coming to her eyes.

The guards moved in to seize Vorga, and I caught the sheriff by the arm.

"Please sir, it's not stolen," I pleaded for him to listen. "Is there a fine? I'll..." I ripped my coinpurse from my belt. "What's the fine? She didn't steal, but if I can just take her home..."

"It's the price of the stolen book, plus a fine to the city." The Searlus turned to me, eyes amused now.

"The book costs ten silvers!" The clerk announced. "I want her prosecuted."

Prosecuted. A rich term. This was the courtroom right here,

and I knew whether they had found her little book or not, they would have captured her in this extortion scam.

"We can pay," I said, holding my money up. "Pay for the book. It's not stolen. I bought it in Oakshire. Just let us go."

The sheriff held out his gloved hand, soft riding leather, coated in fox-fur at the wrist.

"Give it here," he said.

I opened the pouch, fishing out the ten silvers.

"All of it," he said.

I handed the pouch over, and he emptied it into his hand.

"This clears any debts to the city," Sheriff Searlus intoned. He nodded to the jailor, Bellick, and I relaxed finally. Damn the money. If I could just get Vorga home...

"However, bail is another matter..." The sheriff smirked, trading smiles with the jailor. "That isn't my jurisdiction. The orc is in custody now. To bail her out, I'd say..."

"Sixty gold pieces," the jailor growled.

The blood went from my face. "The fine is paid, the book is returned..."

"Bail remains," the sheriff said. He turned from me and waved his hand. The clerk walked up to him, murmuring about the book and probably his cut of the proceeds. But he only received a cold shoulder and a single silver that the sheriff dropped onto the ground.

It was the brazenness of it that threw me.

I ran forward, grabbed the sheriff by the shoulder

"Do not touch me!" he pulled away.

"Please. Just let her go." I was ready to grovel.

The sheriff looked over at Vorga, now squirming in the arms of Jailor Bellick's men at the edge of the bridge. Below us was a hundred foot drop.

"You can fetch her when you bring her bail," the sheriff said and leaned in close. "Though I'd hurry if you prize the girl's teeth. I'd give it a day before the pliers come out. They don't call him Bellick Bloodgums for nothing."

He walked away. They readied the crossbows on us. Elina sobbed and I grabbed her shoulders.

"Get on the wagon," I ordered. I nodded to Brim, saying goodbye, and he knew what was about to happen.

Get her, ugly-man.

The cleric was babbling. "Davik, we'll go to the temple. We'll get her out."

"By tomorrow morning, they'll have done terrors to her, Elina. I'm sorry."

Elina looked confused as I sat her aboard the wagon.

"Sorry?" she asked.

I looked up at her and shut the wagon tailgate. All of a sudden, she knew.

"Davik..."

"Ride, and keep her safe," I breathed.

The cart started advancing, slowly.

"Wait!" I shouted, running towards the jail guards holding Vorga. Every movement tracked by crossbows. "I have jewels. They must be worth more than sixty. Please, let her go."

"Hold." the sheriff looked over from the gate, interest piqued.

The jailor Bellick Bloodgums grinned and nodded to one of his men. "Go see."

The guard squeezed past another wagon, coming towards me.

"Just give me," I said, taking another step closer, digging deep into my pockets.

"What's he have?" the library clerk asked.

"I have it here," I said, taking another step.

"Get on with it!" A guard snarled that held Vorga.

I walked another step closer. "Here it is."

I dug my fist out of my pocket. The guard leaned forward.

I could see her over his shoulder. My eyes locked onto Vorga as he bent to look. I gave her a little smile.

Sorry.

Sorry she had to see this.

I shifted my weight. An old lesson taught to me long ago, when the light dimmed in a forest and I had just started shaving. Shadowboxing next to a crackling fire. The eyes of a troop of thieves watching. The sharp intake of breaths. Pivot, twist, turn. Fists striking a pugilist's palms. *Pick up the earth under your shifting heel, pass it through your hand.* Leverage, speed, timing.

And before all that, a decision.

My hand never opened. I brought it skyward. My knuckles met bone, and the sharp crack of a palate splitting followed by a skyward spray of blood. The gurgle of a tongue bit nearly in half.

"Davik!" Vorga cried out.

There were five city guards near the sheriff. I saw four on the parapet with crossbows. Another four close enough to come running. Two of Bellick's men remained.

If I had a shield, maybe. Maybe I would've made it. But this wasn't a storybook Vorga read. This was life. Where men die from disease and cuts that get infected. Where the heaviest names get stabbed by some nobody in a tavern doorway.

I charged forward, not giving the crossbowmen a stationary target. "He's a liar!" the clerk screamed.

What a funny thing to say.

The guards pulled Vorga towards them. The city guards shot in from my right. I struck out with a fist, knocking a head back, replacing it with two feet flailing in the air and the rattle of armor tumbling to the ground.

I heard the click and whistle of crossbows being loosed.

Adrenaline throbbed through my temples. The world turned into that strange, slow place.

"Fire!" the sheriff shouted at his men. Though they were already firing at me.

Thunk! Thunk!

I sprinted to the men holding Vorga. They held their hands up, fearing I'd strike them down, but I wrenched her away with a spin.

"The wagon!" I shouted to her. If I could just get her close to our wagon, maybe they'd have a chance.

"Ride!" I shouted to Brim as I shouldered another city guard to the ground.

Someone grabbed my leg, stifling my momentum. I stumbled. Vorga sprawled onto the bridge as the wagon moved away. I looked down and couldn't believe my eyes.

"I've got him!" the clerk screamed. He was wrapped around my leg like a child.

I twisted, turning to stomp his skull into mush. Another city guard lunged at me with his sword. I bent forward, making as much space as I could as I tried to turn the blade. It missed its mark. The blade slid over my palm and cut my abdomen instead of planting in me.

"Get her!" I screamed to Elina and grabbed the man who had stabbed me.

The clerk was still on my leg, but now he reached up to my shirt, pulling me down.

Elina fell back in the wagon as bolts landed in front of her. One hit one of the horses, or near it, and it screamed. I saw Brim trying to pull back on the shrieking team of ponies. The clatter of their hooves reverberated on the long bridge.

"Kill him," the sheriff ordered. His voice was contempt. This entire ordeal was apparently beneath him.

Bellick and his two men rushed past me and grabbed Vorga

as a bolt sank into my left thigh. It's never the pierce with crossbows, it's the force of it hitting you. I felt it plunge through my flesh, the muscles in my legs splaying for a moment like the strings of an instrument cut loose.

Pain, old familiar pain, lanced up my body. I roared and head-butted the city guard, denting his faceplate and dropping him. Another bolt thudded beside me.

"Davik!" Vorga shrieked as they dragged her into the city gate. Her legs kicked in the air, her face was one of terror. She was reaching out for me. Not wanting me to die.

I hoisted the clerk up. "Come here, you little rat," I snarled into his face.

"No!" His eyes went wide.

I spun him and held him in front of me. My human shield. Bolt after bolt drilled into him and he cried out like a stuck pig. That sound gave me a sick pleasure as I barrelled forward. More men manned the parapets. A cavalry crossbow would've gone through both of us. But the shorter models don't didn't pack the same punch.

If I made it through the gate before it closed, I'd bring the fight inside the city. Shut the entrance behind me if I could. Maybe take Bellick hostage. Negotiate Vorga's safety in exchange for a date with a gibbet and a well-tied knot.

Bellick turned as I closed on him, eyes filled with panic. I snapped off a protruding bolthead out of the little librarian and stabbed him in the back of his shoulder.

"Gods dammit!" He screamed, reaching for the bolt. I grinned and pushed forward, the librarian taking another bolt to him, one that punched right through his collarbone and into my cheek.

It didn't matter. I was in that red place. The realm of exertion and suffering. I had broken lines of men. Broken armored infantry with a shield and a mace and a killing dirk. My eyes were wild as I charged past Bellick. Vorga was nearly in my arms again. She struggled to stop the two men from pulling her inside.

"Enough," the sheriff grunted behind me.

A mace snaked out. Enchanted. The heavy buzz of its spell-work inside the very metal. My runes told me. And then they whispered their failure to render that enchantment null. It hit like with the power of a demigod. My skull should've broken apart. Splattered across the gatehouse.

I stumbled to the side. The force so strong the world reeled. Sheriff Searlus's calm demeanor broke; he was shocked that I was alive as I turned, half-blind, to tear his jawbone from his mouth.

"Davik!" Vorga screamed. But not for herself. For me.

Another impact. I looked down as I was stopped in my tracks. A bolt planted into my side, right where I had been cut.

"Help me!" the librarian screamed at my feet where I had discarded him.

The sheriff swung again, the mace kissing me just in front of my right ear.

I fell to the ground. It had been a long time since I had been hit that hard. I'd seen flaming swords flicker to deadened steel when swung at me, and witch-cursed arrows shift into nothing but wood and bone when they landed on my shield. But his mace held something else—some higher enchantment. You could take over a city with it. You could become Sheriff of Trinth.

There was clamor everywhere, the parapets, the bridge, the voice of Elina on the wind as the wagon scurried away.

"Bring him down!" Searlus called up to the parapets as he stepped away, staring at the mace that had failed to slay me twice. "And get Bellick to the damned medicae! Put that orc in holding until she's processed and transfer her to the jail! Now kill this bastard!"

I heard the foot-stirrup and hand crank of crossbows being readied.

I looked up at Vorga. The world swimming in my failing vision. Her eyes pleaded with me. Urging me to survive.

Stars slid in my head, my eyes. Everything threatening to go dark.

I pushed myself up.

"Come here," I growled and grabbed the bleeding clerk. I broke off another bolthead and held it to his throat.

"Let her go," I called out to the sheriff.

He turned, eyebrow raised.

"Let her go and I'll walk to the gallows."

Sheriff Searlus sucked his teeth. Bellick screamed for my death.

I held the squirming clerk tight. "Just let her go," I repeated.

The sheriff looked at me, at the librarian. Then he waved to the guards on the parapets.

"Bring him down."

The clerk wailed in my arms. I held him close, the bolt against his neck.

"You're coming with me," I hissed and wrapped my arms around him. We backed up to the bridge.

"What? No!" He cried out. "No!"

"Davik!" Vorga shouted.

Four crossbows raised, training their aim on me.

I'm sorry.

I pulled him back with me. The bridge flew away from us as we plummeted down the cliff, to the deep chasm of the ravine a hundred feet below. It grew smaller and smaller. Like something taken, never to be given back.

CHAPTER
TWENTY

In a prison camp long ago, a group of men sat and starved to death. Across from them, a little sign that had the word *Darkshire* burned into it rattled against an iron railing. The only denizens within were dead men, frozen, staring at you when you looked.

"What's your name?" I said to the man in the cage near mine. He was a pikeman.

He might have told me. But my mind only had the space for suffering. No names. It would swallow them, hoping they were sustenance.

"You got friends? You got family?"

The young man shook his head. Eyes wide, staring at me in winter. He was afraid of me. Afraid of the talking skeleton. That he would look like this soon.

"Have you tried it?" the young man asked me.

"Tried what?"

He looked over to Darkshire. The mound of bodies not even given burial or a ditch. A taunt. I'd seen some take the trip to Darkshire. I didn't look. But I couldn't not hear it. It wasn't just the sound of them eating. It was the moans. The elation as they ate their comrades.

Then you would hear the rattle of battle elves and guard mages laughing, warm next to their braziers. Amazing what war can bring out of any man.

"Never," I said to him. "Neither will you. Listen to me. Hey!"

The spearman looked back at me, terrified.

"I'm not gonna make it," he had said. "I'm gonna die."

"You're gonna make it." The energy to speak was draining. "Listen. The guard we bribed said a week. A week, you hear? You're in the next batch. They'll send you home. Doesn't that sound nice?"

"I'm not gonna make it," the young man repeated. I looked down at the swelling in his belly.

There's a place where you're so tired that the only thing between you and death is your denial. I'd seen it in the cages. And I'd seen it in the faces of those who crawled into Darkshire.

"Yes, you are. You're almost out of here."

I looked back at the other skeletons huddled behind me for warmth. None of us were going to make it. We knew that. But for some gold teeth we had gotten a potato.

"Give it to me," I whispered to the men. Skin and bones, bones and skin. They looked over my shoulder at the pikeman. He had enough meat on him to survive. But he would give up soon.

They murmured to each other briefly. Then the large brown gem of starch, worth more to us than any treasure, was placed in my hand.

I turned, keeping an eye out for the guards.

"Hey," I whispered. I held out the potato. The pikeman's eyes looked down in disbelief. "Take it."

His hand grasped around mine, palming it and bringing it under his single thin blanket. Tears welled in his eyes, and his words came out as choking sobs.

"I... I...you should have—"

"Hey," I said with a wink. I was dying. "Some men go without, so some can go with. Right?"

"I'll remember you. I'll tell them to get you out of here."

"Sure" I replied. One of my cage-mates would be dead that very evening. He wanted to taste the potato, but told us he wouldn't swallow any. *Just want to remember what food tastes like.*

"What's your name?" he asked me.

"Davik," I spoke the words slowly, tasting them as they came out. Every effort, even blinking, was a step closer to my grave. "From—"

I BLINKED. The sound of something banging had roused me. I had lived. But the pain I felt made me wish I hadn't. My skull throbbed with hot lances of red agony. I turned, half-drowned from where I lay and saw the source of the noise.

The clerk from the library hadn't made it. His body was slapping against a cistern to the city, the current bashing him over and over against the metal grate that led to the sea.

I groaned and rolled over into the soft earth. The water was freezing. The light was failing. My mouth was full of blood where the bolt had pierced it. My side was worse, singing with the sharp pain of the bolt that had been torn out during my tumble. My leg was a nightmare of throbbing pain where the bolt stuck out of my thigh.

Vorga.

The chill of remembering made me shudder as much as the freezing water.

The clerk's body kept tapping against the cistern gate. His flesh was bloated. His face was a mask of terror and rigor mortis. In my delirium, I wondered if this counted for Sariel's little spell. Would her ring be glowing red? Would her heart break as Elina raced back to her? I hoped Elina made it quickly. Sariel needed to know what happened.

I had failed. What a fool I had been. Not even a thought about bringing a most-orc into a city of vile dregs. The rules were the same, whether you held the knife or felt it against your throat. Extortion, unfairness, the power to hurt others, that's what made the wheel. It turned on greed. People were just the grease that made it move.

Whatever happened to me, it didn't matter.

I looked up at the rock face. The sea wasn't far. It was eroding Trinth until it sat upon a cliff on this side. High walls, the sheer face of so many crags. How we hadn't landed on any of the sharp stone cliffs was a groaning miracle.

I sat up, resting against the rock. I gripped the bolt and pushed it the rest of the way through my leg. I felt the runes under my skin burning in response. Seeking to see if there was any magic here to counteract, to save me from.

You bastards are too late. Where were you on the bridge?

The bolt came free and blood seeped from my wound. I reached for my shirt and began to tear it for a tourniquet until my eyes settled on the clerk bobbing against the grate on the water.

"Might as well be useful for something," I told him as I took his belt.

I put the bolt in my soaked pocket. I was going to need a sharp edge. I looked up to the crag, the high cliff up to Trinth. Behind me, maybe a quarter mile, the bridge I had fallen from was a small line. We had floated far.

"Keep a watch out for me," I said to the clerk. His blank face didn't respond.

"I gotta go fetch your book."

I started climbing.

IN THE DIM light of a pourhouse, in a section of Trinth where good people didn't go after dark and only the too-curious youth of the city ventured to get themselves into trouble, the buildings were little more than cloth tarps and tents.

Candles flickered in meager lanterns. A dwarven woman smiled shyly at a man sitting in the corner of the winesink. She was older, and the years had been hard, harder now that the sheriff had passed new taxes, fees, and ordinances.

The handsome man winked at her and raised a small goblet of wine, as if this were a beautiful establishment and not a place for last stops. The other tables were occupied by drinkers who sat motionless, clutching the tables like barnacles on a docked ship. Their only noise was the hushed whisper of the doomed, clearing their throats to call for more of the wine that killed them. Those whose entire world revolved around drink and the pursuit of more drink. Who stole in the daytime, or conned their way into honest labor only to disappear after pawning the hammer they had been given to build something for a bottle.

I slid into the booth next to the man, pressing the broken crossbow bolt against his groin and keeping him in place next to the wall.

"You always had an eye for another man's wife, Rushe."

If I surprised him, he did a good job of not showing it. A smile spread across his lips. "Darkshire. I thought I was mad in the street. I thought, there's a man who looks like my old friend. How I do miss him. But that can't be him. That's someone with a nice life. If Darkshire were here I'd know, there'd be dead men everywhere, wouldn't there?"

"Yeah." I glowered and leaned into him.

"Heard them talking a few years back that you opened the gates at Rochdale. They saddled that on you, didn't they? Not that you're not so much a bastard, but I thought, my friend Davik wouldn't miss any chance to get himself killed. How did you make it out?"

"Charm," I said, remembering the sight of the lords of the city I had been charged to defend riding away. I learned later they had negotiated a share of the plunder from their own fiefdom with their enemies. "I lost my temper, too."

"Always was dangerous when that happened." Rushe held his smile under eyes that hadn't seen much sleep. The years had not been kind to him, or he hadn't been kind to himself. "So is this it, Darkshire? Is this the end of your old friend Rushe?"

"Maybe," I said. I was soaking wet. A creature that had emerged from the cisterns, smelling horrid, feeling worse. His eyes darted down at the belt around my leg.

"I heard about trouble on the bridge," Rushe said slowly. He sipped his wine. "Said there was a commotion. Some halfling stole a book, I hear?"

"A most-orc." I glared at him. "And she didn't steal it."

"Mmm," Rushe said. "Not your style, Darkshire. Books. But hey, we each grow new tastes, don't we? You ever keep up with any of—"

I needled the bolthead further against his groin. "Ahh, ahh. Sorry, Davik. Rushe loves to talk. But I can be a fine listener."

"Tell me about Bellick." When the dwarven woman came near, I sent her away with a dark look and turned back to my old compatriot. "Now."

"He's a brute. Ah, easy Davik. I'd like to be a father some-day. They call him Bloodgums. He likes pliers. Likes to take them to anyone cleaner than him, which is everyone. Got a real sadistic streak to him. Corrupt, of course, but not as much as that Sheriff Searlus. Bellick will steal the teeth out of your head. Searlus will help you look for them and charge you for the favor."

"What's he do?" I asked.

"Bloodgums? You don't pay bail when he snatches some-one, the clock starts ticking. A young maiden gets snatched on the road. By the time her father can ransom her, she's destined for a life of soup."

"He's a turnscrew?"

"Have you known one that wasn't?" Rushe backed up against the wall. "Come now Davik, don't pluck the plums from a tree ready to help you."

"What do you know about the jail?" I asked.

Despite the bolthead against his tender flesh, Rushe looked as if he had seen something more horrific than me walk in. His eyes burned as he spoke.

"A friend of mine... got caught. We did a nice job, but, you know rookies. She moved too quick. Sold something too fast. I told her not to..." he trailed off.

I stared at him, waiting.

"Cost me, a lot. To get her out. Took me too long. My own fence tried to run with a jewel the size of an egg. Cost me two days. Had to give him the Darkshire treatment."

"What happened? Your friend get out?" I asked.

Rushe nodded. "She did. They leave them alone the first day, Davik. So you can raise the money. But... it took me four days. I gave Sheriff Searlus the gem. Gods, it was a prize. When she got out, she left. They told me she refused to see me. Left without saying a word."

Rushe reached for the bottle to blanch the pain I saw on his face. I held his hand on the table.

"Gonna need you sober."

He looked more defeated at that than anything.

"I don't think they'll let you bail your friend out, Davik. You hurt a lot of people on the bridge. Heard some might not make it."

"That's okay."

Rushe glanced at me now. He used to look so young. How many years had it been?

"Why is that?" he asked, and he already knew the answer from my grin.

"You're going to help me, Rushe. You **owe** me. Remember?"

Rushe met my gaze, and I saw him resign to helping me. He was always a little bastard. A shit-eating grin and a tongue that got everyone into an argument. But when it came to a tight spot, he came through. And more importantly, when he had been in a tight spot, I came through when no one else had.

"You have some steel for me?" I asked, breaking the silence.

"I don't." He shook his head. "But listen, I know some heavy hitters here in the city. A good boss-man. Better for this type of work. Give you some backup. It'll cost you, sure. Cost you plenty. More than it would be to buy her out, but that's over the bridge, right? Have you got any coin?"

I smiled, the wound in my cheek searing with pain. "Not a copper, Rushe. Not in the mood for new friends. Time is of the essence. But I have something much better."

"What's that?"

"You."

~

WE MET CLOSE TO MIDNIGHT. When quiet footsteps and hands over mouths replaced the warcry before an assault. City patrols walked aimlessly, always alone, with no real order. Rushe had little issue bringing a satchel of highly illegal weapons. Whomever his contact was in the city, some shadowy underworld figure had come through.

"We shouldn't be rushing like this," Rushe whispered as he crept into the park and found me.

"Shouldn't, doesn't factor into tonight," I said and opened the pack he set down.

"Please, help yourself. That cost a lot, by the way."

"Guess you'll have a few more pockets to pick," I said as I rifled through the bag. "What did you find out?"

"Bellick is at the medicae as of an hour ago, but he's heading back to the jail. They say he called for his pliers to be polished and plans to work all night."

"Anyone else do the interrogating?"

Rushe shook his cowled head. Beyond him, the spires of Trinth glowed in the darkening night. "None of the gaolers have a stomach for his craft, anyway. Knew a guard who worked there. He tried to make a brief visit of his own to the cells with some farmer's daughter."

"What happened?" I asked, looking up.

"I guess only Bellick can visit his garden." Rushe smiled. "Last I heard, the guard became a guest of the dungeon."

We had time, but little of it.

"It's gonna be tight in there, Davik."

I loaded a heavy cavalry crossbow, pulling the wire back. The stakes, I already knew.

I'm probably not making it out. But she will. She has to.

I thought of Vorga, alone in some dark cell, terrified. Then I thought of Sariel. The softness of her in my arms. I saw days and seasons with her. Her hair draped over me in a bed.

Walking among the river and ponds. Smiling at each other as the years passed.

At least I got to feel it, even so briefly.

"Did you bring it?" I asked him.

Rushe shook his head to himself and fished out a vial from his pocket. He tossed it to me.

"That leg is going to be a problem," Rushe said.

"Not for long." I opened the vial and drained it, tasting the old bitter medicine. Aelthorn extract was distilled from rare flowers. They used to feed it to us when we were in the war. Field medics would pour it in your mouth when you were wounded, to ease the pain of injuries and to put more blood in your body.

Aelthorn was strong stuff, even at this small of a dose. The screaming in my leg dulled into a whine. I shuddered as the drug took hold, settling into my bloodstream. Expanding it.

The feeling of the drug in me brought me back. I felt the grim resignation come over me, eyes setting on a single task. Survival didn't matter, only victory.

"Horses?" I asked.

"Three near the east gate, if we make that far."

"If I go down, don't wait for me. Get her to Oakshire."

"Will do."

I slid the armor on. It was good leather, with small bands of metal embedded underneath. The reassurance of it felt good on my wounds, holding me together.

I traded my belt tourniquet for a short sword leg sheathe that I bound tightly over the wound. I had stuffed strips of the clerk's shirt into both sides of the wound, packing it until I gritted my teeth in anguish.

My cheek was another matter. A slow trickle of blood was pooling from the puncture. I covered the bottom of my face like a bandit with several wraps of black cloth.

There, standing in dark cloth and armor, my face half covered, I felt at home again. That sunlit valley in Oakshire seemed like a lifetime away. I was back to what I was. Freezing, half-drowned and ready to storm a small fortress.

All dreams end.

"Slow and steady?" Rushe asked.

I handed him one of the several crossbows. "Fast," I said and wrapped the head of the mace he had brought for me in cloth to quiet it. "And nasty."

"Alright," Rushe said. He was holding something back.

"What is it?"

He gave the smallest shake of his head. "Just kind of sad to see you like this again. When I saw you with those girls, I was happy for you. Do you have a woman, Darkshire?"

"I started to," I said, holding his gaze for a moment. "Probably not after this."

"Yeah."

I pulled the last piece of kit out of the small bag. A small kite shield, painted black. As soon as it settled into my left arm, it felt like a wayward family member coming home.

There you are.

"We should have two more guys for this," Rushe said.

"I'm a little short of friends."

"Wish Rayleth was with us," Rushe mused.

"Me too." The mangled elf-in-exile and his swordwork would have been a welcome addition to this meager band. But more than that, there wasn't a better feeling than a solid comrade with you. A wounded fighter turned busboy and lazy thief was less than ideal.

"Coulda ran on you, you know."

"I know," I said. That unspoken thing between men where they may not like each other, but can depend on each other, hung between us. "Thanks."

Rushe grinned. "Never could keep myself out of trouble." He bent low and grabbed a second crossbow. "That was always your job."

～

TRINTH CITY JAIL held sixteen cells in the bottom dungeon. Above that were the interrogation areas on the second floor, and the top floor was street level, held by a heavy door that would take a battering ram to get through.

Or the hands of a good burglar.

I watched the run-down jail in the darkness of our cover. My mouth dried in anticipation of combat.

Sorry Sariel.

Planning is good. It can be the difference between life and death. A good plan is a blueprint, a dream of how things should go. But if you hold on to it too tightly, it's just an anchor ready to drown you.

Rushe wasn't wrong. We needed two more men for what I wanted. Six would've been ideal. With two lookouts outside and a handler holding a team of horses nearby. Another two men on the city gates for when the alarm rang.

You think too much and 'should' becomes a poison. The world is full of should. Should is overrated.

I prefer can.

"Ready?" Rushe whispered.

I nodded.

Two torches burned above the entrance door to the jail tower. In the center of the door was a wicket with iron grating for the man behind it to check who was there before opening.

"The door, then the bell," I reminded him.

"I got it," Rushe said. The swagger of the preening thief was gone now, and the unforgiving look in his eyes was one I had seen in tight situations years ago that always earned him a place around a campfire.

We approached the door in a crouched sprint. Rushe threw a fistful of blackout powder to stifle both torches. He immediately knelt and started on the lock, his tools moving quickly in his hands.

"Open up," I ordered, knocking on the door.

"*Whassthat?*" a groggy voice said inside.

"Open up, bossman' coming."

I looked down at Rushe. He was staring at the lock, spinning and rotating slowly.

"*The hells you mean? Bellick just—*" the swing-through opened and the guard's eyes went wide as I pulled the trigger to the crossbow.

Thwack!

The bolt punched through his forehead, planting itself into his skull. The weapon was built to penetrate plate armor.

The man fell stone dead onto the ground. His air escaped his lips in a strangled death rattle. As it did, my body pulsed with a strange sensation. The deal-struck charm confirming I had violated the terms of the agreement with Sariel.

"Hurry up."

"Don't rush me," the thief muttered as he spun his tools. I heard the click and scrape of his picks on the lock teeth.

"Rushe," I said, looking inside.

"Shut up," he repeated.

I bent low and reloaded the crossbow. Another one was slung on my back.

The door clicked and Rushe pulled the handle down, the three-bolt slide releasing and he pushed.

"It's blocked," he hissed.

The body.

I pressed against the door, my leg protesting even through

the touch of Aelthorn. As I heaved against the corpse, the wet sound of its shifting weight filled the silence. Rushe slipped in. I felt the door budge once he dragged the body away to the center of the guardhouse.

Leaving the dark sky outside, I ducked into the stone tower. I tried to bolt it again, but it wouldn't shut.

"You broke the damn lock!" I hissed.

"You want me to take the time to fix it, or you want to get going?" Rushe snapped back at me.

Slowly, we both turned and saw a young lad sitting at the table, his mouth open in horror. He was in a gaoler's garb, fifteen maybe. His uniform looked fresh, like he had just started his first job.

Rushe swung his crossbow and took aim.

Gods, Davik, he's just a kid. That face from long ago, of the boy pickpocketing me, came back to me.

"No!" I pushed Rushe's weapon off target. The bolt shattered against the stone wall over the boy's shoulder. It was loud. Way too loud.

I rushed the young man, pulling my mace and before he could beg for mercy I dusted his crown, holding back to not kill him, and he went limp at the table.

"What the hells!" Rushe said.

Below us, there was a clatter of metal. The squeal of a door opening. Queries wafting up from the dungeons below.

"Get the bell," I ordered and walked to the stairs.

"We babysitting now?" Rushe scowled and walked towards the alarm bell. It ran down into all the floors in case there was an escape.

He cut it up high with a long knife. Then he grabbed a lantern off the table and dipped the tip of the rope into the flame until it caught. The orange flames climbing to the bell.

I took position at the stairs, waiting. I saw a glint of metal appear and a voice reached out.

"Gull? Ya'alright?"

"Give us a hand," I croaked. "Hurt ma' damn leg."

"On what?" the man walked up the stairs. I leapt behind him and covered his mouth. I slid the long dirk into his left armpit, dipping through his shirt and flesh.

He screamed in my hands, his teeth coming down on my fingers and I held him tight, wrenching the dirk from side to side to open the wound and dip until I found his heart. That macabre squish of the blade sliding into the organ.

When I felt him go slack, I released him slowly to the stairs. The deal-struck charm pulsed again, making me shudder.

I looked over at Rushe, the burning rope behind him. In a few minutes, the smoke might catch attention, it might not.

"Ready?"

"Ready," he answered me, leveling a crossbow.

I took point, walking down the stairs warily. I had my shield on my left arm, the crossbow in my arms and my weapons swinging or sheathed to me.

The world was damp darkness. The smell of excrement. Of misery and despair and terror. I walked down a spiral staircase, boots crunching on old brittle stone.

A guard looked over in a long hallway. To the right was an open area with racks and tables for interrogation.

I fired, the bolt catching him through the jaw. His hand flew up instantly. He stumbled and I rushed him, bringing the mace down on his skull and splattering it as he went down.

My body pulsed again with the charm. Somewhere in Oakshire, maybe Sariel's ring did the same.

"Moving," I called behind me, eyes scanning the dungeon.

"Move," Rushe answered, covering me with his heavy crossbow.

I hurried to the partial cover of a pillar, pulling another bolt. The interrogation area was empty, which could mean we were early or too late.

More voices came, two guards rising from the stairs ahead.

Rushe's bolt flew past me in the dark as I bent to reload.

"Miss," Rushe shouted.

"Intruders!" a guard cried out. He swept forward into the interrogation area, unsure of where he had been shot from. He was ten feet from me. Then six.

"They cut the bell rope!" the other gaoler yelled.

I didn't look up. I was pulling the string of the heavy crossbow, deadlifting it back until I heard the click.

"Bellick!" someone shouted.

I popped out behind the pillar and fired at the gaoler closest to me. The bolt glanced off his breastplate, his head snapped over, finding me.

"Miss," I grunted and threw the crossbow as hard as I could. It knocked the guard down with a clatter.

I pounced on him in the low light of the dungeon and planted my dirk into his ear, he screamed in terror as I buried it into his brain.

Thwack! A bolt sailed over me, bringing a groan from the stairs to the lower level.

"Hit," Rushe confirmed. "Moving."

I stood and pulled my other crossbow from my back. "Move."

The guard that Rushe had shot was wailing on the ground. The bolt had taken him through the belly. Rushe covered him with the crossbow.

I walked over. "Watch the stairs."

"Watching."

I grabbed the wounded man's chest and wrenched him

towards me off the ground. I held the long needle-like blade to his face, still coated with his friend's gray matter.

"Where's the orc?"

"They're coming," Rushe called out next to me, his crossbow trained on the stairs. Thunder sounded like it was roiling up from the caverns below.

"Where?" I shook the man.

"Last cell, downstairs, please—" he grunted.

I planted a fist in his face to silence him. He fell unconscious in my hands.

"Contact," Rushe called and sent a bolt down the stairs. Metal punching through metal. "Hit."

"Moving," I grunted. I moved on my bad leg to the stairs. Balancing the shield and crossbow was awkward, not unlike working the tavern.

"Reloading," Rushe said and bent low.

Two more guards sprinted up the stairs. I fired my crossbow point blank into the closest one. The bolt punched through his heart. I dropped the weapon and rushed the second with my shield.

We clashed. I shoved him back, not enough room to bash him in the tight stairwell.

He swung a cudgel at me. I caught it with the edge of the shield, then grabbed him, pulling him close with my free hand. My grip was impossible to escape.

"Help me lads!" he cried out.

"Ready?" I grunted to Rushe.

I heard the click of a crossbow string finally falling into place. "Yeah," Rushe said softly.

"Boys!" the guard shouted again. He was an older fellow, older than me. His best days were behind him.

Especially since we were here.

"Now," I groaned and spun him around with a trip. He

sprawled behind me, flat on his stomach and I slammed my boot on his back to pin him.

He looked up wildly, trying to rise. Rushe sank a shot into his eye, and his body reeled and twitched under my foot.

"Last one." Rushe loaded his final bolt.

I reached to my leg sheathe, keeping my shield towards the stairs and threw my last bolt to him.

"On me," I ordered.

Rushe came behind me and grabbed my leather pauldron. He aimed the crossbow over my right shoulder and I raised my shield. We locked together, armor and weapon, and walked clinched down the steps.

This was an infiltration and close quarters engagement. A world of corners, of hiding areas, of blind angles. There were dozens of ways to do this. I was several corpses closer to Vorga, that's all that mattered.

But sometimes you have to stick to the basics.

"Clear on the left," I whispered as we descended into the dungeon. I saw four cells down to my left, a single torch lighting a sunless realm. A pair of hands grasped the bars.

"Pivot," Rushe whispered.

I turned in the near-darkness, giving him cover with my shield as we rotated.

A blade slithered out. "Shit!" Rushe grunted. It missed my face, but I heard it strike true behind me and Rushe let go of me as he fell to the stairs.

The guard had been aiming for me. His arm was still over my shoulder when I drove my dirk up. I caught him under the chin guard, skewering his tongue to his sinuses with a needle of steel into his brain.

"Hghh... ghhhh," he wheezed, still upright from the blade.

I dropped the handle and moved back as he fell. I reached

back, feeling for Rushe on the stairs. Eyes glued in front of me, ready for another ambush.

My hands found cloth. "You with me?" I glanced back.

Rushe was groaning, holding his hand over his eye.

"Bastard got me," he whispered.

"Get up," I ordered. "Now."

He didn't argue. Rushe had grit. The grit that saw you die or live on the long march. The grit that got you over the mountain out of the blizzard. The grit I needed with me.

His hand grasped the crossbow, and he pushed himself up, squinting to keep his bleeding eye shut.

"Can't see shit," he hissed.

"Let's move," I said. "Stay right behind me. They're waiting."

We took the bottom steps again. I had my shield raised high to protect us both at the cost of visibility.

"Now!" Bellick's deep voice filled the dungeon.

The air filled with the melodies of three crossbows unloading. Two slammed into the shield in my hands, and one went low, between my legs and into Rushe's shin. He swore and fell to the ground, but twisted sideways, one good eye straining in the dim light for a target.

I lowered my shield, seeing ahead of me. It was narrow down the hall. The gaolers had formed a small formation. In their rear was Bellick, a bandage on his shoulder from where I had stabbed him earlier. The first line of men fell back as the next stepped forward with clubs and blades to cover them while they reloaded.

"She's dead now!" Bellick cackled. "But it'll be a long time coming."

She's still alive.

"Darkshire," Rushe groaned behind me. "Do it."

My body straightened. I looked down; the mace was in my

hands where it belonged. The runes in my skin sang in succession, sensing combat, ready to dispel any sorcerous assault. The strength in me came barreling forth, fueled by a wicked rage and making me shake with anticipation.

It wasn't a warcry that came from me; it was a howl. A terrible thing. The dark greed for blood finally let loose. It had been honed, grown, so many years ago. Years holding a begging bowl, watching the world walk by. It had been fed hauling a cart made for a horse, conscripted into an army. It had helped me survive the engraving to be a Magebreaker. A procedure I barely understood even now. Grown in countless quests and campaigns. It had refused to let me die. Even when I was...

Sitting in a wire cage, starving to death.

I fell on them. I did not fight. I waged war. My mind became a feedback loop of hate and aggression. There were men here, and they had to die. The room needed to empty itself.

I stomped impatiently towards them. There was no time for them to reload. Their cohesion flexed, the formation breaking before I even touched them. They were gaolers, jailors, not soldiers. Their victims were soft people fed to their sharp instruments. Fed to the fist, the boot, the unwanted touch.

War is a lie, and a fool's errand.

Yet there is no sweeter draught than justifiable retribution.

And to see the sweet fear in men who prey on others.

I detonated on their meek little line. The sound of my shield was the war drum of a dark god as I plunged into them.

"Captain!" a gaoler called out as I fell on him, starting in the center.

My mace knocked the cudgel from his hands, reversed, and sent his jaw cocking sideways at an unnatural angle. The force so hard his head wrenched around unnaturally behind him.

The man to his right screamed when my shield swung around, matching the same speed. I felt his neck crack; the vertebrae bursting under the force of the blow as the edge found him.

A bolt flew past me. Rushe was still on the ground and firing the last bolt he had into the man on the furthest to my right. The bolt landed under his eye, protruding out of the back of his head, and I sneered and continued my work.

They tried to crowd me. Contempt was the only thing I felt.

I held my shield high, spinning, pushing, bashing. There were six more men. A blade cut the back of my neck and I answered its owner by driving the head of my mace into his mouth and wrenched it downwards with such force his teeth flew out. Then I caved his helmet in with a snarl.

More blows came, and I felt them all. But I was in that place, the timing was just right. Where you know exactly what you need to do. Where pain is a promise for later, and here and now there was only wrath.

Someone grabbed the cloth around my face and yanked it back, pulling me off balance, but I braced, driving forward and slammed my head into the face of another guard and he crumpled to the ground, dead or incapacitated. It didn't matter.

I stomped his head apart like a swollen fruit.

"Kill him!" Bellick screamed. The fear in his voice was the sweetest thing next to the sound of men and the structures of their bodies collapsing under my mace.

Spinning, I went low. I fed my mace ankles and kneecaps, and when a man fell, I crushed his windpipe with the edge of my shield.

Another gaoler grabbed me, trying to keep me off his friend. I brought the shield skyward and shattered his jaw, then brought it down again and slew him before he fell to the ground.

"Fucking, die!" A man shouted and jabbed a hook into my back. The thick barb twisted, catching in the leather. I snapped it in half with my shield. He held only a broken handle when I butchered him, holding his shirt and hammering his helmet over and over with the dripping mace until his helmet crushed his skull and blood spilled into my hands.

The last guard tried to back up, but he stumbled over a twitching corpse. I buried the mace into his skull, the impact so strong it echoed in the dungeon.

"Aghh... aghh..." he gurgled and spasmed, standing there, his brain wrapped around the head of my weapon.

I stared at Bellick, wrenched the weapon free, and walked towards him.

"I'm unarmed!" he screamed, throwing down a short sword. "She's fine!"

My mace was ravenous, it craved blood and bone. He heard the wood of it creak in my tightening grip.

Rushe groaned behind me in the darkness, wounded and half-blind. An idea came to me, saving Bellick's life in the flickering light.

I prodded my gore-caked mace into his fat belly, backing him to the wall.

"Give me the keys," I spat.

He held them out.

"Where is she?" I asked.

"She's in there!" Bellick stammered, pointing to the cell to my left, second from the last.

"Vorga?" I called out, eying Bellick. We both knew if I didn't hear an answer he would be dead where he stood.

I heard nothing. I raised the mace to slay him.

"She's in there! I swear!"

I held. It felt like the truth.

I limped forward, unlocking the door, keeping my eye on Bellick. He was a big man, and I had plans for him.

I opened the cell, and a thin human girl stared at me. Twenty maybe, with dark hair and skin that was sallow from too little sun.

"Please don't hurt me," she pleaded.

"Come out," I said. "Who else is in there?"

"We didn't touch her," Bellick promised. "Her father said he would pay more, so we took good care of her."

"Looks like top treatment," I said, seeing how thin the girl was. My head snapped back to him. "Where's the orc?"

He was bewildered. "The greenskin?"

They killed her. They thought you were here for the human.

The look on my face brought the answer from him I wanted.

"She's here! Just here. The last cell!"

I guided the girl gently by the shoulder. "Can you do me a favor?"

"What?" she squinted. Even the torchlight was bright for her.

"Grab that crossbow there, yes, that one. Point it at this pig. If he moves, pull the trigger."

The girl reached down and held the crossbow from one of the guards up, her hands trembling.

"Easy now, easy now girl." Bellick put his hands out as if to steady her.

"Vorga!" I coughed the words. "Can you hear me?"

"Davik? Davik we're in here! I'm alright!" Vorga shouted back.

I could have collapsed in gratitude.

I looked over. Rushe had hobbled over to a cell and opened

it. He was kneeling over a body. I figured he was looking for something. A bandage, maybe.

Until I heard the haunted words from his mouth.

"*He was supposed to let her go...*"

Vorga's smiling face came to the wicket as I slid the key into the last cell.

"Davik!"

"Are you alright?" I swung the door open and grunted in pain when she threw her arms around me. She let me go, the front of her dress blanching with blood.

Vorga held my face. "She needs help."

"Who?" I asked.

We turned and peered into the cell. Another woman, this one even thinner than the first I had pulled out. Black hair, the mark of some deity under her ear.

"Is that a Paladin's sigil?" I asked Vorga, but got no answer.

The young woman was gripping the wall, trying to inch forward. She looked starved.

"Davik, she can barely walk. They haven't been feeding her." Vorga's voice filled with sadness.

"We should go," the girl holding the crossbow cried out.

I saw the flicker of crimson when I watched the woman in the cell. Just for a second.

"Give me that," I motioned to the torch burning on the wall. Vorga handed it to me.

"Davik," Rushe breathed my name out.

I stared at the girl in the dark cell. Then I held the torch close to her face.

Short dark bobbed hair, a beauty, once, perhaps. Brown eyes stared at me. They held gratitude, and hope and...

I tossed the torch away, letting the cell fall into darkness. Red eyes glowed in the dark, staring at me.

Hunger.

"She's a vampire," I hissed, pushing Vorga back. "She's crimson touched!"

Vorga's hands grabbed my arm. "I know, Davik. I know. She helped me. We have to get her out of here."

The vampire crept forward. She was wearing rags; she had been here for some time. Closer now, I recognized the sigil tattooed on her. It held three lines under it, denoting oaths. The emblem of Selene, deity of justice and fairness under her neck.

Evidently not present in a place like this.

"A Paladin of Selene?" I whispered.

"Once," her voice was hoarse, as if she hadn't drunk for days. "I won't do you any harm."

"Please Davik," Vorga begged. "There's others."

"Fine," I said. "Past the gate. I'll get them past the gate."

I turned to Bellick and nodded towards Rushe, still kneeling in the cell. "You wanna live? You're carrying him out of here."

The fat man's face went a bit surprised, but then he took in the gore covering me and nodded.

"Oh my gods," the girl holding the crossbow whimpered. I turned to see what she was looking at.

The fallen paladin had crawled over a dying gaoler. Her mouth was at his neck. Long sups coming from her throat. Her red-tinged eyes were closed in bliss.

"We don't have time for this," I told her. I turned to Bellick. "Now pick him up and carry him out of here."

"Davik," Rushe called to me softly.

Time was burning away. I imagined dozens of city guards sprinting towards us.

I walked over, the impending urge to begin a quick getaway driving me up a wall. I glanced in the cell where the body of a woman lay dead in squalor.

"Who is this?" I asked.

"I thought... I never thought..." Rushe was mumbling. "I can't lift her, Davik. I can't. I tried, and I fell." He looked up at me, eyes tinged with something worse than grief.

Shame. Failure.

"I can't leave her. They told me they let her go."

I put my hand on his shoulder. "It's okay. It's okay. I'll handle it... I'll carry her."

Vorga was unlocking the other cells. I turned to the occupants and poor souls of Trinth City Jail and nodded.

"Let's go."

CHAPTER
TWENTY-ONE

W e walked in darkness, three women, Bellick carrying Rushe and me carrying a poor dead girl. Behind us, four other men we had freed from the cells ran into the streets, off to their homes or to escape. I cared little if they were guilty of whatever crimes they were accused of. The state of them was punishment enough.

No alarm sounded. No fire had spread from the burning rope. The tower of Trinth Jail was eerily quiet. But my Aelthorn elixir was starting its fade, and I was moving slower than I liked.

"Are you okay?" Vorga asked me as we crept along in the darkness. Rising from a dungeon into a quiet, civilized city was like waking from a bad dream. She hadn't mentioned the bodies in the dungeon, or the plain fact that I had put them there.

"I'm okay. Are you alright? Did they hurt you?"

"I was only in the cell for a few hours. Nobody touched me. When one of the guards came to the door to taunt us, the woman in there with me shielded me. But they never came in. They just said... things to us."

"We'll be out of here soon," I promised. Whomever had taunted her was dead now. "Walk with the others, help them."

I turned to Bellick. The big man was having a hell of a time carrying my wounded friend.

"Stop slowing down," I hissed in his ear and he winced. "Or I'll bleed you in a gutter and carry him myself."

Bloodgums nodded, sweat pouring down his jowls. Rushe held his throat at knifepoint, and was gritting his teeth from his wounds.

"Davik," Rushe whispered. "We're close."

His good eye caught mine for a moment, a question and answer passing between us within in the space of a single step.

I walked to the three women. "Alright, there's three horses ahead. But we have to hold here for a moment. Who here can ride?"

Only the vampire raised her hand. Of course.

The other girl burst into tears. "I'm sorry, I never tried it. My father just used to have me take the family carriage."

"Shh," I said. "It's okay. Alright. Vorga, You ride with..."

"Lyra," the cursed paladin said.

"You ride with Lyra," I said. Her eyes had dulled their crimson glow, and were now like pale bloodstones in the moonlight.

"I'll ride with you?" the girl asked.

"You'll ride with my friend. He's hurt, so he'll need your help." I looked at all of them as we crouched. "Wait here."

I laid the dead girl down as respectfully as I could and walked back around the bend to Bloodgums swaying under the weight of the rogue in his arms.

"Rushe, most of these girls can't ride."

"I can ride," Rushe assured me. "Just can't get on the damn thing. Or see very well."

I raised an eyebrow in the darkness, staring at the bolt through his shin.

"I said I can ride, Davik."

"Alright," I said. I had felt the charm singing for every time I killed a man. My vow to Sariel was stained in blood and broken. Something sacred had been shattered, and it was my fault. My fault for bringing Vorga here. My fault for all of it.

Bellick looked at me. "Wait! What about-"

I stood and watched, feeling cold, as Rushe opened his gullet. He took a little long with it. Drawing it out. They dropped to the ground, Rushe changing from the wounded man to a murderer over his victim. Bloodgums soiled himself and flopped like a fish on a dry dock.

"He's done," I said. "Come here." I lifted my old compatriot up, taking all his weight and walking back to the girls around the corner. When we got to the girls, Rushe stared at the dead body I had laid down.

"I'll come back and fetch her," I promised before he could say anything.

Rushe's contact had come through. Three horses waited for us where he'd said they'd be. I helped Rushe up first, lifting him like a small child, and motioned to the stirrup where his shattered shin hung.

"In or out?"

"Leave it out," he breathed. There was loathing in his words. Something precious had been robbed in that dungeon. The story he had been told. The girl that got away hadn't got away at all and he hated himself for it.

I beckoned the young girl over, helping her up to Rushe.

"Keep him upright and steady," I said.

Lyra took the other mount, pulling Vorga up with her

cursed strength. I watched her, weighing the genuine possibility I'd have to put her down.

"Wait a moment," I whispered to the riders.

Once I fetched the body of the girl, I took her to my mount. I put her over my shoulder as I climbed up, then steadied her in my arms.

I nodded to the riders. "Don't stop. If someone falls, just keep going."

I took the rear, in case the city guards dropped the portcullis. I was feeling worse and worse every minute. There was a substantial chance my wounds would do me in. If anyone was getting left behind, I'd make sure it would be me.

"Ride hard," I told them.

Lyra nodded. Vorga gave me a sad look as I steadied the body on the front of my horse.

The now familiar silhouette of Trinth's gate loomed before us, the same bridge I had tumbled from. Torches sputtered weakly against the dark, casting long dancing shadows across the open gate and raised portcullis. The night, for all its danger, held the ominous silence of an ambush waiting to fall. The city itself held its breath, bracing for our flight.

We cantered up slowly. As quiet as you could on horseback. The air punctuated with fresh sobs from the girl on Rushe's horse, the strangled cries curling from her throat in fear. I didn't blame her.

The two horses ahead of me snorted, feeling the tension of their riders.

"Now!" I whispered, my words slicing open the silence. We spilled forth like coins tumbling from a cutpurse's touch. Rushe and Lyra urged forward. Hoof cresting cobblestone as we galloped. Then the drum-thud of horseshoes on wood. We rode through the gate; freedom waiting through the bastion of the gate like the jaw of a monstrous mouth threatening to shut.

"Halt!" a voice rose from the parapet. But the riders steeled their mounts. We sprinted through and across. The corpse on my mount was a silent bobbing witness to the liberation we stole. My morbid familiarity with carrying such a silent passenger was as familiar as my grip on the reins.

We crashed across the bridge like crusaders off to a grand quest. Trinth sliding away from us. On the rushing wind, Vorga raised a fist and let out a wild yelp.

Lyra was an expert rider, and as we exited the bridge to the softer trample of a dirt road, she cast a look back to make sure I was still with them. I nodded to her. It wasn't lost on me, the power of her restraint in not feeding on Vorga in the dungeon. It was admirable, truly. She held the poise now of a Justicar of Selene, yet the rapid recovery after drinking the blood of dying men brought the possibility of a dark confrontation later.

We made it one mile, then five. We slowed our gallop to a jaunt, then a surprise glittered in the dark beyond.

"Lights ahead!" Rushe shouted over the wind. "Wagon waiting! Could be an ambush."

"Ride past!" I shouted to the riders.

As we drew closer, the light of the wagon swinging, Vorga shouted in glee, "It's Brim!"

Brim rode slowly towards us in Rober's wagon. A pipe clenched between his teeth and a fiery look in his eyes. There was a kitchen knife stuck into his belt. Next to him was the broad hulking mass of the minotaur, horns absent save for two bony stumps on the side of his skull. He held a familiar wood axe in his giant claw, his leg mended now.

Brim's psionic voice shouted in my head, the noise of it jarring me from my seating.

Ugly-man!

We slowed, circling the two riders to peter out the speed of the horses.

"What the hells are you?" Rushe circled the wagon, eying Brim and his guest suspiciously.

"That's our dishwasher," Vorga said. She watched the minotaur with a suspicion I was glad to see.

I climbed down from the saddle. Brim nodded to me, smugness beaming from him.

"Breaker," the minotaur greeted me after he stepped down from the wagon. The weight of him allowing it to raise up.

"See that leg got fixed."

The beast man looked down and nodded. "Your cleric friend, thought you might need my assistance."

"Do we trust him?" Vorga whispered to me.

"I will not harm you," the beast knelt, as if pledging fealty to a warlord. "I apologize to you, orc. For my behavior at the tavern."

He is okay, Ugly-Man. I vow it. Brim pulsed the words to me. *I would not bring him if not.*

"Davik?" Vorga looked at me.

"We do today," I declared. "If you wish."

"Okay," Vorga said. On the road to Trinth she had been in favor of his redemption, but after a night of false imprisonment I was pleased to see her so shrewd.

"What's your name?" I asked him.

"The men who hired me called me Bull."

"Creative of them, but what were you called before?"

The dark bovine eyes stared at me, the lanterns shining on them like stars. "Kardak. Of the Banehide herd."

Kardak the Minotaur. So be it.

I slid from my saddle, holding the reins to my horse, the body of the girl still slumped over the saddle tack. Vorga hugged me again, jumping from Lyra's mount.

"You saved me," she whispered.

"I almost got you killed." I held her close for a moment. "You did so well in there."

Her words were muffled by her face buried in my chest. "Learned it from you."

"Listen," I said and broke from her, trying not to wince in pain. "You go with Brim."

"Davik, aren't you coming?" Vorga asked, then she looked at the body on my saddle and Rushe staring at the ground. "Oh."

Lyra spoke from her horse, no motion of getting off of it. "They'll be after us, likely."

I turned to the paladin. "Can you go with them?"

"Trust me, now?" Red eyes stared down at me.

"Suppose you didn't touch the girl. Looks like I have to."

The glowing eyes shut for a moment. "It will be done. But I will require sanctuary."

Her syntax and voice were one of authority, a paladin indeed. "You'll have it. Just... nothing happens to them, okay?"

"Nothing will," the vampiric paladin said. "I swear on Selene."

"If it comes over you... just leave. Don't make me find you."

"You won't need to."

I looked at Rushe's mangled leg. He'd probably lose it. "Can you heal him?"

Lyra looked over at him. The regret plain on her face. "I don't have that capability... any longer."

"I understand. Just get them to Oakshire."

"I will," she replied.

Vorga and the girl whose name and father I'd learn later sat on either side of Brim. I watched them roll off. Kardak walked beside the wagon, my wood axe laughably small in his fist. The paladin rode slowly next to them, eyes scanning the road.

Vorga never looked away. She stared back at me in the moonlight as the wagon carried her off to Oakshire, where she belonged.

"You're not going with them?" Rushe asked.

"I'll give you a hand." The blood on his eye had dried. "You see out of that eye?"

"Barely." He pulled on the reins. "But I can ride."

We rode out, and Rushe took the lead, straying from the road. We traveled several miles off the road, splitting from the path. There were no tools on us, except knives, but there in the dark soil of a derelict farm, the city of Trinth far in the distance and the midnight moon above us, we dug a grave with what we had.

There's a silence that exists between men who've known each other for years. Men who may not be friends, but are brothers of war, or the road, or simple hardship. That silence is a weight at times.

That night, it was a small blessing.

It took longer than our escape, but there in the earth we laid whomever this woman had been to rest. I didn't ask questions as we buried her. Rushe was dead on his feet, a branch bracing his leg tied with a filthy cloth.

We stood for a moment, and Rushe shut his eyes. I walked away, giving him his moments. I calmed the horses, keeping my ear out for riders. I hummed and quieted them, so I wouldn't hear his choked words to her.

"Shh," I patted the horses, steadying them. "It's alright."

After a while, Rushe limped towards me, eyes glassy and teeth clenched. His face contorted in fury. He walked right up to me, and I knew what he'd say before he said it.

"You owe me."

∿

IN A VERY FINE house in the city of Trinth that should have had a more sober guard and a much better lock, Sheriff Rodolf Searlus woke to the scrape of dirty boots on his floorboards.

In my experience, it's never a good idea to sleep under the covers of a bed. Someone could light it on fire. It's too easy to get tangled up when you rise and defend yourself.

Or someone like me could hold the sheets down, trapping your arms to your side.

"Good evening sheriff," I whispered. I was in a foul mood from sneaking back into the city we had escaped, and half-carrying Rushe the entire way. But it seemed the city guards hadn't even discovered the jail yet. No wonder Rushe lived in Trinth. The incompetence of the guard protecting their highest authority proved why this was a breeding ground for thieves.

"Gods! Gods! What is this?" The sheriff blinked, trying to clear his eyes. Trying to make this a dream.

I had little qualms coming back to finish this. I wouldn't stand in Rushe's way. Bellick had needed to fall, and I was fine with cutting any trail leading this sheriff back to Oakshire to the tavern. I had told him where we were from on the bridge. He'd remember Vorga. The gnomish engineers could be questioned and spill exactly where the delivery was going.

It's better to live with a heavy conscience than an eye on the horizon.

"You were supposed to let her go," Rushe whispered from above. Sheriff Searlus looked up in horror. Rushe was perched on the bedframe above, a gargoyle looking down on his prey. His mangled leg dripping blood on the pillow next to the man's head.

Rushe glowered. "Remember that gem? 'Buys me plenty' you had said."

"I do! I did! Rooth? It's Rooth, right? I had her released. I told Bellick to let her go, or at least I ordered him to. If he didn't, by gods, they'll be hell to pay."

"Mmm," Rushe murmured, smiling down at the man like a vulture. "I remember when you moved into this place months ago. Always stuck out to me I helped finance it."

"I'm a servant of Trinth!" The sheriff shouted and struggled against me, but there was no escape. He focused on me now. "Wait, wait... you're from the bridge, aren't you? Today? It was a big misunderstanding. The orc!" His eyes lit up. "We can have her released! We were going to let her out anyway. A book is just a trifle thing. Those fucking librarians! You wouldn't believe the goddamn noise they bring."

"She's already free," I told him.

"Gold! I have gold in my office. Tucked away. Let me up, we can make this very easy. Take every scrap!"

Rushe put a finger to his own lips. Then a flash of silver appeared in his hands. I didn't realize he had taken it from the body.

Rodolf Searlus's eyes locked onto Bellick's pliers.

"Now hold still," Rushe whispered. "We should have everything out by the morning."

We looted the house. I found the strongbox in his office as promised. I pried it open myself. It was full of notes and envelopes of payments and ransoms and promissary notes from half a hundred different people. When I reached in to clear it all, I found a necklace with a little gold feather on it.

Rushe's eyes fell when I held it up. I handed it to him and he gripped it in his fist.

"Here's the coin you wanted," I said. Gesturing at the strongbox.

He didn't look over. He was staring at the necklace. "You take it. I don't want it."

Neither did I. There was half a fortune in here. But it was worse than blood money. So much worse. Like finding the treasures of a spider. I took my eleven gold pieces back that Searlus had taken and put the rest of the envelopes into a leather satchel.

My skull still throbbed from the blow he had delivered me. I found the enchanted mace in his vanity, of all places, sitting in a lined drawer next to brushes and waxes. When I picked it up, my runes detected the enchantment, and I felt them struggle to disable it.

"Curious," I said, turning the weapon in my hand. It was plain, finely wrought, but not a masterwork. The head was crested and ridged. Good for denting, for breaking. What hand had made this? It hit like a thunderbolt. I peered at the small maker's etching on the base of the head.

I slid it into my belt. A mystery for another day.

Good arson begins with opening all the windows. Then we burned the house down.

Outside on the street, drinking the only thing we had stolen from the wine cellar, we stood and watched it burn. The flames crept and then roared as they spread through the house. A house purchased with extortion, with countless kidnappings. We passed the bottle back and forth as the heat of it warmed us.

They'd know it was foul play. Bellick and all the guards in the jail would be too high of a coincidence. But maybe word would spread that Trinth needed a better sheriff, that extortion and kidnapping wouldn't stand.

Maybe not.

"Here." I handed the satchel of bribes and bail to Rushe.

"Told you," he said. "Don't want it."

"Neither do I. But I bet the people who paid this and lost their homes to do so would. Track them down, Rushe. Give it back to them."

Rushe shrugged and took it. A deep grief haunted his eyes.

After a moment, he asked, "Does it help? Those girls, that place, after the life? Being with them."

I watched the flames climbing up to the third story of the mansion. People were stirring. A bell in the city's distance sounded. The fire would divert plenty of attention from our escape.

"It does." It was the truth. Now that the sun threatened to conquer the sky, and the dawn light was breaking, I felt dirty. I didn't want to be here. I didn't want cities and jails and corrupt officials and the clinch of murder in tight spaces.

I just wanted pancakes around a wooden table, filled with laughter.

"See you, Davik." Rushe shouldered the satchel and limped down the road.

"See you," I said, watching him go. Off to find a healer maybe, or another bottle, or a new life or an old one. "Rushe."

CHAPTER
TWENTY-TWO

My goal that day was just to die in Oakshire.

By midday my leg screamed in a pulsing throb with every shift of the horse under me, and my side had gone from a dull ache to a frightening numbness.

All those times in the trenches, and it'll be some nameless gaoler that does me in.

It seemed fitting.

Behind me, the city of Trinth was a taste of the past I wanted little of. Enough alleys and sordid dealings. Enough killing. The death of the sheriff, of Bellick Bloodgums and his gaolers didn't bother me. Men who stood by such brutality were just as guilty as those who inflicted it. My heart was not so born anew under the touch of an elven tavern owner that it grew me a new conscience.

No, that hadn't bothered me. Not the killing, but the way I felt when I did it. Like I had returned. Like Oakshire had been a dream that I woke up from.

War's we—

I shook my head, not wanting to hear the song anymore. Not now. Not rolling around in my head if I died today.

If I lived? It didn't matter if Sariel asked me to leave. All that mattered was Vorga was safe. Safe from guards and jailors and cities that couldn't be trusted. Safe from power, and all those sick enough to seek it.

Maybe Sariel would see the heating system once it arrived. Maybe when she touched warm water, she would think of me and smile.

"Come on," I urged the mount forward. Fever danced around my skull, and I shuddered under its maddening touch.

I rode towards Oakshire for hours, the fever growing. My leg stopped aching and felt only coldness now where I had been shot. My side thrummed with every stride of my mount, the blood soaking through the bandages and wetting even the leather armor.

When Oakshire finally came into view, I patted my horse and croaked the words out. "That's Oakshire. I'm going to be buried there."

The street was nearly empty in the midmorning. A rider always brought looks, but when they saw the state of me, several people covered their shocked mouths with hands.

I felt warm in the cold autumn morning when I saw the tavern. And I thought I was mad when Sariel stepped outside, clad in Embrien warplate. Her sword sheathed on her back as she locked the tavern door. The keys clattered to the ground from her shocked fingers when she turned and saw me.

"Davik?" her voice was sweet music to me.

"Hey there," I mumbled and half-fell from my mount. She was there, arms steadying me. Smelling wonderful. She always smelled wonderful.

"Davik!" she threw her arms around me. I hugged her limply. I guess her ring didn't tell her what had happened.

"I'm so glad you got out. I'm so, so glad. Elina rushed back and told us. I thought you were dead. I was headed out to find you. Vorga said you might've been hurt. Elina and I were going to leave to go to the sheriff in Trinth when Vorga returned. She told me you were alive. That you saved her."

I fell into her, just for a moment, before everything would change. There were times in the war where I was wounded and dragged towards a medicae tent, spending hours trying to stay alive just to be seen. More than battle, more than fighting, that had unnerved me the most. When your life hung in the balance, and it was up to you to hold on.

I remembered so many men moaning and crying, waiting to be healed. They called out the names of their loved ones.

There had been no name for me to call. Until now.

"Sariel," I whispered into her neck. Her hair shifted into my face as she gripped me tighter. Of all things, I would savor this moment.

This is what I'll remember, when I leave and go back. Back to the woods. At least in the end I'll have her name to cry out.

Her gentle touch, her embrace. It was everything I'd wanted. I realized in that moment something that had been evading me.

The world is a vast place, and we are blown about by the winds of power and need. Forces greater than ourselves. It's a raging storm. Home is the solace from that. It has to be. The unmoving shelter in the things that change. It's the only fortress that stands in your heart even after it's destroyed.

"Come inside." She dragged me into the tavern and sat me at the closest booth. "We'll get Elina. We'll get you healed up and..." she kept speaking, but I didn't hear her.

Sariel didn't know. I wouldn't have to tell her anything. About the rules that were so important to her that I had broken. Sure, men had died. But I had pulled Vorga out of that dungeon, and she had seen dead bodies but live ones too, and likely wouldn't remember the difference. Even if so, I could say Rushe did it. It could be a secret.

I looked up as she stood to go get the cleric.

"Stop." I grabbed her hand.

I couldn't carry one more secret. Not here, not in this place. This wasn't a bending of the rules. If the distance had been too great for the ring to register what happened, then I would.

"Davik, you need help." Sariel tried to pull away.

"I have to tell you something," I said. My side ached again. Maybe I didn't have much time. "Please, sit down."

Sariel sat across from me, face wracked with worry. I watched the shape of her neck, the rise and fall of her chest under her armor. I burned it into my memory like a wood etching, wanting to hold it forever.

"I killed people, Sariel," I breathed the words out. "In Trinth."

"Davik—"

"Just listen," I said. "I could have tried differently, maybe. By the time we would have gotten Vorga out, the things they would have done to her... I couldn't. I just couldn't. I broke your rule. I slew a dozen men, maybe more, to get her out."

Sariel reached forward and put her other hand on top of mine. "I know, Davik."

I glanced down to where she usually wore her ruby ring. It was absent, and her bare finger was inflamed red from its band.

"It flickered all night. Once Elina told me what happened, it started. I felt you, Davik. I really felt you. I felt your rage, and your violence, and it felt so dark. But you saved Vorga. You did what you had to do."

I stared at her, trying to make myself not say it, but I wouldn't lie to her. "It's not just that, Sariel. I went back with a friend. I helped him murder the sheriff. Even before that, those mercenaries that stopped here? I crept out that night and maimed them. Is that what you want here? I didn't kill anyone. I used a club instead of a blade so it wouldn't violate the charm. I still lied. Look at me. Look what happens. The firewood brought thieves and blood. A trip to the library? Vorga almost died. I'm no good, Sariel. I'm—"

"Dangerous?" Sariel's silver eyes twinkled with the curl of a soft smile, her hand squeezing mine tighter. "You think you're the only dangerous person in Oakshire, Davik? You should see what Vorga brought home with her that's sleeping upstairs, hiding from the light."

"You don't get it," I told her. I felt lightheaded, but I had to finish. "I'm still there. Deep down."

"Of course you are," Sariel said. "So am I. Hells, look at me. This armor. I swore I'd never wear it again. I have dreams all the time that I'm back in command of a regiment. And I see farms burning. I'm always too late to stop it. To stop myself."

"Sariel, it's not just that..."

Sariel stood out from the booth and slid in next to me, never releasing my hands. "Davik, you once told me that the war was over. That I needed to stop running away. Do you think I'm some naïve village girl? I'm centuries old. Do you think I'm sad because I'll have to share you? Not just with others, but with your nature?"

"That's not—"

Sariel shushed me by bringing my hand to her mouth and kissing it. "You've lived hard, Davik. Maybe deep down, there's a young boy begging in a street somewhere. You're not some morsel of bread that can only sate one hunger. Most men are only trickles, and their wives wither away trying to survive with that. You're a river, Davik. And while they may supply so much, they're dangerous. I know that."

She brought my hand over her heart. "This is yours. It belongs to you. Because I chose to give it to you. You know the pride I feel, the contentness, when I see my girls around the kitchen table, fed and safe, protected? Do you think I'd find a river and keep it to myself? Or run away because of how strong its current swept away those who came to harm us?"

Sariel stared at me. I inhaled, trying to stay awake. "This can't be my home..."

"It already is," Sariel whispered. "You bring so much here, Davik. But you think every bad thing is because it's attracted to you. It's just life. Stop running away. Do you know how I felt when that ring was flickering while you fought for Vorga's life? I felt proud. Proud to be your woman. To be under your banner, under your blanket. I haven't felt pride like that my entire life. I pretended my whole life to be proud. Proud of my companies. Proud of victories. It's not perfect, and I'm not interested in fantasies that don't exist. Leave that to the books Vorga reads."

She kissed me, and it was like the first time.

"You're not going anywhere," Sariel gripped my hand. "You've changed so much. We lose our way, sure. But... Davik? Davik!"

I fell back into the booth, my eyes struggling to stay open. This would be a good place, a fine place for it to end.

The door to the tavern opened, and I heard multiple footsteps as my eyes shut.

"Oh hells," a gruff older man exclaimed. I knew that voice... but who?

"Get him on the table. He's lost too much blood," a younger female voice ordered. I heard the tap of a staff on the ground.

Sariel though, I knew her. She never let go of my hand as they lifted my body onto a table.

Then it was dark.

CHAPTER
TWENTY-THREE

When I woke, I was as surprised as anyone to find myself in heaven. It certainly wasn't earned. Maybe I had been shown mercy instead of justice.

The enormity of the feather bed after months of sleeping in a barn was such a contrast it was almost painful. I groaned and sat up. The only thing I wore were tangled bedsheets and bandages.

A window in front of me spilled sunlight into the room. When I shifted, my leg ached and my side held a tightness that didn't quite feel like stitches. If this was the afterlife, they did a decent job of mending me, but they could have at least gone all the way.

Beneath me, I heard a clamor of voices coming through the wood floor. Women yelling at each other, teasing, the stomp of feet.

Next to the enormous bed was a nightstand and a glass pitcher of cool water and bar tumbler. I reached for the glass. My fingers felt like they hadn't moved in a while. The stiffness betrayed me, and the thick tumbler fell to the ground, clattering and rolling.

"He's up!" a voice I knew called down the stairs. The door swung open slowly, the white wood creaking as it did.

Karley stood there, a slim shirt across her chest and in her panties like the same day I had seen her for breakfast. The drow had a toothbrush in her mouth, the feigned bored look on her face.

"How are you feeling?" She popped the toothbrush out of her lips and pointed it at my body. "Look pretty banged up."

I pushed myself up more and whipped a cover over my lap, cutting off her view. "Better, I suppose. What day is it?"

Karley brushed her teeth slowly, the handle of the toothbrush sliding back and forth between her lips. Then she spat into a small cup in her hand.

"Wednesday. You've been down for almost two days. Thanks for all the help at the bar, by the way."

I rolled my eyes.

But Karley didn't walk off like she would usually. She shifted her weight from one bare foot to another; the muscles flexing under the violet skin of her thighs. Her black panties hugged her, and she made no show of modesty.

"Sorry about that. I was detained." I laid back on the pillows.

"Heard about that. Here," she said and walked towards me. She turned and bent over, her thonged ass coming practically onto the bed with me as she grabbed the glass and put it on the dresser for me.

Still a tease, after all. If she was looking for another spanking, she'd have to wait.

"Thanks," I said.

"No problem." Karley turned and spotted a used bandage

on the other nightstand. She climbed over me, her slender body hovering in front of my face.

"Are you the maid now?"

Karley grinned and moved back off the bed, eyes trailing to my groin under the thin silk sheet. Her bare feet shifted on the wooden floor again, her hips rising on either side. For a moment, her hand started to slide down her stomach, towards her panties.

"I've got his breakfast!" Tyra shouted as she stomped up the stairs. For one of the faen, she didn't always move as gracefully as you'd think.

"He's up," Karley said, still staring at me. Then she blinked, turned away, and walked past Tyra, who burst into the room.

"Ew, get your toothbrush away from his food!" Tyra pulled the tray away.

"For a busboy he makes a mess," Karley said and put the toothbrush back in her mouth. I looked away from the heart shape of her rear, the silken black cloth riding between her shapely cheeks, and turned to Tyra.

The faen-girl was glowing. She set the tray on my lap.

"Your favorite!" Tyra giggled. A steaming stack of pumpkin pancakes sat in front of me, with hand-whipped cream and a small glass carafe of her orange blossom syrup.

"Thank you," I said. The smell hit my nostrils, and my stomach growled to be fed.

Tyra sat on the bed next to me, the weight of her impact making us bounce and her large chest jiggle. She had her red hair down, and she put an arm around me in a half-hug.

"I heard what you did for Vorga. I'm so glad you're alright," she murmured into my shoulder.

"It's... thanks," I said. She nuzzled closer to me and I slid my arm around her back. Her long skirt draped over her knees and she reached up and grabbed my face, looking at where my cheek had been punctured and three rough stitches now remained.

"You're even more rugged now," Tyra said with a smile. "Now that you're staying here, I'm sure the drama will increase. But, you know... it's good to have you here. It makes Sariel and Vorga feel safer. Karley too."

"How about you?" I asked.

Tyra's beautiful face split into a smile. "Makes me kind of nervous sometimes. But that's a good thing. Besides... nobody wants to visit a boy in the barn." She winked and stood. Then she clapped her hands together. "Coffee! I forgot the coffee!"

Before I could say anything, she scampered out of the room, a bundle of giddiness. As the door opened, I saw Vorga standing there, looking at me shyly.

"Vorga." I sat up and made sure I was covered. "Come in."

"Are you... okay?" The most-orc girl walked in slowly. Her dark eyes were full of something close to embarrassment. "I helped them with your bandages and cleaning you. I tried to talk to you, but you were asleep."

I nodded, patting the bed for her to sit. "I have to say something to say to you," I said.

"Okay." Vorga sat, crossing one leg to sit and face me. "I do, too."

"Me first," I said. "I'm sorry. I'm really sorry, Vorga. It was foolish to take you to Trinth. I didn't even think... because you're an orc..."

"Davik," she said with a soft smile. "You **saved** me."

I shook my head. "It's my fault. Don't you see? I didn't even think about how you're treated differently. Looked at differently. And the things I did in the dungeon... with my friend. You need to know you never have to fear me. If you want, I can stay in the barn. Actually, I plan to."

"No," she cut me off suddenly, her eyes softening. "Stay

here. So you can recover. It makes Sariel happy... I've seen how happy you make her."

"Vorga, I put you in a situation where something terrible could have happened to you. Something even more terrible."

"Maybe," Vorga said. "Maybe, Davik. But you don't control the cities or the towns or the worlds, do you? You just tried to take me to a library. You didn't make the clerk behave that way. Or the jailor. Or accuse me."

"You almost died."

Vorga smiled. "I may be young, Davik. But that's the world. It's not your fault. We'll be more careful next time. But I don't want to live in a world where I can't go to a library, or to a fair... or be with someone. You were brave in that jail, braver than anything I've seen. You may think you scared me, but you didn't. I'm a most-orc. It made me realize I have to know how to defend myself. How to make friends that can come to my aid."

"If I stay here... how will that make you feel?"

Vorga pursed her lips, and a long ache of longing filled me when she did. The way she held herself in the dungeon, keeping it together, it had shown me how resilient she was.

"I want you to stay. I want you here."

My heart somersaulted in my chest.

"I'm sorry, we lost your book," I said.

Vorga stood, smiling. She glanced at my scarred and muscled chest and then blushed. "I'm not. Mean's you owe me another one."

I laughed. "That's a deal."

Vorga went for the door, but then she turned back to me. "Thank you Davik. Do you think when you're up to it, you can teach me to protect myself?"

"We can talk about it later," I promised. I wasn't sure if I wanted to be in the business of teaching anyone about blades or violence.

"How is he, Vorga?" Sariel's voice warmed my ears asked as she climbed to the top of the stairs.

I almost laughed. For once in my life, I saw her without a lovely dress on. She was wearing tight-fitting trousers, a workman's shirt unbuttoned halfway, and a ridiculously large gardening hat.

"What?" Sariel turned to me. "I was gardening."

"Some nurse you are," I groaned, moving a pillow behind me. "Leaving your patient."

"Be well, Davik." Vorga smiled and walked back downstairs.

Sariel pushed the door shut behind her. It didn't close all the way but stalled in the doorjamb. I'd have to fix that.

She smiled and walked up to me, sitting next to me and rubbing my hair.

"You look good in my bed." The elf kissed my cheek.

"Mind telling me what happened?"

"Elina tried her best with physical instruments, but you were wounded so badly. She stitched you up and gave you some extract that gave you more blood."

"Aelthorn," I muttered, recognizing the bitter taste in the back of my throat.

"That's it. But your wounds were deep. Your leg, your side. Finally, she cast spells to heal you. That's what saved you."

I smirked. "Poor Elina, I've told her before it wouldn't... wait, what did you say?"

Sariel's face was puzzled. "She healed you, or the Mistress did."

"That... can't be." For a horrifying moment, I wondered if my runes had lost their effect somehow. But when I focused, I felt them pulse back to me. They were still there.

"That's what she had said, but she thinks since she's bound to you... the runes in you don't see her as a threat. She said something had been blocking her before. Not just the runes. That healing you was like healing her own body. Does that make sense?"

I reached down and touched the wound on my leg. The hole was mostly healed, far more than it had any right to be.

"Wow," was all I could say. It had been so long since a healing spell had worked on me. Since before conscription.

"Guess the Mistress has your back," Sariel said with a smile.

Sariel sat with me while I ate. Pouring me the coffee that Tyra brought. Then she stood up and walked to her little chest of drawers and undid her blouse, then her brassiere. She slid her pants down, and her underwear.

I watched her with a grin. "Your bed has an amazing view."

Sariel turned and stood in front of me, legs sliding against one another, a hand touching her side and drifting lower.

"Elina says you shouldn't move... which I think makes you my prisoner."

I sat the tray away from my lap.

Sariel crawled onto the bed, her long blonde hair hanging down, her bust finally freed and hanging below her. Her hand reached up to the covers along my waist.

"These look dirty," she said in a pouty voice.

"Filthy. A downright hazard, if you ask me," I agreed.

She slid them off, my cock rising under her transfixed hungry glare.

"Elina's been giving me things to practice... can I try them on you?"

"Practice is the sign of greatness."

Sariel broke her little sultry act and smiled, a bit embarrassed. "I've never done this before. Tell me if it's okay?"

343

"Sariel, if all you ever do is wake up in the morning, I'll die a happy man."

Her silver eyes flashed at me with such lust and need. It was still so new, to be wanted so wholly.

"I love you," she whispered the only spell that would always work on me.

"I love you, too."

Her lips kissed my thigh, and then up, and I groaned. Shifting down into the pillows, watching her as she kept running her lips higher and higher, her eyes never leaving mine.

"Don't move," Sariel whispered. "You have to heal."

"Okay," I said. She reached up, grabbing my throbbing cock and laid flat on her stomach, holding it, staring at it and running her thumb underneath.

"Blessed, indeed."

Her lips kissed the base of me, then higher and higher, until she groaned and shut her eyes, running her tongue around the head.

"Sariel," I whispered.

"Mmm," she responded, but she hadn't really heard me. Her kisses melted into the symphony of her lips and tongue running all over my cock. The elf gripped me and stroked slowly, her eyes glazed with lust.

"Just lay there..." Sariel murmured and then swallowed me. Her warm wet mouth hummed with a groan as took me more and more. She gagged as I hit the edge of her throat and sucked even harder as she slid back up, freeing me from her mouth with a loud pop.

"I've wanted to do this for you," Sariel spoke between devoting her mouth to me, stroking my slick shaft in a spiraling hand motion. Before I could respond, she attacked me as if she was starved for it.

"Gurghh," Sariel coughed as she took me deeper. The saliva poured out of her mouth when she did, but instead of withdrawing, she bobbed her head up and down. One hand was between her own legs, her hips thrusting into her own fingers, her pale calves and feet bending upwards into the air.

"Mmm, mmm," she hummed. Sariel stared at me, wanting me to watch as I tunneled into her mouth, stretching her lips wide.

"Oh Davik," she huffed as she withdrew for air again. Her stroking had turned into a furious churning, her hand sliding up and down. She squirmed against the mattress, her thick cheeks flexing as she ground against her own hand again and again. "I love sucking you."

She got on all fours. Both hands wrapped around me as if in some submissive prayer. Her fists enveloped me, tugging as she dove again, milking and churning me. Sucking so hard, she refused to let it leave her mouth.

I reached down, the stitches in my side stretching as I did and slid my hands between her legs as she knelt. She rose, gyrating against my hand. Her sweet, silken folds mashed down, thighs clenching around my arm as she ground against me.

She tugged on my cock needfully, as if afraid to let it go.

"Ohh, ohh..." Sariel ground harder against my fingers, eyes opening, silver irises locking onto me in a mixture of need and delicate agony. "Can I taste it again? Please?"

But she didn't wait for any word from me. She crawled around, bending down, her ass towards the door and spreading now. I spanked her, sending her cheeks rolling. She groaned with a mouthful of my cock. Head bobbing quickly while I spread her cheeks and slid a single finger inside her.

I shuddered in pleasure from the raw lust fueling this fierce dedication to me. She slammed her head down, trying to take all of me until I pressed against her throat while I toyed with her.

Her hand stroked me as she moaned, and my head turned to the door the instant I heard it creak.

Dark eyes, violet skin. The door was open several inches, and I locked eyes with Karley. She was biting her lip, looking back at the stairs several times, her hand down her panties and rubbing feverishly.

My first instinct was alarm, but as Sariel throated me again and again, I spanked her one more time.

"You like me spanking you, don't you?" I asked.

"Mmhmm," Sariel groaned.

If I was a river, then that's what I would be. I would flow and feed plenty. I knew Sariel wouldn't mind this erotic voyeur. She'd love it.

Karley stood in the doorway, her nipples piercing through her pale cloth undershirt, her panties a slick mess as she rubbed herself.

"That's it." I grabbed a mass of Sariel's magnificent blonde hair and pulled it. "Suck it like a good girl."

The tyrant comes out within all of us... maybe Sariel was right, that we had to be both, we couldn't run from what we were. But the difference now, here in Oakshire, with this beautiful elven woman devoting herself to me, was that it finally felt bright. The sun through the window, the cleanness of her sheets. Just being in her room was like having a glimpse into her soul.

Women are soft, wonderful things. Worth protecting, worth dying for. Worth murdering in a dungeon for. They bring a gentleness into a world that can seem bleak and full of dark things.

Yet there's a beast inside them as well. You've seen it emerge when you're young and worried about moving too fast, but the girl you're kissing is already ripping your belt away.

"Do you like it nice and slow?" I asked Sariel, rubbing her clit. My eyes were locked onto Karley, who was matching my touching of Sariel movement for movement. Like a student watching their instructor.

I rubbed harder and quicker. Sariel groaned again, leaning into my hand. "Or fast?"

The drow followed my movements exactly. She slowly opened her mouth, her lips cascading into an awaiting "O".

"Davik," Sariel murmured. I watched Karley gyrate her hips against her hand, sliding a finger into her mouth, wishing it were me her lips were pursed around.

"That's it," I said, smiling at her. "Deeper."

Sariel slid lower, my cock throbbing in her mouth, and Karley stared at me, eyes on fire as she slid her finger into her throat.

Sariel broke and turned to me. "I need you inside me... I'll be careful. I'll crouch above you."

"I'll help you," I told her.

A vicious grin spread across her face. Sariel spun around, facing the window.

"What if they hear us?" I asked Sariel, casting a look at Karley through the opening of the door.

"I don't care." Sariel stood over me, her tall, voluptuous body glistening with the light sheen of sweat. She looked over her shoulder with a smile, then she squatted down slowly.

Her cheeks spread as she did, her lacquered nails reaching for my cock to position against her entrance. Her legs and calves flexed as her ass came down. I held and steadied her, so she wouldn't drop her weight on me. She was a tall woman, thickly proportioned, but in my hands she felt like a light plaything with enough meat on her to grab and toss around.

"Are you ready for me?" I asked, turning once again to watch Karley.

"Yes," Sariel groaned. She squatted lower. Her heavy breasts crested against her body as she rubbed me on her and...

"There," Sariel murmured as she took me. Warmth and tight heat enveloped me. My cock slid into her slowly. She moaned with a hundred years of waiting.

"It's big," Sariel groaned. Inch after inch slid home until she took most of me.

"You're so tight for me, aren't you? Just feel how wet you are."

"Ugh, Davik. It's yours. It belongs to you. I need to ride it. Is that okay? Just a bit?"

I gave her another spank. She bounced up and down, legs planted on either side of me.

Sariel rode faster, milking me. "Oh fuck, oh fuck."

I cast a look at Karley. Whatever semblance of restraint she had was gone now.

"That's it," I said to both of them. "Give it to me."

"Yes, baby. Oh Davik, fill me. You're stretching me. It's feels... fucking... good."

Sariel bounced down and up, clenching onto me. I felt her shudder and reached around with my fingers, playing with her clit as she impaled herself over and over.

"Fill me, Davik. Please. Please fill me. I need it."

I turned my head over to Karley, who was watching in a lust-drunk haze. Over the sound of Sariel's flesh slapping against mine, I could hear her wet adulation as she played with herself. "Show me. Show me you can take it," I ordered.

Sariel groaned and rode faster. "I can take it! I can take it!"

My eyes were on Karley, a wolfish grin across my face. She took her free finger out of her mouth and slid her panties down.

"That's it, show me what that pussy can do," I ordered, spanking Sariel again. My eyes were transfixed on the drow in the doorway.

"Ohh," Sariel moaned.

Karley spread her legs. Standing in the doorway, she rubbed her breast over her tank top, one black fingernail twirling on her shaved pussy. She was biting her lip, going faster and faster.

"Take it," I ordered Sariel.

My lover fell to her knees finally. All regard for my injuries vanished. Her lust took over as she sat down, and my side ached as she ground back and forth, her meaty ass against my pelvis and back arching high. The bucking swing of her breasts as she rode spurred a new fire in me.

"Do you want it?" I asked both of them.

"Yes, baby. I want that come so bad." Sariel tossed her hair back and rode faster.

Karley nodded to me in the doorway, begging me, pushing her hips out so I could see her tight pussy.

"I'm going to..." I groaned.

Karley fell to her knees. Racing to catch up. She spread her legs, panties stretching between her knees as she gyrated her hips into the air frantically. She bit her bottom lip, brows furrowing as she watched me.

Sariel cried out in pleasure as she came. In a breathless whisper, she begged me, "Fill me, my love. Give me all of it!"

Karley had her mouth open, tongue out as I came, begging me.

"Davikkkkk," Sariel moaned.

My climax came crashing down. This room, this woman, the drow in the doorway, writhing at the sight of me filling her landlord—it all slowed as I came.

We broke into a cascade of groans and exclamations as

Sariel's cunt clenched around me, arriving a moment before I did. Then I broke, filling her, spasm after trembling spasm, grabbing her hips to hold on to her.

I rose from the sheets, holding her from behind. Sariel wrapped my arms around her chest, pinning me there, inside her, full and swollen.

I kissed Sariel's back. She shuddered at the sensation. When I looked over in the doorway, it shut quietly as Karley snuck away.

Sariel looked over her shoulder, smiling at me. "Ready?"

"Yes," I said, and she withdrew and fell into the sheets next to me. Her erect nipples heaving under her rapid breath. I ran a hand over her shoulder, pulling her in for a kiss.

"Looks like our visitor enjoyed herself," Sariel said with a wicked grin.

I shook my head. "I knew you left the door open on purpose."

"You can't prove that." Sariel fell into the pillow, staring at me. "Voyeurs are infesting this house."

I smoothed her hair behind her ear, holding her chin. "Maybe there's just an exhibitionist in this room."

She giggled. Then a quiet moment passed between us. We looked into each other's eyes.

"I love you Davik."

"I love you," I told her. The truth felt invincible when I spoke it.

"I'm so glad you found me. I was locked away," she whispered, her eyes wetting with the threat of tears when she said it.

I took her hand and brought her into my arms. "There's no place I'd rather be."

Sariel nuzzled into my chest. "I moved your things from the

barn. You're staying here now. Elina will be by later to check on you."

"I should get—" I began to rise.

"Shh," she quieted me.

I didn't know what to say. It was the most anyone had ever shown me they wanted me near them. I was accepted. Needed.

Sariel pulled me back down, resting her head on my chest. "Stay still, busboy. You're not going anywhere."

CHAPTER
TWENTY-FOUR

We stalked through the forest, spears up, eyes quiet and watching everywhere. In autumn it was hard to stay silent in a world of dry twigs and leaves under your foot.

We moved into the wind, following the signs of our quarry. He was big, there was no doubt. Dangerous too.

Ahead of us, in a morning-lit canopy, several rotted fruit trees shifted.

I nodded to Vorga, and she readied her spear. I moved to the right, hunching down, my body ready for the kill. My hands tightened on the shaft of the spear. I didn't breathe. I was the hunter, the bringer of death.

Vorga crept forward, the spear in front of her like I taught her.

The wind reversed suddenly, and I froze. Vorga looked over at me. I shook my head as the bushes beyond us rustled as our quarry fled.

"Damn," Vorga growled. It was pleasant to see her so eager, that new frustration of those on their first hunts seeing an animal run. The boar tore off into the woods.

"Don't worry, they're rutting right now." I walked up to her and we rested our spear handles into the ground. "They can't hide forever."

Vorga had taken to hunting with a fervor that would have made any teacher proud.

"We tracked him for an hour!" Vorga groaned.

I shrugged. "That's hunting. Long frustrating hikes, with nothing but a sore set of legs to bring home."

"This is the second time, though!" Vorga protested. "We didn't even see any yet! We just track them and they run away. Did you even see his fur? I didn't."

I laughed. "That's hunting."

She shot me a bratty look. In our time since Trinth, she had opened up more. I hadn't expected someone whose nose was planted in books to take so strongly to stalking prey. Vorga was full of surprises.

"You think she'll stay?" Vorga asked me.

She meant the vampire staying at the tavern. The other girl we had freed from the dungeon was already gone. Elina had seen to her wounds, and within a day, someone got word to her father while I was unconscious and she went home.

"Lyra? I don't think so. And I don't think it's safe if she does." I thought of the few times I had seen her, dropping off broth and what little food we had. She always shut the door quickly.

"She won't hurt anyone."

"Lyra isn't a pet," I told Vorga. "She's dangerous, even she knows that. She knows it more than anyone. A Justicar of Selene is a straightforward as it gets."

"She told me in the cell how she lost her powers..."

I nodded, not responding. I was watching the beautiful young woman in front of me, the autumn wind casting her dark hair that always escaped her ponytail over her face.

Vorga reached out to my chest and grabbed my waterskin. She yanked me forward and opened it.

"Careful now," I warned. "You could break me."

Vorga rolled her eyes. "Sure, Davik. Little old me could break you."

She smiled and drank. Then shook it at me with a smile. "Looks like we'll need a refill."

"That pond had a stream we passed, lets go refill on our way back."

Vorga didn't let go of the waterskin. She held it like a tether that pulled on my neck. The playful look on her face vanished.

"The thing that scared me the most in the dungeons was that I thought you died. When I saw you fall from the bridge."

"Hey." I touched her hand. "I'm still here. It'll take more than a dive into the water to keep me away."

It also took the body of a library clerk who should've minded his own fucking business to break my fall, but that was between me and where I'd left him circling the cisterns.

"I thought I'd be down there forever..." Vorga murmured, her eyes flashing back to her night in the dungeon. I understood how it affected her—how it felt to be wrenched away from safety, thrown into a strange place, and not know if murder or torture awaited you.

"I know," I said. "I... was once kept in a prison for a long time. After the Summoner War. Sometimes when I dream, I'm there."

Vorga nodded. "I get nightmares. I'm always afraid in them. But Lyra isn't there. Someone is... someone is coming towards the cell. I want to be brave, but I'm not. I just stand there, petrified. The jangling keys..."

I watched her sad eyes, and a surge of rage rose in my heart. For myself, for allowing it to happen. For not getting there quicker.

For leaving anyone alive at all.

"Then the door opens, and it's so bright. It hurts my eyes. But when I look, it's always the same." She looked at me. "It's always you. You always save me."

"It's going to be alright," I promised. "They go away."

"Did yours?"

"They mostly did," I said. "Once I came here."

"Is it because of Sariel?" Vorga asked, her breath a little quicker at blurting out the words.

I looked at her. The urge to lie rose in me, to deflect, but I wanted to be honest with her. "It is. And you. And the others. This entire place."

Vorga smiled.

We walked to the pond and backtracked up the running stream to where the water would be cleanest. This was the last of the mountain runoff, the bright snowcapped mountains beyond Oakshire getting whiter each day.

"It's so cold," Vorga laughed as she held her waterskin under the stream.

"It's the—"

Crack!

I thought it was a crossbow for a split second. It was a heavy branch. I had been too lost in thought. Too focused on something else.

The boar came squealing out of the woods right at us. I pointed my spear and dug my heels in as it charged towards. Like infantry bracing for a cavalry charge.

Then it snorted and dove to my left, where Vorga squatted near the stream. She scrambled up, dropping everything and grabbing her spear.

No.

"Watch out!" I screamed.

The old boar charged, slipping past me, and I plunged the

spearhead into his ribs. I grunted, my muscles straining as I surged forward. The boar thrashed wildly, his powerful legs kicking, desperate to dislodge the spear embedded deep in his side. I pressed him against the jagged stones in the stream. Water splashed as he kicked and slid towards Vorga, the blood trailing behind him.

"Get back, Vorga!" I yelled, my voice hoarse. I couldn't see her, but I hoped she'd listen. The boar's anguished cries pierced the air, as desperate as they were loud. He bucked his head and swung his neck, trying to impale me with a tusk as long as a dagger.

"Ugh!" Vorga grunted as she thrust her spear deep into his chest.

The boar squealed as the blade entered him. He thrashed even more wildly.

"Again!" I shouted.

Vorga roared a warcry and stabbed him again. And again. The blade plunging in and out the cavity of his chest until the thick glop of his heartblood sang forth. His movement halted. His cries turned to huffs, lowering their volume with every beat of his failing heart.

With a boot on his flank, I yanked my spear free and drove it through his eye into his brain, silencing him.

I dropped my weapon and turned to her, running my hands all over her to check for wounds. "Are you alright?" All that mattered was that she was safe.

Vorga was breathing fast rapidly. Every muscle in her body was solid under my touch. My own heart was pounding from the thrill of the kill.

Vorga grabbed my bloodstained hands and slowly raised them to her lips.

"Vorga," I whispered.

She stared at me and sucked the blood from my fingers.

The heat of her lips and tongue stifled the breath in my chest. Then she stepped back towards the lake and kept stepping, watching me. She shifted her dress strap off of one shoulder, then the other.

She stared at me as it slid to the ground in a bloody mess.

Her perky breasts heaved, her jaw set, eyes fiery like a bloodstained goddess of the hunt. Her abs glistened with the exertion of what we had just done, and the trimmed hair of her untouched quim shone like a dark invitation.

I watched her as the sun broke through the canopy, lighting the pond with light.

"I want you," Vorga said.

I walked towards her.

"I want you," she repeated as if it was something she had known for a long time and it was time to speak it aloud.

I came closer. And closer. Like a wayward prince in the books she liked to read. Falling to the magical woman who rose from an enchanted lake.

We kissed. The feel of her tusks on my jaw was strikingly sensual. Our lips parted, spreading, our tongues slid back and forth with impatient eagerness. She sank into my arms, nude, and pressed against me.

"Davik," she murmured, kissing my neck, biting me softly with her tusk.

She wasn't the only one affected by the kill. I matched the feral look in her eye. I held the back of her neck as I kissed her, my hand running over her breasts, pulling her towards me. I bit her neck in reply, sliding my hand between her legs, over the softness of her mound, to her wet lips.

She tore my shirt away and clawed at my belt. We fell onto the ground, my feet on the edge of the pond bank. Vorga opened my trousers and gripped me, pulling me towards her, legs wrapping around me, threatening to never let me go.

"Take me," she demanded.

We were covered in blood. Her body felt feverish in the cold autumn air. The sun painted us in light as I took her. I entered her, the strain of entering her was an immense pressure. There was no chance of gentleness for her sake. She pulled me into her, demanding I break what stood between us. In a flush of pressure, I sank into her, claiming her, and she growled in pleasure. She ground against me as her crest broke, breath leaving her body, eyes hungry for more.

Vorga raked my back with her nails, gripping my ass to give me all of myself. I did. She stared into my eyes. The first man to feel the wonders of her, this brutal and exquisite gift.

It was animalistic. So unlike what I had thought it could be. And yes, as she writhed under me, I admitted to myself all I had denied. That I had thought about her. She had drawn me in.

I fucked her, and she panted for more. Always more. There was no delicate thing under me, wrapped around me. Her body was strong, like mine, and I pinned her there and ravaged her as she moaned my name and when she came, she pulled my face into hers and kissed me like the only man on earth.

"Davik," she purred.

I spread her legs wider, tethering her to the soft earth in that autumn grotto. Vorga growled. I strode into her, taking her with strong urgent slaps of flesh, her moans interrupted by my violent thrusts. Each wail escaping from her lips was both a sign of pleasure and a challenge for more. She was mine, if I could claim her, and so I did.

When I was close, I made to pull out, but her legs locked around me.

"Inside," she groaned. "I need you, inside."

We stared into each other's eyes and we came together, both of us exclaiming, and the tightness of her fueled my lust

—the shield she had carried within, gone and broken now. I leaned forward as my end came, growling louder as I claimed her in a torrent of desire pouring forth into her.

"Yes!" was all she said. Demure brown eyes held my gaze while my body locked at its pinnacle. Then I fell into her.

She ran her hands down my back, legs still around me. The most-orc smiled down at where my head lay on her chest. Finally, she shifted, and I spilled from her.

"Vorga," I said with a surprised smile.

But her hand was already around me, coaxing me back to life. I responded.

"Again," Vorga whispered.

CHAPTER
TWENTY-FIVE

That night, there was someone I needed to see.

I knocked on the door of the tavern guest bedroom in the late evening, close to closing time.

"*Come in*," Lyra answered.

I walked inside. Lyra was seated on the floor, cross-legged, her wrists resting on either knee. Black hair, cut short to a bob, was pulled back into a straining ponytail with a leather throng.

"How are you feeling?" I asked.

The fallen paladin looked up at me, her eyes hungry. "In truth, I thirst. I have not... fed since the night in the jail."

"Does food do anything for you?"

"Somewhat. But it does nothing for the thirst."

"May I sit?" I nodded to a chair next to her bed. The room was so meticulously clean and orderly it looked like no one had been in it. The sheets were pulled tigh in a military fashion, ready for inspection.

"Yes." Lyra watched me. Despite her sitting passively on the floor, I knew how fast those of her affliction could be.

"Want to tell me how you ended up in that jail?" I watched her, alert for any quick movement.

Lyra regarded me for a moment. "I interfered with an unjust tax collection when I first arrived in Trinth. I was arrested after assaulting several guards. Once Bellick saw I was sun-cursed, he threw me in the jail. Maybe to sell me? Maybe to ransom me back to my temple? I don't know. Not that they would have lifted a finger for me."

There was bitterness in her voice. I leaned forward, feeling the blade tucked into the back of my waist, ready if needed.

"That's a nice story. Very heroic."

"They left me alone because they were afraid of getting close. I think Bellick wanted to see me turn the girl, Vorga." Lyra began to push herself up.

"You're fine there," I motioned for her to stay seated.

The paladin held a smile for a second that held no mirth. "I figured that's what this was. Should we dispense with the questions Davik of Darkshire? And get to what you came here for?"

"What's that?" I eyed her.

"Slaying me. I'm sun-cursed. Or a vampire. Or crimson-touched, as you keep saying. Above being a paladin of Selene, a Justicar of faith, I'm afflicted. That's all I am. That's all any see. That... and failure."

"Have you ever known a vampire that didn't turn into a fiend or a monster?"

"Never," she replied, eyes settling on mine.

Having Lyra here was beyond dangerous. Dangerous to the travelers, the customers, and dangerous to the girls here. Lyra may have been a great and just paladin, but the sun-cursed change when they fall to darkness. And as lovely or pleasant as she might be, I had no qualms about ending her life if it meant saving them. Selene could take it up with me in the afterlife.

"Maybe. What will your god have in store for me once I end your life?"

Lyra laughed. "She'd likely send you a boon. I wouldn't know. She doesn't speak to me anymore. She stopped when I broke my oaths. When I failed her."

"How is that?" I asked. "You're not welcome in the temple? Why? Because of your condition?"

Her red eyes flashed at me in the offense she took. "The Order of Justicars is not so petty. They serve for life. Beyond maiming. Beyond wounds and curses and afflictions."

"But you don't," I countered.

"I..." Lyra stared at me, but she didn't really see me. She was far away somewhere. "Was attacked. By a powerful blood fiend. A feeder. One who would make me his thrall. I hear him, sometimes. Whispering my name in the dark. Laughing. I fought him, but I was betrayed. My companions fled. He held me, laughing. Threatening to despoil me, to take me further from my god."

"I'm sorry."

"He pinned my arms, my chest. Then he called his thrall over. She slid along the ground, half-crazed in thirst. The very girl I had meant to rescue. And he told her to turn me. It interested him, to see if his power was enough that I would submit to his thrall."

"And this bite severed you from Selene?"

"No," Lyra shook her head. "I shouldn't speak of this. But it's been so long since anyone spoke to me, truly. And honestly. Even if they plan to kill me."

"What happened?"

"I cried out for help. I felt her touch recede, her blessings fell from me as my oath was betrayed."

"That's it?" I raised an eyebrow. "Selene abandoned you because you asked for help?"

"You don't get it."

"I don't."

"I asked for help for **myself**. My faith wavered. Justicars serve. But not themselves. Vows of chastity. Of poverty. Of silence sometimes. But before all that, the first oath is to serve. To ask nothing for ourselves. I didn't cry out for help to stop this fiend from terrorizing more souls. My ask was selfish. I wanted only to save myself from a terrible fate. Not to help others. And in that moment, I broke my oath."

I didn't know what to say to that. What did you call a paladin deserted by their god, but still upheld their ideals? Still worshipped them?

"She turned me, and before anything else could happen... they left me. The fiend, I won't speak his name. He abandoned me when he felt my blessings vanish. He wanted me to feel as he did. A thing of darkness, cut off from all light. So that I would go to him willingly. He wanted my other vows to be given to him freely."

"But you didn't?"

"No," Lyra said and looked at the ground. "I found every door shut to me I had ever walked through. I was a failure. Not even given the chance of penitence. Nowhere in the world was open to me but the arms of the one who turned me." Her eyes looked up at me. "I will die alone in the dark before I give him the satisfaction."

"Do you feed on people?"

"Would you believe me if I said only those guilty of death? I doubt it. You can do your duty now. To protect your flock. I didn't feed on the girl, despite starving for weeks. But I can see that means little to you."

I stood, reaching for the blade behind my back. I'd pin her to the ground, staking her, and then remove her head. I'd burn her and leave her charred corpse in sunlight.

"Enough." I looked down at her. "I'm sorry for what happened to you. And I thank you for your help in getting Vorga home. I'm not here to kill you."

"No?" Lyra asked. Looking up at me, wearing her half-plate. Eyes hungry. "I was hoping you would. Many have tried. I've bested them all."

"You won't best me."

Lyra smirked. "I wish it were true, Magebreaker. I do. I've tried to submit before, but the creature, this curse in my blood, it won't let me die. I tell you this now, because the moment you make your play, your blood will flow."

I shifted, reaching out for her in feigned slowness.

She was fast. Very fast. Lyra flew across the room, hands poised like claws, ready to grab and dig to hold me while she fed. It was like a blur.

Yet I was made of sterner stuff. I caught her throat in my hand and slammed her against the beam of the wall so hard I heard it splinter.

"Fool," Lyra hissed at me.

I closed my hand around her throat. She ripped at my arm, but it was a beam of iron. My body was stronger. It had been getting stronger and stronger since coming here. Stronger than I had been in the war.

"This is so you know," I said, staring into her sad crimson eyes. "That you can't best me, paladin. If I see a slain citizen of Oakshire, if one of the girls here gets even the strangest feeling that you're watching her..."

Lyra coughed, but I kept my grip up, pinning her to the wall, her feet half a foot off the ground.

"You'll kill me? Do it now, Darkshire. Do it."

I shook my head. "No. I'll wipe the entire order of Selene from the realm. I'll burn every temple. I'll spend my life murdering every Justicar. I will lay waste to your beloved religion. I don't deal in justice, paladin. I don't do revenge or eyes for eyes. I deal in desolation. If you harm any of these people here, I'll climb into the heavens and strangle your beloved goddess."

I dropped her to the ground.

"You didn't fail your god," I told her and reached down, giving her my hand. She blinked, eyes full of tears.

Vorga wanted her alive. And a debt was owed for her help, despite how dangerous she was. I saw myself in her too. Alone. Wandering. A stranger among your own kind, a shame so deep you didn't know what to do. But you don't treat isolation with more hiding. You can't solve shame by nurturing it.

"Your god failed you. If I were you, I'd find a new oath."

Lyra stared at me proudly, standing up straighter. She impressed me. Holding her thirst at bay. Still adhering to the oaths she supposedly failed.

"Come down for dinner now. I bled a boar for you. Tomorrow we can figure out where you go from here. Though Vorga wants you to stay and work in Oakshire."

I turned to the door and walked into the hallway.

"What work would that be?" Lyra asked.

I stopped. "Town needs a new constable."

"Why don't you do it?" Lyra asked. "You could. I saw your work in the dungeon."

I shook my head. "I already have a job."

CHAPTER
TWENTY-SIX

I never moved back into the barn.

In the mornings, I woke in Sariel's bed and made love to her until she gripped the sheets and moaned my name. Afterwards I would head downstairs to a freshly made breakfast, now complimented with bacon from the boars Vorga and I hunted. It wasn't the same sweetness as a hog, but the meat made for a new tavern menu as winter approached.

Vorga wore the tusk of her first kill around her neck. Our first union.

"It looks lovely, Vorga," Sariel said with a glow at the breakfast table.

"Now we have to get Karley a necklace," Tyra said as she set down the fare for the day.

Karley rolled her eyes. Even despite the growing chill in that autumn promised, she still walked around most mornings in her underwear. The other girls teased her for it, but that didn't stop her.

"You should get to sleep earlier," Tyra told her.

"Or maybe someone shouldn't be creaking against the bedposts all night," Karley muttered.

"No idea," Sariel said with a smile and a handful of toast. "What you're talking about, dear. It's an old house. It makes all sorts of noises."

I drank my coffee and rose, helping clear the table with the dishes.

After breakfast, Sariel would pull me upstairs again. Her hunger was that of a new lover, of centuries without ever being touched, and I was here to make up for lost time. She'd fall to her knees near the end, swirling and slurping on my cock, and wouldn't let me leave until she milked me into her mouth. Sometimes when we made love, she would whisper her love to me. But in the late evenings, when I woke to her kissing me, she wanted it more illicit. I'd stride into her from the side and she'd urge me to tell her about Vorga in the forest. Or Karley, who had watched us.

I obliged her. I was the champion of her heart, and even if I left her bed, I always returned to it.

Several times that week, Vorga and I headed out to hunt boar. The forests were full of them, and our goal was to stock enough meat for winter. To fill our storage for travelers and townspeople so they could eat cheaply when the snows came.

Sometimes we were lucky. Other times, when the tension between us was simmering, we'd drop our spears the moment we were in the woods and fall into one another. There, with her wrapped around me against a tree, we melded. It felt divine to be inside her. Her passion always surprised me, this bookish girl. When she had a spear in her hands, or my flesh, the fire in her shone. I warmed myself with it in those chilled forests.

Once at work, in the middle of a shift, she ambushed me in

a supply closet. I had walked in to get a mop for a broken flagon, and her green hands shot out and pulled me in.

Life was good.

When the water heating system came, it transformed the tavern to a new level. Jessa, the part-time human waitress, had left by that time. She was off to visit family before her wedding, which we would all attend in the spring.

The installation took a better three days, and Sariel and Karley both were worried so much about the holes and pipes being punched through the entire tavern that I finally had to send them home so the gnomish contractors could work in peace.

In the end, the pyrocrystals were set, the differing tubes and tanks and pipes were installed on the side of the tavern. I gave them more gold for an additional installation and service, which they were very glad to take.

"Come on out!" I shouted to the girls in the tavern. They came filing out from where I had told them to wait in the back of the kitchen, and I grinned widely as I called them over to the shower.

"Turn it on," I said to Vorga with a nod.

All of us were standing in the shabby little shower area. Vorga spun both handles. The water came forth instantly, and steam rose as she yelped in surprise. Then she held her hand out to feel.

"It's hot!" she giggled. "Come feel!"

"Holy hells!" Tyra laughed. "How much is there?"

"As much as we want," I said with a smile. I turned to Sariel next to me. "Now, I won't have to carry bucket after bucket to your bath. And you don't have to worry about using too much firewood."

Sariel reached for my hand, holding it in front of everyone. We stood shoulder to shoulder as Karley, Vorga, and Tyra turned the spigots on and off. "I can't thank you enough, Davik. This will change so much. It's in every room?"

I nodded. "Every room. Not a shower, obviously. But a tap for water, cold and hot. We'll need to buy crystals in two years, which costs ten times the amount of all this piping. But you're now the proud owner of the only tavern in the Midlands with hot water in every room. And in the shower out back."

Sariel shook her head, gratitude shining in her eyes. "Davik, you didn't have to do this."

"Of course I did," I said. "We have meat. We have firewood. Now we have hot water. But there is something you won't like."

"What's that?" Sariel asked. I pointed to the gnomes carrying pipe and wood to the front entrance.

"What are they doing?" Sariel wondered, a little manic. I held her hand tighter to keep her from running inside.

"They're ripping up the floor. It's a new feature I paid them to do, well... they had the idea. The hot-water pipes are going to circle everywhere in the bottom floor on a separate control. It's going to heat the tavern! Heated floors for the winter. I think that will drive a new customer base, don't you? You're about to have the coziest place in the Midlands."

Sariel's mouth was open, both in wonder and horror at her tavern being ripped apart.

I pulled her by the hand to face me. "They'll be done by the time we come back from the harvest festival. Brim is staying behind to oversee. And the new constable is going to keep an eye on things... and her deputy."

Sariel shook her head. I could see how much this bothered her. It was like doing battlefield surgery on her own child. But she nodded. "I trust you Davik, I do. This is... a lot. Everything is going to change."

I smiled. "Speaking of, I think this shower and tub need to

go. The system is so powerful, and your wells are so full... I'm thinking before we do the outside seating area in spring, that maybe a little bathhouse is in order. Not just for travelers. I think a lot of Oakshire residents would appreciate a steam room, a hot body of water to sink into."

"And where did you get this idea?" Sariel asked.

"He stole it!" Vorga laughed, now splashing Karley with water. "From the baths in the temple of the Mistress. Elina and I saw him naked!"

"Guilty as charged," I said.

"Hmm, I never heard about these baths you took..." Sariel winked at me. "Hiding something, Davik?"

"Oh, you know me," I said. "I'm full of tricks."

We left for the harvest festival in Tawney in two wagons. Elina had already left, bringing her own stall and small shrine to the festival, sharing a wagon with the bookstore owner Helena. I knew because I had lifted the damn thing into the wagon.

For our own journey, Sariel drove one wagon, and I the other. We left the tavern closed for the week, in the hands of Brim to oversee the floor installation. It had taken the rest of my gold, and I cared little for it. Sariel had laughed when I reminded her I was due my silver for the week.

"I think a different payment plan is in place, Davik. I can't let you spend so much on the tavern."

But I had refused that. Nor any claim to the building or lease. Besides, the timber business would be picking up again soon.

We were two former enemies, newfound lovers. She came from cities older than time. Families that were as much military legions as they were relatives. Sariel had walked away from that. Now a bit of hot water coming from a tap made her happy, and that smile of hers made me cherish something I had never truly had. A home.

I drove the wagon with Karley and Tyra and all the barrels of ale and casks of wine. I led the procession, cutting the way to the fairgrounds, my eyes flitting among the trees for any signs of ambush or banditry. Yet word had already come that the roads were cleared by the mysterious new constable who you only saw at night.

Whenever I looked back to see if Sariel and Vorga were faring well, they were shoulder to shoulder like sisters chatting and giggling. Often casting me knowing glances and needful looks for my attention.

The hills of Oakshire and the mountains beyond slid out of view as we traveled. We cut through the hills until we came along the great rivers and forests. Autumn's chill was here, and it felt like the last day of warmth. The end of a grand and brief summer. The best I had ever known.

The season intended to die in glory, the sun baking us as we rode while the girl's covered themselves with hats. Next to me, Karley seemed to be having the hardest time.

"You alright?" I asked her as the cart bounced and bobbed, the two carthorses tugging us along dutifully.

"I prefer it indoors." She shielded her eyes under her large sunhat. The drow was struggling. "Damned sun."

"Did you grow up in the depths?" I ventured. I knew little of Karley's background. Over time, I had come to accept this wasn't just a day job for most of the girls, it was a place of solace. I wasn't the only one with secrets and a past they wanted to flee from, or ignore.

"Not exactly." Karley's shoulders swung back and forth, knocking into me. In the back, Tyra was having a much better time. She was lying on top of the barrels, palms and feet out, basking in the sun. When I glanced at her, her skin sparkled like the sands of a shoreline.

"We'll stop soon, get some shade, and make camp." I pushed the team on to climb over a break in the road.

"So, how long do you plan on staying?" Karley stared at the road.

"At the tavern?"

"In Oakshire."

"I'll die in Oakshire," I answered. "What about you?"

Karley nodded, both of us glancing at one another.

"I'd like that," she said. Whether she meant she liked my answer, or it was her own, I didn't know. "Crowded in the house, though, lately."

I smiled. That much was true. The split-level along the lake was cramped for all of us. Before we left, I had made one last visit to Mabel's timber fields and begun felling large trees. I left the giant oaks where they fell to season. Expansion was coming, and some of the wood might be useful for its construction.

"Because of me," I said.

"Yeah." Karley swallowed.

"You know, if it bothers you me being there…" I let the words hang.

"Then what?" the bartender turned her head to look at me.

"Then you can move out," I laughed. "I know a good barn someone would rent to you."

Karley rolled her eyes. If she expected me to offer to vacate the premises on her account, she was mistaken. I wasn't here to displace anyone. But I wasn't shy or dancing around the relationship I had with Vorga and Sariel. Tyra seemed amused by it all, and lately she and I still went out for breakfast when she didn't feel like cooking. But in those early mornings, I felt there was something she wasn't telling me.

I saw Karley burning with jealousy and resentment at times. Another better man would have sat her down and had a conversation about it, felt out her feelings.

Karley was a brat in many ways. But underneath that was a yearning for something else. Something more. The encounters we'd had, all those nights in the bar. The pointed words. When she watched Sariel and I.

"I don't pass up good things, not anymore. I spent too much of my life chasing the wrong things. There's room for all, plenty for everyone. I get it, though, if you want to move out."

I knew she didn't. Her job, her life with Sariel, was too sweet.

"Why would I want that?" the resentment creeping into her voice.

"Maybe you don't like to share. Maybe you want to keep it all for yourself."

"As opposed to you? The benevolent bringer of upgrades and renovations?"

"Oh, I'm worse. I'm quite territorial."

Karley rubbed her eyes as the sun poked through the tree-line again. "So your new lovers belong only to you, is that it?"

I looked at her, driving the point home. "Yes. They belong to me fully. Mine to cherish, mine to protect, mine to devote myself to. But in a more candid way to get this across to you, Bartender of the Underdark, no hands interested in living touch what is mine. Ever."

Karley held my look. Our eyes locked together. I could see how nervous she was in this moment. In some ways, I had told her exactly what she had wanted to hear. "Sounds like property rights."

The barb didn't unsettle me in the slightest. "I don't think you believe that. You don't seem to mind watching the camp-fire when its burns."

She blushed at that.

"I don't think you're asking how long that campfire lasts either," I continued.

"Oh, yeah?"

"Yeah," I answered. "You just want to know if there's room for you."

"I don't! You're a—"

I cut her off. "And more than that, you might want to know if the fire is enough. If it doesn't warm all of you. Maybe you're worried you'll be left half-out, subject to the cold."

The cart moved on, grumbling against the gravel on the road. The silence came down between us.

"And?" she asked. Wanting me to assuage her fears. She wanted a morsel of promise. Some sweet underhanded assurance.

"Nothing is guaranteed in life," I said to her. "But there are chances worth taking."

Karley turned away sullenly.

"Time for camp," I said and pulled the team off to a glen near the river line.

We circled the wagons in a half moon, shielding us from the road, and unpacked. Karley stormed off into the woods. Maybe she wanted someone to chase her, but she was the type that the more you rewarded her tantrums, the worse they'd become.

Sariel and Vorga hopped down and began fetching the tents. Tyra yawned loudly behind me. The faen girl sat up as I threw the brake on and put a hand on my shoulder, her red hair cresting down to my neck as she whispered in my ear.

"Not bad, Davik. Not bad at all," she said.

"Sounds like you were in quite the slumber."

Tyra laughed, hopping down from the cart and spinning, her long multi-colored dress turning. "I knew she wanted to talk to you. Figured I'd take the appropriate nap. Can't help it if I hear things when I sleep!" Then the cook flitted off, running to the other cart to get the makings for dinner.

We setup the two tents without Karley, which was typical. Sariel never reprimanded her. She had a soft spot for her, and I wasn't sure why.

Maybe you should punish me.

I shook my head, smiling at the memory.

I helped Tyra bring her cookware down on a makeshift wood slab table we would use for our stall at the fair. Once we had a fire going and I strung her chain and pot. She began cubing the boar meat we had brought.

"I love this meat," Tyra giggled. The little redhead looked stunning, her pale freckled cleavage spilling out of her blouse as she held up a piece of bloody meat. She inhaled it, her eyes shutting before opening and smiling. "You can smell the... passion that went into its capture." She winked at me. "A bit of a hint of oak, pressed oak."

"Boars rub on trees. Maybe he was scratching his back," I ventured.

Tyra sent me a wink. "Oh, I think the oak helped satisfy many urges. Absolutely." She set to chopping scallions, her amber necklace swinging back and forth to her chest.

Sariel stretched, standing after putting her things in one of the tents. "Such a journey. I'm out of practice."

Vorga walked out from the trees where she had gone to relieve herself. She smiled at me, looking me up and down. "Swim could be nice, don't you think, Sariel?"

My Elven lover smiled at me, pulling her hair from her headband and retying it to lift off her delicate shoulders. "Sounds fabulous."

"Oooh!" Tyra looked up from chopping. "I'll join too once I get this in the pot."

"Where's Karley?" Vorga looked around.

"Off twenty yards in the trees, sulking." Tyra didn't look up from the steady blur of the knife on vegetables in her hand. "**Not** doing chores."

"I'll grab her," Sariel offered.

Vorga shook her head. "Leave her, Sariel. She'll catch up."

Tyra threw tallow into the heating pot and seared the chopped boar pieces. The smell of it made my mouth water, and I eyed the meat pasties she had on the table that she would serve with dinner. The faen glanced up at me.

"Oh, no you don't, wolf! Stay away from this flock until it's ready." She turned and grabbed a bottle of broth and emptied it into the pot, submerging the meat, and then began adding red wine to the stew. "Off you go."

I turned, seeing a marvelous sight. Vorga and Sariel were walking nude into the soft riverbank that flowed south. The river ran off towards the direction of the fairgrounds a day away.

Vorga's green skin, the muscles in her back that flexed all the way down to her thick buttocks, drew me in. The light brown freckles that dusted her nose ended at the back of her shoulders. That gentle frame that held such a hidden strength was a marvel.

Beside her, Sariel turned as they stepped into the water, bathed in sunlight, shuddering from its icy touch. Her thick hourglass figure, now free of her binding dress, spilled forth. She was sculpted like a goddess, her heavy breasts spreading across her chest. Blessed are the never-aged.

She turned, casting a soft smile at me as she stepped into the water. It was like an oil painting made lifelike. Her quim was manicured, the soft v-shape of it between her thighs dipping into the blue river.

She and Vorga turned, coming closer to one another, until their bodies were like a wedge, two women waiting for me.

My lust rose, my cock pressing against the confines of my pants.

"Water looks real nice," Tyra murmured behind me. I turned, and she was smiling at me. "Leave your clothes here, Davik. I'll have them hung up to dry."

I stripped there, walking towards the water where two beauties waited, like water nymphs. They bobbed with smiles in the water. The cold crept into my muscles as I walked in, the sun burning the skin on me, the water icy as I plunged in.

"This river is freezing," Vorga laughed as I swam towards the two of them. Sariel stood, her breasts coming from the water, pink nipples fully erect from the cold.

"Come over, Davik." Sariel smiled. "Do you think there's enough dinner for all of us?"

Sariel pulled me towards her, until I was between the two of them, their backs to the rocks and shoreline. Her hand slid under the water, grabbing me. Vorga giggled, pulling me against her, feeling me with her hand. Both of them tugged on me gently, their fingers meeting, interlocking around each other.

"Yeah, Davik," Vorga said softly, her eyes going lustful. "Is there enough?"

I shivered, feeling the touch of two women gripping and pressing on me from either side. I felt the warmth of their two bodies enveloping mine in the frigid water.

"I think so," I said with a grin.

We drifted against the shoreline rocks, fighting the gentle current.

Vorga wrapped her legs around me, and I carried her in the

water as she ground against my abdomen. Sariel slid her arm around my lower back, then stroked my cock and angled it, sliding against Vorga's mound.

"I want to watch first," Sariel whispered in my ear with a kiss. "But save some for me." Then she pressed me forward.

I pinned Vorga against the shoreline, where she floated against me, and I slid into her.

"I think there's plenty," Sariel whispered.

Vorga pulled me into her with a lustful groan. Our hips circled. I pushed into her, her flesh spreading and swallowing me. The grip of her was so tight she was pulled from the shore when I withdrew and moved back when I plunged in again.

"Yes," Sariel murmured, a tongue sliding into my ear.

I lifted Vorga's hips, holding her so Sariel could see me enter her. The most-orc's eyes flashed in carnal hunger as I took her steadily. Our bodies continuously separated and reunited, mirroring the constant ebb and flow of water near us, never ceasing.

CHAPTER
TWENTY-SEVEN

The Harvest Festival at the Tawney Fairgrounds was a city that rose once a year in a flurry of carpentry, peaked frantically, and withered away to dust in the space of six days. Leaving behind a battlefield of empty tankards, banners, and signs.

We hit the fairgrounds with a day to launch before opening. The leisurely mood we had enjoyed on the road shifted into the full-blown chaos of a dinner rush. There was no time to visit the town of Tawney.

I hammered the stall together. A makeshift bar and food counter. Karley and Tyra started arguing immediately. Vorga found that we had forgotten serving trays of all things, which meant it would be a rapid all hands on deck every day.

It was perfect.

Amid the pandemonium, between fifty other merchants of other taverns, blacksmiths, jewelers, and bakers and anything else you could think of, I fell into a ceaseless stream of work.

The bar was off kilter, so I shimmed it. Someone misplaced a hammer, so I borrowed one from Aron the blacksmith two stalls down. Tyra couldn't find her flour, so I searched high and low until I saw Karley standing on it, using it as a cushion at the bar, which sparked another giant argument.

Sariel ran back and forth all day, arguing with the fair groundskeepers about the stall, about permits, about the ability to serve wine and beer and spirits simultaneously, which somehow now cost more. Apparently, this was a change. It wasn't until I interjected, telling the man we were not only duly permitted, we were serving lunch each day to all his compatriots free of charge, that he relented.

"That'll cost us," Karley made her nineteenth bitter remark that hour.

"Not as much as the permits, fool!" Tyra shouted from her makeshift kitchen.

"Knock it off," Sariel barked at the both of them. As the stresses of the day went on, you could see more of the old military commander arise from her.

"Hey," I rubbed her shoulders. "It's going to be fine. Trust me."

Sariel smiled and did not believe that one iota. "Some days, I swear these lot are harder to manage than a starving army."

"Worse," I said. "Can't whip these ones for not doing their job."

Sariel chuckled at that. "Alright, what else needs to be done?"

I had taken charge once things started devolving into argument-hell. Even among my crews in the past, we had never bickered as much as these girls did.

"Kegs are set, stand is set. Roof is rattling, so I'll put some more nails up in the stall. Other than that, there's a meet and greet tonight for all the vendors, right? Why don't you take the girls out a bit?"

"Davik my boy!" A grizzled old voice rang out that I was

glad to hear. Sariel and I both turned to greet Rober, who was a few pints deep already in the early morning.

"Off to the races I see." I nodded to his cup.

The old boy winked at me, his cheeks rosy. "Got in with a vendor badge. Figured I worked at the tavern too. Family is at the inn in town, not as nice as our place, but it'll do."

He made a point of looking around the stall, nodding appreciatively. "Looking good, looking real good, you two. Plenty of coin to be made this festival."

"I hope so," Sariel said and kissed my cheek. "I'm going to take the girls for a lunch we don't have to make. Maybe a bit of a walk-around. What do you think?"

"Please," I begged her. "I banish you for a few hours. Don't return upon pain of death."

Rober shook the stall a bit, noticing its wobble. "Hmm," he looked over at me with a raised eyebrow.

"A bit of coin suit you?" I asked.

"Oh yes," Rober grinned. "The wife and children will run me back to poverty once the fair and harvest festival opens. Women have a special power of draining a man's gold before his eyes. The worst is that it's your own hand that dips into your pocket. I hope you brought some yourself, Davik. You've got some shopping to do."

Sariel waved as she and the three other girls walked off to the stalls to take a break. As soon as they disappeared, I rolled my sleeves up.

"I don't have much time, Rober. Give me a hand. There's silver in it for you. Meals, drinks. I have to fix this stall before they return and I'm tripping over them."

Rober nodded, as if he were the wisest sage on women, and rubbed his chin. "Aye, I figured. Too many hens in the coop, my boy. I don't know how you do it. But sometimes a man's gotta put them to pasture to fix up the—"

"Here." I cut him off and handed him a can of nails. "Give me a hand, you greedy old man."

Rober laughed and took the nails. "Away we go."

I was up into the late hours getting everything ready. After they returned, I sent Sariel away again with Karley and Vorga, and kept Tyra, who wanted to sort everything out for the kitchen and get the next day's food ready.

Rober had been a huge help. As had Elina. The cleric showed up not long after he left to assist Tyra. But as the night wore on, she had to leave us.

We worked under a harvest moon. Tyra focusing so much that she wasn't even smiling.

I came up behind her as she worked, folding, powdering, setting meat pasties into trays to be stored.

"Take a breather, Tyra."

She shook her head. I had never seen her this frazzled. There was a lump in her voice as she spoke. "There's so much more to do. You go ahead, Davik. Just get some rest. I should've prepared more... Jessa was supposed to but as soon as she quit the tavern she went to visit her in-laws... I wish Brim was here to give me... oh..."

Her voice trailed off as rubbed the muscles between her shoulders. Her back was tight with tension. Aside from hunching over a stove all day, Tyra's chest was heavy enough on such a small figure it likely caused her some pain.

"Oh Davik, you might need to switch from clearing dishes to shoulder rubs."

"You're just stressed," I said, kneading her flesh deeper and deeper. She shuddered and leaned back against my thumbs. "Is that too hard?" I asked.

"No," she murmured. "It's... oh yes... right there. There. Oh, thank you."

"You're working too hard," I told her. "Let's call it a night. Everything is going to be fine."

Tyra smiled, laying her head back onto my chest. "It feels that way when you say it."

I gazed at the freckled mounds of cleavage. The slight sparkle in her skin of the faen. She slid against me, eyes opening in a smile.

"It's nice to not run everything," she murmured. "Nice to have you around. Someone strong."

"Helps me carry all your ingredients." I smiled. But her faen eyes were floating beneath mine. I felt the thickness of her body, the cool air around us warmed by the small oven and baking pasties.

"Sometimes we just need a hand." Tyra smiled softly. She fell into my arms and I held her.

"Come out here. I want to show you something." I led her out of the stall and had her to sit at one of the small tables and stools we had rented from the fairgrounds.

"Look," I told her.

We watched the makeshift street of vendor stalls, lit by stringed lamps. Everything was bathed in the light of the harvest moon.

"It's like a faen village," she murmured and sat on the bench. It was just her and I. She leaned back into my hands again, laying against my chest as we stared at the street. What she felt poured into me with her faen-magic. The same essence that found its way to all her food. I felt her exhaustion, her worry, and her need to be held.

"It does, doesn't it?" I put my head next to hers and wrapped my arms around her. It was like a tide of feeling, holding onto her. Worry lapped at me in a cascade of emotion emanating from her. Then it receded, and I felt the undercurrent of desire. The riptide curling towards us in sensual need the more I held her.

"I like having you here," Tyra said. I felt it, all those mornings she came for me, how she looked forward to it. It wasn't unrequited love. It wasn't a hidden thing. But it had changed. Like an ingredient of hers, mixed with all these other feelings. Of all things I felt radiating from her, desire was strongest. Tyra served others. With her smile. Her helpfulness. Her cooking and labor.

Sometimes I can't cook another thing.

"I don't want to disrupt anything that Vorga and Sariel..." she whispered.

I slid my hand down to the neckline of her blouse. Slow, like stirring one of her pots. She exhaled, a pulse of lust coming from her as I filled my hand with the plumpness of her right breast. I freed it from her shirt, cupping it in the night air and caressed it as she ground her rear against me.

"Davik, I... there's something you should. I want to... but I can't do *everything*. Not yet..."

"Shh," I whispered. I kissed the side of her neck, and I felt her feelings pulse in excitement. It was like a lighthouse in a shoreline, guiding me to where she wanted me to go. What she needed. I slid my finger across her the lips of her mouth and she sucked on it, moaning.

As she did, I slid my other hand down her hip and lifted her skirt. Out there in the open, looking like two lovers just watching the lights, she spread her legs, her body pulsing to me in its sightless magical way what she wished. I traced the edge of her panties, the heat and wetness of her making me hard.

It was slow. It was hidden and perfect, out there on that bench. My fingers teasing her sopping quim, cradling her from behind. Until my touch found the melody she wanted. Somewhere between comfort and lust. She ground against me, and I withdrew my fingers to taste her, and she gasped when I did. Then I returned my touch to her needful thighs.

I held her there, where all she had to do for once was feel good. Nothing more. Nothing less.

"We all just need a hand... sometimes." I whispered in her ear.

THE FAIR AND festival turned into a river of coin. Once the first day dawned, and all the crowds came and clamored for beer, for ale, for wine and meat pasties, everyone fell into a steady rhythm.

Vorga and Sariel flew back and forth between taking orders. Karley twirled around the bottles of spirits and the drinks, calling constantly for casks and kegs to be fixed or replaced.

Tyra never stopped cooking. I ran among the rented eating area, moving people along when they finished, taking the empties back to the kitchen.

Rober and his family came each day, as did Elina, to help, to visit. By the end of each day of the festival, we made more than we did in a week of strong business at the tavern. You could charge more here, and it had been a great harvest. People had money to spend. There was a real mirth in seeing families together, old friends reuniting under the banner of one of our beers.

We went through five boar, over six hundred meat pasties, and we sold out on wine and beer. We emptied twenty two full kegs in total and countless casks of wine. By the end of the festival, we only had bottled ale and hard spirits, which led to interesting and messy customers.

Every species of humanoid walked the fairgrounds. Tieflings, gnomes, draconic bloodlines. Elves that hailed from the woods, the high cities, the sea, and the darkness within the earth. The dwarves drank less than I thought they would, but the halflings were the first to buy their own barrel, declaring any that held the mark of their clan were to drink from it for free.

There were mercenaries. There were thieves and cutpurses. The constables of the Midlands raced around constantly, chasing people, thumping heads. There were soldiers from different domains, some on duty, some looking for trouble. I broke up my share of fights.

I became well acquainted with the groundskeepers and security forces for the Tawney Festival Grounds.

A group of faen hailed Tyra one evening, bidding her to share a drink with them. The four women spoke to her about all matters of things. It was the first time I saw her so nervous about speaking to someone. She eyed their wings with a mournful reverence. When I asked if she was alright later, she smiled at me and said nothing.

Vorga was the star of the show. She took to the tables, the screaming children, the overtired parents like a medic on the battlefield. At least Oakshire citizens demanded she sing her song for them, and I would lift her onto a table while she shyly tried to deny them. Orders flew from the kitchen under Sariel's organized watch to get everything out.

By the end of the last day, most tourists had left the festival, their coin depleted, their trinkets purchased. The crowds thinned.

On the last evening of the last day, it was Vendor Night. The organizers of the festival invited everyone who owned or manned a stall. Lanterns were strung up across a makeshift dance floor. There were jugglers and actors and bards. A band broke out. Everyone put forth their last casks of ale or libation for the workers and merchants.

I waited, a cup of strong liquor in my hands as the girls arrived. Sariel, Vorga, Karley and Tyra. Each wore a beautiful dress that Sariel had purchased for them, a gift for their hard work.

"You," I said, taking Sariel arms. "Look lovely."

Lovely was too meager of a word. Sariel was picturesque. She wore a dress of emerald green, and despite my protestations, she pulled me onto the dancefloor.

"I've got you now," Sariel laughed, but I swept her hand in mine and led her in the slow, lilting tune.

We moved together, gliding, twirling, and I spun her and then brought her close.

"Davik of Darkshire," she murmured. I didn't seem to mind that name when she said it. "You are full of surprises. Where did you learn to dance?"

"From a thief," I told her. "She said picks were for locks, but to steal a woman's heart, dancing was the best tool."

"Mmmhmm," Sariel said as she nuzzled close to my neck. "I'm sure it was hearts you were after."

"I've missed you," I said and brought her close.

Sariel ran a hand down the back of my neck. "Awful, isn't it? We're next to each other all day, but never time for a word between us. I've missed you, my love."

I glanced over at Tyra and Vorga and a sullen Karley, all looking beautiful in dresses of red, green and dark blue. They shooed away any brave enough admirers trying to entice them to a dance.

"Looks like you have your work cut out for you," Sariel laughed.

"It's… a lot. Are you sure that you don't—"

"Shh," Sariel shut me up with a kiss. "You're our river, Davik. Now show them how to dance."

The songs changed as the night went on to bawdy tunes. Most dances were in groups, where the entire floor held hands and kicked back and forth, moving left and right in large circles. Everyone cut loose. The hardship of the week was over. People laughed, they fell, they spun in drunken glee.

But towards the end of the night, when the casks went dry, and the lights seemed hazy and the braziers had that special glow, things slowed down.

I walked towards Karley. She had never looked better. I had danced with everyone except her. Her dress was a blue so dark it was almost black, her violet skin shining under the lanterns. Dark eyes edged in red makeup regarded me with a feigned annoyance.

"Take my hand," I said, holding it out.

Karley glowered, but she took it and I pulled her in brusquely. She gasped for a moment as we glided into the center of the dance floor around a dozen other couples, and I held the small of her back against me.

"How are you?" I asked. We hadn't talked since the road, more than barking orders at one another.

Karley looked away, but she folded her hands around the back of my neck as we danced.

I slid in closer to her, feeling her tight body against mine. All that silk. We melted into each other somewhat, more of an embrace than a dance. She glanced at me, the scowl on her face threatening to disappear.

"You smell nice," I whispered.

Karley laid her head on my shoulder. We floated under the lanterns. The strings of the instruments were slow and sad, like the girl in my arms. A soft smile crested her lips.

Despite it all, all the outward demeanor, all that attitude. This was just a girl afraid of boys, afraid of herself. She was a romantic. I felt it in the way she fell into my arms. She wanted the fairy tale, the prince, the soft movement under the stars.

I saw the lanterns reflected in her eyes. The drow stared up at me, nuzzling closer, her small breasts sliding against the muscles of my chest.

"Davik," she said my name. As if tasting it, trying it out for size before purchase.

I slid my arms along her back. Over her shoulder, I saw Sariel and Vorga dancing slowly, watching us, the soft hint of a smile on them both. Karley glanced that way, but I spun her.

"It's just us," I told her.

She stared at me shyly. Violet lips tinged the deepest red, eyes so dark you might never find your way out. She blinked expectantly, afraid. Tilting her head up...

I leaned in.

A hand grabbed my shoulder. "Oh hells! It **is** you! Fucking Darkshire!" A drunken voice laughed.

Karley jolted in my arms, the entranced moment broken. I spun, irritated, staring at a man my age. Slightly balding, a bit heavy.

"You're mistaken," I told him.

"Nah, wait..." he leaned in, not letting it go. His drunken eyes looking at me, then they went wide. "It's you. I knew it! It's me, Darkshire. It's Emmer! I was a pikeman. Fourth company, remember?"

Karley slipped from my fingers, turning away and disappearing past the other dancers. The moment gone, burned away like a speck of snow falling above a burning brazier.

Emmer... Emmer...

"Fourth company... third line?" I asked him.

"That's it!" Emmer clapped my shoulder. "Didn't recognize

you at first. But I saw you, I thought to myself. There's a big bastard. Tall as an evergreen. Even with that little beard I knew twas' you! C'mon!"

He pulled at me in the impatient pleading of the drunken. "The lads aren't going to believe this."

There's no brushing some people off. I followed Emmer, mortified at being wrenched from my world and ladies of Oakshire. I should've denied him again, but I was so caught off guard. And I had had my share of spirits.

At the edge of the grass clearing used as a dance floor, there were a dozen soldiers for hire standing around drinking. I recognized the green and silver of their uniforms. They had been working security for the festival on the opposite side of where we had been.

"Lads, I fuckin' told you! It's him. It's Darkshire!"

"You're right! Look at him!" A man reached out and shook my shoulder.

"Great to see you all," I lied. I turned to Emmer. "So, what brings you here?"

He motioned with an empty flagon. "Ah, easy security work tween' jobs. Lot of us are working for this new outfit." His face broke into a grand revelation, eyes going wide, motioning at me. "Oh hells, you should *join* us Darkshire. They'd have you in a minute. Probably give you top-tier pay, a share and a half, maybe."

"Unless you're busy?" another voice spoke.

I looked over at a sober soldier my age, obviously a veteran. His face was very familiar. Another pikeman.

Then I remembered. A skinny lad, talking to me through cages.

I'm not gonna make it.

"Alain," I said, sticking my arm to him. "Good to see you."

"You too," he shook my arm in the embrace of our old

legion. We weren't the same company, nor the same occupation, but a veteran will always make space at his table for others. "Was always glad you made it, Davik. Out of Darkshire."

"Yeah."

Emmer's voice grew louder. "What have you been up to? I've heard stories from all over. Darkshire this, Darkshire murdered a prince. Rochdale fell under his blade. He'll knife you for a loaf of bread." He chuckled.

"Just stories," I assured him. I wore the uncomfortable grin we all know too well, the one when you should be glad and you're anything but. This wasn't a trip down memory lane I was interested in strolling.

"Lot's of stories," Alain spoke softly. I noted a corporal's mark on his shoulder. His eyes probed me.

"So..." I ventured, trying to kindle enough conversation to excuse myself. "What are you lot up to after the festival? Off somewhere?"

"Oh hells, the new campaign is delayed. Told us to fuck right off till they need us again. Kept our uniforms and Alain got us a security gig here... but... go on, tell him Alain." Emmer pointed his cup.

"Tell me what?" I asked.

Alain's calm eyes regarded me for a moment. "We spotted someone during the festival. Few of the boys did. An old Summoner commander. An Embriel she-elf."

I felt my blood run cold. Alain stared at me with a knowing look. There was a heaviness between us.

He continued, "Commander Sariel. I remember her, because we had those little playing cards they used to hand out. She broke the lines at Breakspear."

"Is that so?" I said slowly. My heart screamed in my chest. A fevered panic set upon me, and my stomach churned with acid. I glanced around at the merrymaking, the drunken lean and nod of the soldiers and mercenaries in his group. Now wasn't the time, especially unarmed. But everyone has to sleep.

Not everyone needs to wake up.

Emmer joined in, "Said she runs a tavern er'sumtin. Fucking whore. So we're thinking we pluck her off the road. Nice high tree and a short rope, for the boys, you know? For all those didn't make it..." Emmer trailed off, his eyes going maudlin. Every veteran of a war is different, and every veteran is the same.

Alain watched me. "If it is her, that is."

I'd find them, I decided, this evening. Send the girls off in the darkness. A few knives in my belt, maybe palm a sword from an empty merchant stall. It wouldn't be easy work, but I'd make it quick. I owed them that. A sudden shame washed over me at the thought of murdering my old comrades, even if we hadn't been close.

But to protect Sariel and the others, I'd kill everyone I ever met.

"Could definitely use a Magebreaker," Emmer murmured, eyes lighting back up. "Damn Embriel are tricky."

I looked back to long ago, to that place I don't like to think of. That act of generosity had been one of the few good deeds I ever did in the war. Now it came hurtling back to destroy everything I held dear. If I hadn't saved Alain, this wouldn't be happening. How could a good deed turn so horrid?

"I never told you, did I, Emmer, how Davik here saved me?" Alain asked, but his eyes never left mine.

"What'sat? Nah, ye didn't Alain."

"See," Alain said slowly, his eyes shrewd and knowing. "My batch was the next to be released. They fed us, sure, but not much. We were still dying. Not as fast as the Magebreakers, who they didn't feed at all. Bunch of men lying around, skeletons with bloated bellies."

"Goddamn Summoner War," Emmer chimed in.

Alain continued. "That's right. Well, the Magebreakers didn't have much, but a few of them had gold teeth. So they plucked them out of their heads and traded a guard ten teeth for a single, moldy, potato."

"Bastards," Emmer grumbled. "I'da never survived."

"Few did," Alain said, watching me. "One of them knew a single potato meant nothing to men bound for death. And they knew I was to be released soon. So they handed that potato over, through the cage, to me. I had given up, you see. Given right up. But when I ate it, I tasted what so many men gave for me. It steeled me. Made me decide to make it. More than anyone had done for me in the war. More than protecting my back in battle, more than pulling me along in the march."

"Heroes," Emmer said. "The lot of them. Bad break the Magebreakers got."

"None worse..." Alain said, his eyes intense now. "I always carry one, even now. Feel nervous without one. Isn't that funny? Keeps me from feeling... fidgety. And when I do find an old enemy from the Summoner War, I feel it like a weight in my pocket. All those men who died, pulled their own teeth out so me, some nobody, could live. How practical, how objective of them. They may not have been heroes to many, but they were to me."

Alain reached into his pocket, pulling out a single potato. He stared at it. "Sometimes feels like a burden, all that weight. It feels heavier each day. Always figured I could never pay it back. What some men go without, so one could can go with."

My old comrade held the potato in his hands, staring at it.

"Maybe it's time I set it down," Alain mused. "Maybe it's time I forget some things."

"Wish we'd all forget," Emmer murmured, eyes shutting in intoxication.

"See things sometimes," Alain said as he held out the potato to me. "Things that aren't there. People who aren't who I think they are. That ever happen to you, Davik?"

I reached out and took the potato. "Used to."

Alain let it go, smiling sadly to me. "Maybe I'd like to pay it back one day. What some men go without, so one man can."

I stared at him. He nodded. "Don't think we'll be seeing you again, Davik. We're heading south after this."

"South?" Emmer hiccuped. "What about the she-elf?"

Alain watched me. "Aint her, Emmer. She died long ago. Didn't she, Davik?"

"Yeah," I said. "I think she did."

"Lotta men probably would die anyway, trying to get her. What do you say Davik, you hold on to that for me?"

I nodded and reached out, clasping his arm. We shared a knowing look, one of a debt fulfilled that no one else would ever understand.

"Take care of yourself, Davik of Oakshire."

"You too, Alain."

"Everything alright?" Sariel asked sleepily as I crawled into our tent. Vorga was asleep next to her.

"Everything's fine," I whispered.

"Saw you run into some old friends. Figured you'd be out drinking for a spell. Was it nice seeing them?" Sariel's eyes were closed. The last of the festival had exhausted everyone.

"It was nice. Yeah," I said and threw my shirt off. I climbed under the covers between the two of them, their bodies warming me in the night air.

"You should invite them to the tavern," Sariel murmured as she dozed off to sleep, and arm wrapping around me. "Show them all the work you've done. You think they'll come visit?"

I watched her face in the tent's shadow. So peaceful. Vorga snorted and spun in her sleep, putting her arm around me. Her tusk rested against my shoulder.

"Maybe another time," I whispered to Sariel.

Vorga shushed me, then nestled closer to my chest.

The End

EPILOGUE

I t was winter in Oakshire. Even with the snows we were busy. Guests from close and far came to see the novelty of a tavern with heated floors. Or take up the chance to stay in rooms that had hot water.

Rober had sold most of the remaining firewood. Business slowed. But there wasn't an empty fireplace in the valley. Harvest was over, and now was the time of survival. Some farms had done better than others. Sometimes we fed the poorer residents of Oakshire for free.

Elina grew busier. Our meetings became quicker. Rushed at times. One morning, Sariel joined me and the three of us sated our desires on the temple altar of the Mistress. They had clasped hands, holding one another as I took them.

I had ripped down the wooden shower shack and moved the bathtub at the beginning of winter. Now I laid stone, building a stream room and bath that might finish by the time winter ended. The outdoor seating area for spring would be the next project.

"Again?" I asked. I looked up from the stonework of my

bath house as Elina smiled and walked towards me. Inside, the lights were bright, the smoke wafting from the tavern chimney.

As the people of Oakshire battled winter with their stores of grain, of wheat, of meat and stews and ale, sickness rose. Elina was busier than ever. Sometimes I drove her out to the distant farms, saving the halfling from trudging there in the snow.

"Two more babies have fever, Davik." Elina walked up to me. I embraced the halfling in my arms, pulling her cloaked body close to mine. "And I have my own needs... to be close to the man I'm bound to."

I hugged her in the snows. "I told you, you should think about joining us at the house for the winter. Sariel will make room."

Elina kissed me. "I'd like to. But it's too far from town for when people need me."

On my way back from dropping her off at a young widow's house, whose husband had fallen ill in the spring the year before and had an infant, I spotted Lyra, standing cloaked on the road.

"Need a ride?" I called out.

The town constable turned, then nodded, climbing aboard. The light was dimmer in winter, and she traveled covered and cloaked when she braved daylight. I saw the redness in her eyes.

"Kardak was late to his post this morning," Lyra said, ever the Justicar. "I saw him coming from your tavern."

I shuddered, and not from the cold. "It seems the minotaur and Brim have a special...relationship. One that I unfortunately walked in on in the deep storage."

"That needs to end." Lyra shook her head. Keeping her

furred cowl down. "A day-constable need to be prompt. Chaste, true."

"He's not a paladin, Lyra." We traded glances. "Not everyone is chaste, true, and whatever else."

"Mmm," the vampire said with a scowl next to me. "Maybe."

"How's your roommate?" I asked.

"Mabel is...opinionated. She speaks often that I need a husband. Despite my explanation of my vows."

I chuckled at that. My timber business partner hadn't blinked at the idea of having a crimson-touched boarder. Often I stopped there to bring fresh blood from the boars we had slain for Lyra to sate her thirst.

"But it is...warm and safe. Thank you."

My interactions with the county night-constable, a new term we had made up to justify her and Kardak's shared posting, were frigid at best. It wasn't her affliction that made her this way. It was the grief of her failed oath. To hear thanks from her was no small thing.

"Vorga visits, you know," Lyra continued. "Or you should know. If that's alright."

"She asking you to teach her the sword?" I asked.

Lyra nodded. "Mabel and her talk much. She's inquisitive. There's a deep devotion in her, an oath almost. I can feel it."

I agreed, but didn't say so. That devotion was to me. The dynamic at the house had been amplified because of the snow confining us. Karley was still distant after the festival and our spurned dance. Vorga and Sariel both had needs I tended to.

As winter came, Tyra seemed much less cheery, the landscape affecting her. Cold wasn't to her liking, nor the absence of sun. I half-hoped the bathhouse would be something to lift her mood.

"Trying to coax her into Selene's path?" I asked.

Lyra shook her head. "There are...activities...Vorga would never wish to surrender. She has spoken to me about them. Elina visits me as well. She wishes there was something she could do for me. But her optimism is... refreshing."

"Sounds like you enjoy being a constable." I snapped the reins of the cart and we moved faster.

"It is a duty..." Lyra said slowly.

"What is it?" I asked her.

"I miss the sun's full embrace."

"I don't blame you," I said, not helpful whatsoever. I still had my guard up around Lyra, but the more I was near her, the less I worried about anyone's safety. She had brought several thieves to justice, driving them from town. Kardak's help didn't hurt either, I'm sure, in a tight spot. The day-constable walked around with horns bound together by iron bands. And he did spend too much time at the tavern, waiting on Brim. "There's no feeling like it."

"I have to come to terms with something. What you said once may be close to correct."

"What's that?" I asked.

Lyra looked at her gloved hands. "That perhaps I was failed by Selene... that maybe it's time for a new oath. Or a new faith."

"If you slay the fiend who turned you, will you revert?" I asked.

"Maybe." Lyra stared straight ahead. "It is uncertain."

"Spring brings many things, Lyra."

We passed the beginning of town, near Elina's temple, and Lyra raised her hand. "I'll get off here,"

"Elina's not in. She's at a farm for the night."

"I'm aware," Lyra said and climbed down from the cart, careful to stay covered. "I...visit the garden of the Mistress, sometimes."

"Good luck to you, Constable." I pulled the edge of my hood. "Come to the tavern. Don't stay cooped up."

"My thanks," Lyra said. As she stood, her cloak spread across her armored body. Her red eyes found me. A new hunger there. "I will see you soon."

I nodded and reached for the brake.

"I don't like women, by the way."

I turned. "What?"

"In case you were wondering, that that was the reason I liked the women visiting me. I am not... of that persuasion."

"That's... fine to know Lyra."

"Just so you know." Her crimson eyes shone with sudden worry. "Or worry. About... predatory behavior."

"Just don't bite anyone," I said, eager to be out of this stilted conversation. "That's my main concern."

"Good. Well, then. See you." The constable turned to the temple to visit the garden.

As I rode back to the center of Oakshire, I felt him, immediately. The runes snapped my attention towards the tavern like a dozen howling hunting dogs.

Mage.

Every part of me was aware of his location. Powerful. Very powerful. I cracked the reins and pushed the wagon towards the tavern.

It's likely nothing. A traveler. There's a thousand mages in the lands...

"Davik!" Karley emerged from the back of the tavern near the woodpile when I arrived. Her face told me enough. "There's a guy here..."

"Go to the house," I ordered her and climbed down.

"Do you want me to—"

"Go," I ordered. "Tell everyone to stay put. Take the wagon."

I walked past her and into the rear of the tavern. The place was empty, which wasn't unusual for a morning in winter. The closer I got, the more my skin itched from the power of whomever waited within.

A high elf sat at the table. His appearance reminded me of someone, but I couldn't remember who. Golden hair sat poised above a face of cruel immortality. He was playing with a set of dice. Rolling them on the table. His eyes fixated on me. My bones were practically vibrating.

I walked towards him slowly, one heavy step after another.

"Need a refill?" I placed my hands on the chair across from him.

The high elf smiled, rolling the three dice in his hands.

"Just playing. Fancy a game?" he asked.

"Sure." I threw my leg over the chair like a saddle and sat. "What are we playing?"

"Ladies and Liars," he said.

"You need five dice for that."

"Hmm," he said, eyes flashing up. They were silver, but unlike Sariel's, they were like cooled metal. The tips of his ears were blackened, as if he had wandered too close to the void, pulled too much power. His riding cloak spoke of a lifetime of wealth. "Perhaps you can lone me one of your precious die to roll around with?"

"I don't share," I said.

We stared at each other, his thin smile curtailing his lips.

"A pity. That which isn't shared is often taken."

"That which is taken isn't shared," I answered, leaning forward at the table. "How can I help you?"

The elf grinned, reaching his hand down slowly to the pommel of his sword and raising it up, still sheathed. The blue and gold filigree; the curve of it. I recognized it immediately.

Last I had seen it, I had left it in the woods for Ciaran and Nellie.

"A young couple, quite skinny, tried selling this. You can imagine I became...quite inquisitive with them as to its owner. Not its *original* owner, since I know the untimely fate that fellow met. But the person who owned it before them. They had quite the tale to tell me. Full of adventure, of betrayal. A ship and an ambush. The Silver Hands even made an appearance. Can you imagine?"

"Is that so?" I said, gripping the table. "How *inquisitive* did you get?"

"Oh, I droned on and on." The elf smiled wickedly. "They could barely keep their eyes open by the end. That is my way. Conversations can be so exhausting."

"Especially when you're tied to a chair screaming."

The elf sipped his wine, his eyes lighting up in agreement. "Especially then."

"What do you think? Should the sword go back to its owner, so to speak? That why you're here?" I asked.

The mage smiled. His cloak was blood red, his black-tipped ears adorned in many earrings. It reminded me of a friend I had named Trith, a spellslinger and sorcerer who chased more skirts than gold.

But where Trith had a lust for life, my visitor seemed to hold only a disdain for it.

"See, you might think so. But what hurts more? Killing a man living a quiet life?" The elf raised the dice between his fingers. "Or tearing that life apart?"

I stared at him, waiting for him to continue.

"See, what you did was very naughty, Davik of Darkshire. My poor brother was only taking a nap, and you murdered him in his bed and took his sword. For what? For gold? He had already paid you."

I leaned back, letting the little dance between us go on. "I didn't murder him for gold."

"Oh, no?"

"No." I smiled smoothly at him. "I murdered him because he was a cunt. And I see now that it might run in the family."

The elf kept smiling, but his eyes held a furious wrath.

"Imagine," he said, leaning forward. "A little tavern, full of lovely girls. All their own little stories. Their own little histories. Guarded by a great warrior."

He raised his hand and dropped a single die onto the table, where it clattered. "But what if an old betrothed was alerted to his love's whereabouts?"

Another die fell, spinning on its side. "Or a particular enclave who would be keenly interested in knowing a certain drow's location?"

Another die dropped, this time clattering against the goblet. "Or even, say, a creature of particularly cruel tastes... learning exactly where his *thrall* was living."

He clapped his hands together. "Or a faen king! Finally learning—"

"Enough," I cut him short.

He looked disappointed. Then he slid all the dice together on the table and stared at me.

"Or certain old enemies, learning where Davik of Darkshire was trying to lead a quiet life."

"What do you want, exactly?"

"Just to watch you sweat," the elf said with a smile. "My name is Vilas, by the way. I was Venthren's brother. Now I have no brother, how sad. Just this old sword to remember him."

"It's very sad," I agreed. I looked at his hands, they were shaking. I felt the power of a spell readying from him.

"See Davik, I wanted to let you know. It's all going to be undone. Everything you've built. Everything you've loved, you cherished. All the old debts come crawling back and they say one thing." Vilas held the dice up to his ear as if they were whispering to him. "*Settle me! Settle me!*"

"Where's my die?" I looked around the table. I picked one up, dropping it towards him. "Brother who swore vengeance comes calling to put the villain to justice."

Vilas's eyes smoldered, they crackled with witchlight. "I like that one," he hissed, his voice layered by five others through magecraft. "Do you want to beg, Darkshire? Beg for one of those dice to be lifted? To not be rolled? If you ask nice enough, before the end, I might listen. You might save one woman."

I looked at the table, then grinned. "I find the older I get, I'm indecisive. You and your brother didn't talk much, did you?"

Vilas smirked, his eyes glazing with sorcery. The power emanating from him stank. It was vile to me, as was his existence as a blue and black mage.

"We never did get along," Vilas growled. "He used to do *this* to me!" He grabbed my wrists and power erupted from him.

It's a terrible thing to be electrocuted. I saw a cart horse struck by lightning once. There are few fates grimmer—I've seen men tortured by electricity, a slow and agonizing demise. The face of a mage twisting in concentration, channeling a searing current into their flesh. Always a sickening satisfaction in their eyes. The skin blisters. The muscles seize, and the air reeks of burning hair and roasting meat.

Vilas was a master architect of that agony. His hands clamped down on me like iron vises, his face contorted in a scream as he unleashed the spell. The grip sent a jolt through me, the onslaught of pain and sensation horrific. It felt as if every muscle in my body was straining under the agony of lifting a mountain.

The runes etched within me reacted. They found the tune of the spell, like a player joining a melody, and matched it. Bringing it low. The pain was agony. The damage, less than what he intended. Far less.

With a maniacal grin, Vilas summoned his power in a final surge. When he finally released, his gaze lifted to meet mine, eyes shifting from a wrathful black to their cold gray. The shock in them was palpable. I reveled in his astonishment.

"Magebreaker," he whispered, not believing it.

I grabbed his arm and wrenched him forward with a grunt. His limb snapped at an odd angle. Vilas howled, but I stunned him with a blow to the skull and grabbed his other hand.

He knelt as I twisted, driving him to the floor.

"Should've spoken with your brother more." I grinned. My body was bright red with small burns and blistered flesh. I twisted his forearm like wrenching a keg tap, spinning the connecting bones free from his elbow. The mage screamed under my punishment. I picked him up and hurled him against the stone fireplace so hard I heard his spine break against the cracking mortar.

His spell had damaged me. But the runes in me hadn't just counteracted with resistance. They had absorbed part of it. I stared down at him as the strength flooded my body.

Vilas raised his ruined hands. "Burn!" he screamed. Flames poured forth from them, a river of fire. His arms were so mutilated that the spell flooded out, uncontrolled and chaotic.

My clothes burned, my skin seared slightly. The table cracked and split under the heat. When he finally stopped, only I remained amidst a smoldering clump of furniture.

I looked down at him. The runes in me were full. They thrummed with the need to empty. I shook my head. "Should've tried with the sword. Should've done your research." I reached down and grabbed a smoking table leg.

It would do.

Vilas screamed at me. "That was no jest! The dice! They tumble towards you! They'll come for you!"

I grabbed Vilas by his shirt and lifted him to me, the table leg smoking in my hand. My veins pulsed with a ferocious bloodlust, the mage's magic boiling within me, a tempest eager to be unleashed upon its master.

"They'll come..." he gasped through shattered teeth, blood trickling down his chin.

I brought the hissing table leg to his face, close enough for him to feel the heat of his own magic flowing from me into it. The enchantment trickled from it in flaming droplets. Lightning danced in a blue crackle along the scorched wood. "Let them come."

I let him drop, his body hit the ground with a thud.

Then I caved in his skull.

WHERE TO FIND ME

Thanks for checking out *Magebreaker*! If you've enjoyed the book, please consider leaving a review.

To receive a free bonus story and keep in touch with new updates you can join my newsletter (http://subscribepage.io/declan-court-newsletter)

To learn about new upcoming projects, get early previews on Magebreaker 2, or just to show support—be sure to sign up for my Patreon!

Any support goes a long way. There is also a free tier if you just want to be notified of updates.

About the Author

Declan Court pens tales of fantasy, speculative fiction, romance, and asshole gnomes.

He lived in Seoul after college to teach students the finer points of English and what a hungover American looks like. He returned to the states to grab an MFA.

Currently he spends his time in the southwest writing.

ACKNOWLEDGMENTS

Firstly, thank you to the readers.

A novel is a big commitment, and I deeply appreciate the energy and coin you've invested in these pages. Time is the most valuable currency, and I'm grateful you chose to spend it here.

To my Patrons on Patreon—I am incredibly grateful for your early support. I hope to always strive to be worthy of it. You are awesome.

A big thanks to Jessica at Royal Guard Publishing, and Marcus Sloss who does so much for this genre. Thanks for being great to work with on the audiobook project. And to the narrators Melisandre Verte and Patrick Dubois— thank you for your passion and bringing this tale to life for listeners.

I also want to acknowledge the authors that came before who created and developed this genre. Your work and support makes newcomers like me possible.

Made in the USA
Thornton, CO
01/02/25 18:54:10

2dd5278a-7dc7-4d0a-a2cc-fe1ac09aa5b6R01